Deadly Medicine

By

Orson Wedgwood

Acknowledgements:

I would like to thank all those who have helped me with this book. Not having the support of a professional editor has meant relying on the keen eyes and helpful suggestions of the following people: Claire Blain, Simon Portsmouth, Simon Lewis, James 'Rabs' Elliott Daren Packham, Joan Campbell, Sabine Kinloch, Nicky Mackie, John and Loraine Lovell, Sue Lawson, Jess Wingate and Saione Greer (cover art). I would especially like to thank my wife Kirsty, who as well as lighting up every day I spend with her, has provided excellent editorial advice. I am also very grateful for the endless support that I receive from my parents, Brian and Brigitte. In addition I would like to single out Louise Taylor for special gratitude, as she spent many patient hours weeding out the worst flaws in my writing.

Some background:

I'm married to Kirsty, who is also a writer. We live in Brighton, where much of the action in Deadly Medicine takes place. It's a great city, and we wouldn't live anywhere else in the UK.

I've spent many years working in HIV, which is one of the reasons why I chose this therapy area to set my novel in. I have never encountered such a highly motivated group of patients and doctors, and it has been a real privilege to work with this community. I've also worked in the lab designing HIV drugs as part of my Ph.D. in organic chemistry. It was during this time that I started to really think about the origins of life. I worked every day for three years with the key chemicals that determine the code for life (Nucleic acids in DNA) and the molecules that DNA codes for (amino acids in proteins).

Other than writing I have several passions in my life, including windsurfing, photography and travelling, but probably my greatest passion is for the truth.

"There is grandeur in this view of life, with its several powers, having been originally breathed by the Creator into a few forms or into one; and that, whilst this planet has gone circling on according to the fixed law of gravity, from so simple a beginning endless forms most beautiful and most wonderful have been, and are being evolved."

Charles Darwin, *The Origin Of Species*

Chapter 1

Adam pushed through the crowds of Christmas shoppers and hurried to the end of the block.

Small drops of rain began spattering his glasses. He took them off, squinted into the icy drizzle and tried to make out the blurred numbers on the street sign.

Fifty-First Street: three more blocks to go.

The walk sign began flashing. He ran across the street and collided with a red-faced man on the other side. Adam's hand instinctively darted inside his coat pocket. The panic subsided when his fingers closed around the reason he was in New York: a secret worth millions of dollars and millions of lives.

He rushed across Fifty-Second Street, leaning his shoulder into the stream of people that flooded towards him. He'd never seen the city so busy. Maybe the subway would've been better, but there were more pickpockets down there and more chances of not making his meeting.

Two minutes later he reached Fifty-Fourth Street and headed west up the even numbered side. After a hundred yards he arrived at the black marble entrance to 274.

He paused in the doorway and looked up at the reflective wall of steel and glass that stretched into the murk above. He stepped into the revolving door and was swung into the subdued lighting of the lobby.

There was a wide granite reception desk flanked by two tall glass cylinders filled with polished pebbles. The overweight security guard looked up from the afternoon edition of 'The Post'.

"Can I help you?"

"I'm here to see Helen Richardson."

"And you are?"

"Adam."

The guard picked up the phone and dialled a number.

"Doctor Richardson? An Adam here to see you…right away." He put the phone down. "She's on the forty-third floor.

She'll meet you at the elevator." He picked up his paper, shook it straight and resumed reading.

Adam walked over to the bank of chrome doors on the rear wall and called the one with floors thirty-to-fifty written above it. He stepped inside and pressed the button for Helen's floor.

"This is it," he said, and took a deep breath.

It seemed only a matter of seconds before the lift was slowing down and a soothing feminine voice announced its arrival. The doors slid back.

"Helen," Adam said. He didn't move; he'd forgotten the effect her looks had on him.

"Are you going to stay there?" Helen said.

He stepped out, holding back the closing doors.

"You do have it don't you?" she asked.

"Do you think I'd have come if I didn't?"

"Let's go inside then." She turned and led him to the end of the passage where a door was left ajar.

He followed her through the lobby into a large corner room lined with floor-to-ceiling windows that commanded panoramic views of the dense midtown skyline. There were two black leather sofas and a glass coffee table, arranged to best appreciate the scenery. A series of three contemporary paintings hung on the wall at the back of the room, one with a sideboard beneath it.

"Nice place," he said. "They must be paying you well."

"They are." She pointed to one of the sofas. "Take a seat, would you like a drink?"

The roof of his mouth dried up. If ever he needed a drink it was now. "Mineral water."

"Water?" she gave him a look of disbelief.

"I've quit."

"For how long?"

"Since the last time I saw you."

She shook her head.

"Well you won't mind if I do," Helen said, and walked over to the sideboard. She opened it and pulled out a bottle of Gordon's, poured some into a tumbler, added a splash of tonic, then returned to Adam and put the drink on the table in front of him. She smiled then left the room.

He stared at the clear fizzing liquid for a few moments before closing his eyes and slowing his breath. He unbuttoned his coat and felt inside the pocket again. The USB drive was where it'd been all day. He withdrew his hand as Helen came back. She put a tall glass of water next to her gin and tonic.

Adam took the glass and gulped greedily until he'd drained it.

"Did you run here?" Helen asked.

"The whole area's gridlocked. I left my cab in the thirties."

"Why didn't you take the subway?"

He shook his head, leaned back into the creaking leather and studied Helen. She was a walking lie, a lie he'd once believed, and one his eyes were begging him to believe again. His fingers tingled at the memory of her long auburn hair slipping through his grip; now she restrained it in a tight ponytail. He moved his gaze across the elegant lines of her face, avoiding the allure of her eyes, and focused on her left eyebrow.

Helen's left eyebrow was the one imperfection he could find. It slightly disrupted her facial symmetry by being permanently raised in a questioning curve. When he first met her that question had been a seductive challenge, now it was one whose tainted answer he didn't care to know.

"When's he coming?" he asked.

"Four-thirty."

"Why did you want me here at four sharp?"

Helen pulled a cigarette out of a packet of Marlboro Lights, lit it and blew a long plume of smoke in Adam's direction.

She shrugged. "Guess I wanted to see if you'd changed your mind about us."

Adam shifted in his seat. "Why would I?"

Helen looked at him then at the floor. "I thought the time away from each other might have softened your feelings."

"No," he said. He felt his eyes being pulled towards hers, but resisted. "We're not suited. We want very different things."

"I just needed a little time," she said. "I could've changed."

"I doubt that."

"You never gave me the chance."

"You made your choice when you left Oxford," Adam said.

"It wasn't really a choice."

"There's more to life than money."

"Hypocrite."

Adam shook his head and looked out of the window. "I'm not doing this for the money."

"Right."

"After today there isn't a research centre in the world that would hire me. If I don't take the money I'll have nothing." He looked back at her. "But that's not why I'm here, this can't be kept secret."

"You could've gone to the government."

"Too bureaucratic, they'd get tied up in law for decades. I need a company that will develop this drug and run with it."

Helen reached across the table to flick her ash. "Is it really as good as you said?"

He nodded. "So far."

"I can understand why Marivant want to bury it then."

"But it goes against everything I believe in, everything I've worked for," he said.

"So your love affair with the pharmaceutical industry is over then?"

"My passion was always for research, they just happened to be the best at it."

"Research costs money, you know that," Helen said. "A billion dollars to bring a drug to market."

"There's a balance that needs to be struck, and they've gone too far with this. I can't work for an organisation that puts profits before lives. I'm glad to be getting out."

"What are you going to do?" she asked.

Adam leaned back and looked out past the glittering towers at the dreary sky.

"Head South. The weather in Florida should still be good. Maybe Brazil or Peru, travel for a while, clear my head. Three million's enough for me to live off for the rest of my life."

"Travelling by yourself can be very lonely." Helen stubbed her cigarette out, looked at him and smiled. "My commission for this is pretty good."

Adam made real eye contact for the first time.

"I'd rather go alone."

Helen finished her drink. "Excuse me." She stood up and left the lounge.

* * * *

Helen headed for the bathroom. She locked the door then put her hands on the sink and gripped the rim tightly. She stared at her reflection in the mirror.

"Get over it!" She stamped her foot on the tiled floor. "Focus on the money."

It was no good; the tears had already begun to form.

She pulled the medicine cabinet door open and grabbed the small plastic bottle she'd hoped she wouldn't need. She sat down on the cold floor and popped two pills. The effect was immediate: the pain and guilt evaporated as she became detached from her emotions. She closed her eyes and allowed its power to spread through her, sharpening her senses to the point where she felt invincible. She could have soaked in the feeling for hours, but it was only a few minutes before reality intruded with a knock at the door.

"Are you alright?"

"Fine," she opened her eyes, "just needed to freshen up."

"OK."

She listened to Adam's footsteps padding back down the passage. She got to her feet and reapplied her make-up.

"Perfect," she said.

She returned to the lounge and poured herself another gin and tonic.

"You haven't changed a bit have you?" Adam said, shaking his head.

"I haven't had a reason to."

"You should always want to improve yourself."

"Don't bother. I'm quite happy as I am," She said.

"Are you? I mean, look at what you do."

"There's nothing wrong with what I do."

"Cutting shady deals for faceless companies?" he asked. "What happened to the talented researcher I knew? Where did your passion for science go?"

"It never went, I just hated working in the lab."

"You should've done something different. Someone with your talents could do anything, why this?"

"If it wasn't for 'this' your drug would be a secret forever. Just think how much good I'm doing by arranging this deal."

"You're not interested in the ethics, it's pure greed."

She looked at her watch. Four-twenty. She stood up and walked over to one of the windows. South? Perhaps she'd go south too, dive in the Caribbean. Or maybe she'd spend the winter snowboarding in the Alps. She pictured herself cutting through the icy snow, then practising her French as she spent her evenings flirting with the locals. Diving could wait. She'd go back to Europe where she could live in the style she'd always dreamed of.

She sat down next to Adam and looked into his eyes. If only he'd said something, one small reason to hope, then everything could've been avoided. There'd still been time, but not now.

She wanted something from him before they parted, an emotional souvenir to carry in her memory.

"There's something I need to tell you as I may never see you again."

"What?"

"You do know that I loved you."

Adam shook his head. "Don't do this. There's no point."

"Do you want to know the real reason I went away?"

He sighed.

"I left because I couldn't tell you the truth."

"The truth?"

"I was pregnant." She paused and allowed her revelation to penetrate before continuing. "I went overseas because I was carrying your child. If I'd stayed, you'd have insisted on getting married." She suppressed a smile as she watched his face turn as pale as the dead baby's skin.

It was a while before he spoke.

"You should've told me." His voice was barely audible.

"I couldn't. I just wasn't ready for two-point-four children and a Mondeo in the drive."

"But you still should've told me." The hostility was gone; his resistance was fading.

"He's well and happy, being looked after by my mother." She lit another cigarette. "He's got your eyes."

"A boy?" Adam's eyebrows lifted. "What did you call him?"

"Josh."

"After my father?"

She nodded.

"I thought you didn't get on with him."

"Only because he was such a devout Catholic." She cringed at the memory of dinner with Adam's family. "I always felt he was judging me, but at least he practised what he preached."

The confusion in Adam's eyes was final confirmation that her ruse had worked.

"Can I see him?"

The doorbell rang.

She got up from the sofa and walked into the lobby, closing the door behind her. She brushed her skirt down with the palms of her hands and fixed her hair in the mirror. She opened the front door.

"Luke," she said, and stood aside to make way for the tall Irishman.

Instead the visitor stood his ground. He grabbed her hand, pulled her towards him and kissed her.

It wasn't looks that drew her to Luke. He was more than twenty years her elder, had a crooked nose that had been broken in a rugby game and thick black hair. The outline of his heavy winter coat could have hidden the pampered body of a well-fed executive, but she knew better. His bulk wasn't fat; she'd felt his immense strength as he'd held her by her wrists.

"Is he here?" Luke asked.

She nodded.

"And the data?"

"Of course, I told you he'd bring it."

Luke stepped inside and they walked down the passage to the living room. He opened the door and gestured for her to enter first.

"Luke Martin," Helen said. "Adam Sandford."

Adam got up slowly and the two men shook hands.

There was silence for a few moments. Luke looked at Adam and raised his eyebrows in expectation.

Adam produced a USB drive and put it on the table.

"Everything you need to know about Spiravex is on there," he said, sliding it across the glass.

Luke took a laptop out of his shoulder bag, booted it up and inserted the drive.

"Password?" he said, looking at Adam.

"Undetectable."

Luke typed it in and began browsing the document.

Helen looked at Adam. For the first time since they'd been reunited, he smiled at her. It caught her off guard as it penetrated the drug-induced blockade. She opened her mouth to say something, but it was too late, a .45 calibre bullet shattered Adam's left temple and his smile was gone forever.

Luke turned round and replaced the Glock in his jacket pocket. "You know I'm not one for small talk."

Helen smiled. She'd got her memento and a million dollars.

Chapter 2

Julia's hand still felt warm. She looked small and vulnerable under the sterile lighting. Ben wanted to hug her, protect her, but it was too late for that.

"Take as much time as you want," the mortician said.

Ben stared at the face he'd loved from the moment he first saw it twelve years ago. Even in death she was beautiful, but the kindness that warmed her smile and the love that filled her eyes were lost forever.

"I'll leave the forms with you."

Ben nodded but didn't look at Steve, who put a clipboard on the aluminium table beside him and walked away.

Ben was too shocked to feel anything. A decade ago it might have been expected, but not now, not since potent combination therapy came on the scene in the late nineties.

"They said it was a heart attack," he said. But how could it be? She was only thirty-four.

Steve's footsteps stopped. "It looks that way."

"It's crazy, there's not an ounce of fat on her."

Steve appeared by his side again. "I was going to ask you something later, when you'd had a bit more time to come to terms with things."

Come to terms with things? Was that the same kind of banal expression he used when comforting bereaved relatives?

"What?" he asked, turning away from Julia's face for the first time since Steve had pulled back the sheet.

"Were you still treating her HIV?"

He was the only one who ever had. Her trust in his judgement had been absolute. He'd also been the one who held her tight when the tests said she was positive; he'd lain awake by her side that first night as their minds filled with thoughts of their stolen future only weeks after they'd met and fallen in love. Then, as the years passed, their relationship began to focus beyond the daily regime of pills and side effects to the possibility of a normal life together. Would he have been such a good HIV physician if Julia had been negative? He'd never know, but since her diagnosis he'd read every article published on the subject.

"I made sure she never missed a pill," he said. He tried to think like he would about any other patient, but all that went through his mind was the songlike tones of her voice as she'd called goodbye on her way to work that morning. "It can't be the drugs. I took her off proteases last year when her lipids started to shoot up."

"What did you switch her to?" Steve asked.

"Spiravex." 'The industry's best molecule ever', that's what the head of the British HIV forum said when Ben had attended the first study investigator meeting. As the results came in from around the world, he became inclined to agree; they were so outstanding that putting Julia on it when the proteases played up was a no-brainer.

Steve looked puzzled. "Didn't you get the amber alert?"

"About Spiravex?"

"It went out last Tuesday."

"We were on holiday." A dreamy week on the Amalfi coast, morning strolls through ancient streets, afternoon espressos in bustling coffee shops, a glass of Chianti on a restaurant terrace as they watched the sun set across Sorrento.

"Two patients from the trial recently died of heart attacks, not enough at that stage to make the FDA shut it down, but if any more came in, it would reach statistical significance."

"The drug killed her?" Ben said.

"Three heart attacks from the same study? It's hard to see how you could come to a different conclusion."

"But she's been taking it for months. Surely some effect would have shown itself by now?"

"I really don't know Ben," Steve looked down.

A terrible realisation formed in his mind. He'd all but signed a death sentence for her when he wrote that first script for Spiravex.

The door to the morgue opened, they both turned round.

"They told me what happened in casualty," Ruth said rushing across the room. She reached the bench with Julia's body and put her hand to her mouth. She shook her head then turned to Ben, tears filling her eyes. She stepped towards him and put her arms around him.

"I'll come back later," Steve said.

Ben's sister squeezed him tight and cried into his chest, just like she had twenty years ago at Heathrow Airport, and just like then, his emotional reflexes pushed the pain deep inside.

"This isn't happening," she said.

"It is," he replied, "and it's all my fault."

Ruth took a step away, wiped her eyes and looked up at him.

"What are you taking about?"

"I killed her," he said, barely able to get the words out. "I killed my wife."

Ruth looked confused. "They said it was a heart attack."

What had he done? Every thought he'd had since he met Julia was for her. It had never once occurred to him to leave after her diagnosis. His only thought had been how they would fight it together. Life without her wasn't an option, only now he'd made it reality.

"The drug I prescribed killed her."

Ruth put the palms of her hands on Ben's cheeks.

"You silly man. You mustn't think like that, it wasn't your fault."

She was wrong. There'd been other drugs available. If he hadn't tried to be such a hot shot Julia would never have taken Spiravex. He shouldn't have believed the hype. No drug was completely safe, he should have been more careful, waited till the trial was over and it had been used more widely.

He turned to Julia one more time. She was the meaning of his life and he'd killed her.

Chapter 3

Six months later

Ben sat in his stuffy office finishing the notes on the last patient he'd seen. He put the file on top of the growing number he'd dealt with that morning and buzzed through to his secretary.

"Debbie. Has David Walters shown up yet?"

"I don't think so. I'll go check in the waiting room."

Ben stood up, fought with the sash window behind him until it was about a foot open, and sat back down. The room filled with the mechanical rumbling of traffic from the street below, but it was worth it to feel the fresh air cooling his back.

The speakerphone crackled with the sound of Debbie's voice.

"He's not here Ben, but Tamba's turned up early."

"Send him through…and Debbie, could you give David a call. It's not like him to miss an appointment."

He pulled out Tamba's notes. Like all of his patients Tamba was HIV positive. Unlike the majority of men attending the clinic, he was heterosexual. He'd been infected in Uganda after having sex with a woman he met in a bar.

There was a light knock at the door.

"Come in," Ben called.

The door opened and the shiny crown of Tamba's head appeared in the gap.

"Hello Doctor Williams."

"Hi Tamba," Ben said, waving the slender African into the room. He gave Tamba a brief smile and gestured for him to take a seat. He returned to the notes he'd been flicking through and stopped at the page with Tamba's latest lab results. He raised an eyebrow.

"Bad news Doctor Williams?" Tamba asked.

"No, the opposite. Your CD4 immune cell count is above three hundred for the first time, which means your immune system is recovering, and your viral load is undetectable."

Tamba's broad grin reminded Ben of why he loved his job.

"You're taking your drugs on time and this is the result." He put the file down.

"No more TB?"

"Shouldn't be if you keep taking the combination correctly."

Tamba's smile faded.

"What's the matter?" Ben asked

"My asylum claim failed."

Ben closed the file with a sigh. They both knew what that meant for his treatment. "Are you appealing?"

Tamba nodded. "I'll find out in three months."

Ben shook his head as he looked back to the first time he saw Tamba, when he was admitted to the acute ward with TB. Being from Uganda his HIV diagnosis was almost taken for granted, but with the powerful drugs now available, the team were able to nurse him back to full health.

On return to Uganda he might be one of the lucky ones to get on the new generic combination provided by the World Health Organization, but it was a lottery. If he didn't get any treatment then all that effort and the tens of thousands of pounds spent on him would be wasted. Within a year of returning to Africa Tamba would be dead. If he stayed in the UK he'd probably live till he died of old age.

The speakerphone buzzed. He picked up the receiver. "Debbie?"

"Just spoke to David's partner. It's sad news, David's dead."

"What?"

"He died three days ago."

Impossible, AIDS doesn't sneak up that quickly, the virus had been undetectable at his last check-up. "Are you sure you've got the right David?"

"There's only one David Walters on our system."

This was crazy. "Did Robin say how he died?"

"I didn't really want to pry. He sounded awful."

"I don't get it." Ben glanced up at Tamba. "Thanks Debbie."

He put the receiver down and stared at his computer screen. He'd known David for years, he'd been one of his first patients at Brighton.

"What will happen to me if I lose my asylum case?" Tamba asked.

Ben looked at him. "You'll be deported."

"Will I get TB again?"

TB, pneumonia, fungal infections that turn your mouth into fur and eat your genitals alive.

"Let's hope your appeal is successful."

* * * *

The last patient finally closed the door twenty minutes after the clinic was due to end.

Ben leaned back in his chair. It was the first chance he'd had to get his head round David's death and compose himself to call Robin. David had been more than just a patient, he was like a comrade in arms, fighting a war against the relentless march of the virus. Just as it looked like they were winning, David had caught a stray bullet. The suddenness of his death stirred dormant feelings about Julia, that he'd managed to keep a lid on since November and he had no desire to confront them now. The trick was to forget the past and focus his mind on the present. Right now that meant contacting Robin.

Ben looked at the phone. What should he say? He'd met him a couple of times, but they'd never really hit it off. Still, there was no choice, he needed to know the cause of death for the unit's records.

He reached forward and dialled the number. It rang four times then went through to an answer machine. It still had David's voice on it. Ben hung up before it reached the beep.

Maybe he should go round in person, but what if Robin didn't want to see anyone yet? Ben certainly hadn't wanted company after Julia's death. No, it was best to phone first. He redialled the number; this time it was engaged.

He put David's notes to one side, picked up the other patient files and carried them through to the relative cool of the north-facing secretaries' office.

Debbie sat at her desk nibbling a piece of cake. She was losing the eternal battle she fought against sugar, not that it harmed the way she looked, the extra curves suited her.

He put the files on her desk.

"Not going down the beach to have your lunch?" he asked.

"I'm working through," she replied. "I need to get away a bit early." She moved the files to one side and picked up an open notebook. "Tony from MSD called to confirm your meeting next Tuesday, and Ruth left a message asking if you were windsurfing this afternoon."

Ben looked out of the window at the trees. The boughs were nodding back and forth in the spring sun, but they needed to be bending over in submission before he went near the water.

"Cheers Debbie."

He turned to leave but the exit was blocked by Keith, his boss. The bloke really needed to lose weight if his dignity was going to survive the summer. Sweat trickled down his reddened face into his black beard, and the white shirt that stretched over his stomach had turned pink as it clung to the mass of damp flesh beneath.

"Fancy a pint?" Keith asked in his thick Yorkshire accent.

He didn't really, but it beat sitting at home battling dark thoughts for the next two hours.

They left the clinic and walked down the street of terraced houses that separated the hospital from the beach. At the bottom they descended a flight of steps to the lower promenade, which had undergone major regeneration over the past decade. The once derelict arches lying beneath the busy seafront road had been converted into fashionable bars and restaurants. Rotting nets and dilapidated fishing boats were replaced by shiny aluminium tables and chairs, which spilled out onto the wide path meandering along the length of the shingle beach.

Ben and Keith strolled past several busy cafes before they were able to find a table outside a bar next to a volleyball court. A group of students shouted in foreign accents as they threw themselves about in the sand to keep the game alive.

Ben felt his disease-filled morning fade away as he sat down and allowed the beachfront atmosphere to lift him.

A waitress arrived, smiled at Ben and took their order.

"Hope this weather lasts." Keith said.

Ben followed his gaze out to sea; a slight swell was building and flashes of white broke the surface beyond the shoreline. He shifted in his seat.

"Be nice if it did," he said.

"Bloody country, you get a bit of sun early on, makes you feel like you're living somewhere decent, and then it pours with rain for the rest of the summer." Keith frowned at Ben. "Are you alright? You seem a little distracted."

"One of my patients died suddenly," Ben said.

"Rare event these days," Keith said, shaking his head. "Mind you Ian Jenkins died a few weeks back, totally out of the blue. Nothing to do with AIDS though, his CD4 count was well up and his viral load was undetectable."

The name was familiar, probably because his case had been discussed at the Virtual Clinic.

"David Walters was undetectable too."

"David's dead?" Keith said.

"You knew him?"

"I saw him while you were at the Milan conference," Keith replied. "Nice chap. He was training for the London marathon, came in looking for sponsorship."

"And a month later he's dead," Ben sighed.

The waitress returned with their drinks and Keith's food. The plate had barely hit the table before his fork was lifting a large sausage to his mouth. "Bit of a coincidence," he said, still chewing.

"What is?" Ben put his hand round the cold pint of beer and lifted it to his lips.

"Two of our HIV patients dying from non-AIDS related complications."

"I don't know for certain it wasn't AIDS," Ben said.

"There was no way it could have been if he was undetectable. Either way, find out. If it wasn't you should check their notes. Might be a drug interaction no one's spotted yet." Keith looked up from his food and raised his eyebrows. "Could be a paper in it."

The guy was unbelievable. Two men were dead and all he could think about was raising the profile of the unit. That was why Keith was Head of Department and Ben would never rise above Senior Consultant. Sniffing out opportunities to impress others and attract corporate interest were just the kind of antics he was desperate to avoid.

Still, Keith did have a point, there might be a connection and Ben owed it to David to find out.

"How did Ian die?" Ben asked.

A gust of wind suddenly hurried along the seafront sending a flurry of coasters flying off the tables and carrying Keith's answer with it. He decided to put work out of his mind; he had an afternoon on the water ahead of him.

* * * *

By three o'clock large thunderheads were building inland. To fuel their expanding bulk they sucked in moist air from the sea, bringing a steady force five to the coast.

Ben was standing in the strip of wet sand between the steep shingle banks and the water's edge making some final adjustments to his rig. He lifted his kit up and walked into the surf. He dropped his board, a Viper 110, into the sea and pulled the sail into position, then effortlessly stepped on and headed out through the breakers onto the rolling swell.

The board built speed and lifted out of the water. He hooked his waist harness onto the boom, dug his feet into the foot straps and really started to fly. The waves were building into steep ramps, and when he caught a bigger gust, he aimed the Viper up the face of one. He leapt off the other side, allowing the wind to lift him high into the air before landing in the trough. The salt water splashed against his tanned skin and matted his hair. His spirit was free from the shadows of urban life and his mind focused on the next move rather than fighting the relentless march of a virus.

He took his feet out of the straps and banked the board at twenty knots, then flipped the rig and headed downwind towards the beach. The shorefront, at first distant, grew rapidly. Lines of Regency terraces with columned facades merged into modern hotels and apartment towers near the centre of town. Beyond the coastline, Brighton's red roofs climbed up towards the sun-covered grassland of the South Downs, which were dwarfed by the dark clouds whose wind he was stealing.

As his board bumped and juddered beneath him, his peace became disturbed when he remembered what Keith had said. The disquiet over David Walters' death returned.

Suddenly a strong gust hit his rig and pulled him violently upwind. The board's fin sliced out of the water and the front dug into the top of a wave, catapulting him forward. His legs clattered onto the boom and he found himself under the sail, still hooked in. The waves lifted everything up and down on top of him. For a moment he lost control of his feelings and wanted to succumb, maybe death would reunite him with her.

Julia! The trial! How could he have been so dumb? He managed to unhook his harness and feel his way along the boom. He finally surfaced and gasped in a lungful of air.

"Spiravex!" Ben shouted at the blue sky above him.

He knew why he remembered Ian Jenkins' name; it wasn't just that Keith had mentioned him at the Virtual Clinic, but because both Ian and David had been on the Spiravex trial, the same trial that Julia had been on. He'd been so focused on trying to block out any thoughts about her death that he'd stopped himself from making the connection with the trial.

He knew patients had suffered heart attacks whilst taking the drug, but he hadn't heard of any long-term cardiovascular damage. Even so, he was willing to bet that both Ian Jenkins and David Walters had suffered the same sudden death, and therefore other patients needed to be warned. Keith may have been wrong about a drug interaction, but he was right about the deaths being related.

Ben swam round the front of his submerged kit, grabbed the mast and pulled the sail across the wind, causing it to resurface and lift out of the water. He moved his hands to the boom and looked upwind in time to see a gust rushing towards him as it harried the lumbering swell. He pushed the sail up and in a second was levered back onto his board.

* * * *

"Bit too much for you?"

Ben looked up from the job of dismantling his kit to see his sister standing over him.

"Something came up at work," he said.

"Out there? You were flying," Ruth said. She put her board on the beach. "I was hoping we could have a race."

"I can't, I remembered something I have to deal with that won't wait."

"Don't get many days like this."

He was tempted by the thought of racing her across the Channel for an hour or two, but knew that once he'd got something on his mind he wouldn't be happy till he'd dealt with it. "Another time."

"There's always an excuse." Ruth knelt on the sand and yanked open one of the foot straps on her board. "You're never around when I need you."

"For windsurfing?"

Ruth shook her head and adjusted the strap. "You can't even be bothered to reply to my messages."

"Chill out Ruth, we can have a race next week."

She closed the strap and looked across at him. "I wanted to go for a coffee after, I need to speak to you about something."

"We can talk now, I've got a few minutes."

"That's all you've ever got," she said, her eyes narrowing with resentment. "I was there for you."

He looked away.

"You know what my work's like."

Ruth shook her head again. "I need to talk to you properly. Are you doing anything later?"

He looked back. She had him. "Nothing much."

"Can we meet in the Tin Drum at six?"

"I guess, but why is it so important you can't talk about it now?"

"Just is." Ruth clipped the mast foot into the board. "Nasty wipe-out," she said, looking at his right knee.

He glanced at the two-inch gash that oozed a steady trickle of blood down his leg. "Catapulted in a gust. Be alright in a day or two."

"You're the doctor." Ruth stood back up and lifted the sail, pulling it to and fro against the wind. "What sail did you take out?"

"Six metre. Bit overpowered at times, but I like it that way."

"I'm on a five-five, should be about right." She manoeuvred her board to the water's edge. "See you at six then?"

Ben nodded.

Ruth pulled her kit into the water. Within seconds she was cutting a perfect wake across the surface of a large breaker that wasn't nearly quick enough to catch her.

* * * *

An hour later Ben was back in the stifling heat of the unit. He headed for the records room. He entered the pass code and hit the light switch. The aisle labelled 'I-P' was right in front of him. He walked down it and looked for the Js.

He pulled out Ian's notes from a shelf at the end of the row then walked to his office. He put the bundle of papers next to David's file and turned straight to the final page which was a copy of a death certificate. Cause of death was Myocardial Infarction. Bingo, Ian had died of a heart attack, now all he had to do was find out about David. He thought of phoning again, but decided to go round in person; it was only a five-minute walk from the unit.

He headed back out into the fresh air. The wind had really filled in now. The clouds that he'd seen mustering behind the Downs had begun their march seaward and threatened to block out the late afternoon sun.

He soon found the lilac painted terraced house where David had lived with his partner. He hesitated for a second. He could almost sense the grief coming through the walls, it was the same sensation he'd had as his headmaster had walked with him to his grandparents front door in 1979. He knocked a couple of times before the door was answered. Normally perfectly groomed, Robin was barely recognisable: he had thick stubble and his clothes were grimy.

"Doctor Williams?"

"Hi. I'm sorry, I should've called before coming round."

"No, it's alright. Come in."

Ben followed the skinny five-footer into the gloomy house, closing the door behind him. Robin shuffled down the hall into the kitchen.

"Cup of tea?"

Dirty mugs and glasses were scattered everywhere. Saucers full of cigarette butts filled the gaps, and several empty whisky bottles crowded round the overflowing bin by the back door. It was a far cry from the immaculate home Ben had visited a year ago when he'd been called out to see David in the middle of the night.

"Yes please."

A picture of David and Robin standing in front of the Eiffel Tower sat lopsided under a penis-shaped fridge magnet.

"When did you take this?" Ben asked.

"Last August. It was our tenth anniversary."

"He looked so well."

"Sugar?" Robin asked, pouring boiling water into a large mug.

"No thanks, just milk."

Robin finished making the tea and led Ben into the stale air of the lounge. There was a three-piece suite with a half empty bottle of whisky standing next to the sofa and more makeshift ashtrays crammed with their rank residue. The curtains were drawn, making it hard to believe such a perfect spring day had ever existed beyond them.

Robin sat down on the sofa and moved a crumpled blanket to his side. Ben chose the nearest armchair.

"Thanks for coming round Doctor Williams."

Ben took a swig of the tea and tried to ignore the brown crust his lips encountered on the rim. "I just wanted to say how sorry I am to hear about David. I only found out this morning."

"It's so unfair," Robin said. "David had inherited some money in January. He paid off the mortgage last month and we were planning to go to Thailand later this year. We were so happy."

Ben peered into his tea and took another unwelcome sip. When he looked back up he saw Robin staring blankly at the curtains, his mug tilted, tea dripping onto the carpet.

"You must have loved each other very much," Ben said.

Robin gave him a desolate look. "He was the most amazing man I've ever met; so creative, so talented, and so mindful of others. It's not right, there's no God."

Robin seemed to drift off again and Ben realised he was going to have to bring up the subject himself.

"Do you mind telling me what happened? The last time he was in the clinic he was perfectly well. His CD4 count was above a thousand. Most healthy people don't have a count that high."

"It wasn't AIDS," Robin said, "I could deal with that. It was a car that killed him."

"Not a heart attack?"

Robin gave him a funny look. "Heart attack? David jogged ten miles every morning. He was fitter than most men half his age."

That was true, the blood pressure record in David's file was excellent, but that wouldn't stop an MI if it was caused by the drug. A car though? "Was it a drunk driver?"

Robin shrugged, then rummaged around under the blanket, pulled out a packet of Rothmans and lit one up. "They never caught him."

"A hit and run?"

Robin nodded and blew out a stream of smoke. "If I could get my hands on the bastard…"

Robin was no Arnold Schwarzenegger, you wouldn't put money on him against some drunken yob from the local council estate, yet there was such bitterness in his eyes that it may not have been totally impossible.

The ash on Robin's cigarette grew.

"Are you taking anything?" Ben asked.

Robin looked down at the bottle of gin.

"If you come into the clinic tomorrow I'll write you a prescription."

"I don't take drugs."

"It's better than booze."

"Thanks Ben, but I'll deal with this my way."

"Your choice, but if you change your mind, call me, even if it's just for a chat." Ben put his hands on the chair ready to lift himself up. "David was a great guy, I'll miss him."

Robin didn't seem to be listening anymore.

"I guess I'd better head off." Ben stood up and lingered for a second. "I'll see myself out."

He closed the front door quietly behind him and walked back to the unit.

Once at his desk he looked at Ian Jenkins' and David Walters' files again. Both men had been enrolled onto MVT084, the phase II trial for Spiravex, a drug made by Marivant that stops the virus from entering human cells. Along with Julia, they were the only patients from Brighton on the drug and they'd all responded well to the treatment. Ian and David were taken off Spiravex the day Julia died and the FDA shut the trial down. In the end, a total of eight of the one hundred patients from around the world had suffered heart attacks attributed to Spiravex. All eight had died.

According to the notes Ian Jenkins had also died of a heart attack. However, without corroborating evidence it was hard to see how his MI was linked to Spiravex. Six months after coming off the drug was a heck of a long time. It had to be a coincidence.

He looked back and forth at Ian and David's files, and imagined Julia's on top. Even though the two men had died from different causes, it was still a fact that everyone from Brighton who had been on the Spiravex trial was dead. What were the chances of that?

The small clock on top of the desk beeped. It was six o'clock.

"Damn!" He'd forgotten all about Ruth.

Chapter 4

Ben stepped off the crowded number six bus onto Church Road. It had just started raining, and with each step the drops grew faster and harder causing the air to thicken with a dusty smelling mist that rose off the hot pavement.

He turned down Second Avenue and ran the last fifty yards to the Tin Drum. He joined the large group of people crowding into the entrance, carrying plates and glasses as they abandoned the pavement tables. His rain soaked shirt was cold against his skin, but that compensated for the lack of air-conditioning in the hot bar.

He scanned the crowded room. Ruth wasn't at any of the dozen wooden tables in the rustic-style restaurant section to the left, nor was she in one of the comfy-looking sofas to the right. In between lay a large area filled with damp diners who were now forced to eat standing up. He picked his way through the chattering throng and spotted her standing with her arms folded at the bar.

"Sorry," he said.

"Was someone dying?"

He looked at her blankly.

"Why are you so late?" she asked.

He glanced at the clock above the bar, six thirty. Half an hour was bad, even for him. "Someone did die. I got involved in finding out why."

"Not happy just being an HIV consultant?" Ruth asked.

He raised his eyebrows.

"You're not a coroner in your spare time are you?"

"Oh." Ben shook his head. "What are you drinking?"

"I'm fine," Ruth replied, holding up a glass of red wine. "You're a real pain, you know that?"

He gave her his scolded puppy look. She smirked and looked away. It never failed. He smiled and took the place of a young woman leaving the bar with a tray of multi-coloured cocktails. He ordered a bottle of Belgium beer then rejoined Ruth.

They looked around. It was standing room only.

"I had to give up our table in the restaurant," she said.

"How long till we can get another one?"

"I know the waitress. She said she'd come and find me if one became free again." She sipped her wine. "So why were you playing coroner?"

He explained what had happened to David and Ian and that they'd been on the same trial as Julia.

"Looks like a connection is unlikely though," he said. "I wasted a perfect afternoon on the water."

Ruth shook her head. "I wouldn't say that. Robin might drop into the clinic and get himself back in shape. Besides, just because David Walters didn't die of an MI doesn't mean other patients in the trial aren't at risk." She paused. Her brow furrowed with concern. "I know you don't want to rake over what happened, but..." She looked at him for help.

"Julia died of an MI too?" he said.

She nodded. "I mean, it's an obvious connection, and it wasn't just Julia."

"It might seem obvious, but their deaths were half a year ago. If David had died of an MI then there was a chance something was going on, but I think Ian's death is just a coincidence."

"If only one patient from each unit died after the study was stopped, it's unlikely anyone would make the connection between Spiravex and the heart attacks, but that doesn't mean the connection isn't there," Ruth said. "If David hadn't died you wouldn't have given Ian's death a second thought. Maybe it's serendipity that you made the association. Other patients could still be in danger."

She had a point. Even though it seemed unlikely there was a link, he should be sure before totally dropping it. It wasn't good medicine to draw conclusions from flimsy evidence, but discounting theories without being certain was even worse.

The crowd next to them parted as a harassed-looking waitress appeared.

"Do you still want a table Ruth?" she asked.

"If you have one soon," Ruth said.

"A booking didn't turn up. There's one free now."

They followed her to the table and sat down.

Ruth started fiddling with the knives and forks.

"What's the matter?" Ben asked.

"Nothing."

He remembered their conversation on the beach. "What did you want to tell me?"

Ruth shrugged and continued playing with her cutlery.

He watched her, and waited. That was the only way to deal with Ruth's silences, you needed to make sure she knew she had your full attention.

After a longer silence than normal, she spoke. "Would you mind if we didn't go to Kampala this year?"

Ben's eyes widened.

"It's so morbid. I've found it pretty depressing for years now, but after what happened last November I don't think it'd be good for us" she continued. "I don't want to forget them, but I think we need to move on."

"You've never said anything before."

"I know. I didn't want to upset you in the past, but…it's different now." Her voice was soft, and compassionate, as it always was when she referred to Julia's death.

Ben smiled. "I only went because I thought you wanted to."

"Are you serious?" Ruth said. "I was so afraid of telling you, I was worried you'd think I didn't care any more."

"Of course not, I feel the same as you, it's horrible. I don't want to forget Mum and Dad either, but I want to stop reliving all the heartache we went through when they died."

Watching Ruth stand by the graves and cry was the worst part. He always focused on her rather than thinking about what their deaths meant to him. He'd never really been to that place, that's where Robin was. How could he be strong for Ruth in that state?

She reached out and squeezed his hand. "Can we just have a quiet dinner together instead?" she asked. "I still want to pay my respects in August, and us being together is the best way I can think of."

Ben nodded in reply.

"I wonder what they'd be like if they were alive," Ruth added.

"The same. They'd probably still be in Africa. Dad would be trying to convert the lost and Mum would be trying to heal their diseases."

"Do you ever think about moving back?"

"It'd be hard now," Ben said. "I did my time out there, and to return for anything longer than a year would mean sacrificing my career in the NHS." He looked down. "But there are times when I feel my training would be of more use in Africa than the UK."

"So what's really stopping you?" Ruth asked. "Career and ambition were never a big deal for you before."

Ben looked up. "Guess I'm too comfortable here. You know what it's like being an ex-pat."

"It's not that bad."

Ben cringed. "Spending your evenings down the club, knocking back the hard stuff and moaning about the locals? No thanks. Anyway, you've never moved back."

Ruth shook her head. "Not really much demand for art when people can't afford to eat."

"That wouldn't stop you if you thought you could make a difference."

Ruth looked away for a moment. "To be honest I'm scared," she said. "Dad seemed invincible when we were growing up. Knowing that he was hacked up with a machete like bush meat…" She stopped and breathed in hard. "Life has no value."

"It's not as bad as it used to be."

"Maybe, but I've grown used to feeling safe."

"So you're not going to be a missionary after all?"

Ruth smiled. "We need missionaries here more than they do in Africa. England's lost its faith."

"That's called progress Ruth."

"You think our society with all its worship of wealth and fame represents progress?"

"I think a society not ruled by superstition has progressed. God died when Darwin wrote 'The Origin Of Species'." Ben beat his fingers on the table.

"Darwin proved nothing."

"You're an artist Ruth, you're not really equipped to argue about science."

"Just because I didn't study it, doesn't mean I'm incapable of reading. There's plenty of literature out there challenging atheism."

There was no doubt that Ruth was every bit as intelligent as him, which made it all the more frustrating that she clung to her outdated beliefs. It was even more bizarre considering that she had experienced and witnessed the same sort of suffering he had, worse in fact. It was a paradox. "Like I said, you're not really in a position to judge the scientific integrity of that literature."

Ruth's face reddened. She opened her mouth but no words followed as the waitress arrived to take their order. Once she left, he steered the conversation away from the flashpoints of their parents' deaths and religion, towards windsurfing. The years they spent learning the sport in Worthing had brought them close together, and in some ways were among the happiest of their childhood, in spite of the cause of their relocation. Maybe it was because for the first time they weren't living in the third world, or constantly moving around. By the time the food came Ben had restored his little sister's natural good humour.

"Do you fancy going somewhere else for a drink?" Ruth asked when they'd finished eating.

Ben frowned.

"Ben?"

"You've got me thinking about those patients on the Spiravex trial," he said. "It's starting to bug me."

"So?"

"So I won't be happy till I've got to the bottom of it."

"You can't do anything now," Ruth said.

"Of course I can."

"But the clinic will be closed."

"I'll use my laptop." Ben ignored the look of disappointment on her face. "If you hadn't put the idea into my head then I'd be up for going somewhere else, but now I need to find out if other patients had heart attacks after the trial ended."

Ruth's nod was one of resigned defeat. "Will you come out another night instead?"

"I'm really busy at the moment."

Ruth rolled her eyes.

"Make time Ben." She pulled her coat from the back of her seat. "You're my brother, all the family I've got, and the only time I see you at the moment is when you're doing loops in a force six." She put her coat on and stood up. "I'm sure you just see me as an inconvenience. Would you prefer it if I'd been hacked up with a machete or died of a heart attack too?"

Before Ben could reply she turned and disappeared into the crowd. He called the waitress and settled the bill.

He left the table, pushed back through the busy bar to the entrance and stepped outside into the cool dark of the evening. The rain had stopped, but the air was still damp and heavy. The dusty smell had been replaced by a leafy fragrance rising up from the well-tended gardens that lined the street.

Ruth was sitting on a wall a short distance from the front of the bar.

He stopped in front of her.

"I'm sorry," she said, and stood up. "That was out of order."

Ben shrugged. "It's the Welsh half, I'm used to it."

Her reaction wasn't totally undeserved. Ever since Julia had died he'd buried himself in his work. He'd hardly been out at all. There was another reason he avoided her too, she always asked if he was OK, or made some sympathetic comment that would remind him of what had happened. He didn't want to be reminded, he just wanted to get on with his life.

"I'd got myself so worked up about telling you I didn't want to go to Kampala that I was ready for a big scene," she continued. "I think I needed to create one just to get rid of the pent up emotion."

"You don't have to explain yourself," Ben said, then took a deep breath. "I'm always going to be busy Ruth. If you want a night out, you'll have to arrange it, you've got a lot more time on your hands than I have. Just check with me first."

She leaned up and kissed him on the cheek. "Thanks Ben."

They walked up to Church Road and stopped before going their separate ways.

Ruth's worried expression returned as they faced each other. "Are you sure you're OK about not going to Africa?"

Ben nodded and smiled. "Of course. The meal will be enough."

Ruth looked relieved, but her eyes had started to glisten. He put his arms out and they hugged.

"Just thinking about it sets me off," she said.

"It always will," Ben said into her hair.

* * * *

In his apartment Ben made himself a strong coffee to sharpen his beer-softened mind. His espresso machine was one of the few items he'd brought with him from the home he and Julia had shared.

He sat down at the breakfast bar, which divided his modern kitchen from the open-plan living space that lay beyond. The few visitors he'd had awkwardly joked about his apartment being a typical bachelor pad with its laminate flooring, brown leather couches and plasma TV; but to him it was simple, functional and spacious. Like his windsurfing, it was a vital antidote to the chaos and overcrowding that invaded his life at work and in the city. It was very different from the elegant townhouse he'd shared with Julia. That had her touches all over it.

He booted up his laptop and accessed the web through his wireless network. He logged onto the hospital website, entered his personal drive and opened the file on the MVT084 study. It was the first trial to use Spiravex in positive patients. The study's recruitment had been completed, and some of the participants had even reached the halfway point before it was pulled.

The results looked impressive at twenty-four weeks. All the patients had undetectable viral loads and their CD4 counts had risen dramatically. Then everything fell apart the previous November when the eight deaths were reported within three weeks of each other. Julia's death was the tipping point. The study was stopped abruptly, and the surviving patients were switched to alternative anti-retrovirals. Spiravex disappeared onto the billion-dollar trash heap of undeveloped drugs.

Ben looked at the report by the Chicago-based Principal Investigator, Professor Richard Cook. There were six patients from the UK: the two from Brighton, two from the Chelsea and Westminster Hospital, and two from Guys Hospital. Ben opened a separate file where he'd stored the details of the UK investigators. He noted down their phone numbers so he could call them in the morning, but he wanted to learn more about the overseas patients now.

He looked at his watch. It was still early afternoon central time. He found the contact details on the back of the report, picked up the phone and dialled the number for the Chicago University. The switchboard transferred him to Cook's secretary. Ben gave her his name and was put on hold.

A minute later Cook's deep African-American voice came on the line.

"Doctor Williams?"

"Hi."

"Didn't we meet at ICAAC last year?" Cook asked.

"That's right, at the investigators' meeting." Ben was impressed that he remembered him.

"How can I help?"

"I'm after some information."

"About MVT084?" Cook asked.

"Kind of. I'd like to find out what happened to the patients after they were taken off Spiravex."

There was a long delay before Cook answered.

"I don't have that information. They were told to change regimens as soon as the study was discontinued, after that Marivant took over monitoring the data." Cook paused again. "Why do you ask?"

Ben was about to reply when Cook jumped in ahead of him.

"Have you had any patients with problems after coming off Spiravex?"

"Just one," Ben said.

"Send his details to Marivant, they've got deep pockets. None of the relatives who sued are complaining about the settlements they've received."

Ben was happy to see Ian Jenkins' family get compensation, but that wasn't why he was calling.

"Have you heard of any other patients from the trial dying after the study ended?"

"Dying? Of what?"

"Heart attacks."

"Like I said, Marivant have dealt with all post-study complications."

Ben knew the likelihood of Marivant even hearing about a case like Ian Jenkins' was remote. As Ruth had said, no one at Brighton had connected Ian's MI to Spiravex until David's death caused them to dig deeper. Doctors tend to only consider the drugs patients are using at the time of death, not six months earlier. Even if Marivant had heard from the odd ultra-observant physician, would they invite further lawsuits by announcing there might be long-term problems? Unlikely. He needed to find out for himself.

"Would it be possible to have a list of all the centres and investigators involved in the study worldwide?"

"Why?" Cook asked.

"I just want to know if anyone else in the trial had the same complications."

"If they had, I'm sure it would be public knowledge," Cook replied.

"All the same, I'd like to check for myself, so I can put my mind at rest."

"For the third time Doctor Williams, Marivant have all that information. I am involved in dozens of studies each year, I wouldn't be able to recall even one centre that participated in MVT084. If you want to put your mind at rest I suggest you contact Marivant."

There was enough sharpness in Cook's tone to make Ben back off.

"I guess I'm worrying over nothing," he said. "I'll do what you suggested. Thanks for your time."

"No problem."

Ben hung up and stared at the computer screen in front of him.

If he didn't have such a high regard for Cook's reputation he would have accused him of lying. The PI was able to remember an obscure doctor from the south coast of England, yet he couldn't name a single unit from the most disastrous clinical trial in the history of HIV research.

Chapter 5

Ben ignored his conscience the following morning and swapped his bus pass for the keys of his TT; he needed to get in early.

After a ten-minute drive along the misty seafront, he parked up behind the two-storey concrete slab that housed the GUM unit and used his swipe card to get in through the out-of-hours entrance. He hit a switch causing a series of halogen strips to flicker to life and pour their stark light on the deserted main corridor. The door to his office was fourth on the left. He put his rucksack on the desk and pulled out the notes he'd made the night before.

Mike Procter was first on the list of names to call. He'd spent a rotation training under Mike at the Chelsea and Westminster Hospital. His old mentor had a legendary work ethic He'd put money on him already being at his desk.

He dialled the number for the bespoke HIV research unit at the hospital and asked for Mike's direct line. The phone was answered after two rings.

"Mike, hi, it's Ben Williams."

"Ben," Mike said in his brisk London accent. "How's things?"

There was the sound of fingers tapping on a keyboard in the background.

"Not bad, and you?" he said.

"Busy. I'm on holiday in Egypt for the next couple of weeks. Got loads to sort out. What's up?"

"It's about the Spiravex trial."

"Yeah?"

"You had two patients in it didn't you?" Ben asked.

"If you say so."

"What happened to them?"

"Switched therapies as soon the trial was aborted," Mike replied.

"How're they doing now?"

The tapping stopped and there was an impatient sigh.

"Wouldn't have a clue. They weren't my patients so I don't see them anymore," Mike said. "Where's this going Ben?"

"I know you're snowed under, but I really need to find out how they are."

"Why?"

"One of our patients had an MI more than six months after being taken off Spiravex. I'm worried there might be a pattern of long-term damage."

"I'll get my secretary to look into it," Mike said. "Is that everything?"

"That's all, cheers Mike."

Ben hung up and glanced at the clock: eight-fifty. He still had ten minutes before his morning clinic. He looked at the other number he'd scribbled down from the Spiravex file. It belonged to Professor Rachel Milbank.

He knew everyone who was anyone in the close-knit British HIV community, and everyone knew that Rachel's husband, Neil, was the UK medical director for Marivant. When they'd married, he'd been a registrar with her at the Royal Free. Ben had met him a couple of times at training courses and conferences, and knew he was sick of the politics in London hospitals, so wasn't surprised when he quit the NHS.

He flicked the corner of the sheet of paper as he debated calling Rachel. Maybe he didn't need to yet, maybe Mike's patients would reveal something.

He put the sheet to one side. He had a long day ahead: more patients than he could fit into the morning, and a meeting that would take up the whole afternoon. For the moment his suspicions about the Spiravex trial would have to be put on hold.

* * * *

Helen reined in her Porsche Boxter as she rounded a hairpin bend on the road between Malaga and Ronda. She allowed the engine to idle as she admired the view across the steep rocky valley to her two-storey villa perched halfway up the other side.

Her gaze fixed on the unfamiliar car parked in the drive. She gunned the eager 3.0 litre engine and a few minutes later pulled up next to the red Mondeo.

39

Helen couldn't see the driver or any passengers. She leaned across, opened the glove compartment and felt around for her Beretta. She pulled it out and checked it was loaded. She took the safety off then slipped it into her shoulder bag.

She got out and examined the Mondeo. It had Malaga plates and a small sticker on the windshield bore the Hertz logo: an airport rental.

She walked towards the cedar and iron front door, then veered left onto the path that followed the whitewashed walls round to the back of the house. She stepped cautiously onto the paved yard with its wooden furniture and terracotta pots filled with bright flowers.

There was no one. Whoever rented the car must have let themselves in.

She stayed close to the rear wall and looked through the kitchen window. It was empty. She reached into her bag and gripped the pistol, then eased the backdoor open and slid inside.

It took a few moments for her eyes to adjust from the bright morning sun of the Sierras. She scanned the room.

Since she'd left for the coast three hours earlier, the work surfaces had been wiped clean and the pile of plates she'd left on the central island had been cleared. But her maid would be long gone by now.

Helen slipped her shoes off and moved silently from the kitchen down the cool hallway. All the doors were closed except one at the end of the passage. She peered into the spacious lounge and instantly recognised the thick black hair of the man sitting on the sofa.

"Luke," she said, and walked round to face him. "What are you doing here?"

"You've spent your money well," Luke said, nodding towards the French windows behind Helen.

She turned and looked at the view; the reason she'd bought the place. From its thousand-foot vantage point the villa looked down the valley, past numerous mansions that clung to the rocky slopes, to the coastal town of Marbella. On a clear day the panorama extended beyond the Spanish resorts that lined the dark blue Mediterranean to the shadows of the Atlas Mountains guarding the gateway to North Africa.

She turned back. "I said we were through."

Luke laughed. "You think I came all this way to chase after you?"

"Why are you here?"

"You still work for me," he said. "Marivant phoned last night."

Helen's heart sank.

"I don't want to be involved with that anymore."

"You're involved until I say you're not."

"I'll do the kind of jobs I did last year," she said.

"You don't have a choice."

"That's not what you said when I agreed to work for you."

"Look at it as a promotion." He smiled. "It's clear I've allowed you too much time to enjoy your money, but I didn't need you before, now I do. You're the only UK agent who can do this job."

"What about Anne?"

"She's already doing the background and surveillance work."

"Can't you use a subcontractor?"

"Why would I do that when I have you?" Luke said.

Helen looked down.

"Is it a relative?"

"Yes, but with complications," he replied. "I got the call last night. The PI in Chicago phoned Shackleton directly. A doctor in the UK was asking too many questions. They want someone to investigate him immediately. He has a unique motivation for being inquisitive, his wife was in MVT084."

"Do you want me to take him out?" Helen asked.

He took in a deep breath and stretched his arms along the back of the sofa. "Do you normally let your visitors go so long without offering them a drink?"

"What do you want?"

"Iced water," he said. "We'll discuss details when you get back."

Helen returned to the kitchen and filled a glass with bottled water from the fridge. She pulled the ice tray out of the freezer and slammed it on the counter.

She cursed and stared at the frosty mess of shattered ice cubes. She thought she'd finished with Marivant in November.

Her dream of a new life on the Costa del Sol revolved around kitesurfing, shopping and clubbing; it didn't include the shadow of Luke's presence, nor did it involve killing. The ghosts of Adam and her baby already haunted her dreams; she didn't want any others waking her up in the middle of the night.

She returned to the lounge and handed Luke the glass.

"How long will I be in the UK?" Helen asked.

"Just pack for a few days and buy clothes when you need them."

"Where am I going?"

"Brighton."

A silver lining. It could have been Swindon or Luton.

"I've booked two seats on the four o'clock to Gatwick," he said. "We'll go straight to our base in Surrey and get a heads-up from Anne. She's finding you an apartment as we speak. You'll be armed and briefed then it's up to you."

"Is it up to me whether I kill him or not?"

He shrugged. "If you feel he knows too much, you'll have no choice."

"And how am I supposed to get close enough to find out?"

He glared at her.

"You want me to be a whore too?" she said.

"Grow up. You're a professional, act like one."

Helen shook her head and left the room to pack. Letting Luke tempt her into Slade was proving the worst move of her life. She'd been naïve to expect that commercial espionage merely involved trading envelopes under a table. The lying and stealing in her earlier assignments had been easy, but this was a whole new level.

Slade now had more leverage over her than the initial enticements of money and excitement; they'd overseen her complicity in her ex-boyfriend's murder. How much more of her would they own once she'd actually pulled the trigger herself?

* * * *

It was gone six before the doctors piled out of their airless meeting room. Ben headed back to his office to collect his bag. He turned his mobile on and found a text from Ruth asking whether he was busy on Saturday night.

He started replying then noticed a post-it on his desk. The handwriting was Debbie's:

'Mike Proctor phoned. Call him as soon as you get this message.'

He dialled Mike's clinic number. There was no answer; he'd probably gone home. Ben began scrolling through the directory on his mobile but soon put it down. He was wasting his time, he'd recently upgraded to a different network and only transferred active contacts.

He tried directory enquiries for Mike's home number but he wasn't listed. There was no choice but to wait till the morning.

He grabbed his rucksack, turned off the lights and headed out of the unit into the evening drizzle.

After several attempts he manoeuvred the Audi out of the cramped car park and began the crawl home through the rush-hour traffic. Following up the Marivant trial was like sitting in a jam and not being able to see how far ahead the cause was, it felt like if he was making any progress at all it was only a few inches at a time. Not being able to contact Mike meant he'd have to wait another night before he could get any closer to resolving this.

He craned his neck to see the queue went to the roundabout by the pier. The large sign above the entrance added welcome colour to the grey evening as the words 'Brighton Pier' rippled back and forth in alternating red, white and blue. Beneath it a smattering of tourists browsed the brightly coloured fast-food stalls.

"Damn!" He hit the steering wheel with the palm of his hand. "He's going away." He may even be going tonight. It'd be weeks before he'd find out any more about Mike's patients.

The driver behind sounded his horn. Ben filled the gap that had grown between him and the car in front.

He didn't want this hanging over him any longer. Until it was resolved it would constantly be there, acting as a reminder of all that he'd lost. He just wanted to get on with his life and this would drive him crazy.

He edged another car length closer to the snarling hub of the jam. There had to be a way of getting Mike's home number. He made a decision. He flicked the indicator and began moving into the right-hand lane. There was no way he was going to wait two weeks.

Chapter 6

"I thought there was a heat wave?" Helen said, as he took her holdall and put it in the boot of his Mercedes.

"There was, it ended yesterday." He closed the boot and they got in the car.

A few minutes later they'd left Gatwick and were in the fast lane of the M23 heading north towards London.

The dark sky and fine drizzle made it feel more like autumn than spring. Helen turned the heat up on her side of the car and looked out of the window at the motorists they were overtaking.

A stressed businessman ranted into his hands-free; a mother screamed at her brawling kids on the back seat; an old couple chatted, oblivious of the impatient queue that jostled to pass them in the middle lane.

She'd drifted into the middle lane when she was with Adam and nearly surrendered her dreams of adventure to the British goal of a career, a house and a family. Then she saw the meaningless lives of those who had sleepwalked down that path before her. Huge mortgages enslaved them to a pile of bricks and soulless corporations. Looking into the abyss of a life whose only purpose was to reproduce, she panicked.

Joining Slade gave her the chance to break the mould; it promised wealth and adventure and she jumped without thinking. Adam didn't understand and broke off their relationship. She'd lost the one man she'd loved and was now sitting in a car she didn't want to be in, on a job she didn't want to do. She was just a different kind of slave.

They reached the M25 and Luke steered the car westbound into the eighty-mile an hour evening rush home.

"How's Maria?" Helen asked.

Luke didn't reply.

"How did she feel about you flying to Spain to visit me?"

"Don't flatter yourself with the thought that my wife would be jealous of you," Luke said.

"Shouldn't she be?"

"With you it was just sex. That doesn't bother a woman like Maria."

Helen looked away. "If she was more of a woman than me she wouldn't be able to share you."

"Maria is superior to any woman I've met. She recognises it's unnatural for a man to be monogamous. She was able to share me, why weren't you? You're inferior in your thinking by always wanting to be the only one."

"You wouldn't feel like that if it was the other way round," Helen said to the window, and folded her arms.

She wished she'd kept her mouth shut. She'd made it look like she still wanted him, but she didn't. She was attracted to his powerful charisma, but ultimately she was a jealous woman and wanted no part in a three-way relationship.

They took the Leatherhead exit and exchanged the bland motorway scenery for the hedge-lined lanes of rural Surrey.

She felt a pang of nostalgia for her homeland as they passed through a succession of ancient villages with their timber-framed cottages and cricket pitches. Neither the weather nor her mood could dampen the pleasant effect of the gentle scenery.

They left the village of Lower Waldron, the closest to their destination. Did its Middle England residents, whose biggest problem in life was getting a seat on the morning commute, ever imagine that one of the most ruthless organisations in the civilised world had a base on their doorstep? Probably not. More likely they'd think the property was owned by some vulgar trader from the city who was too rude to get involved with local life.

They pulled onto a gravel track about half a mile west of the village. An unlocked farm gate with a 'No trespassing' sign stood across their path. Luke looked over at Helen. The pretence of chivalry had disappeared now her body was out of bounds.

She sighed and stepped out into the drizzle to open the gate. The Mercedes glided through. She looked down the lane in both directions; it was empty. She closed the gate and got back into the warm car.

They proceeded slowly down the track, which passed through thick woodland. The roof of the car thudded with the sound of large drops falling from the branches above. After about four hundred yards the trees thinned out and they arrived at another barrier.

The security was more obvious than on the lane. There was a twelve-foot high black iron gate that formed part of a spiked fence encompassing the entire property. Evenly spaced surveillance cameras swivelled back and forth.

"The remote's in the glove box," Luke said.

Helen found the small black fob and pressed the button.

There was a loud clanging as the barrier began to open. The moment the gap was large enough, Luke eased the coupé through. The gate juddered to a halt then began closing automatically behind them.

The gravel driveway turned to the left and arced round an area of hedged lawns that stretched a hundred yards to a perfectly preserved Tudor manor.

The large E-shaped brick house was latticed with black timbers. Three broad chimneys towered above the tiled roof, one at each end of the building and one above the centre. The windows were composed of dozens of small diamond-shaped panes separated by thin lead mullions.

As they drew closer, two silver cars came into view in front of the porch. One was a brand new SLK, and the other a vintage Aston Martin.

"I see Anne still thinks she's Bond in a skirt," Helen said.

Luke didn't respond and brought the car to a halt next to the SLK. They both got out.

"Is the Merc mine?" Helen asked, running her fingers along the sleek lines of the bonnet as she walked past.

"Ask Anne. I left the logistics to her."

Helen and Luke passed through the thick stone doorway into an arched entrance hall. They walked along a poorly lit passage to the back of the building where an oak-panelled corridor stretched between the two main wings. They turned left and strode past a series of portraits of dignitaries connected to the house.

At the end of the passage was a broad flight of stairs. They stopped at the bottom next to an open door on their left.

"I need to check my messages," Luke said. "Join Anne, I'll be down when I've finished."

46

He started up the stairs and Helen stepped through the door into Slade Bio's main communications room. She'd been told that it once formed part of a great hall, but the inserted plasterboard partition made the high ceilings look out of proportion to the modest floorplate.

On the right-hand side stood a bank of scanners and printers. At the end of the room, two leather armchairs and a Chesterfield looked out through large stone-framed windows to the lawns in front of the house. Four workstations were positioned along the wall to the left; three LCD screens hung above them, flicking through a series of live external images.

Anne was sitting at one of the workstations. She still had short bleached hair but her physique was even more muscular than it had been the last time Helen saw her. Anne did spend most of her free time in the gym though. It was a bit OTT. A reasonable level of fitness, good weapons and martial arts training, combined with curves in the right places, were a better combination for success in their profession. Three trips a week to the gym was fine; it left more time for playing. Their attitude to working out aside, they'd become good friends while training together at Slade's campus in Namibia. Anne was the only one who'd been there for her when she and Adam split up. Before starting in the field they made a pact to watch out for each other. They needed to. They were the only two female agents in the firm's UK Bio division.

"Hi Helen," Anne said, not looking up from the screen. "Won't be a sec."

She typed for a few moments longer and hit a key. A laser printer to Helen's right whirred to life and began spewing pages into a tray.

Anne got up and opened her arms. Helen returned the hug. This was the first time they'd met since the Marivant job started.

"It's good to see you," Anne said. They let go of each other. "How's life on the Costa del Crime?"

"Fine till this morning."

"Tell me about it. I got a call at five am."

"I was hoping the whole Marivant thing was over and done with," Helen said.

"Wasn't everyone? I guess we knew something like this might come up though." Anne returned to her workstation and typed in a few commands. An inkjet began snapping back and forth.

"I've got some pictures already," Anne said. "When you see them you might feel more enthusiastic."

"Really?"

"I definitely would." Anne winked at Helen.

The rear wall thudded with the sound of footsteps descending the stairs next to it. Helen turned to see Luke enter the room.

"Are you ready to get Helen up to speed?" he said.

"Just printed the report," Anne said. She retrieved the pile from the printer, put them in a document wallet and handed it to Helen. "Something to read tonight."

Helen opened it and looked inside. There must have been at least fifty pages. "You've been busy."

"Most of it's bank statements and credit card stuff," Anne replied. "I downloaded a couple of research papers he published and wrote a brief summary of his family and career. There are a few gaps, but I'll fill them in over the next few days. I guess you know his wife was one of the patients on MVT084?"

Helen nodded.

"Have you seen a way in yet?" Luke asked.

"Not sure. Helen might have some ideas after she's read the file, but that's something I'm going to be looking out for when I get to Brighton."

She went to the inkjet, picked up the photos and handed them to Helen. "I downloaded these off a windsurfing club website."

"Windsurfing?"

"I found a direct debit on his bank statement. The pictures shouldn't be too out of date, he only joined four years ago."

Helen looked at the first picture.

"See what I mean?" Anne said.

Helen nodded. The picture was of a tall well-built man holding a surfboard under his arm. He had short blonde hair and a deep tan. His confident smile etched firm lines across his face; he looked fun. The second picture was taken through a zoom lens. It caught him halfway through a jump, suspended from his kit above a stormy sea.

"Wow, great air," Helen said. "He must be good."

"So's his sister," Anne said.

"Sister?"

"Next two. Her name's Ruth."

Helen pulled the third photo to the front. "They don't look like brother and sister." There was a nervous honesty in Ruth's expression. Maybe she didn't like having her photo taken. "She's a bit ginger."

"Let me see," Luke said.

Helen gave him the photo.

"It could be your way to Williams." He handed the photo back.

"Where does she live?" Helen asked.

"In Hove, not far from her brother," Anne said.

"Anne, split your time between the two," Luke said. "It'd be less obvious if Helen got to him through his sister. Find out what she does, where she goes…everything."

"What if they aren't close?" Helen asked.

"Read the file," Anne replied. "I'd bet my life on them being inseparable."

"We need to know as much about them as possible," Luke said to Anne. "You're going to be very busy the next few days."

"What about me?" Helen asked.

"We need to design your cover to entice Williams," he replied. "Then we can discuss how you eliminate any threat he poses. First I must eat."

* * * *

"Ben?" Mike said, his expression caught between surprise and irritation.

"Sorry to come round without phoning," Ben said, "I've lost your home number."

"What the hell are you doing in Notting Hill? You live in Brighton."

"I need to find out what happened to those patients," Ben replied. "It can't wait till you get back from Egypt."

"I forgot what a pain in the arse you are when you've got something on your mind," Mike said. "I haven't got time now, I was just about to call a cab for the airport."

"Where are you flying from?"

"Heathrow."

"I'll take you, I came by car," Ben said. "We can talk on the way."

Mike's eyes widened.

"Are you mad? Heathrow's the opposite direction to Brighton," he said, and then shrugged. "Guess it'll save me thirty quid."

Ben helped Mike carry his bags from the narrow hallway of the terraced house to the TT.

They clambered in and began the journey out of central London to the airport.

"So why are my patients so important to you?" Mike asked.

"If either of them died of an MI, it could link one of our patient's deaths to Spiravex and imply long-term heart damage."

"Are you worried about being sued?"

"Why would we worry about that?" Ben asked.

"You bloody well should," Mike replied. "Are you insured against legal action?"

"The trust looks after that kind of thing."

"The trust? You're having a laugh. Get yourselves proper protection."

"Why would the patient's family sue us?" Ben asked. "Surely they'd go after Marivant."

"Did you suggest he go on the trial?"

"He was Keith's patient, but we all made the decision through the Virtual Clinic, but the patient didn't have a choice. He'd been on anti-retrovirals since the early nineties, had resistance to just about everything else."

"Wrong Ben, he did have a choice. A lawyer will tell a jury that you made him take an experimental drug without him fully understanding the risks."

"But he would have died without it."

"How do you get on with Jerry?" Mike asked.

"The Marivant rep? All right I guess, we all do, he's a nice bloke."

"Takes care of you does he?"

"Look Mike, we make sure we spend an equal amount of time with all the reps."

"I saw you guys at the Robovir launch in Dubai. How much did it cost Marivant to fly you lot out there business class and put you up in the Burj Al Arab?"

"They can't send us business class or use five star hotels anymore."

"That's now, I'm talking about five or ten years ago and how well they looked after you then."

"Alright, I get the point."

"And so will the lawyers. They don't care about realities, they care about perceptions. That's why the industry has become so anal about any sponsorship now, they need to look whiter than white. But the lawyers don't give a damn about reality, they'll say that you were putting patients on the Spiravex trial because your department were indebted to Marivant. They won't look at the fact that Abbott flew you to a conference in Budapest or the BMS sponsored a workshop in Prague. They want to win their case."

Ben steered the TT onto the Chiswick flyover and joined the M4. The rush hour was over and the traffic was moving well. It wouldn't take long for them to reach Heathrow.

"Red tape and compensation culture, that's what the NHS is about these days," Mike said. "Why can't they just let us get on with our jobs? You'd think we spent six years at med school to deliberately kill people."

Ben joined the fast lane and brought the Audi up to eighty. It wasn't far to Heathrow now, and he needed to find out what had happened before he dropped Mike off.

"We can't afford to get sued," Ben said. "Did Spiravex kill either of your patients?"

There was a long silence.

"You're off the hook."

"Really?" Ben said.

"No MIs."

Ben smiled. No more deaths, no tussle with Marivant and no lawsuits from David's family. "So they're both fine?"

"I didn't say that," Mike replied.

Chapter 7

"This is our turn," Mike said.

Ben moved the car over to the inside lane and joined the slip road.

"What's wrong with the patients then?" Ben asked.

"Don't worry, they didn't have heart attacks, you're not going to get sued," Mike replied. "Bit of a wasted journey if you ask me."

"Not really," Ben said, and pulled up outside Terminal Two. "I'd have spent the next two weeks worrying about it."

He got out and pulled Mike's case from the boot.

"No you wouldn't," Mike said, taking the suitcase from Ben. "Guess I should have told you at the house, Claire's emailed you the patients' notes." He hauled his suitcase onto a trolley. "Thanks for the lift though."

Ben got back in his car. He'd made the right choice to come up. Neither of Mike's patients had died of an MI, meaning that he was one step closer to confirming that Spiravex didn't cause long term heart damage. If he could find a way of learning about Rachel Millbank's patients without her knowing, then he could walk away from Spiravex with his conscience as clear as it could be. He'd always have to live with the decision that he put his own wife on the drug in the first place, but at least he would have fulfilled his responsibilities towards the other patients in MVT084.

He revved the engine and sped away from the terminal, he was finally on the home straight with this business.

* * * *

"How are we going to build my cover?" Helen said, and took a sip of her black coffee. She rested the cup back down on the arm of the Chesterfield.

"What have you learned?" Luke asked.

"Stick as close to reality as possible." That's what they'd been taught in Namibia.

"Exactly. That way you're unlikely to make a mistake," he said. "Keep your story the same until you joined us. Change the name of your college at Oxford, and the title of your Ph.D. We'll steal the identity of someone with a similar profile who wouldn't be known to your targets. You may need to do background reading on the Ph.D. Williams might only be an MD, but he'll be able to talk confidently about science."

"I doubt it," Helen said. "Most doctors I've met don't have a clue what goes on at molecular level. They rely on the reps to educate them."

"Not in HIV," Luke replied. "You must assume he knows everything. With regard to your career at Pharmagen, we will find a company that floated around the same time you left and make out you owned a lot of share options."

"A biotech millionaire," Anne said.

"Afterwards I travelled a bit, then moved to Brighton," Helen added.

"Hove," Anne said. "Your flat's in Hove."

Helen turned to Luke. "So what am I doing now?"

"What were you doing these last six months?" Luke asked.

"Enjoying my life for the first time in years." Until it was ruined by an arrogant Irishman.

"That's your answer. We'll add details once we know more about Williams," he said.

"You've already got the kitesurfing," Anne said.

"He's a windsurfer," Helen replied.

"Same thing."

"Not at all." How could someone so sporty know so little? It was like saying that skiing and snowboarding are the same.

"It's of no importance," Luke cut in. "You have a good reason to be on the same beach."

"Do you think he'll be expecting surveillance?" Helen asked.

"I doubt it," Anne said.

"I wouldn't be so sure," Luke said. "There's a lot about conspiracy theories on TV. Many people are paranoid today. Williams backed away when Cook pressed him, he may have felt threatened. That's why we're here now. We must assume he knows something. If he does, he would be wise to be afraid. That's why Anne is doing the reconnaissance and you're not. With your looks you stand out too much. He must only notice you in a way that is a natural coincidence."

"So what else am I going to do besides reading this file and going over some biochemistry?"

"Building your cover is more than just facts," Luke said. "Become familiar with Brighton. Find favourite restaurants and bars. Your apartment should have the touch of a woman. Use your Amex, there's no budget."

Helen raised her eyebrows. This was going to be fun after all. She could spend hours wandering the lanes and spending money on luxuries and fine food.

"That's how I managed to get you the SLK," Anne said, and smiled. "Same goes for your flat. According to the property agent I spoke to, it's the dog's."

"If it's obvious you've lived in Brighton for more than six months, there's no chance he'll guess a connection to Marivant," Luke said. "But that's only half of the battle. We need him to fall for you."

"I was thinking about that during dinner," Anne said. "He's spent a lot of time in Africa, and if he's like most doctors he'll be driven by the desire to help others. His wife was doing volunteer work in a Médecins Sans Frontières clinic when she met Williams. That's where she got the needlestick injury that gave her HIV. I think Helen's history should include a stint with an HIV charity in Namibia."

"Good," Luke said, then turned to Helen. "With your knowledge of HIV and Namibia you'll think of something."

"It might be a way of getting him to open up about the Spiravex trial," Helen said. "It'd be natural to talk about which pharmaceutical corporations are stepping up to the plate and which aren't in the developed world."

"Focus on Marivant. They've spent a lot of money building hospitals, training doctors, and making their drugs available at below cost price" Luke added. "If you mention these things, it might prompt him to tell you any bad things he knows about MVT084."

"And if I find out he's close to the truth?" Helen asked. "Do I kill him then?"

Luke cocked his head and glared at her.

"Anne, leave the room," he said.

Anne's look of confusion lasted only an instant. "I'll be in the kitchen." She stood up and left.

Luke got up and walked out of Helen's view. She stared straight ahead at the windows. Her heart was pounding at double speed. The faint reflection of Luke's figure grew behind her in the glass. A ring of cold metal pressed against her right temple.

"I could kill you right now," he said.

Helen breathed in slowly. "But you're not going to."

He didn't reply. There was a click that jolted the pistol's muzzle deeper into her skin. The safety was off.

"Are you sure about that?"

"You need me. Shooting me would screw up the whole operation." Keep cool, that's all she had to do. There was no way he'd kill her. The image of Adam's skull exploding flashed before her mind's eye. She just had to keep cool. "Quit messing around Luke, we're wasting time."

The gun was withdrawn from her temple.

Helen stayed completely still.

"The point is I could kill you. I could do it without a second thought."

"Congratulations, you're a hard arse."

"Are you?"

"Am I what?"

"Hard," Luke said, and walked round to face her. "Why do you always ask if you'll need to kill Williams?"

She held his searching look. "I've never killed anyone before."

Luke tilted his head. "Are you sure about that?"

Helen opened her mouth to say yes, but closed it and looked down. He knew. She'd told no one, not even Anne, yet he still knew.

"You have not killed an adult," Luke said.

He definitely knew.

"The thought of putting a gun to a man's head and pulling the trigger is a problem for you?" he asked.

"Shouldn't it be?"

"You can remember the conversation we had when we first met?"

She pictured the bar in San Diego two years earlier at a conference on nucleic acids. Luke was posing as an executive from a biotech company. Conferences were where he scouted for new agents and clients. That's why he'd sat next to her. She was already loosened up with a few vodkas. He patiently listened to her describing her disillusionment with research and the pain caused by her father's suicide. They discussed the pointlessness of life and she remembered drawing strength from his pragmatic outlook.

"We talked a lot," Helen said.

"What did we say about religion?"

"Neither of us believes in a god."

"Do you know how rare that is?"

Helen shrugged.

"Less than three percent of the earth's population are true atheists," Luke said. "Slade deliberately looks for people who have no religious allegiance, or potential for any. Our organisation is founded on the principle that morality is irrelevant. Our clients come from all sections of society. We have done jobs for the church and for drug cartels. We work for money, not a cause. Our agents need to have liberated their minds from traditional moral dogma. That requires mental discipline."

"But it's obvious to anyone who understands evolution."

"Only to someone who understands the weakness within. We have evolved to believe in a god and to have a conscience. It's a genetic trick that has made man superior to other animals by forming strong communities that rely on this mutual sense of responsibility. Religion and morality are a product of evolution. The discovery of the 'God gene' proves this."

"But I'm still stuck with a conscience."

"That's where mental discipline comes in," Luke said. "Take Maria. She does get jealous, but she's able to rationalise that feeling by understanding its evolutionary roots. Jealous women are protecting their genetic investment by ensuring they receive all the provision their male partners can give. Jealous men are making sure it's actually their genetic future they are working for and not some other male's. Morality is a result of the conscience as much as monogamy is a result of jealousy. Both come from evolution and both are redundant once you know the truth. The conscience is like a psychological appendix, it's useless and potentially dangerous. It's an unnecessary hindrance to our having exactly what we want in this life."

"Anything goes."

"As long as you don't get caught," he said. "Slade recruits people who can learn how to silence the irrational voice of their conscience. The first step towards achieving this is to realise no gods exist and there are no eternal consequences to your actions. The rest is a logical progression."

"I'll learn."

Luke nodded. "I know you will, I can see it in your eyes." He smiled. "You are a natural predator."

Helen felt her pulse race again.

"However, we know the mind still plays tricks on us so we provide some help," Luke continued. "Those pills I gave you are designed for this purpose, they were developed by one of our clients for military use. They suppress the release of chemicals that cause this sense of conscience. They stop you doubting yourself and bring about a state that is closer to the pure human form, the way we would be if this 'God gene' didn't exist."

"Just like animals."

"We are animals, and animals aren't held back by moral codes."

Helen nodded. She'd concluded this herself after reading 'The Selfish Gene' as an undergraduate, but her heart was still saying otherwise. She needed to learn how to suppress that internal voice.

"You ask about killing Williams," Luke said. "Once you know you need to, will you do it?"

"Yes."

"Very well. If you have any doubts, take the drug." Luke sat down in one of the armchairs. "However, a consultant's death isn't going to be easy to hide. We should avoid killing him if it's possible."

Helen nodded. She finally had her answer.

"Call Anne back," Luke said.

Helen got up, left the room and went to the cavernous Elizabethan kitchen that lay on the other side of the staircase. She found Anne smoking a cigarette.

"Luke wants you."

"Did he give you the god and conscience talk?" Anne said.

Helen nodded.

"What do you think?"

"Makes sense."

Anne stubbed the cigarette out on a plate and they returned to the communications room. Anne went to the workstation she'd been using and pulled a briefcase from under the desk.

"Here's all the kit you'll need for now," she said, and handed Helen the case. "I've put a Berretta and a few boxes of ammo in there. There's a key for the flat too."

"Is it ready to move into?" Helen asked.

"The agent said it was fully furnished. I asked them to put a few basics in the fridge."

"Thanks." Helen turned back to Luke. "So you don't want me doing any reconnaissance at all?"

"No. You'll meet Anne in a few days and go over anything new she's learned."

There was silence. Helen looked at Luke, then at Anne. "Have you got the car keys?" she asked.

Anne smiled, went back to her workstation and returned with her bag. She produced a set of keys and handed them to Helen. "I'll drop by tomorrow."

Helen turned to Luke. "You've got my bag in your car."

"I'll come with you," he replied.

They left Anne and walked back through the shadowy passageways to the front of the building. Helen popped the boot of the SLK and slung the case inside before transferring her holdall from Luke's car.

"This job is important," Luke said. "There's a lot at stake."

"Have I let you down before?"

"You have not worked alone before."

"Don't worry, I'll be fine."

Luke nodded.

She got in the Mercedes and watched him walk back through the stone entrance, then looked around to familiarise herself with the controls. She started the engine and reversed the car out of the space. She pushed the gearshift into drive and looked ahead. The deepening dusk was transforming the lawns and woodland into seamless shades of darkness. Brighton was an hour away. She had fond memories of the city but she wasn't going there for a hen party this time.

Chapter 8

Ben was sitting on his sofa reading Claire's email when the entry-phone rang. He looked at his watch; it was ten-thirty.

He put the laptop on the coffee table, got to his feet and walked into the hall. He pressed the intercom button next to the front door.

"Hello?"

"It's Ruth."

"It's really late, what's up?"

"You said to check with you if I arranged a night out, and seeing as you appear to have to lost the use of your thumb, I decided to come round in person."

Ben remembered the text message and groaned. He'd forgotten to send the reply.

"Are you going to let me in?" she asked.

He buzzed her into the building, opened his front door and waited for her. He watched the display above the lift scroll from one to five. There was a ping and the doors opened to reveal his sister glaring at him.

"Have I done something wrong?" she asked, striding towards him.

"No."

"Why haven't you replied to my text?" She pushed past him into his flat.

"I've been busy all day," Ben said, closing the door behind her.

"How long does it take to text someone?"

They walked into the lounge. Ruth sat on the large couch, Ben chose the two-seater.

"I was going to reply earlier but I got distracted," Ben said. "I only walked in the door quarter of an hour ago."

"You were working all this time?"

"Not exactly. I went to London after I finished at the clinic."

"What for?" Ruth asked.

"To find out what happened to a couple of patients in the Spiravex trial."

"Learn anything useful?"

"No more than if I'd come straight home. I was just reading an email from the guy I went to see."

Ruth leaned forward and put her hand on the laptop. "Can I?"

"Go ahead."

She moved the screen round and began reading.

"It just confirms Mike's patients didn't have heart attacks." He said, watching for her reaction as she scanned the email.

Ruth frowned. "But one of them still died."

He knew she'd pick up on that. He had.

"Of an OD."

"And the other's missing," Ruth said. She rubbed her forehead, then looked up at him with a perplexed expression. "They may not have had MIs, but don't you think it's even more worrying that three of the four patients we know about from the Spiravex trial died within the space of a month, and the fourth has disappeared?"

She was echoing his first reaction but it was a big jump to go from suspecting the patients were killed by a drug's side effect to them being murdered. He had to be absolutely certain before he started down that road, playing devil's advocate with Ruth might just tease out any flaws in any murder theory.

"If they were diabetics or from a coronary unit I might be concerned, but we're talking about HIV patients. The girl who died was a heroin addict, so having an OD was tragic but hardly surprising. The bloke who's missing is an asylum seeker, they go AWOL all the time."

"What about Ian Jenkins and David Walters?" Ruth asked. "There may be nothing suspicious about a heart attack, but a hit and run?"

Exactly. Finding out that David Walters had been killed in a car crash had initially dismissed any chance of their being a connection between his and Ian's death, but now it felt like a signpost to something far more sinister.

"What are you suggesting? Someone killed them?"

"I don't know," Ruth said, shaking her head. "Maybe."

"But why? There's no reason to kill them. You're reading too much into it Ruth. There are lots of uninsured drivers who wouldn't stop after an accident. The other deaths are just a coincidence, you're adding two and two to get ten."

"And you're getting one. What about the other UK patients?"

"I don't know."

"Are you going to find out?"

He nodded slowly. "I have to, don't I?" he said. "The truth is I was a little shocked when I saw the OD too. I just wanted to see if you thought the same, and that I wasn't over reacting." Ruth was frowning again. "What's the matter?"

"I think you should go to the police."

"We haven't got enough yet, it's just circumstantial evidence. Besides, the police won't lose much sleep over a couple of gay blokes, a junky and an asylum seeker."

"That's not very nice," she said.

"It's just the truth. They've got other stuff on their minds."

"But what if there really is something going on?"

"There's no real evidence. They won't take us seriously."

"I'm not talking about telling the police now, I'm talking about you," she said. "If these patients were murdered, then whoever the killers are could come after you if you keep sniffing around."

"Your artist's imagination is working overtime now Ruth." And maybe his was too. "I think we're reading too much into this."

"Can you be sure?"

He took a deep breath. "No, I can't, but..."

"Exactly," she said. "Don't put yourself in danger, go to the police."

"But I can't even think of a motive."

"Maybe Ian's death was caused by Spiravex. Maybe Marivant know there are long-term problems and they've killed the other patients to avoid future lawsuits."

"That idea occurred to me but then I remembered that when I phoned the principal investigator he all but insisted I seek compensation for Ian Jenkins. It doesn't sound like they're worried about being sued. Big companies are well insured, they wouldn't need to kill anyone."

"Maybe they want to avoid bad publicity."

"It's too extreme. Corporations don't do that kind of stuff."
He suppressed a yawn. He needed to get a good night's sleep, he'd
think straight in the morning. "Listen, I'm knackered, and I've got a
load more emails to sift through before I go to bed."

She nodded and stood up. "What about Saturday night?"

"Depends what you have in mind," Ben said.

"Don't you trust me?"

"It's nothing to do with church is it?"

"No."

"I'll come then," he said.

"Good. We're meeting in Santa Fe at seven."

"Why so early?"

"Is that a problem?" Ruth asked.

"I guess not." Ben stood up and walked her to the door.

"You will be careful won't you?" Ruth said in the hall.

Ben nodded and opened the door to let her out. "See you
Saturday."

He returned to the lounge and sat in front of his laptop.

A doctor doing his job well will identify a specific illness
after a process of elimination through differential diagnosis. A
patient would describe a list of symptoms that could be caused by a
number of different conditions. A good physician would only arrive
at the correct conclusion after dismissing all the other possible
causes through further investigation.

Ben knew of colleagues who'd misdiagnosed serious
diseases like cancer because the symptoms could come from a more
common and less threatening source; lives are lost because doctors
perceive cancer as unlikely and they miss it by not carrying out
thorough tests.

Ben wasn't like that with his medicine and he wasn't going
to be like that now.

He drummed his fingers on the base of the keyboard. He
still believed there was a possibility the deaths were random, but
until he could prove it beyond doubt, he had no choice but to
consider the possibility the patients were murdered. As with cancer,
if the improbable became reality, catching it early was vital. To do
that he needed to find out what had happened to every patient in
the trial.

He typed a reply to Claire's email, asking for the asylum
seeker's details together with his last known address. He sent the

message and began emailing Rachel Milbank to find out what happened to her patients from MVT084. He stopped halfway through as Ruth's parting words came back to him.

Milbank's close relationship with someone from Marivant meant that any enquiries he made about the trial may get relayed to them. If his sister's concerns proved to be more than paranoia, it wouldn't just be the patients on the study who were killed. Adding a doctor to the list of dead or missing would be small beer. Ben closed the message without sending it; he didn't want to end up being part of someone else's investigation.

Chapter 9

"Is this for real?" Ben said, and looked up from Amy Taylor's notes.

Simon, a tubby health advisor with a goatee and tattooed forearms, nodded and lowered his eyes.

"And she didn't know till this morning?"

Simon shook his head.

"Unbelievable." Ben slapped the file down on his desk. "What did she say?"

"She wouldn't listen to me. She asked to see a doctor, a real doctor, not 'some kid'."

Ben ran his fingers through his hair and frowned. It was the least he could do, but his Friday morning clinic was already running late and this would make it later still. He was desperate to put the whole Marivant business to bed by the weekend, but at this rate it would be dragging into next week.

"Give me a couple of minutes then send her through," he said.

"Thanks Ben." Simon stood up and left the room. Ben flicked through Amy's notes again. He saw plenty of tragedies in his job, but this was one of the most senseless; it never should have happened.

He closed the file and checked his emails, nothing from Claire yet.

There was a knock at the door. Simon led a blonde woman in her late twenties into the room then left. She was slim, wore tan trousers and a cream jumper. If she hadn't looked so tired, she would have been pretty. She was trembling.

"Take a seat Amy."

"Is it true?" she said, not moving.

Ben held eye contact for a few seconds then nodded.

She slumped into the chair opposite his desk. "The bastard." She started to cry.

Ben wanted to hug her, but knew better.

"Would you like a nurse in here as well?"

She shook her head, wiped her nose with a crumpled tissue and looked up. The red whites sharpened the blue of her eyes.

"Alex too?"

"I'm afraid so."

She started crying again.

When breaking news like this it was best to just sit silently and wait for the patient to ask questions in their own time.

"Can they do something for him?"

"There are drugs," he said.

"I didn't know I had it," she said. "I had all those blood tests when I was pregnant. Why didn't they pick it up?"

"Your sample got mislaid in the pathology lab. It was only tested for HIV in the last two weeks."

"But they took my blood six months ago."

Ben nodded. "The results are normally back in a week or two."

"Would he still have got it if you'd known before I gave birth?"

Ben breathed in deeply. "The chances of transmission would have been lower."

"How much lower?"

"With anti-retroviral drugs, and no breastfeeding, it falls from over thirty percent to less than two."

Her mouth fell open. "I was told to have a natural birth."

"The midwives didn't know."

"You said there are drugs, is there a cure yet?" Amy asked.

"Not so far, there may never be, but the drugs we do have allow us to treat the disease chronically."

"In English please."

"It's not a death sentence. If you take the drugs properly you'll live to see your grandchildren."

"Will Alex see his grandchildren?"

"It's possible."

"Possible?" She shook her head and her face started to fill with anger. "He's ruined our lives. I'm gonna kill the bastard!"

Join the queue. Her husband was well known at the GUM clinic. He was a long-haul pilot who'd been diagnosed with HIV a couple of years earlier but never mentioned he was married. He was obviously too spineless to tell his wife; that would mean letting her know how he'd become infected.

"My baby," Amy said, then stopped sobbing. "What about compensation?"

The word that seemed to be on the lips of every patient who entered the hospital. For once someone had good reason to use it.

"There'll be an investigation, but on the face of it, it seems obvious it was the Trust's fault that your son was infected," Ben said. "I doubt you'll need to go to court, the lawyers will sort that out."

Her shoulders sagged. She shook her head and started crying again.

He hadn't felt this awful about his job since the days when he had to tell haemophiliacs they'd been infected by contaminated blood. The majority of his patients now caught the virus through unprotected sex. For some it was just the result of a one-off drunken encounter. That was bad luck. Then there were those who were just too sexed up for their own good, and went to events like dark rooms. Top prize for senseless infection went to the bug chasers though. He really struggled to sign the script for a man who'd been to a gift party, where the gift was HIV through sex with a known infected host.

Amy's case was right at the other end of the spectrum. Not only had her mindlessly selfish husband infected her, but because of some freak cock-up in the path lab her baby would suffer needlessly for a lifetime. What kind of God allowed things like this too happen? This was why his hackles rose whenever his sister brought up religion. You had to be blind or stupid to believe in a benevolent God. He was either some ruthless sadist who took pleasure in watching suffering, or he didn't exist. Period.

He looked at Amy's shaking shoulders. Her prospects may be better than her son's. Being born with HIV was a tough break, but with modern, better tolerated once daily drugs and well developed professional pediatric support, there was hope. The trick was adhering to the drugs, if he let that slip, resistance would set in and just at the point when he should be starting to plan for the future, some doctor would tell him he'd exhausted all the therapy options and he only had a few years left to live. However, if he got into his teens without blowing too many drugs, then he could look forward to a near normal life, and yes, even one day have grandchildren.

Amy wiped her eyes. Ben reached into his drawer, pulled out a box of tissues and passed it to her.

"Thank you," she said, and blew her nose. The tears continued to flow.

He mulled over the Spiravex trial again. A question she'd asked was bugging him. Maybe he was looking at the deaths from the wrong angle. If Ruth was right and the patients had been murdered, then it may have nothing to do with heart attacks or lawsuits. A theory formed in his mind, but it was so unspeakably evil he was inclined to dismiss it immediately. The deaths had to be a coincidence, but he couldn't be sure until he'd learnt about the other UK patients.

Amy was looking into her lap, but her sobs were less frequent.

He glanced across at his computer screen. He couldn't see any new emails in his inbox; Claire still hadn't got back to him.

If only he could be sure Milbank wouldn't say anything to her husband then he'd have his answer in a few minutes. But he knew he couldn't, she wasn't someone he'd ever got on with, and he'd heard that she treated her staff like personal servants, and the unit as a means of feeding her academic ambitions rather than a place to improve the lives of patients.

There was a knock at the door.

"Who is it?" Ben called.

The door opened. Simon looked inside and raised his eyebrows.

Ben nodded.

Simon entered with the adherence nurse and walked over to Amy. He put his arm round her shoulder.

"Come with us love," he said. "Now you've spoken to Doctor Williams the nurse needs to have a chat about taking the medication."

Amy looked up and slowly got to her feet.

Simon steered her towards the door then looked back at Ben. He raised his hand and mouthed the word 'thanks'.

Ben nodded and looked down at the notes in front of him. He read two words then lifted his head sharply. "Hang on Simon, didn't you work at Guys before you came here?"

"For five years."

"How well did you get on with Rachel Milbank?"

Simon grimaced. He stepped back inside the room and closed the door.

"What about the research nurse?"

"We were good mates, she's a real laugh."

"Does she owe you any favours?" Ben asked.

"No, but she wouldn't need to. She'd do anything for anyone."

"Even if it means going behind Milbank's back?"

"She hates her. I reckon she'd jump at it, as long her job wasn't at risk."

"Milbank will never know. I need some information about two patients on MVT084."

"The trial with all the heart attacks?" Simon asked.

Ben nodded slowly.

"What information do you want?"

"Their current clinical data and all their personal details, where they live and so on."

"I can only ask. When do you need it by?"

"As soon as possible."

"I'll get on to it straight away." Simon left the room.

Ben leaned back in his chair then noticed the screen flashing: 'You have mail.'

He clicked on the open icon; it was from Claire. After reading three lines he knew Simon was his last real hope of learning any more about the patients from the trial.

* * * *

"So what do you think?" Anne asked Helen.

"I couldn't have chosen better myself," Helen replied.

She led Anne into the bright living area of the eighth-floor penthouse. The furniture, although not quite to her taste, was modern and relatively well scattered across the beech floor, giving a good sense of space. All she needed to make the flat feel like hers was a couple of vases and a few candles.

Once again she'd been blessed with great views. Large windows overlooked an urban jumble of tiled roofs, chimney pots and trees that led to the sea; the occasional church spire and apartment block climbed above the low-rise skyline. The whole scene was speckled with the white flashing of seagulls as they wheeled over the buildings and chanted their monotonous mantra.

Anne sat on the cream fabric sofa. Helen made some coffee, lit a cigarette and sat in one of the armchairs.

"Have you read through the stuff I gave you?" Anne asked.

"Of course," Helen replied. "I think you're right about them being inseparable. After what they've been through, who wouldn't be?" She paused to pick up her notepad from the coffee table. "I've also come up with a couple of ideas about getting to Ruth."

"Go on."

"She's a Bible-basher right?"

"Don't see why else she'd give a tenth of her salary to the church," Anne said.

"She's probably the type who's always on the lookout for potential converts."

"And you're going to pose as bait?"

"Why not?" Helen asked.

Anne laughed. "Just make sure you don't get suckered in. I'm not sure Slade's the right place for Born-Again Christians."

Helen smiled. "If that doesn't work I've got another idea, salsa dancing."

"Where did you get that from?"

"There are payments of five pounds going out of her account every Wednesday and Saturday to a Club New York. Turns out they give lessons."

"Sounds a bit corny to me," Anne said.

"Better than church though."

"Are you going tomorrow?"

Helen rolled her eyes and took a long drag of her cigarette. She sighed.

"What's the matter?"

"Just wish I wasn't here at all."

"You don't have a choice do you?"

"No," Helen said. "I'm beginning to realise that."

"I did ages ago," Anne said. "Once you know too much they've got you for life. At least you got into the Marivant job early, it'll be ages before they allow me near so much money."

"That was only because I knew Adam." She flicked her ash into a saucer.

"It must have been hard to betray him," Anne said.

"It would have been a lot harder if he hadn't dumped me while I was in Namibia."

"I know you loved him," Anne said. "I remember what a mess you were while we were training."

"I know, but I've come to realise that in my heart I always knew it wouldn't last." Helen took another drag then stubbed her cigarette out. "I was attracted to his idealism, it reminded me of better days, but by the time we met we weren't suited. I just wanted to party and he wanted a family."

"You told me it ended because you joined Slade," Anne said.

"Not specifically Slade. It was more because I decided to leave research and make some real money. He wanted to be with someone who shared his values."

"Killing him's a good way to get your own back."

"I didn't kill him," Helen said. "Luke did."

"You knew what was going to happen."

"Not when I first discussed it with Luke. I'd only ever been given small assignments, I didn't know how vicious Slade could be."

"You knew by the time Adam arrived in New York."

"I didn't lure him there, he contacted me. He thought I was in America as a commercial negotiator, he wasn't to know Slade worked for Marivant."

"And you saw a chance to land a place in the millionaire's club."

Helen nodded. "Once I realised they were going to kill him it was too late. They would have done it with or without me." She twisted a loose strand of hair round her finger. "I nearly didn't go through with it."

"You had a crisis of conscience?"

"Something like that. I offered him a way out, but he didn't take it."

"Did you take the drug?"

Helen nodded. "I couldn't have done it otherwise."

"It's powerful stuff," Anne said, "and dangerous. You know about the team working in Afghanistan don't you?"

Helen nodded. Two guys out of a team of seven who had taken the drug while on a mission had suffered heart attacks. But the drug was out of reach of the FDA and there was just some mutterings about not taking it at altitude. There was never any suggestion of withdrawing it from company use.

"You've used it though?"

"A couple of times." Anne lowered her head. "More after the event than before."

"To get rid of the guilt?"

Anne raised her eyes. For a second Helen was looking into a mirror revealing all the turmoil, fear and darkness that haunted her own dreams.

"Do you really think Luke's right?" Anne asked. "Is it really possible to silence the conscience forever?"

Helen looked away. She'd gone over it in her head a dozen times, Everything Luke said made sense, but if he was right why were both Anne and her struggling so much? She wasn't in a position to question it though. She looked back.

"I don't know," she said, "but having a villa in Spain and a new Porsche helps."

The vulnerability in Anne's eyes receded back into the shadows. "I can't believe you got a full million for the tiny amount you did."

"Luke and I were getting on much better then. Besides, Slade didn't have much on me, the money needed to be big to make sure I'd deliver."

"What happened with you and Luke?" Anne asked.

Helen shrugged. "Just fizzled out."

"Probably for the best. It's never a good idea to be shagging your boss."

"Hypocrite," Helen said. "I know you've been sleeping with him too."

"He told you?" Anne's cheeks turned red.

"No, but you just did." Helen smiled at the sight of Anne's jaw dropping. "Are you still screwing him?"

Anne folded her arms and slowly closed her mouth.

"You are aren't you?" Helen said.

"No," Anne said. "No, I'm not, and even if I was I wouldn't let him kill my ex-boyfriend."

"If Slade decided to do it, you couldn't stop them."

Helen watched Anne as she struggled to regain her composure.

"Would you still join Slade if you knew as much then as you do now?" Anne asked.

Why was she was digging again? They were stuck there and that was it.

"I don't know much more about them than when we started, which was next to nothing. Have you managed to find out anything while you've been in HQ?"

"Only snippets," Anne replied. "They're not exactly Tesco or HSBC, they don't put you through a cheesy corporate induction day."

"But you have learnt more than we knew in Namibia?" Helen asked.

"I know they're not a new company. They go back at least to the beginning of the Cold War, possibly further."

"What about our section?"

"No, the Bio division was formed in the eighties. It's one of the smallest parts, yet it makes a huge chunk of their profits. The other sections deal with criminal organisations, or 'alternative industries' as it's called in the accounts, but the largest amount of work is done for governments."

"I bet they don't find agents for that at science conferences," Helen said.

"They mainly recruit ex-cons for the crime work, and ex-servicemen for the government jobs."

"What do they do? Same stuff as us?"

"Apart from the military coups," Anne said. "All the dirty jobs that can't be traced back to politicians or other public figures. That's where Luke worked before he was made head of the Bio division."

"Slade must make a fortune," Helen said

"They do. If you thought you were well paid for delivering Adam, think again. That was just a tiny fraction of the money they've made from the Marivant job."

"But if the truth got out it would ruin them."

"Precisely. With a hundred billion turnover, they can afford a few tens of millions to keep a secret." Anne pulled out a plastic A4 wallet from her bag. "Which is why we're here now."

"What's that?"

"Luke's asked me to work on contingency plans. These are details of some of Williams' patients."

"You won't need a contingency plan," Helen said. "I've got it covered."

"Always plan for the unexpected." Anne opened the folder and started looking through.

"Haven't enough patients died?" Helen said.

Anne put the file down; her expression became very grave. She looked Helen straight in the eyes.

"Is it definitely over between you and Luke?" she asked.

"Absolutely."

Anne breathed in deep.

"What's the matter?"

Anne said nothing and continued staring at Helen.

"You're freaking me out now," Helen said. "What's wrong?"

"You didn't really answer me when I asked you if you thought the conscience could be silenced."

"I said I don't know."

"You also said that Luke's talk to you about evolution and the conscience made sense when I asked you at HQ. Do you really believe that?"

"It seems extreme unless you're an atheist, then it makes perfect sense," Helen replied. "But once you've started down that road there's no turning back."

"Exactly," Anne said. "You begin with a few small things, the odd lie, a bit of cheating, stuff that others would call wrong, but you don't believe in right or wrong, so you ramp things up and move on to extortion." She paused. "Or worse."

Helen nodded. "Then you reach a point where you've done so much that to think in terms of morality is all but impossible. You wouldn't be able to face up to yourself even if you wanted to."

"And you've reached that point now?" Anne asked.

"I was there before I joined Slade, that's why Luke was able to recruit me so easily. A bit of lying and cheating was no worse than I'd already done."

Anne looked disappointed.

"That doesn't mean I'm happy about killing people," Helen said. "I might be able to rationalise the fact that there's no good or evil and therefore there's no such thing as sin, but that doesn't stop the growing feeling of sickness I have inside of me."

"It doesn't get any better." Anne looked down. "Wait till you've gone all the way."

"You've actually killed someone?"

Helen was just able to perceive a nod.

"A security guard." Anne looked back up. "I'd broken into a biotech firm in Zurich and was raiding their mainframe. I didn't hear him coming. It was either him or me."

There was a long silence.

"At least it wasn't cold-blooded murder," Helen said.

"Wasn't it? He was just doing his job."

"So were you."

"That's different."

"Why? When he puts on his uniform and carries a gun, he's making money from the fact that he may have to kill someone to protect the profitability of a corporation."

"It didn't feel like that," Anne said. "He didn't look like a killer. I read about it in the newspaper afterwards, he had three kids. Even if you use some perverse argument to justify what I did, can you do the same for Ben Williams?"

Helen bit her lip. "This is going nowhere. We don't have a choice, Slade's got both of us now."

"What if I found a way out?" Anne asked.

"What do you mean?"

"A way in which we're able to leave Slade and guarantee they won't touch us."

"How?"

"I can only tell you if I'm sure you're up for it," Anne said. "We promised to watch each other's backs. I need you to do that now, in case I get caught."

"Caught doing what?"

Anne looked hesitant for a few moments, and then spoke.

"Why did Slade hire me?"

"You're a hacker."

Anne nodded.

"You've found information you could use against them?"

Anne raised her eyebrows.

Helen didn't know what to think. Namibia was a long time ago and they'd both changed since then. Was this some scheme cooked up by Luke to test her loyalty? Was it actually possible to break free?

"I'm not sure."

"Forget what I said." Anne put the folder back in her bag.

"I can't really, can I?" Helen said.

Anne lifted the bag onto her lap and put her hand inside. "Are you going to tell Luke?"

It was catch twenty-two. If Helen said no and Anne was under orders from Luke, she was dead. If she said yes and Anne was for real, she was still dead. Decision time.

"I won't say anything," she said. "I promise."

Anne's expression didn't change. She pulled a mobile out of the bag and got to her feet.

Helen stayed put and watched her leave. As soon as the door closed she picked up her own mobile and dialled Luke's number. It was engaged.

Chapter 10

A red light on the edge of Lewisham gave Ben another chance to look at the address Simon had given him. He turned the A-Z on the passenger seat so he could read it; he didn't have far to go.

He glanced out of the open car window at the shoppers strolling along the pavement. That's what he should have been doing with his Saturday afternoon, not tracking down an HIV-infected prostitute called Leticia. But there was no alternative, especially now he'd thought of a theoretical reason for Marivant murdering the patients.

Leticia was the key; she was the only UK patient he didn't know about. According to the research nurse she'd last visited the clinic in March and her next check-up wasn't until June.

The other patient from Guys had died of an MI. Two days earlier that would have been all the evidence he needed to confirm Spiravex caused long-term heart damage, but he wanted more than that now. To disprove the new theory he had to be certain the overdose and the hit and run were a coincidence.

The lights changed and he entered central Lewisham. He knew this area of South-East London well. He'd been a locum at Greenwich Hospital for six months after coming back from Kenya. It was very different from the part of the city Mike Procter lived in. The Mercedes and Porsches were ten years older, and instead of smart coffee houses and expensive delicatessens, there were scruffy launderettes and Indian take-aways.

He looked at the map again as he came to the end of Lewisham High Street. After another set of lights, he turned up the road given in the address. It was lined with run-down terraced houses.

He found a space fifty yards from the number he was looking for, and walked back up the street.

All the houses would have benefited from a coat of paint, but the exterior to number fifty-five looked beyond repair. There was a small front yard full of litter and weeds. The window frames were flaking and the brickwork was crumbling. An old BMW with blacked out windows straddled the curb in front of it.

Ben hesitated at the end of the path then strode up and knocked on the door. A steady beat was coming from inside, but there didn't seem to be any movement. He knocked louder. The music stopped, but still no one came to the door. He knocked again. A light came on, revealing the filth on the frosted glass of the door. A shadow grew as someone approached, finally obscuring the light completely. The door opened, and Ben found himself looking at a broad muscle-filled T-shirt with two black arms folded across it. He looked up at the unfriendly face glaring down at him.

"What?"

"Is Leticia here?" Ben asked.

"Are you the police?"

"No."

The man stepped out of the house, making Ben take a step sideways. He looked up and down the street, and then back at Ben.

He flicked his head towards the corridor.

Ben looked inside. It was everything he'd expected: the wallpaper was peeling off the walls, revealing holes in the plaster; the colour of the threadbare carpet was invisible under the muck that covered it.

He slowly stepped inside. The door closed behind him.

"Wait in there," the man said, pointing to a door immediately to the left of the entrance.

Ben grabbed the handle and pushed the door open. The room was dark inside. He felt for a light switch and flicked it on. There was a double bed against the far wall and a pile of crumpled sheets lay on the floor next to it. He walked up to the bed. The mattress was covered in stains of human origin, there was no way he was sitting on that. He turned round. There was a TV sat in the corner with a pile of DVDs underneath. The images on the covers drew his eyes like fleshy magnets.

The sound of voices came from further inside the house. A deep voice was shouting. His heart raced. Why wasn't he doing his weekend shopping, or flying across the water on his Viper? This was crazy.

He crossed the room to the doorway and looked down the hall. The door at the end opened and the man who'd let him in appeared. He stopped once he saw Ben.

"Are you a punter?" he asked.

Ben shook his head. The man turned and leaned into the room behind him. He said something inaudible then looked back and repeated the flicking gesture with his head.

Ben walked towards the door. The air became thick with the smell of weed. He stepped past the doorman.

This room wasn't suffering from the same decay that beset the rest of the house. What once might have been a typical dining room and kitchen area, now extended into a much larger space. Parts of the kitchen remained, but a bar had been added along the right-hand side. Two tall speakers sat against the opposite wall, between them was a wide sofa where two black men sat either side of a skinny white girl. The thick layer of make-up didn't disguise the fact that she was probably under sixteen.

The man on the left looked about twenty. He was clean-shaven, wore baggy jeans and a red American-football shirt with the number twenty on it. The man on the right of the girl was much older. He had short hair, and a well-kept beard. He wore cords and a black shirt. He looked like the boss.

"You're really in it if you've let a pig in Lance," the youngest one said.

"Shut up. I told you, he's not a pig."

"Who are you then?" the man with the beard asked in a strong Caribbean accent.

"A doctor."

"Why do you want to see Leticia?"

"She hasn't been in the clinic for a couple of months and we need to speak to her."

The man stroked his beard and frowned at Ben. "You're a bit keen aren't you?"

"Sorry?"

"Since when do white doctors bother to make house calls on black hookers on a Saturday afternoon?"

"Leticia was in a trial that's been causing some problems," Ben said. "I tried phoning her mobile, but the number doesn't work."

"Problems?" the man said.

"I really need to speak to Leticia."

Ben's eyes locked on the handle of a gun protruding from between the cushions on the sofa. Not going windsurfing was turning into a disastrous decision.

The bearded man glanced down to where Ben was staring and pulled out the pistol.

"Guns make you nervous Doctor?" he said, putting it on his lap. "You got a name?"

Ben lifted his eyes slowly to meet those of the boss. It wasn't guns that were the problem, he'd handled plenty in the Cadet Force at school; it was the man holding the gun.

"I asked you your name."

"Frank Dean." It was the first name he remembered from Guys.

"Do you recognise him?" The boss said to the girl.

"Never seen him," she said. "But then I always ask for lady doctors."

"Lance. Go check on the internet whether a Frank Dean works at Guys."

"I only want to know if she's alright," Ben said. Lance paused in the doorway. "Some of the patients on the trial have had heart attacks."

"Leticia has no problem with her heart," the boss said. "Lance, do what I said."

Ben stood still. The girl crossed her legs and started grinning at him. What was her story? She'd probably been in care since she was born, then bounced around various foster homes before becoming fully institutionalised by the time she was a teenager; ripe pickings for the man sitting next to her. Treat her nice at first, buy her clothes and make her feel special for the first time in her life. Break her in gently with one of his friends and reward her with some extra pocket money, then get her hooked on crack. Her parents had never missed her, and the state wouldn't miss her now. He'd met hundreds like her in the GUM clinics of London.

He looked at the clock above the bar and watched the second hand go round twice.

Lance walked back into the room.

"There is a Frank Dean at Guys," he said.

The boss nodded then put the gun on the arm of the sofa.

Ben relaxed a little. If there'd been a photo he would have had a problem; Frank was bald.

"Leticia won't be coming to see you any more."

Ben gave him a puzzled look. "Is she going somewhere else for her meds?"

"You ask a lot of questions."

"I need to know in case the company organising the trial want to get hold of her."

"They won't."

"If she gets ill there might be compensation." After all this, there was no way he was going to leave without answers.

"She won't need any compensation. She's dead," the boss said, with as much emotion as a mechanic describing a car breaking down.

Ben tried to look shocked. "I'm sorry to hear that," he said. He ignored the raised eyebrows of the boss. "How did she die?"

"What difference does it make to you?"

"Like I said, there might be compensation if it's related to the drug."

"It was nothing to do with the drug." The boss raised the gun and pointed it at Ben. His pulse surged as their eyes met in a line with the sights. The tip of the gun lifted in the air. "Bang."

Ben watched the grey steel until it was resting back in the man's lap.

"Shot?" he asked.

The boss nodded.

"Do you know who killed her?"

Big mistake. The boss leapt off the sofa and strode towards Ben. His free hand closed around Ben's throat and pushed him against the wall.

Ben felt his windpipe closing. The muzzle of the gun was forced into his cheek. He looked into the man's eyes. There was nothing, no emotion at all. Taking a life would be no different to eating a hamburger or going for a dump. David, Ian, Julia. They were just names. Their hopes, their dreams, their families meant nothing, as did he.

The man relaxed his grip and let him go.

"See Doctor Dean out Lance."

80

Lance grabbed Ben's arm just above the elbow, pulled him out of the room and shoved him down the hallway. He opened the front door and manoeuvred Ben out.

"We don't know who killed her," he said. "Now get lost." He slammed the door leaving Ben standing in the street.

A grey mist had formed, adding to the depressed atmosphere of the area.

He walked away from the house, got in his car and closed the door. He sat still and stared at the steering wheel.

The balance of evidence had shifted. There were six patients on the Spiravex trial in the UK, one was missing and the other five were all dead. Three of those five had died in suspicious circumstances. Other than coincidence, the best explanation he could find was the idea that had occurred to him while speaking to Amy, but it was so greedy and evil it still seemed impossible.

It would have been relatively easy though. The forty or so hospitals running the trial were scattered across the globe. There were no more than one or two patients from each unit, most likely seen by different physicians. There'd be some like Leticia or the IV drug user from the C & W. Or they'd be asylum seekers and illegal immigrants, statistical shadows living on the periphery of society. Gay men rarely had children to leave behind, and they'd be lucky if their deaths made a line in the local newspaper. One hundred human beings wiped off the face of the planet by a mixture of random killings, overdoses and heart attacks. Even the MIs could have been murder, induced by a drug that leaves no chemical signature. Was that how Julia had died? Had she been murdered too? The grief and guilt that he'd silenced so successfully began to stir inside and a new emotion formed: fury. He had to stay calm though, if he lost his objectivity and focus he'd get nowhere.

He took a few long deep breaths and forced his mind into the present. He started the engine. Where did he go from here? If he was persistent he might be able to get the authorities to listen to him. However, the heart attacks aside, an investigation would only reveal a series of coroner reports that showed unlinked causes of death. His theory wouldn't fly without solid evidence to support it.

He pulled his seatbelt across his chest. If the authorities would see a connection as unlikely, maybe he should still be thinking that way too. What had really changed from an hour earlier? A prostitute killed in a turf war between two London pimps? It was only because he'd been looking for a link that he'd found one, the three deaths could still be a coincidence. Maybe the sight of the gun had provoked his imagination into forcing the connection, and maybe subconsciously he wanted someone else to blame for Julia's death and this was adding to his inability to distinguish fact from fiction.

Whichever way he looked at it there was more reason than ever to persevere with his investigation. If he didn't, he would be no better than the GP who continued to dismiss cancer even after a new and more sinister symptom appeared.

He turned the fog lamps on; the dashboard lit up in front of him.

"Damn." It was six-fifteen; he'd never make it back to Brighton by seven. He sent Ruth a text saying he'd be late, then pulled out into the road.

The front door to number fifty-five opened. Lance stepped out and glared at him. Ben sped up as he passed the house. He looked in his rear view mirror and saw Lance write something on his hand.

Chapter 11

Helen sat on a stool next to the bar and ordered a gin and tonic. The Club New York website advertised lessons starting at eight-fifteen, but it was already ten past and there were only two other people there. Both were men at least ten years older than her.

She took a sip of her drink and looked everywhere except at the two men; she could feel their stares and didn't want to encourage them with eye contact.

The club was a large rectangular room with high ceilings. One wall was lined with warped mirrors and another had various murals of New York City that predated nine-eleven. There was a bar and a DJ booth on the wall by the door. The upbeat rhythm of salsa music and the Latin appearance of the staff made it feel like somewhere in South America.

An overweight black man wearing a bowler hat entered the room. He walked confidently across the floor and stepped into the DJ booth. He put some headphones against his ear and fiddled with the decks; a new track began playing. He looked out of the booth across the room. His eyes locked on her; she quickly looked away.

If Ruth Williams didn't turn up soon she was out of there.

Three girls in their twenties entered and crossed to the other side of the room. They sat down on a long leather bench and chatted while they pulled dance shoes out of their bags.

By eight-fifteen a few more people had drifted in and dumped their bags around the room, but there was still no sign of Ruth.

The DJ clapped his hands. "Everyone line up!" he shouted from his booth.

He strutted out across the dance floor and motioned for people to join him. Helen stayed put. The man came over to her.

"I'm Havi," he said in a Latin accent. "This is your first time?"

"Here," she replied.

"You have danced salsa before?"

"A couple of times."

"We will look after you."

"I'm not sure…" Helen was about to make her excuses when another small group arrived, three women and a man. Ruth Williams was easy to recognise, she looked just like her picture.

"If you stay for the lesson, I give you a drink on the house," Havi said.

Helen nodded, took the hand that he offered and joined the growing line of dancers.

Havi marched away from her and took his place at the front of the dance floor. He clapped his hands again. Helen used the mirrors behind him to watch Ruth's progress across the room. Havi demonstrated the basic steps and told everyone to copy him. Helen joined in as Ruth and her three friends started a new line behind the first.

* * * *

The warm-up lasted about twenty minutes and by the end she had worked up a glow.

There were at least fifty people by now and more were turning up all the time.

Helen returned to her seat at the bar. Ruth and her friends came and stood next to her and began ordering drinks. Should she try to speak to her? Not yet, it would be better to wait for a more natural opportunity. She turned away and watched a couple who were brave enough to dance on their own.

The man was tall and English looking. He knew the moves and could keep the beat, but there was something about the way he danced that was reminiscent of Monty Python and the Ministry of Silly Walks.

Havi suddenly appeared next to her. She made ready to go to the bathroom, but she didn't need to, he turned to Ruth instead. He took her hand and led her onto the dance floor. The bulky little Cuban was at least three inches shorter than the tall athletic figure of Ruth; this was going to be even more comical than the Monty Python impersonation.

They began dancing and Helen's eyes widened with surprise. In the space of a dozen beats he was transformed from repugnant night club creep into a God of dance. It wasn't just that his timing was perfect, but that he seemed to have so much time. Unlike the tall Englishman, he wasn't struggling to squeeze a move into each set of steps. His attention was fixed on Ruth, and while his body rippled with masculine authority his touch was smooth and subtle.

After the song ended, there was another clap of Havi's hands. He told all the beginners to go to the far end of the room and the rest to join him near the DJ booth. Ruth walked over to the experienced group.

Helen got off her stool. Although she'd only done salsa a couple of times in Spain, this might be the best chance she'd get to speak to Ruth all night. She had no choice but to join the same lesson. She positioned herself next to Ruth in the forming circle.

"Hi," Helen said to her.

"Hi," Ruth replied, then looked over her shoulder at the door.

"It's my first time here," Helen said.

"The beginners' class is the over the other side." Ruth replied, still looking at the door.

"I've salsa danced before."

"Oh."

"Find a partner everyone!" Havi shouted.

A chubby Arabic-looking man, with a film of sweat across his forehead, came and stood in front of Helen. He put his arms out. She lifted her hands slowly and let him take hold of her with his clammy grip.

Havi pulled a girl out of the circle and demonstrated a routine.

"Right," he said. "We start with one cross-body."

Everyone began to dance. Helen was immediately out of her depth and she wasn't alone in noticing, Havi was looking straight at her. She'd been rumbled.

"You have lessons before?" he asked.

Helen shook her head. She swallowed hard as the circle stopped dancing and twenty pairs of eyes turned to her.

"You should go to beginners' class," he said.

Helen crossed the room. It was a truly cringe-worthy moment, like doing the walk of shame in 'The Weakest Link'. She joined the beginners, whose instructor was a young Mediterranean woman with black hair tied up in a bun. Helen looked around for a spare man, but there was already an excess of women.

"Dance with Tina," the instructor said, pointing towards a large woman in her late forties.

This was turning into the night from hell. It would be so easy just to walk out of there, but if she gave way to cowardice now it'd be all but impossible to return. She'd just have to grit her teeth. Although she might not make progress with Ruth tonight, this club gave her a great chance to access her target's sister twice a week.

She took a breath and focused on mastering the routine the class was grappling with.

* * * *

"Salsa?" Ben repeated.

"The lesson's only just started," the girl at the pay desk said. He handed over a fiver and dragged himself up the poorly lit staircase leading to the club. The sound of stamping feet and shouting grew louder with each step. What had Ruth got him into?

If he hadn't been in trouble with her already he would have bolted, but he couldn't let her down now. He stepped through the doorway and looked into the busy club. Two circles of men and women were dancing at opposite ends of the dance floor. He scanned the room for his sister. His eyes fixed on the knockout brunette dancing with another woman on the far side of the room.

"Ben." Ruth's face appeared in front of him. "Where have you been?"

"London," he replied.

"Don't tell me," she said, "you were looking into something."

He nodded, and gave her a look that said 'you've got me'.

"The Spiravex trial?"

He nodded again.

"Tell me about it in the break."

"Ruth," Ben said, and looked around. "I'm not really up for this."

Her expression made it clear he didn't have a choice. "The beginners' class has only just started, I'm sure you'll be able to catch up. It's over there." She pointed to the group at the far end of the room.

86

He looked where she was pointing and his eyes caught the brunette's; she was staring directly at him. Result. He ditched his coat and joined the group. The instructor paired him with the woman the brunette had been dancing with, and then demonstrated a turn with her partner.

It looked easy. The class tried to follow their example; he wasn't the only one to fail. The instructor repeated the move emphasising the need for the man to lead the woman. After a few attempts Ben managed to pull it off. The women were told to move round one place in the circle. He was next in line for the brunette, only when she arrived, it was clear she wasn't a brunette; her hair had a rusty tinge. Up close she was even better to look at.

"What's your name?" he asked.

"Try the turn again," the instructor said.

Ben held his left hand up and his new partner gracefully placed her right hand in his palm. He closed his hand around hers and felt her fingers match his grip. He then put his right hand in the small of her back and pulled her towards him, closer than he had the previous woman who was as lithe as a sack of King Edwards.

"Helen," she said, looking up at him.

Was it his imagination, or was her expression deliberately seductive?

"One, two, three," the instructor said.

Ben began the move; it felt completely different with Helen. Before it had been an awkward equivalent of human origami, now it was fluid, organic and sensual. The fraction of an inch that lay between their moving bodies felt as though it was charged with a million volts.

"Change partners!" the instructor shouted.

"Thanks," Ben said to Helen.

She smiled and moved to the next man in the circle.

Dancing had never really been his thing before, but maybe he'd been wrong. As the lesson progressed the moves started to feel easy. It took about ten minutes for Helen to make her way back round the circle and by then he had mastered a couple more moves and was building a small repertoire.

"Your first time here?" he asked, half way through the routine.

"Is my dancing that bad?" Helen said, with a look of hurt on her face.

"No, that's not what I meant…"

"Change partners."

He was left with a teasing smile.

They were taught another couple of moves, then just as Helen was about to join him for a third time, the instructor from the other class clapped his hands and announced a break.

* * * *

"Not bad big bro," Ruth said as she joined him. "You looked good, you must have been enjoying it."

"It's OK." There was no way she was going to get away with ambushing him that easily. "Wouldn't have chosen to come here myself."

"Don't give me that, I saw you dancing with that girl. I haven't seen you grin that much in ages."

She was right, but why did she always have to remind him of what had happened? No wonder he'd rather work than see her.

"She's called Helen."

Why did he feel so guilty just saying her name? He'd only danced with her for crying out loud, and more to the point, Julia was dead. He shouldn't feel guilty about being attracted to someone else, was he supposed to join a monastery or something?

"You got her name? I bet you're glad I brought you now."

"Even though it was under false pretences?"

Ruth raised her eyes and shook her head. "So what happened earlier?"

"I went to London to finally settle this Marivant business."

"And did you?"

"Ruth," he said, lowering his voice, "have you talked to anyone else about this?"

"No," she said. "Why would I?"

An image of the Boss holding her by the throat with a gun to her head flashed before his eyes.

"Don't. Not a word. Not to anyone."

"What's the matter Ben? Was I right?"

"We'll talk more later," Ben said, looking around, "I'm not sure, but there's a chance you might be, especially about being careful."

Ruth's friends joined them and one handed her a drink. She introduced Ben, but he kept the conversation to a polite 'hello'; there was someone else he'd rather speak to.

A bit of Dutch courage was in order first though. He headed for the bar, bought a beer and looked around. Helen was standing by herself near the DJ booth looking at the dancers. He took a step towards her but was stopped in mid stride when she was joined by the fat instructor from the other class, who handed Helen a drink.

Ben changed direction to rejoin Ruth and her friends. He chatted with them for a few minutes, all the time glancing over at Helen. She was enjoying the flat bloke's company a bit too much, but the next time he looked over they were no longer talking and Helen was walking towards him.

"Ready for more punishment?" she said, as she came up to him.

A loud clap was followed by the order for everyone to get back to their classes. Ben walked with Helen to the far side of the room. The next thirty minutes were an intermittent combination of torture, as he wrestled with the other women, and pleasure, as he moved in time with Helen. At the end of the lesson the formal circles dispersed and the dance floor came alive.

Ben continued to dance with Helen. There were moments when he felt like he'd been doing it for years, but this illusion was only maintained if he didn't look at any of the more experienced couples dancing near them. It was entirely different to the combination of awkward shuffling and beer-induced fits of flailing his arms in the air that constituted his previous experiences on the dance floor. Modern nightclub dancing wasn't designed for intimacy; with salsa it couldn't be avoided. He could feel Helen's stomach muscles tighten and loosen as he held her waist during one of the moves they'd learnt. His eyes pored over her slim form as he made her turn in front of him. Then he pulled her close so their bodies touched as they moved to the beat; it was like foreplay with clothes on.

Time lost all meaning as one song blended into another. He could have carried on till the club closed, but he suddenly caught Ruth glaring at him from the edge of the dance floor. He stopped dancing.

"I just need to talk to my sister," he said to Helen.

"Your sister?"

"Over there." He pointed to Ruth.

Helen smiled.

"I was worried she was your girlfriend," Helen said.

Ben smiled back. That had to be a good sign. "I'll only be a couple of minutes."

He walked over to Ruth.

"I thought we were going out so we could spend time together," she said.

"You shouldn't have arranged salsa dancing then."

"I wanted you to get to know my friends."

"Are they Christians?" Ben asked.

Ruth reddened. "What if they are?"

Ben frowned at his little sister. "I know you mean well, but stop trying to set me up with your church buddies. It's a bad idea, I don't have anything in common with them."

"I'm not trying to set you up."

He knew her better than that. "Anyway, I've already found someone I like."

"I can see that, she's very pretty."

Ben nodded then looked over to where he'd left Helen, but she'd moved.

He looked around the room and spotted her on the dance floor. Nightmare, she was with the chubby instructor.

"Who's she dancing with?" he asked.

"Havi. He's Cuban, a natural," Ruth answered.

How could she dance like that? She was a beginner too and hadn't done those kind of moves with him. He looked more closely and saw what was going on. It wasn't that she had suddenly acquired advanced dancing skills in some Matrix style mental download, rather it was Havi's tight leading. In fact she was struggling to keep up, but that didn't stop her looking like she was in raptures.

Havi had complete control over her body. Ben suppressed an urge to walk across the floor, rip the guy off her and deck him. Not only would it have been the most uncool thing he'd done in his life, especially after only knowing Helen for, oh, ten minutes, but it was also against everything he believed, and he hated himself for even feeling violence towards someone else. Still, some primeval part of him felt as though he were watching the woman he wanted being ravished by a man with a foot-long penis.

He looked away. He'd forgotten what a nightmare the singles game could be. A bubble of pain popped up from where he'd been suppressing his feelings. If Julia was still alive he wouldn't have to go through this...he'd just go home, make love with her and fall asleep with her head on his chest.

"We're moving on," Ruth said. "Are you coming?"

"Where are you going?"

"Casablanca," she replied.

Ben looked back at Helen. He didn't exist any more. No bad thing, women like that are usually trouble.

"Won't do any harm, I guess."

Ruth went over to her friends and they began collecting their belongings. Ben grabbed his jacket. He was adjusting the collar when he felt a hand grip his arm.

He turned to see Helen.

"Leaving already?"

"I'm supposed to be spending time with my sister."

Helen looked disappointed. She also looked incredible. He'd be a fool not to give her another go.

"You could come with us if you like," Ben suggested.

"No, that's OK. You need to be with your sister."

"She won't mind, she's got her friends."

Helen looked over to Ruth and her companions. "Are you sure?"

"Of course,"

Ruth joined them.

"Helen's coming with us," Ben said.

A flash of annoyance was followed by a nod.

Helen left them for a few moments then returned with her coat. Ben looked at the instructor, alone in the DJ booth. Those fancy moves weren't much good now were they?

They piled out of the sweaty club into the crisp May evening. Ben and Helen walked a few paces behind the rest of the group.

"Do you live in Brighton?" he asked.

"Hove."

"Where abouts?"

"Grand Avenue."

"That's not far from my flat."

Ben looked at their reflection in a shop window; they looked good together.

"Do you work in Brighton?" Helen asked.

"At the hospital."

"You're a doctor?" Helen turned towards him.

"Yep," Ben said.

"Cool."

He smiled. That was worth more than a hundred salsa moves and a Ferrari. Women loved Doctors, a fact that he'd established very early on in his medical career.

"And you?"

"I'm not working at the moment," Helen said.

"Looking for work?"

"Not really, I'm too busy learning to kitesurf."

He looked sideways at her. She had the aura of wealth, but he wouldn't have taken her for a spoilt rich kid. He'd seen enough of those when he'd been sent to private school at the age of eleven.

"Alright for some," he said.

"I got lucky."

"You inherited some money?"

"No, I was a researcher for a biotech company. They sold up and I cashed in my stock options. I made silly money. That's why I've been able to spend the past few years pleasing myself instead of some giant corporation."

They stopped at a crossing on West Street, Brighton's equivalent of the Las Vegas strip. It certainly matched the gambling Mecca's kitsch with its slot-machine arcades, nightclubs and fast-food outlets. What made it different from Vegas were the shabby unkempt buildings, the litter and the threatening atmosphere created by hundreds of drunk teenagers stumbling up and down the pavements.

"You've just been kitesurfing all that time?"

The lights changed and they crossed the road.

"No, I spent the first year travelling and then a year doing charity work. I moved here because I was sick of living out of a suitcase."

"Charity work?"

"I helped HIV orphans in Namibia."

He was speechless. Any previous negative prejudices were immediately vaporized. Not only was she so hot that she'd blown him away on first sight, but she was incredibly smart, a scientist, and to top it all, had a heart that beat for others. You don't just meet people so perfect in random encounters. Maybe there was a God after all!

They followed Ruth and her friends into a traffic-free warren of boutiques and restaurants.

They arrived at Casablanca and joined the end of a queue that snaked into the street.

"So what brought you to the club tonight?" Ben asked.

"I was bored," Helen replied. "I split up with my boyfriend a few weeks ago and since I only moved to Brighton in January, I haven't made many friends here yet. Thought salsa might be a good way of meeting people."

"Seems to be," he said. "Would you go again?"

"Depends if I still need to meet anyone."

Ben looked away and suppressed a grin. Steady on mate.

"What about you?" Helen asked. "Are you hooked on salsa?"

"Depends who I'm dancing with," he replied.

It didn't take long to reach the doorman.

Ben offered to pay for Helen, but she refused and handed a tenner to the cashier.

They entered the main room. There was a long bar with a seating area that looked through large windows onto the street. On the other side lay a small dance floor with the front half of a VW Beetle forming the DJ booth. He was playing tracks from the seventies and a rowdy group of women in fancy dress had taken over the dance floor.

Ben looked at the bar. Ruth gave him a 'come here' look. He asked Helen what she wanted to drink and headed for his sister.

"Are you going to talk to any of us tonight?" she asked.

"Stop busting my balls," Ben said, but then decided conciliation was a better approach. "Let me get a round in for you and the others."

It was a while before he reached the bar and was able to order the drinks, but it was worth it, Ruth appreciated the gesture.

Helen was still standing by herself in the corner. Should he wave her over? Nope, that would mean sharing her with the others.

He looked at his sister with a pleading expression. Her frown quickly yielded to a smile. "Go on then, but behave yourself."

"Yes Mom," Ben said, and gave her a grateful nudge with his elbow. He held the bottles up and pushed back through the group of drunken dancers towards Helen.

"I don't think your sister's happy about me stealing you away," Helen said. "Do you think we should join them?"

"No, she's all set. Besides, they're friends from her church. Do you really want to hear a sermon?"

"Is your sister very religious?"

"Goes to church twice most Sundays."

"Wow."

"Have you got any religion?" Ben asked.

"Not really, each to his own," Helen said. "I'm a scientist by training so I find it a bit far-fetched."

"You need to switch your brain off to believe what they do," Ben said. "If there's a God then why's there so much suffering?"

"Exactly. Why are babies born disabled?" She shook her head. "I'm always interested in what people with faith have to say, I just don't like it when they try and spoil everyone else's fun."

She flashed him that teasing look again. He smiled.

"Anyway, religion's a bit heavy for a Saturday night." She grabbed his hand and pulled him towards the dance floor.

* * * *

Ben fiddled with a crease in his trousers as he sat next to Helen in the back of a cab. He looked out of the window as they sped past the shuttered shops of Church Road.

"Do you think your sister will forgive you for tonight?" Helen asked.

He looked at her and shrugged. "If she doesn't it was worth it."

They turned up Grand Avenue.

Helen leaned forward and put her hand on the seat in front.

"This'll do," she said to the cabbie. "Next to the big block on the left."

The cab pulled up.

It was over twelve years since he'd last been in this kind of position. What the hell happened next? Had sexual politics changed so much in that decade? Did he just assume he was going up to her flat with her? God knows he wanted to, tonight had awoken feelings that had been dormant for months, and he felt like he was going to explode if he didn't get some action soon.

Helen opened her bag and pulled out a pen.

"Do you have a piece of paper?" she said to the driver.

"Will a receipt do love?"

"Perfect."

Helen took the yellow slip and scribbled a number down.

"If you fancy a dance or something," she said, and handed the number to Ben.

He took it. It was a shame the night was ending, but there was no way he was going to blow it with someone this special by pushing too hard so early on.

"How much is the fare so far?" Helen asked the cabbie.

"Don't worry, I'll get it," Ben said.

"I don't like being paid for," she said to him, and turned back to the cabbie. "How much?"

"Six-fifty."

She handed Ben a fiver.

He took it and put it in his jacket pocket. Helen leaned over to Ben and kissed him on the cheek then opened the door.

"When shall I call you?" Ben asked.

"As soon as you like. My diary's not exactly full at the moment." Helen stepped out.

"Salisbury Crescent," Ben said to the driver.

* * * *

The taxi reached Ben's building. He paid the fare, climbed out and stood on the pavement breathing in the fresh air. He hadn't felt like this in ages, it was like being a teenager again. He sauntered over to the entrance.

Rather than using the lift he climbed the five flights of stairs to his floor. He was slightly out of breath when he reached his flat. He pulled his keys out of his jacket pocket, opened the door and felt for the light switch. He pressed it, but nothing happened. The bulb must have blown. He closed the door behind him and made his way down the hallway. He tried the living room light. Nothing. The bulb going had probably tripped the fuse. He began walking across the open-plan space to the kitchen to find the fuse box. He saw the shadow too late to stop the punch aimed at his stomach.

Chapter 12

Ben fell to the ground gasping for air. A light came on. He was grabbed by both arms and hauled onto the sofa.

"Don't move," an Irish accent said.

Ben finally managed to straighten up and look around. Two men in balaclavas sat either side of him; the skin on their hands was black. A tall white man with a crooked nose stood opposite him, leaning against the work surface that divided the kitchen from the lounge.

"Who are you?" Ben said. "I don't keep any cash."

"We aren't here to rob you Doctor Williams," the Irishman said.

He was kind of hoping they were.

"It is Benjamin Williams isn't it?"

Ben nodded.

"So why did you call yourself Frank Dean?"

Ben looked at the two men in balaclavas. They were about the same size and physique as Lance and the boss from Lewisham.

"Don't worry about them," the Irishman said. "It's me you're dealing with now. Why did you lie?"

"Get out of my home."

The Irishman shook his head, then nodded at Lance. Ben was lifted to his feet and launched across the room. He fell hard onto the glass coffee table; it shattered beneath him.

"Why did you lie about your name and why do you want to know about a patient that was never yours?"

Ben was pulled upright and held between the two men in balaclavas. He could feel blood trickling down his right cheek. He winced as his left arm was pushed against a shard of glass that was embedded in his side.

The Irishman pulled a gun out of his jacket pocket and pointed it at Ben's chest.

"Start talking!" he shouted.

"I just wanted to know if Leticia was OK," Ben said. "I was running a trial in Brighton, the same study she was on, one of my patients died unexpectedly of a heart attack and I wanted to find out if there was a link to the drug in the study. The only information I could get from Guys was Leticia's contact details, they hadn't seen her for a couple of months so I decided to make some enquiries myself. If I'd known she'd been killed I wouldn't have followed it up, I was only interested in her if she'd had a heart attack."

The Irishman looked at the boss from Lewisham and raised his eyebrows. The boss nodded.

"Why lie about who you are?" the Irishman continued.

"I didn't think they'd help me if I told them I was from a different hospital."

There was silence. The tension seeped out of the room.

"You shouldn't put your nose in other people's business."

"I'll know better next time."

"Good, because I don't ever want to see your face or hear your name again." The Irishman moved closer. "If I was you, I'd forget all about that patient of yours."

"I will," Ben said, holding eye contact with him.

The man's right shoulder swung back. His fist crashed into Ben's stomach.

Ben was left to sink to the floor. He heard broken glass crunching under foot and looked up to see the intruders leaving the room.

It took a while for him to recover his breath. He slowly got to his feet and crossed the lounge. He peered down the hallway; it was empty. He closed the front door then returned to the living area and looked at the destruction they'd left. The chaos of the outside world had invaded his home; it was no longer his sanctuary.

He stepped into the kitchen to make a drink.

"You got to be kidding!" They'd even jammed up his espresso machine. They must have got bored of waiting and tried to make a coffee. They hadn't got far; burnt grounds blocked the filtration system.

He put the kettle on; he'd have to make do with instant.

He wished he hadn't told Ruth anything now. What if the violence he'd awoken reached her too? He couldn't live with himself if anything happened to her. The thought that it wouldn't be entirely his fault since it was Ruth who'd persuaded him to investigate the trial in the first place, wouldn't be much comfort. He'd held himself together all these years for her, what would happen if she was gone? It didn't bear thinking about.

He glanced at his watch, it was two-thirty. He should get some rest, but it would be hard to sleep now. He made a mug of coffee and took it to the bathroom. He opened the cabinet above the sink, pulled out his first-aid kit and sat on the edge of the bath to clean his cuts. The worst was caused by the piece of glass in his side. There was a heck of a lot blood. The last thing he wanted was to join a long line of drunks in Casualty. He gently wiped the wound. The antiseptic stung like hell, but once the mess had been removed, it was clear he wouldn't need stitches.

He pulled a pair of tweezers out of the kit and dipped them in the antiseptic. He sucked in a sharp breath as he fished around inside the cut. It took less than a minute to remove the glass. A junior doctor at the County would have taken an hour, and created a hole the size of a shark bite. He dressed the wound and wrapped tape around his chest to hold the pad in place. He cleaned the small cut next to his right eyebrow and wiped the blood off his face.

He eased his bruised body off the rim of the bath and walked to his bedroom.

The mess was even worse than in the lounge: drawers balanced on the ends of their runners, a cupboard door was hanging on one hinge, and his clothes were scattered across the floor. He picked up the backpack he used for work; it felt light. He opened it and looked inside.

"Damn!" His laptop had gone.

He sat heavily on the bed, put his head in his hands and pushed his palms against his eyes. He was in way over his head.

Those men had been sent to scare him off; whatever doubts existed before had been completely blown away. His theory was the only explanation that made any sense, but if he was going to prove it he needed a living patient.

Claire's email said the asylum seeker had returned to Africa leaving no forwarding address. At the time it had caused him to rule the guy out. Everything had changed now. None of the other UK patients were alive and he was unable to find out about the other study centres from the rest of the world. He'd go into the unit first thing to read the attachments Claire had sent, that might help narrow down where Mike's patient had gone.

He stood up and began picking his clothes off the floor. He cleared half the room, then lifted a jumper and revealed his laptop lying open; the battery light flickered red.

He grabbed the backpack from the bed, pulled out the power cord and plugged it in. The screen lit up and the password prompt appeared. He typed it in; the screen announced it was resuming Windows. Several folders were open on the desktop. How had they got his password? Could they have found anything on the hard drive that contradicted his story? There was nothing he'd downloaded from the hospital server, and more to the point, if they had found anything he'd have ended up with more than a couple of cuts and some bruises.

He accessed the hospital server and entered his email account. He clicked on the message Claire had sent and opened the attachments.

He double clicked on one of Esau Kimani's files. It was a psychiatric evaluation. The document ran to over fifty pages and included extensive notes on sessions with a counsellor. The words rape, murder, Moi and Kanu jumped out of the pages as he skimmed through. It was a familiar story about the political persecution of a Kenyan opposition supporter from the Moi years.

He then opened the file containing Esau's medical notes. There were details of all the examinations and lab results since Esau had started receiving treatment in the UK. He had a similar clinical profile to other African patients.

He continued going through the chronologically ordered notes. There had to be something pointing to Esau's whereabouts.

The last page was a missed appointment form that had been scanned into the file. It was four months old. Esau had failed to turn up for two consecutive bookings and no one had managed to get hold of him. There was a comments box at the bottom of the page:

> In my opinion Esau has returned to his hometown of Nakuru in Kenya. He was very excited in his last consultation: President Moi had been voted out of power a number of years ago and his own tribe had been in control since, removing Moi's network of

officials and informers. This meant Esau was able to go back to his homeland safely. He seemed uninterested in his drug regime as he believed God had healed him.

Ignorance must be the greatest killer in HIV. There were hundreds of Africans in Europe who'd died because they'd listened to an over enthusiastic pastor rather than medical experts. They were in the same fold as those who heeded the Pope's council on prevention and avoided using condoms. It was all very well going bareback if both partners had always abstained from extra marital sex, but for the ninety nine percent of people who didn't live perfect Catholic lives, a little bit of latex could save your life. If you're going to sin, you may as well sin safely.

He closed the document.

Esau was his only hope of finding a living patient, but surely Marivant would have got to him by now? Even if they hadn't, without HIV drugs, he might have died from AIDS already.

But if Marivant hadn't killed him, and his theory was right, Esau would be alive regardless of the lack of medication. The theory didn't need any God induced miracles for that to happen, it was all science. There was only one way he was going to learn the truth though.

He exited the hospital server, opened a web browser and typed in the address of a budget airfare site. The cursor flashed in the destination box. He typed the word Nairobi.

Chapter 13

"Are you sure they won't come back?" Ruth asked.

"I don't think so," Ben replied, and handed her a mug of tea. "They seemed to believe me." He sat down.

"And the Irish guy told you to forget about your patient?"

"At gunpoint."

"He wouldn't have been so forceful if they weren't trying to hide something."

"Exactly. If I'm right then even the patients who died of heart attacks were murdered." Ben put his mug on the floor where his coffee table had been. All that was left was a deep scratch in the wood. He looked at Ruth and waited for the significance of what he'd said to penetrate.

"Julia too?"

He nodded.

"What are you going to do?"

There was no point in keeping anything from her now. She already knew too much, cutting her out of the loop would only make her worry more.

"I'm going to Kenya to find the missing asylum seeker."

"What if he's dead?" Ruth asked.

"What if he's alive?"

"Is it really that important to see him?"

"Yes."

"I don't want you to go," she said. "You know what it's like in Africa, Marivant could do anything to you."

"After last night I'm not sure I'm safe anywhere." He put his hand on his side and felt the cut.

"Then drop it. Forget about the whole thing. If you listen to what that guy said they'll leave you alone."

"I can't. Not now I've found out you were right to be suspicious." Maybe pointing out the fact that she'd encouraged him to dig deeper would soften her resistance to him going further.

"I didn't know what I was talking about. Get on with the job you're best at, treating people who are sick."

"I can't believe I'm hearing this," Ben shook his head. "After all I've learnt, do you really think I shouldn't do anything?"

"What difference will it make? You said yourself that the patients are probably all dead. Let it go. You could be killed, and for what? A few men might go to prison, but nothing more."

"You don't think that justice is worth making sacrifices for? What about Julia?" he said. Ruth's eyes fell. "Do you really expect me to let them get away with murdering my wife?"

"Then go to the police," Ruth said, looking back up "Surely you've got enough now?"

"You're right, a dead prostitute clinches it."

"It might. Just tell them everything you know, and let them deal with it."

"That's just it, they won't do anything."

"At least you will have tried," Ruth said. "Please Ben, if not for me, for Mum and Dad. They wouldn't want you to die as well."

Ben lifted his coffee cup off the floor and pictured his father at Kampala international airport. He was eleven years old and leaving Africa to go to school in England. He was crying because he wouldn't see his parents for three months. His father told him to be brave. It was the last time he saw him.

He'd taken that advice to heart and he had the perfect role model. His father hadn't been Hollywood brave, but he'd given up everything to live in one of the most dangerous countries in the world to help others.

"What would Dad have done if he was me?" Ben said, staring into his coffee.

"That's not fair."

"Yes it is." He looked up. "Dad died for what he believed in. Would he be proud of me if I walked away from this? Would I be proud of me? It's not just the people who are dead, it's the people who are going to die."

"Who's going to die?"

Ben sighed, it was time to tell her his theory. "I didn't want to say anything. I'm still not certain it's the right explanation, but I can't see any other."

"What are you talking about?"

"Why a blue-chip corporation would slaughter a hundred vulnerable men and women."

"Their motive?" Ruth said.

He nodded.

"Have I ever told you how much HIV drugs cost?" he asked.

"No, but I guess it's a lot."

"In the West they're pretty pricey, not as much as cancer drugs, but still by no means cheap. One drug can be as much as seven or eight hundred pounds a month, and most patients are on at least three different drugs. Marivant has a whole range of anti-retrovirals, I don't have anyone on treatment who hasn't taken one of their drugs. The key thing is that these patients won't just be taking them for a month or two, but for the rest of their lives."

"Because the drugs aren't a cure?" Ruth said and took a sip of her tea.

"Exactly. They have to be taken continuously, otherwise the virus comes back."

"Why don't they destroy all the HIV?"

That was a question that had been bugging scientists and clinicians alike for many years. It was still unclear as to exactly why it was that the drugs couldn't completely eradicate the virus, and trying to explain in layman terms wasn't easy, but he'd give it his best shot.

"A small amount of the virus is archived in a way or in a place that the drugs can't affect them. If a patient needs to come off treatment for some reason and the drug is removed from the bloodstream, these hidden particles seep out unchallenged. HIV replicates at a phenomenal rate, and within a week or two the virus has swamped the immune system again."

"What's all this got to do with the patients in the trial?"

"A couple of billion dollars a year," Ben replied. "All the patients in the study had undetectable viral loads at twenty-four weeks. That's good, but not particularly unusual in trials of HIV drugs. Most of my patients remain undetectable from one year to the next."

"So why would Marivant want to bury it?"

"Just let me finish Ruth," Ben said. "Imagine if one patient in the trial stopped taking the drug and the virus never returned."

"What do you mean?" she asked.

104

"After they'd stopped taking Spiravex the HIV never came back." He paused, then tried again. "The virus had been completely destroyed, even the hidden particles."

"You mean they were cured?" she asked.

Ben nodded. "I think that's why they killed all the patients in the trial, including those who had MIs. It was the only way they could hide the study results."

"I can't believe anyone would think of doing such a thing."

"Greed makes people do the unthinkable," he said. "Marivant faced losing two billion dollars a year. They need HIV."

"But they'd make a fortune from a cure."

"Wrong, they're making a fortune now from Western countries. Spiravex would have destroyed that. The amount they'd make from saving the millions of patients in Africa would be miniscule in comparison to their current profits."

"That's..." Ruth shook her head.

"It's genocide Ruth, and on a scale greater than Hitler and Stalin combined. There are over forty million people with HIV in the world and that number is growing every year. Africa's falling apart because of this disease."

"I don't believe any company could be that greedy."

"Until now I believed the pharmaceutical industry was better than most," Ben said. "It's not like they're oil companies, they don't make the world a worse place. They don't do back room deals with those in power to suppress climate change policy, or buy up and bury renewable technology patents just to keep their gravy train rolling. I always felt that Big pharma and the biotechs created life enhancing products that made the world a better place. OK, it was only better for those that could afford it, but that's life, I never saw them as being morally bankrupt. But obviously I was wrong, Marivant have taken a step down the same road as Big Oil by suppressing the Spiravex trial."

"It's a huge step though."

"And one that would have stayed secret if you hadn't confirmed my belief that the deaths were connected because of the study itself and not just the heart attacks."

"I wish I'd kept quiet now."

"You don't really mean that."

Her eyes pleaded with him. "You're my brother. I don't want anything to happen to you."

"But what about all those millions of people?"

Ruth looked down. "I know," she said.

"The only way I can prove my theory is to find a patient from the trial who's still alive and not taking HIV drugs. Esau Kimani is that patient. If I don't find him, or he's dead, then Marivant will get away with it and we'll lose the cure to the most dangerous disease of our times."

"Can't you use some of the drug on your current patients to test the theory?"

"It's not that simple. Even if I could persuade a patient to try a drug that everyone believes is deadly, I still wouldn't be able to get hold of it. Marivant recalled all the trial drug. We had to account for every last pill that had been issued. I remember them being more anal than usual about protocol. They even insisted on having CNS samples from the patients after they were taken off Spiravex, now I know why."

"I thought the virus affected the immune system not the central nervous system." Ruth said.

"The CNS is one of the HIV sanctuary sites. We were told they wanted the samples to ensure the drug had been completely washed out. They were lying. They wanted to see if the virus had been destroyed, and once they knew it was they killed the patients. That's why I have to go Africa, I need a sample of Esau's blood."

"Wouldn't you need a CNS sample?"

"No, the blood sample will be enough because Esau hasn't been on anti-retrovirals. If there was a single viral particle hiding in the CNS, the moment he came off therapy it will have entered the blood stream and started replicating. Marivant only needed a CNS sample because the patients were switched to other therapies and the blood would be undetectable."

"So when are you going?"

"I've booked a flight for Tuesday morning."

Ruth frowned. "What about work?"

"They'll cope."

"But you could lose your job."

"People will lose a lot more if I don't go."

"What if you're wrong? It will have all been for nothing."

Ben shook his head. "The more I talk about it the more I know I'm doing the right thing. What would you do if you were in my shoes?"

"I don't know."

"I do. Your faith is all about putting the needs of others before yourself. Didn't Jesus make the ultimate sacrifice and lay down his life so others would know God?"

"Ben, you're not a believer."

"How would you feel if millions died because you stopped me going?"

Ruth closed her eyes and folded her arms.

Ben stood up, walked over to the kitchen and looked out of the window. The words of his father, 'be brave', had always stuck with him. They were there when the headmaster of Lancing College called him into his office on an autumn night to tell him his parents had been killed. They were there when Steve had pulled back the sheet to reveal Julia's face and they were there now, telling him his duty lay beyond the instinctive boundaries of family.

He'd made his decision, there was no going back now, so no point in discussing it further.

He walked back to Ruth. It was time to get her views on the other matter that had been pre-occupying his thoughts.

"What did you think of Helen?" he said.

"She's alright,"

"Is that all?"

"Not my type," Ruth replied

"But you have to admit she's gorgeous."

"It's not just looks that attracts me to a woman," Ruth said.

"And you don't think Helen's got more to offer?"

"I only spoke to her for a few seconds."

"But you can normally suss people out."

"That's because I'm a woman Ben, I'm able to empathise." She finished her tea. "Are you going to see her again?"

Ben nodded. "She gave me her number."

"You didn't stay the night?"

"No, but I wish I had."

"Be careful Ben," Ruth said. "It's not that long since you lost Julia. Don't you think you need to give yourself more time before you commit to someone new?"

Ben frowned. "I'm not going to ask her to marry me."

"I know what you're like. You think sex is only harmless fun."

"Sex is just sex Ruth. Besides, you're hardly one to lecture on morality."

"Because you think I'm gay?"

Ben held a hand up. He wasn't going down that road again.

"I haven't got time for this," he said. "I've got a load to do if I'm going be ready by Tuesday morning."

"I'll leave you to it then, you never listen to me anyway." Ruth stood up. "You always think you know best." She turned and headed for the door.

There was no reason to get up, she knew the way out. Every time he saw her they bickered, he was getting sick of it.

The front door slammed.

He shook his head. She spent her life hounded by guilt because her desires conflicted with her faith. He wasn't bound by the same shackles, and he wasn't going to let her archaic values cramp his style. He picked up his mobile and dialled Helen's number.

Chapter 14

Ben waited for Helen at a table in the middle of Orsino, a restaurant in Hove. He continued with the appearance of reading the menu even though he knew what he wanted. It was better than risking uncomfortable eye contact with the diners who surrounded him.

He took a sip of his Italian beer.

A table of men, who'd been noisily celebrating a birthday, fell silent. Ben glanced over. They were all staring at the door.

His eyes crossed the busy room to the cash desk by the entrance. One of the immaculately dressed waiters was removing Helen's white leather coat. Ben raised his hand. She caught sight of him and walked over. She was wearing a simple cocktail dress that was tight enough to draw attention to her firm curves, but loose enough not to flaunt them.

His memory had failed to do her justice. She was truly awesome.

He stood up.

"Hi," she said, as she reached the table and gave him a kiss on the cheek. "Sorry I'm late."

A waiter was standing behind her chair ready to help her.

They both sat down.

"Nice place," Helen said.

He took a fresh look at the tastefully decorated Italian restaurant. It was divided into two sections by a large central bar. Thin Venetian blinds hung over the large windows, creating an air of intimacy without removing the diners from the outside world.

"I like it," he replied.

Their waiter handed Helen a menu and took her drinks order, a martini.

"Are you packed?" she asked.

"Just about. I have to leave the flat at six in the morning."

"Did you say it was a holiday?"

"Yeah," he replied. "I've been meaning to visit some friends in Kenya for ages. If I get the chance I might do a bit of windsurfing too."

"Kenya?"

"I worked out there for a few years after I qualified."

"How long are you going for?"

"A week. That's all I could get off work at such short notice," he said.

Helen looked surprised. "When did you arrange it?"

"Over the past couple of days."

"It wasn't something I said the other night was it?"

Ben smiled and shook his head. "I just woke up yesterday morning and decided I needed to get away. I've had a bit of a tough time recently."

Helen gave him a sympathetic look. "Nothing to do with that cut?"

"No, I fell on my coffee table on Saturday."

"You didn't seem drunk."

"I wasn't. The lights weren't working."

He hated lying, but felt bad enough his sister was involved; there was no way he was going to rope Helen in as well. It was time to change the subject.

"So what made you choose research as a career?" he asked.

"I wanted to save the world," Helen replied.

"From what?"

"HIV."

"Now that would be something."

The waiter put Helen's drink in front of her.

"AIDS was a big deal when I was a kid," she said." I can remember all the adverts with the tombstones. I was only about eight. It frightened me more than the idea of a nuclear bomb."

"It's killed a lot more people too."

"As I got older I thought about becoming a doctor. I had the grades."

"So why didn't you?"

Helen looked down into her drink and moved the olive round the glass with the cocktail stick.

"It sounds pathetic now, but I couldn't stand the thought of all that blood." She looked up. "And the smells."

"I don't think any of us ever grow to like it."

"It wasn't just that. I realised I couldn't make a big enough impact as a doctor."

"What do you mean?" Ben asked.

"How many lives do you reckon you've saved?"

"Blimey, I don't know. Lots I guess."

"How many of those were without using drugs?" Helen said.

He thought about it for a moment. The answer was obvious, one, but not while he was working, it was an incident on holiday in Venice.

"I did CPR on a man once. He would have died if I wasn't there."

"Only one?" Helen said.

"There may have been more when I did a rotation in casualty, but there would have been some drugs involved."

"See what I'm saying?"

"Doctors are useless?"

"Of course not. Doctors make the diagnosis, they tell you why you're ill, and they know how to treat it. But without drugs, most of the time, that's all they can do."

"So you became a research scientist instead."

"As a doctor I could help a few thousand people in my lifetime, but through chemistry I could help millions."

"And did you?" Ben said.

Helen lifted her drink and took a sip. She shook her head.

"I spent years making useless brown gunk, then years more separating the components. I'd send the compounds for testing, each time hoping this would be the one. Eventually I realised I wasn't going to be Marie Curie. That's why I didn't continue in research after the takeover, I thought I could be of more use on the ground. Hence the year in Namibia helping HIV orphans. Kind of wish I had become a doctor now."

"I wouldn't say that. You probably helped others find powerful drugs by eliminating the weak candidates."

"Very frustrating though," Helen said. "If you're not careful it can make you cynical."

"I can imagine."

He watched her skewer the olive and put it in her mouth. Her lips looked extremely kissable.

"You told me you'd split up with your boyfriend recently," he said. "Was it serious?"

"No. I'd only been seeing him for a couple months. Just a bit of fun." Helen leaned forward with her elbows on the table, put her hands together and rested her chin on her knuckles. "And you? Are you with anyone?"

"No," Ben replied. "Haven't been for a while either."

"I find that hard to imagine."

"Why?" Ben asked.

"You're a classy guy, a doctor and very attractive."

He tried to smile, but felt his cheeks burn instead. He picked up the menu.

Helen laughed. "There must be someone."

"There isn't. I came out of a long-term relationship last year." He didn't want to complicate things too much so early on. Mentioning Julia's death could put distance between them, and he didn't want that. "I've been too busy since then."

"Long term?" Helen lifted her head from her hands. "You haven't been married have you?"

Now she was worried he was divorced with a brood of kids lurking in the background. Lying, or rather not telling the entire truth, was a complicated business, but it was better to stick with it for now.

"No I haven't," Ben said. He fixed his gaze on the menu then saw a waiter approaching out of the corner of his eye. He lifted his hand to get his attention.

"We're ready to order now," he said.

Helen looked confused as she picked up her menu. She opened it then put it back down. "You choose for me."

This wasn't going how he'd planned. It was a shame he couldn't start the evening again.

"What do you like?" he asked.

"Guess," Helen replied.

"You're not vegetarian or anything are you?"

"No."

"What if I choose something you hate?" Ben said.

"Maybe it'll be a sign!" She laughed. "Let's hope you don't."

There was nothing he could do but play along, he was the one who'd signalled to the waiter. He looked at the menu. What on earth should he get her? She was in good shape, maybe a salad, but then she might think he was suggesting she needed to lose weight. There was pasta, but should he choose seafood or meat?

He put the menu down.

"A plate of teriyaki chicken wings and a garlic ciabatta to start. For the main course," he said, looking at Helen, "two fillet steaks."

The corners of Helen's mouth lifted a little.

"How would you like the steaks done sir?" the waiter asked.

"Both rare," Ben said, not taking his eyes off Helen.

"Very rare," Helen added, and smiled.

The waiter closed his notepad and left.

Ben remained silent and continued looking into Helen's eyes. There was more to her than beauty. She was intelligent, adventurous and wanted to make the world a better place. She even had a good sense of fun. His love for Julia was sacred, but maybe it was possible to feel strongly for someone else again.

"Where are the ladies?" she asked.

"The other side of the bar."

"Excuse me," she said, and stood up.

She disappeared behind him. He let out a breath.

He was alone again, but looking around now was a less uncomfortable experience than when he'd first arrived, everyone now knew he was dining with the most beautiful woman in the place.

The unease returned after she'd been gone ten minutes though. Maybe she hates steak after all? He sat up and turned towards the coat rack by the door. He could see a flash of white leather between two dark jackets. He looked forward again. Maybe she's doing her make-up.

Helen returned a minute later, just as the waiter was bringing their starters.

They were more at ease for the rest of the meal, and once they'd finished a second bottle of Marques de Caceres, it was like they'd known each other for years.

After dessert he glanced at his watch. "I don't believe it," he said, "it's five to eleven."

"I forgot you have to get up early tomorrow."

"I know, but I'll be fine." It was going to be two weeks till he her saw again. He wasn't going to wait that long. "I'll sleep on the plane."

She smiled that smile of hers, the one that felt like it was just for him and full of meaning, but just what, he wasn't sure yet. It was time to find out. They paid the bill at the cash desk then stood at the entrance for a moment.

"I'll walk you home," he said. She didn't decline the offer, she must have been thinking along the same lines.

They strolled along Church Road past an endless parade of restaurants, pubs and small shops. As they drew nearer to Grand Avenue he felt her hand brush against his. He opened it up and joined her willing fingers with his. It was a total thrill becoming just that bit more intimate with someone new. He'd forgotten what dating was like: the excitement, the uncertainty and then the anticipation of what might lie ahead.

It took no time to reach her apartment block.

"You coming up?" she asked, putting her key in the door and leaning against it to push it open.

He smiled, there was definitely no uncertainty now.

He followed her into the unfamiliar surroundings of the quiet lobby. He was crossing into her territory.

She called the lift.

They stepped in and she pressed the button for her floor. The lift juddered and started its assent. Her lips were less than a foot away from his, but they may as well have been in New Zealand. Where had his bottle gone? Fifteen years ago he would have grabbed her, hit the emergency stop button and done it right there in the lift.

The torture came to an end when they reached the top floor. They crossed the small tiled hallway to a door. A brass plate read '807'. Helen pulled her keys out of her purse and they entered her flat.

"Very nice," Ben said, looking around at the large living room.

"Thank you," Helen said. "Drink?"

"I'll have a coffee please," he replied.

"Coffee?"

"Yeah, I don't want a hangover when I arrive in Nairobi."

"Coffee it is then," she said. "Make yourself comfortable."

He sat in the deep sofa and took another look at the room. It was simply decorated, with a couple of modern paintings and a few stylish ornaments. The combination of white walls, wooden flooring and a frameless mirror created a sense of space. After the weekend, he'd fallen out of love with his flat. It felt good to be somewhere else.

Helen returned with the coffees. She sat next to him on the sofa, close enough so their legs touched. She smiled, but said nothing. She looked at him with an expression that was serious but inviting. It was now or never. He leaned across and kissed her on the lips. In the space of one second he said goodbye to twelve years of his life. The taste of someone else's mouth and the unfamiliar movement of her tongue spoke of a new future. He felt her fingers slide into his hair and grip it.

He pulled away for a moment and looked at her. Was this real? Even close up she was flawless.

"It's a shame you're going away so soon after we met," she said.

"I won't be gone long."

They kissed again, with more urgency. His hand moved down to her hip. It had been months since he'd made love. He needed this.

Helen gently pulled away. "I have to go to the bathroom." She got up and walked out.

He looked at the space she'd left on the couch. No matter what Ruth said, he was ready for this.

A phone rang. A handset lying on the armchair next to him lit up. Ben leaned across. The name Luke appeared in blue writing. It was five-past eleven, a bit late for a work colleague or mate to be calling.

It went dead, but left the sound of doubt ringing in his ears.

He'd dated beautiful women before. He'd be crazy to think he was alone in the chase. Maybe it was just a friend though, but it could be an ex-boyfriend, possibly even a husband. How could he be sure Helen hadn't been lying to him? He hadn't exactly been honest himself.

Julia had been in his life for over a decade, and he trusted her absolutely. He'd only known this woman two days and had no idea what he was getting in to. Another bubble of pain broke the surface of his conscious. Making love to Julia had never been boring. The fact that they trusted each other absolutely created a cocoon of security inside which intimacy could flourish. That was real love-making.

He caught a whiff of stale smoke. He looked on the floor to the side of the sofa and saw two cigarette butts crushed into a saucer.

She came back and sat down.

"Do you smoke?" he asked.

She looked shocked at first, then bit her lip and nodded. "Does it bother you?"

"Not really," Ben said. "I'd rather you were honest about it though. Was that why you were in the toilet so long?."

"I didn't want to put you off," Helen said, "but I was desperate."

"Your phone rang."

"The mobile?"

"Land line," Ben said.

"Do you mind if I check for messages?"

"Go ahead."

Helen picked up the handset, got to her feet and walked out of sight into the kitchen.

What else was she hiding?

He shook his head. He knew nothing about this woman, and the fact that she'd already hidden her smoking showed she could be deceitful. He'd waited six months, he could wait a little longer.

She returned.

"Sorry about that," she said.

Ben gulped down his coffee and stood up. "I'd better head off." He put his jacket on. "I've got a long day tomorrow."

She looked surprised, and disappointed.

"I'll call when I get back," Ben said.

"I'd like that," she replied, then led him into the hall.

He followed her to the front door and stepped out, then turned back to take another look at her. What was he doing? She was stunning. If his mates knew what he was turning down, they'd say he didn't deserve his manhood, but they weren't living his life, and this was the right thing to do.

"I'll see you in a couple of weeks," he said. He leaned across and kissed her on the cheek. "I had a great time tonight." He looked at his watch.

"I know," she said, "the flight."

Ben turned and headed for the staircase, he didn't fancy an awkward wait by the lift.

* * * *

"Why the hell did you call me?" Helen shouted into the phone. "You knew I was with him tonight, you ruined everything."

"You have my message then?"

"Of course, but he'd already told me about Kenya. It would have helped if you'd let me know earlier."

"Anne only found out this evening," Luke said. "They didn't process the credit-card payment until today. Did he say why he was going?"

"Holiday," Helen replied.

"I don't believe him," he said. "It's not normal to arrange a holiday at such short notice."

"It happens."

"You were convinced?" Luke asked.

Helen thought about the past few hours. "I wouldn't say that, but why would he lie? He doesn't know me."

"Did he say anything about Saturday night?"

"I asked about his cut. He told me he fell on a coffee table."

"And nothing else?" Luke asked.

"No, but that doesn't mean anything. Maybe he was scared the truth would put me off."

"But he didn't tell you the whole truth, so he could be lying about Kenya too," Luke said. "It can't be a coincidence that he's going to the one place on the planet where the last Marivant patient disappeared."

"Yes it can," Helen said. "He's spent half his life in Africa."

"I'll organise a team to keep an eye on him."

"Are you going to order them to take him out?" The thought of it sickened her, but not like before. Sure, guilt would be a part of it, but there was more to it than that. Ben was an awesome guy, and the thought of him not being alive was horrible.

"I don't know," Luke said. "It'd be a lot easier, but if he's looking into MVT084, he might be able to find Esau Kimani."

"When we couldn't?"

"Perhaps. You managed to get him to talk about Marivant or Spiravex?"

117

"No. But I might have, if you hadn't ruined everything," Helen said. "What do you want me to do while he's out there?"

"Work on his sister."

"Still?"

"Yes."

"We didn't exactly hit it off."

"I don't care. Find out if she knows anything. You know what to do if she does."

The phone went dead.

Chapter 15

Ben was awoken by a loud knocking. He sat up and tried to place the unfamiliar shadows.

"Housekeeping," a female voice called.

The Hilton.

"No!" Ben shouted.

A crack of light appeared as the door opened.

"I said no!"

The maid looked into the room.

"Later," Ben said.

"Sorry sir." The door closed.

He felt for the lamp on the bedside table, found the switch and turned it on. He grabbed his watch. Seven o'clock. Bit early for housekeeping.

"Damn." He'd forgotten to put it forward. It was ten in Nairobi. He'd wasted half a morning.

He got out of bed and drew the curtains to reveal the view across the capital of East Africa. From nine stories up, the foreground was a jumble of shiny corporate towers, bland government buildings and fading colonial architecture. Beyond, exclusive residential suburbs tried to distance themselves from the teaming slums. The tinted windows made the city look cloudy, but sharp shadows cast by the downtown skyscrapers told a different story.

He stepped back from the window. Heights weren't his thing.

He needed to eat. The last meal he'd had was on the flight; it'd been too late to get anything by the time he arrived in the city.

He picked up the hotel brochure and flicked through till he found the dining-room times. Breakfast had finished. He'd have to go to a restaurant.

After a shower he picked up his mobile and scrolled through the directory till he found the number he wanted.

The phone was answered after four rings.

"Jake, it's Ben."

"Jambo Ben." Jake's voice sounded asthmatic. "Are you in Nairobi now?"

"Arrived last night."

"When can I expect you?" Jake asked.

"Later today, or tomorrow. Depends how you've got on."

There was a thick chuckle on the other end of the line.

"Ben, this is Kenya. You only gave me the guy's name on Monday. These things take time."

"I haven't got time." Ben tried not to sound impatient. "I'm only here for a week."

"I'll have something by then."

That was no good.

"This is really important. I need to know where this guy is now. I've got nothing, and you're the only one who can help me. Can't you get things moving any faster?"

"I'll try to have something by Friday, but I don't have the same clout I used to. Things have changed."

Friday was better than nothing.

"Thanks Jake. I'll see you later."

He hung up.

A two day delay was a real pain in the backside. He'd expected to have information from his old friend as soon as he arrived. He scanned his memory for other Kenyan contacts. There were plenty, but none better placed than Jake to get access to government information. What was he going to do? He could always go to Nakuru and just start asking around, but that wouldn't get him anywhere.

"Damn it."

He stowed his valuables in the safe, grabbed his wallet and left the room. He nodded to the maid in the corridor as she collected toiletries from the top of her trolley then took the lift to the ground floor where he stepped into the broad circle of brown and white marble that formed the lobby. He began walking towards the entrance. Halfway to the door he noticed a man staring at him from a table in the bar area. Ben looked away, but his peripheral vision caught the man standing up.

Ben left the hotel through the revolving doors and turned left at the base of the steps. He kept his gaze forward and increased his pace. After a couple of seconds he turned back. The man from the bar had just walked out of the hotel. He was black, lean and about six-feet tall with short hair. He was wearing a beige suit and a dark tie.

After about a hundred yards Ben stopped at one of the street vendors and began browsing the curios that were on offer. It was the usual collection of second-rate wood and stone carvings. He showed a bit of interest then looked back up the street towards the hotel.

"American?" the vendor asked.

Ben nodded.

"You like?" The vendor pushed a carving towards him.

Ben ignored him. The man from the hotel was putting coins into a machine in the wall. Maybe he was buying cigarettes.

"I give you good price."

Ben turned back.

"Another time," he said.

"Twenty shillings."

He started walking away.

"Fifteen."

He shook his head and continued down the street.

After another fifty yards he came to a restaurant with a modern looking façade. He tried to see through the smoked glass, but could only make out shadows.

A brass menu, about five-feet tall, stood at right angles to the entrance. It contained the usual international fare: beef and chicken dishes, salads, pizzas and pasta. He positioned himself by the menu so he could observe the busy sidewalk discreetly.

The beige suit was twenty metres away, smoking and looking in a window. As he turned briefly towards Ben, his jacket opened to reveal a flash of black metal and a leather shoulder strap. Ben's eyes darted back to the menu. The guy might not be subtle, but he meant business.

Saturday night had marked the shift from mere suspicion to dangerous reality. He needed to get off the street; he'd feel safer inside. He stepped into the air-conditioned restaurant. Jazz music blended with the gentle rumble of civilised conversation coming from its well-dressed clientele having brunch or morning coffee. Lucky choice.

A young waitress with long frizzy hair came up with a menu.

"Table for one?"

"Can I sit by a window?" Ben asked.

He was led to the only window table that was free. He sat facing back up the street towards the hotel.

He kept his eyes on the constant stream of people that passed by. There was no sign of the beige suit. He picked up the menu and began reading. Five seconds later he'd made his choice. He put the menu down and looked out of the window again.

He caught a glimpse of beige across the street. He waited for another gap in the melee of people and traffic that swarmed past the window. For a fleeting second he saw a beige pair of trousers protruding from beneath a newspaper.

"You ready to order?"

Ben turned round. "Steak and eggs please, and a large coffee."

He looked back across the street. Another gap. The newspaper had been closed and the man took a drag of his cigarette.

If only he was being paranoid, but he wasn't. Somehow Marivant knew he was in Kenya. They'd probably tailed him from the airport. Maybe they were keeping tabs on him in Brighton and followed him to Gatwick. He'd never have noticed. They could've seen where he checked in and hired someone local to keep an eye on him.

That's not how it happened in modern spy films though. They wouldn't have needed to follow him in the UK. It would've been easy to keep track of him by monitoring his credit-card accounts.

His coffee arrived. He took a sip and put it back down on the table. What the hell was he doing there? He was on his own, in a violent and corrupt country, up against a ruthless organisation with limitless resources. He should get a cab straight back to the airport and catch the first flight home. He'd do what Ruth had suggested and go straight to the police and tell them everything. If they didn't follow it up, he wasn't to blame, he'd have done all that could be expected of him.

But what about the people walking past the window? According to the UN statistics every sixth person had a death sentence hanging over them. The barefoot boy in shorts pushing the rusty bike; the young woman wearing a bright head scarf with the baby strapped to her back; the skinny middle aged man with a beaten leather briefcase. Within the space of a minute more than fifteen people had walked past who were infected with HIV. The virus was decimating sub-Saharan Africa, leaving a trail of crippled economies and broken hearts in its wake. Then there was Julia. He'd have died for her while she was alive, how could he live with himself if he hadn't got to the bottom of this. He just needed to hold his nerve and have faith in the fact that he was doing the right thing, and if he failed, so be it, death was better than a lifetime of shame.

He stared out of the window. Another gap. The suit had been replaced by a young woman eating a sandwich.

"Excuse me."

Ben turned to see the waitress ready to put his steak in front of him. He lifted his elbows off the table to make room for the plate.

"Thanks," he said, and looked back across the street. The guy had definitely been tailing him, but he'd vanished. He began eating, all the time keeping an eye on the street.

The beige suit didn't return for the rest of his meal but the young woman was still sitting on the bench when he finished his last mouthful. He paid the bill and left. He waited outside the restaurant for half a minute surveying the street in all directions. Nothing. Maybe he'd been wrong.

He returned to the hotel and went to the reception desk. A thin young man in a blue blazer smiled at him.

"Can I help sir?"

"What time's checkout?"

"Twelve."

"I'm going to need my room for a few more hours," Ben said.

"What's your number?"

"Nine-two-one."

The receptionist tapped on a keyboard in front of him. "That's fine Doctor Williams."

Ben turned and walked to the elevators. He pressed the call button and watched the numbers descend. A flash of light from the revolving door drew his eyes across the lobby. An attractive young woman entered; the same one who'd been sitting on the bench. She headed for the bar.

The elevator pinged. Ben stepped inside and pressed the button for the ninth floor.

He'd been right about being followed, only there were two of them.

The adrenalin returned. His heart beat faster and his mind whirred with scenarios. The lift arrived at his floor; he stepped out and walked to his room. A trolley stood in the doorway. He squeezed past it and found the maid making the bed. She looked up with an awkward expression.

"You're alright," he said, holding up a hand. "I'll just sit over here."

He walked over to a chair by the window and sat down.

How much danger was he really in? What had he said to anyone else about MVT084? Other than with Ruth he'd only ever linked the deaths to heart attacks. Even on Saturday he'd been consistent, so there was no way they could be certain he'd rumbled them. As long as there was doubt over how much he knew, there was a good chance they'd limit their actions to surveillance. But there were no guarantees; they'd already killed a hundred people.

It was time to rethink his plans. Fear might bring out the coward in everyone, but when your back's really against the wall it makes you think outside the box. He wasn't going to run from danger, so he needed to neutralise it. To do that Marivant had to believe he wasn't looking for Esau.

He had two days before he could make any real progress with his search. In that time he needed to act like he really was on holiday, and hope that would be enough to shake them off. If they were more persistent he needed to find another way to slip out from under their noses. That wasn't going to be easy. He didn't know Nairobi as well as other parts of Kenya. This was their city; they knew their way round better than he did. It was difficult to see how he could gain an advantage, even in the countryside. Car chases might work on TV, but not when you've got a pothole the size of the Rift Valley every few hundred metres. But there was one place he had the upper hand.

"Thank you," the maid called, pushing her trolley out.

He looked up and nodded. She closed the door.

It required careful planning, especially when using his credit cards, but it might just work. He needed to get moving, he had to be in Nakuru by Friday at the latest.

* * * *

Ben sat on the end of his bed, his holdall packed on one side of him and his rucksack on the other. It was two-thirty.

Don't be late, you're never late.

There was a knock at the door.

He jumped up and crossed the room in a couple of strides. He looked through the spy hole. The fisheye view showed a tall man standing alone. Ben opened the door.

"Harry. Good to see you." He peered over the visitor's shoulder. The corridor was clear. He let the fair-haired Englishman enter. "Thanks for coming at such short notice."

"No problem. Bit of a surprise though," Harry said. He took his jacket off and put it over the back of a chair. "How long's it been?"

"The last time I was over here," Ben said. "Eighteen months ago."

"That long?" Harry frowned. "Sorry to hear about Julia old boy."

Ben nodded. He didn't have time for this. "Did you do as I asked?"

Harry leaned over, pulled an envelope out of his jacket pocket and handed it to him. He sat on the bed and emptied the contents. There was an Amex, a passport, and an airline ticket. He opened the passport.

"I don't look anything like you," he said, closing it and putting it back down

"They never check on internal flights. Even if they do, we all look the same to them."

Ben picked up the Amex. "Thanks for this." He slipped it into his wallet, and then opened the ticket. It was one-way from Mombassa to Nairobi and was dated for Thursday: tomorrow. Take off was two in the afternoon. He'd be back in the capital by three, which gave him enough time to reach Jake's ranch by nightfall. Perfect.

"Are you going to tell me what this is about?"

Ben looked up from the bed at his friend. "It's best you don't know."

"What are you into mate? You've always been above board."

"It's nothing illegal. I'm being followed and I need to lose them."

"Not the police? You don't want to mess with that lot, the prisons here are vile."

"I told you, it's nothing illegal."

"Then why won't you tell me?"

Ben glanced at his watch. Two-forty. His flight for Mombassa left at four. He wouldn't be checking any luggage into the hold, but he still needed to get moving.

"I haven't got time now, I'll tell you tomorrow," Ben said.

Harry didn't look satisfied.

"How long have we known each other?" Ben asked.

"Lower fifth of junior school."

"Then trust me," Ben said. He picked up the holdall and handed it to Harry, who lifted the strap over his shoulder and draped his jacket on top.

"You'll meet me at the airport with that tomorrow?" Ben asked.

"As arranged, and I'll have a four-by-four ready."

"I'll settle up afterwards," Ben said. "You've got to go. I need to leave in five minutes and they can't see us together."

Ben led Harry to the door. He opened it and looked outside. No one.

"See you tomorrow," he said, then closed the door.

He picked up the hotel phone and dialled the concierge.

"I need a cab for the airport in five minutes."

He hung up and sat on the bed. Had he covered all the bases? He'd paid for a return flight to Mombassa on his credit card, leaving today, returning the following Monday. If Marivant were tracing his movements electronically, that should help convince them he was on holiday. He'd also booked the Diani Lodge for a week. Harry had paid for Thursday's return flight in his name and would hire the four-by-four. All he had to do was make Marivant lose the scent in Mombassa and he'd be free.

He slung his rucksack over his shoulder and headed downstairs. As he walked up to the concierge desk he caught sight of the woman from the bench still sitting at the bar.

"I ordered a cab," he said to the concierge. The elderly man glanced over to the bar area. When people are dirt poor, they're easily bought. It was worth holding tight to that thought for the rest of the trip.

"This way." The concierge led him outside into the hot afternoon sun.

A new Mercedes was waiting at the bottom of the steps. The driver stood by the open boot. Ben handed him his rucksack and looked up the steps to the hotel entrance. No sign of the woman. He got in the Merc and leaned back into the welcoming leather. If his plan worked, he'd be able to search for Esau without looking over his shoulder any more.

Chapter 16

Ben was greeted by a blast of tropical air as he left the arrivals hall at Mombassa airport.

He joined a queue for taxis and put his rucksack down.

He hadn't checked whether he'd been followed since leaving the Hilton three hours earlier; it was better to look as unaware of them as possible. But now he was in Mombassa it would be good to know if he'd managed to shake them off. Everything had been done at such short notice, maybe he'd taken them by surprise.

There were hundreds of people milling around on the pavement. Porters pushed trolleys loaded with suitcases; pale Europeans stood in bewildered groups looking at each other wearily; tour operators held clipboards high in the air; and countless men watched the proceedings furtively from the shadows. Any one of them could have been there to spy on him.

After five minutes he reached the front of the queue.

A young driver jumped out of an old VW and beckoned Ben to give him his rucksack. He obliged and got in the back seat.

"Where to Boss?" the driver asked.

"Diani Lodge."

The driver manoeuvred the car through the scrum of taxis and minivans.

Ben looked out of the back window.

"Flight good?"

"Yes thanks." A red Nissan with tinted windows pulled out and followed a short distance behind. He turned forward.

"You come from England?"

"Not today. I flew from Nairobi this afternoon."

They reached a junction and turned left. After they'd travelled about half a mile Ben turned round again. The Nissan was a hundred yards behind.

"How far to the hotel?" he asked.

"Twenty minutes. Thirty if we wait for the ferry."

Ben looked out of the side window. The Western sky was glowing brightly. The sun would set soon. Night would follow fast; there were no long dusks in the tropics.

The scenery on the coast was very different from the areas surrounding Nairobi. Instead of grassland dotted with broad Acacias, skinny palms towered over a lush layer of undergrowth where banana trees fought for space with giant cheese plants.

The vegetation soon gave way to the scruffy outskirts of Mombassa, humble one-storey huts lined the road.

After another ten minutes they reached the schizophrenic heart of the city. Wide avenues, flanked by colonial buildings, paraded to the edge of the old quarter, in which ancient whitewashed houses leaned across narrow cobbled passageways. Mombassa's split personality wasn't merely architectural. It was both a busy commercial hub and a laid-back tourist hangout. Even its soul was divided between Mohammad and Christ.

The sight of men in white cotton robes and caftans walking alongside overweight tourists in shorts and baseball caps, brought back memories of the holidays he'd spent in the city with Julia. What he'd give to turn the clock back to then.

Shortly after the taxi had negotiated the chaotic traffic of the centre they arrived at the ferry on the southern edge of the island. It was loading on the opposite side of the harbour; they'd have to wait.

Ben checked behind them again. The red Nissan was two cars back. For once he could do without the adrenalin rush, for once he'd prefer an anti-climax, but it wasn't going to be. It looked like Marivant were still with him.

He turned forward. The rusting hulk of the ferry was lumbering back across the hundred metres of water. Its open deck was full of pick-up trucks. Some were stacked high with cages full of chickens, others had been converted into Matatus and were forced to sit on their axles by the impossible number of people crammed inside.

He'd spent many an hour squeezed into the corner of a Matatu, barely able to breathe, with some big mama's butt in his face. He'd never mastered the contortion act required to fit inside with any degree of comfort.

The ferry unloaded, and before long they were on the other side of the river. Another fifteen minutes brought them to the neat

129

gardens surrounding the Diani Lodge. A security guard manning a barrier checked his passport and chatted to the driver in Swahili. Ben glanced behind them along the poorly lit road that led back towards the harbour. The Nissan pulled in fifty yards away and switched off its headlights. Any doubts that might have lingered about being followed were blown away. Plan B was now the only option.

The gate lifted and he was driven down the wide drive lined with rhododendrons.

* * * *

He checked into his room, then undressed and lay on the bed. He dozed for about an hour and a half before getting back up. He refreshed himself with a shower. He'd only packed his surf gear, so had no choice but to put on the same stale pair of Khakis and a short-sleeved shirt that he'd worn all day. He used his fingers to comb his hair before heading out for dinner.

The dining room was a wide circular building set away from the main hotel. Its walls were made of thick bamboo, and a vast central tree trunk supported the high thatched roof. The headwaiter led Ben through the busy room to a table set for two, and removed the surplus cutlery.

There'd been plenty of occasions when he'd dined alone in hotel restaurants, but that had been while attending conferences. Then he was just one of hundreds of solitary diners, now he stood out like a hard-on in a convent, everyone else was either in a couple or a family.

A skinny waiter with a moustache appeared at his table, notepad at the ready.

"Would you like soup or salad to start?"

"Salad," Ben replied. "And the chicken for main course."

"And to drink?"

"A beer."

The waiter scurried away.

Ben looked at the other diners with envy. They'd be playing in the water tomorrow, not risking their lives.

"Do you mind if I join you?"

Ben looked up to see a thickset man in his forties wearing a Hawaiian shirt and holding a beer.

"It's just that I saw you were on your own, and I am too."
There was an antipodean twang to his accent, probably Aussie.

The thought of spending the evening with a drunken Neanderthal from down under appealed about as much as having his eyeballs poked with a red-hot poker, but he couldn't think of an excuse quick enough to fob him off. He nodded.

"Vernon Walker," the man said, extending his hand as he took his seat.

"Ben Williams."

Vernon's face was deeply tanned. Below the neckline the tan was obscured by a dense covering of black hair. He had a broad friendly face but his eyes looked hardened by booze or disappointment, or both.

The waiter turned up with his salad and beer. He looked at Vernon in confusion.

"Just moved from over there," Vernon said, pointing to a table on the other side of the room. "I'll wait till Ben here has finished before I have the next course."

Ben began eating. "Where are you from?" he asked between mouthfuls.

"Nairobi."

"You're not here on holiday then?"

"A mixture," Vernon said. "I did some business in town yesterday, and thought I'd take it easy for a few days."

"What line of business are you in?"

"Air conditioning. I supply units to hotels and office blocks."

"Must be lucrative."

"Can be," Vernon replied. "And you? Where are you from?"

"The UK. Brighton."

"You here on holiday?"

"Yep. Windsurfing," Ben said. He took his last mouthful of salad and finished his beer. He looked up to see Vernon waving at a waiter. He held up a beer bottle with one hand and signalled two with the other. The waiter nodded and headed off.

"Have you always lived in Kenya?" Ben asked.

"For the last twenty-seven years. Before that I was all over the place. My father was a pilot."

"So why settle here?"

"Money. The tourist industry was taking off in the late seventies. Most of the hotels only had fans, and cheap air-con units were becoming available. I saw a gap in the market."

"Have you done well?"

"I did at first, made a killing. But it's been much harder recently. Less tourists, less money sloshing around, fewer hotels willing to splash out on replacing their ageing units." Vernon started peeling the label off his beer bottle. "What do you do?"

"I'm a doctor."

"Really?" Vernon looked up in surprise. "You know I wouldn't have taken you for a doctor."

"Oh?"

"You look too healthy. You've seen too much sun. Most doctors I know are pasty white, they hardly ever seem to get out."

"It's the windsurfing," Ben replied. "How long are you staying for?"

"Not sure. I've got no reason to be back in Nairobi till next Monday. Depends how bored I get down here and whether I get any action." Vernon winked and looked towards two middle-aged women on a nearby table. He looked back at Ben and grinned.

"You're not married?" Ben asked.

"Not my bag. You?"

"No," Ben replied.

The main course and more beer arrived. For a while the conversation was relegated to second place in preference to food.

Once the meal was over they headed for the bar. Vernon wasn't such bad company and was proving a good distraction from the worries about the next day.

* * * *

Helen stood at the bar in Club New York waiting for her drink. She turned round and saw Ruth standing on her own by the DJ booth.

"That's two-fifty," the barmaid said.

"Can you wait a second?" Helen asked.

This might be the one chance she got to speak to Ruth all night. She walked over.

"Can I get you a drink?" Helen said.

Ruth looked surprised, then smiled. "I'll have an orange juice please."

Helen got Ruth's drink and joined her. There was an uncomfortable silence.

"I'm sorry we didn't get a chance to chat on Saturday," Helen said.

"That's alright." Ruth's smile dispelled the awkwardness. "It was very busy in Casablanca and Ben didn't bother to introduce us."

"Your friends aren't here tonight?"

"No, they only come on Saturdays," Ruth replied. "Ben told me you had a nice time."

"On Monday?"

"Monday?" Ruth said. "He didn't say you were going out again."

Ben couldn't have spoken to his sister since the weekend, there was only so much information she was going to get out of her.

"We had dinner in Orsino," Helen said.

"Did you enjoy it?"

"The food was good."

"Only the food?"

"I don't think your brother was very happy."

"I wouldn't worry. It's probably nothing to do with you. He's got a lot on his mind at the moment."

Maybe this wasn't going to be a waste of time after all. She needed to probe further. A loud clap of hands put paid to that idea though, it was time to dance.

"If you're not doing anything after, do you fancy going for a drink?" she asked, it would be easier to get Ruth to talk if they were alone and the drinks were flowing.

Ruth nodded. "But I can't stay out too late, I need to get an early start."

* * * *

After the class they walked across Churchill Square, the soulless shopping centre that stood testimony to the local council's crass stupidity. On the other side they entered a pub with wooden floors and a modern bar area.

Ruth bought a round and they sat down on a bench.

"So what do you think of my brother?" Ruth asked.

Helen smiled. "Not a loaded question at all."

"I've just seen him go through so much, I don't want him to get hurt."

"To be honest I'm not sure it matters what I think. He seemed a lovely guy, but he cut me short on Monday night. I couldn't work it out."

"He can do that, especially if he's preoccupied with something else."

"All I know is I met him on Saturday and the next day he books a holiday. Doesn't make a girl feel wanted."

"Don't worry, the holiday's nothing to do with you. He just needed to get away." Ruth said. "From what he said to me on Sunday, I think he's quite taken with you."

"Really?"

Ruth nodded, but her expression clouded over.

"And that bothers you?" Helen asked.

There was a pause.

"Did he tell you about our background?" Ruth asked.

Differentiating what she'd read in his file and what he'd told her wasn't easy. "Bits and pieces."

"Did he say anything about our parents?"

"Only that you grew up in Africa."

"They were missionaries." Ruth said. "Christians."

"I think he may have mentioned it."

Ruth looked at her as though there was something highly significant in this fact. Of course! She donated money to church, and Ben had told her in the nightclub that his sister went twice every Sunday.

"You don't approve of him dating a non-Christian?"

"It's not that I don't approve, I just want him to be happy." Ruth looked down. "I know my brother has lost his faith." She looked back up. "But I believe he will come back one day, and more to the point, Mum and Dad would want him to be with someone who believed."

Ignorance was passed from one generation to another like a genetic disorder. She was standing in the living laboratory of psychological evolution and Dawkins' meme theory was being played out before her very own eyes. It was pathetic and deserved the derision that educated society poured on it. But this wasn't the time to go down that road. If anything this was an opportunity to get Ruth to relax and open up, get her talking about something that made her feel good. She could even use the idea of posing as a potential convert that she'd suggested to Anne.

"So you only date Christian men then?"

Ruth examined her for a few moments, then said, "I don't date men."

Helen gave her a puzzled look.

"I'm not into guys," Ruth explained.

Helen's eyes widened.

"You're gay?"

"Yes and No."

"Well you're either one or the other."

"It's possible to be somewhere in between," Ruth said. "My brother says I'm gay, but that's only because he saw me holding hands with another woman once."

"So you have relationships with women?" This was an interesting development. "Doesn't that go against your Bible?"

There was sadness in Ruth's eyes. "Actually I'm not sure it does. The Bible says a bit about men having sex with men, mainly in the Old Testament, but it has very little to say about same sex relationships between women."

"So you have lesbian relationships then?"

Ruth shook her head. "No." The sadness intensified. "There was someone once, a woman who I loved very much. I just wanted companionship, some intimacy, but she wanted to take it that step further. I didn't feel right about it."

"But you just said that the Bible doesn't have much to say about same sex relationships between women."

"I know, and I could have used that as an excuse, but I have straight friends in relationships that are holding out till they're married and male friends that are attracted to other men, but because of their faith, they don't get involved in sexual relationships. I want to stand with them."

This was too much, she couldn't hold back any longer. "I think you're all crazy. If it's in your nature to be attracted to someone of the same sex, then what's wrong with it? You're denying yourself love, and for what, a few words written by suppressed men two or three millennia ago. Didn't they also say you should stone adulterers to death? Your church doesn't approve of that does it?"

"Of course not," Ruth said. "The Old Testament does contain some arcane rules that the church no longer follows."

"Exactly. So why do you still apply them to yourself?"

"It's a matter of priorities," Ruth explained. "What comes first, gaining pleasure from sexual gratification or being right with God? To me being close to God gives me more joy than anything else I know so it is the number one priority. If I have any doubt about whether a way of behaving might affect that relationship and disturb that joy, then I would rather abstain than risk losing what is most precious to me."

Helen shook her head. Bonkers.

"It's all about the conscience," Ruth continued. "When my conscience is clear, I feel at peace, I'm light on the inside and am able to access this awesome consciousness or Holy presence that I believe is God. When I've done something that troubles my sense of right and wrong, my experience of that presence diminishes and my life feels darker and emptier as a result."

For a second Ruth's words resonated with something inside, a desire to feel that lightness and peace after all the darkness and emptiness. "But what if you've done something really bad, like killing someone?"

Ruth smiled.

"It sounds odd, but that might actually make it easier."

This was getting more bizarre by the second. "How so?"

"Most people think they're fine, that they haven't done anything really bad so they don't need forgiving so they don't bother with God. The truth is everyone of us falls short at some point. There is no one alive who has never done anything wrong to someone else, even if it is was only something small or not doing something that they should have. But it's the people who have done something seriously wrong who find it hardest to shake off the guilt, and therefore have the greatest need to be free of it. From what I've seen the only effective way you can be free of guilt is through a fresh start through the cross of Christ. It's ironic that they are the ones who then end up having all the benefits of a relationship with God, whereas those who feel they have little to forgive miss out. Forgiveness is the big difference between the Christian faith and others like the Muslim or Jewish faiths."

So this is what it felt like to be preached to by a Christian. If it meant getting the job finished quicker it was worth it, she'd endured worse. Besides there were questions she'd always wanted to throw at someone like Ruth. "So they end up in hell even though they don't deserve it, just because they don't believe?"

"That's what the Bible says. Some believe that you are able to put things right after you die, but Jesus doesn't say anything about that, so why take the chance? After all, if you were God what would you do with someone who turns up on your doorstep who's never shown any interest in you in spite of the fact that this person has been told the truth at some point in their lives but chose to ignore it?" Ruth moved a coaster around on the table. "The fact is though, we aren't God, so he wouldn't react like us, but it seems kind of unjust if someone who has spurned spirituality all their lives gets the same eternal destiny as someone who has devoted themselves to a relationship with God and following his ways. I believe you make your choices in this life. If you choose the material world, whether that be sex, money, power, hobbies, success…whatever…and don't give a second thought to God then it only seems fair that you'll end up not being with him when you die."

For a brief moment, her words made sense. The desire to be rid of the darkness inside and the discovery of a potential means for doing that made it tempting to believe Ruth, but the feeling didn't last. She was talking rubbish. The sense of darkness, of the emptiness of reality, was the cold shower of the truth that there is no God, no after life. Darwin had proved that.

It was time to move things on. She'd played the potential convert long enough and trying to have a rational discussion with someone who believed in completely irrational notions would drive her crazy if she went on much longer. The sooner she got the information she needed, the sooner she could put this nonsense behind her and be back in Spain.

"Do you think he went away at such short notice because of the mugging?" she asked.

Ruth looked stunned. "He told you about that?"

"Some Irish guy or something?"

The risk was calculated. It was highly unlikely Ruth would guess at her true identity given the way they met.

"He told me to keep it secret," Ruth said.

"Me too."

"So what else did he tell you?" Ruth asked, eyeing her cautiously.

"I didn't really get it all, but he mentioned something about a drug trial, and some company. Moravent?"

Ruth's eyes widened. "He talked about Marivant?"

"That's it."

"I don't believe him. He told me it was too dangerous to tell anyone."

Game over. That one line told her everything she needed to know: Williams wasn't on holiday in Kenya, he was there investigating the trial. How easy had that been? She wouldn't even need to get her hands dirty, Luke could get one of their operatives in their African division to take care of things. She was already basking in the Spanish sun. Still, she had to be absolutely certain.

"Aren't you worried about him in Africa?" Helen asked.

"Yes. Very." Ruth looked down. "I'm worried they'll kill him if they know what he's up to."

It was time to call this in.

"Excuse me a second." Helen got up. "I need the bathroom."

She walked into the ladies, stepped into a cubicle and rang Luke.

"I'm out with Ruth Williams," she said.

"Yes?"

"I got her to open up. Williams isn't on holiday. He's out there looking into the trial."

"How did you find out?"

"I said to Ruth that he'd told me on Monday."

"You said what?"

"That he told me on Monday."

"You stupid cow. What do you think you're doing?"

Helen held the phone away from her and looked at it. He wasn't supposed to react like this, he should be chuffed to bits. She put the phone against her ear again.

"I got the information," she said, "Williams is onto us. Isn't that what you wanted?"

"Not if you risked blowing your cover."

"What does it matter now?"

There was a sigh and a pause.

"Marivant are getting cold feet," Luke said. "Killing Williams is now the last resort, they hope he'll lead us to Esau. But you've left me no choice. If the team lose him and he talks to his sister, he'll guess what is happening and go to the police. I can't allow that to happen. There's too much at stake."

How was she supposed to know Marivant had changed the rules? Still, there was nothing she could do about it now. The best thing to do was get on the right side of Luke again.

"I'm sorry," she said. "I just saw an opportunity and took it."

"Talk to me before you take chances again," he said.

She bit her tongue.

"What about the sister?" Helen asked. "She knows too. What do you want me to do with her?"

"Nothing. Just keep close to her. I have to go, I need to clear up this mess you've made."

"You're going to have Williams killed?"

Luke hung up without answering.

Helen opened the door to the cubicle and froze. Ruth was staring straight at her. There was a second of hesitation, then Ruth ran for the door.

Helen felt in her handbag. The Beretta was still there. She followed Ruth into the pub but she was already at the door. Ruth turned and looked back, then bolted out.

Helen pushed through the bar, yanked the door open and ran onto the pavement. She looked up and down the street. Ruth was crossing the road. She was heading for a taxi rank; there was one car waiting.

Helen sprinted across the road after Ruth.

A couple appeared from an alleyway and rushed for the taxi. Ruth arrived a second too late. There was an exchange of words. The young man gave Ruth the finger, got in the car and slammed the door.

Ruth turned and stared at Helen in confusion before running down the alley.

Helen had trained for this. She focused on her quarry and accelerated. Within a few seconds she was behind Ruth. She grabbed her hair, yanked her to a halt and pushed her up against a shop window.

She looked from side to side. They were alone. She pulled the gun out of her bag and shoved it into Ruth's stomach. Their eyes met as they both tried to catch their breath. For a second she felt her resolve flinch as she pushed the hard metal into Ruth's soft flesh.

"Who are you?" Ruth said, her voice trembling.

"No questions. Just do as I say."

Ruth was shaking. "You can't kill me."

"Why not?" Helen said. "Besides, you don't want your brother to die do you?"

Ruth's eyes filled with panic. "Don't kill him. He's all I've got."

Helen grabbed her by the elbow and pulled her back up the alley.

"My car's parked up the hill. If you want to see your brother again, you'll make it easy for me."

What a complete disaster. Luke was going to freak.

* * * *

Ben had lost count of the number of beers he'd drunk. He sat by himself at a table in the bar watching Vernon chat up the two women they'd seen at dinner.

"I need to go to bed," he said to himself. He felt drowsy and wasn't interested in either of the women. They were no match for Julia, or even Helen for that matter. He picked up his key and slowly got to his feet.

A phone rang with the same innocuous tone as his. He fumbled with his pockets then realised he'd left his mobile in the hotel safe. He looked at the table. Vernon's phone lit up as it rang again.

He glanced at Vernon who had his arms round both women; he wouldn't want to be disturbed. He picked up the phone and looked at the display. The screen contained one word: 'Luke'.

Chapter 17

The phone stopped ringing.

It took another second to join the dots. He'd seen the same name on Helen's mobile.

The bitch! He was such a sucker. He knew she was too good to be true, she'd been so easy and now he knew why.

He had to forget his wounded pride for now, he had a more immediate problem. He looked at Vernon again. He was still flirting with the women.

His face didn't seem so friendly now.

The phone beeped. Ben held it down by his side and read the display: 'You have one voice message'.

He slipped it into his pocket and walked over to Vernon.

"I'm just off to the gents," he said.

"Thanks for telling us," Vernon said, giving him a derisory look, then laughing.

Ben walked round the semi-circular bar to the toilet. He stepped inside a cubicle and pulled the phone out. He accessed the message menu, selected voicemail and put the phone to his ear.

"There has been a change of plan. Eliminate the target," the Irish accent said. "Call me once it is done."

Ben hung up. He stared at the green paint of the cubicle door, his mind empty of all thoughts but one. He was dead.

He slumped onto the toilet seat and took a deep breath.

Speculating about dying was one thing, but to know that a man less than fifty yards away had specific orders to murder you was something else.

What had changed? Why weren't they happy just following him? Had he said something that evening to give himself away? Not that he could think of. He hadn't mentioned Marivant to Helen either. How had they found out what he was up to?

He jumped to his feet.

Ruth. They must have got to Ruth. He had to warn her about Helen.

He yanked open the cubicle door and took two steps towards the exit before stopping dead. He looked at the phone in his hand. If Vernon didn't get the message it might buy him some time. He walked back into the cubicle, lifted the lid off the cistern and dropped the phone inside. He hurried back out to hear angry shouting. The loudest voice was Australian. Ben walked round the bar. The seats where Vernon and the two women had been sitting were empty.

He slowed down as his assassin came into view. Vernon was holding a waiter by his shirt collar.

"Where is it you thieving bastard?" He started shaking him.

A security guard ran in from the reception area and put his hand on Vernon's shoulder. Vernon spun round. He looked like he was about to take a swing.

"What's up?" Ben said, as he joined the three men.

"Have you seen my phone?" Vernon asked.

Ben shook his head. "It was on the table last time I saw it."

Vernon turned back to the waiter. "Give me my phone."

"I haven't got it," the waiter said.

The security guard pushed between the two men. "Empty your pockets," he said to the waiter.

Vernon stood back and folded his arms.

The waiter put his tray down on the table and pulled out a pen, a notepad and a mobile phone.

Vernon leaned forward and shook his head. "Not mine. Where have you hidden it?"

"You can search anywhere. I haven't taken it."

Vernon turned back to Ben. "Are you sure it was here when you went to the toilets?"

"I think so. But I've had a few beers. I might be wrong."

Vernon's shoulders sagged.

"We'll look for it after everyone's left," the security guard said. "I'll check the staff's pockets and lockers. If it's been stolen by anyone here, I'll find it."

Vernon gave him a resigned nod.

"I'm off to bed," Ben said.

Vernon looked at the staff with disgust. "Me too."

They walked away from the bar and began crossing the reception area.

"Mister Walker!"

They both stopped and looked at the pretty receptionist.

"There's a message for you," she said.

Vernon turned to Ben. "I'd better find out what it says," he said. "See you later."

No prizes for guessing who the message was from. There was no doubt at all he'd be seeing Vernon again.

* * * *

"Switch it off," Helen said to Ruth, as she drove carefully up the gravel track.

Ruth leaned forward, picked up her handbag and pulled the mobile out. She held it in front of her.

"I said switch it off."

Ruth didn't seem to be listening. The phone stopped ringing. Helen slammed on the breaks. She wrenched the mobile from Ruth's grip.

"Start playing ball," she snapped. "Have you any idea who you're dealing with?"

She threw the mobile onto the backseat and eased the car forward again.

They drove through the dark woodland in silence until they reached the black iron gate. It would have been good if she had a remote of her own, then she could slip in and wait till the morning before dealing with the mess, but only Luke had been issued with one. She took in a deep breath and pressed the buzzer then waited for a minute. No answer. She pressed it again. After about thirty seconds the floodlights above the gate lit up. She shielded her eyes from the glare. The intercom crackled.

"What are you doing here?" Luke asked.

"Let me in," Helen said.

"You'd better not have screwed things up even more."

"Just let me in."

The gate slid back and Helen drove up to the front of the house. Luke was standing on the steps with his arms folded.

"Wait here," Helen said, and removed the keys from the ignition.

She stepped out, locked the car and walked up to Luke. He was staring past her at Ruth.

"This is a joke, right?"

"She overheard me while I was talking to you."

Luke shook his head. "You're unbelievable."

"What are we going to do with her?" Helen asked.

"What's going on?" a voice said from behind.

Luke and Helen turned round. Anne was standing in the doorway. She was dressed, but looked like she'd just got out of bed.

"Helen's screwing everything up, that's what's going on," Luke said. He looked back at the car. "You've not even blindfolded her."

They all stared at Ruth. She had her head down.

"Get her out of there and put her in a cell," Luke said. "We need to find out how much she knows."

"I'll give you a hand in case she tries anything," Anne said.

Helen and Anne marched to the car. Helen pulled the door open and pointed her gun at Ruth.

"Out," she said.

Ruth slowly got out of the car. They led her into the house, turning left once they reached the central passage. At the end they walked into the kitchen. Anne opened a small door immediately to the left of the kitchen entrance. She turned a light on to reveal a set of narrow stone steps that descended in a spiral. Anne led the way. Helen made Ruth follow, and then brought up the rear.

At the bottom of the steps was a poorly lit corridor. The masonry was crumbling and there was the damp smell of mildew in the air. Along either side of the corridor were two grey metal doors; each had a small glass window protected by a metal grill.

Anne opened the second door on the right and turned the light on. There was an iron bed and two buckets. The flaking cream paint on the walls was covered in faint red smears. A padlocked mesh cage guarded the light bulb.

Anne pushed Ruth into the room and closed the cell door. She locked the cell using a keypad on the door.

"So?" Anne said.

"I messed up. I was on the phone to Luke and she heard everything."

"I didn't mean that," Anne said. "I was thinking about our chat on Friday."

Didn't they have enough to deal with? Surely this wasn't the time to be talking about jumping ship.

"Would you still be here if I'd told anyone?" Helen replied.

"Do you want out?" Anne asked.

"There's no way out," Helen said. "Unless in a coffin."

"I told you, I'm onto something."

"Information?"

There was a sound behind them. "What information?"

They both turned. Luke was balancing on the last step. He tipped forward, then walked slowly toward them.

"What information?"

He came up close and leaned down, looking first at Helen, then at Anne.

"Information about Williams," Anne said.

"What information about Williams?"

"I've found something in his credit cards that suggests he knows more than he's letting on to."

"Too late Anne." Luke straightened up. "He'll be dead by tomorrow evening."

He looked through the window of Ruth's cell. "She looks better than in the photo." He smiled, entered the code and pushed the door open. "I might be a while."

Helen caught a glimpse of Ruth sitting on the bed hugging her knees, her face tight with fear.

"What are you going to do to her?" Helen asked.

Luke stopped and looked back. "What do you care?" He turned away and stepped into the room.

This was too much. She didn't care anymore if her conscience was an evolutionary quirk or not, she couldn't live with herself if she allowed this to happen. She stepped forward. Anne grabbed her arm and shook her head.

"But I brought her here," Helen pleaded.

The door closed.

Luke smiled through the glass. "You girls want to watch?"

"Let's go," Anne said. "There's nothing we can do."

Helen watched helplessly as Luke crossed the room. He took his jacket off and stretched. Ruth backed up against the wall, but there was nowhere for her to go.

Chapter 18

Ben pulled the chair from under the handle and cautiously opened the door to his room. He looked up and down the corridor.

A couple walked past and smiled. He smiled back. There was no one else. He stepped out, closed the door and walked to the reception area. Three Germans with expensive looking luggage were checking out. No sign of Vernon. He strolled over to the main entrance and scanned the tranquil gardens for any hint of a breeze. There wasn't a breath. The sun needed to break through the thin layer of cloud before the wind would pick up.

He took a few paces outside where he had a better view of the car park to his left. There were four cars. One was the red Nissan. He went back inside, returned to his room and ordered breakfast. He didn't want to eat in the restaurant. The longer he avoided any chance of bumping into Vernon, the greater the possibility he'd lose him altogether.

He tried Ruth's mobile again. It diverted straight to her voicemail. He left the same message as before, telling her to get in touch as soon as possible.

Twenty-minute's later room service arrived.

What kind of breakfast would a man on death row have on the morning of his execution? It must have been better than the stale croissant and miserly chunks of tropical fruit that sat on the tray before him. Maybe going to the restaurant would have been worth the risk.

He finished eating by eight forty-five then hung the clothes he'd worn from Nairobi in the wardrobe. The maid would sell them or give them to her family. He dressed in a pair of blue surf shorts, a grey Lycra T-shirt and a baseball cap.

Other than his rucksack the only possessions he had with him were the two passports, the airline ticket, his wallet and phone. He put them inside a waterproof bum-bag he normally reserved for keys when he windsurfed at home. He clipped it round his waist.

He looked at himself in the mirror. His eyes were bloodshot and the lids were grey. Not surprising, he'd barely slept all night. He had to put that behind him: he needed to be at his best for the day ahead.

He slung his rucksack into the wardrobe and left the room then walked across the neat tropical gardens lying between the hotel and the beach. Most of the people up that early were gardeners and cleaners in brown canvas uniforms. A few guests dosed on sunloungers or read newspapers, but most of the sun beds were occupied by expectant towels.

He passed through the gate that protected the residents from the pushy traders and opportunistic thieves who prowled the public beach. He nodded at the tall security guard standing next to it. He walked a few paces down the beach then stopped and looked around.

As expected the cloud had already begun to burn away, but there was still no breeze. The listless waters of the Indian Ocean spilt the odd ripple onto the long beach, but without any help from the wind it was just a token gesture. It was easy to see why it was such a popular destination. The scene was postcard perfect. Palm trees leaned over the white sand which led to the bright turquoise waters of the sea.

He walked towards a cluster of thatched huts a hundred yards away. A movement by the hotel wall caught his eye. A young Kenyan with a sports bag and a large carving of an elephant by his feet was talking into a mobile and staring at him.

Ben turned back and continued on his way.

The largest hut housed the windsurf centre. He approached the wide counter. A lanky white guy with blonde dreadlocks was reading a book. A blackboard at the back of the hut gave the hire rates and the name of the manager on duty.

"Hi," Ben said. "Hans?"

The guy looked up, put his book on his lap and nodded.

"Are you hiring?" Ben asked.

"There's no wind dude." He had a slight German accent.

"Do you think it'll pick up?"

Hans got to his feet, leaned over the counter and looked out to sea.

"Maybe in an hour or two. Hard to say." He sat back down.

"Was there any yesterday?"

"None all week."

Great! Why couldn't something go his way just once?

"I'll be back later if it picks up," he said.

He headed back towards the hotel. The Kenyan with the carvings had moved along the wall close to the huts. Unlike the other traders he didn't seem interested in any of the tourists who passed by. It didn't really matter. There was no way him or Vernon would try anything on the beach, there were too many people, even at this early hour. Aside from staff like Hans, there were a few traders staking an early claim, and a steady procession of couples enjoying an intimate morning stroll.

He found a sunbed shaded by an umbrella and sat down.

With the current wind it would take the rest of the day to travel the five miles he needed to. If the conditions didn't improve he'd have to deploy his back-up plan. That would cost a few thousand pounds rather than a few hundred. He'd only accounted for trashing a windsurfer, not a jet ski.

There were other problems with using a jet ski. The Marivant agents might see it as a realistic means of escape and would keep a closer eye on him. They'd be less likely to worry about him making a break for it if he was just windsurfing, especially after he'd been sailing back and forth to the reef for an hour or two.

Ben lay back and pulled his cap over his face. All he could do now was wait.

* * * *

"Ben?"

He pulled the cap off his face and squinted at the silhouette standing over him.

"I thought it was you," Vernon said. "How are you feeling this morning?"

"Bit tired." He sat up and looked at his watch. No! It was nearly eleven.

"Hungover?"

"Yeah."

Vernon sat down on a neighbouring sunlounger. "Thought you'd be on the water. You sounded pretty keen yesterday."

"There was no wind when I came down."

That wasn't the case now. There were at least fifteen to twenty windsurfers flying in and out on the messy chop.

"Guess I'd better get a few runs in before lunch," he said. He lifted himself off the sunbed.

"Do you fancy a trip into town tonight?" Vernon asked. "I've got my car here, we wouldn't have to mess about with cabs."

Ben looked into the reddened eyes of his enemy. "As long as your taste in women improves."

Vernon laughed.

"Quantity, not quality, that's my motto," he said. "Meet in the lobby about seven?"

"Sounds good. See you then," Ben replied.

He walked across the hot sand to the windsurf centre.

"Hey dude, where have you been?" Hans asked. "I thought you'd be here ages ago."

"Fell asleep."

"That's too bad."

"What've you got left?" Ben asked, noticing the empty racks behind Hans.

"All gone."

Ben shook his head. What a prat, all he had to do was stay awake an hour or two.

"Someone might come off the water soon," Hans said.

"I wouldn't if I was out there."

Hans gave him a sympathetic look. "How good are you?" Hans asked.

"I can carve, helitack, duck-gybe. I've been sailing since I was a kid."

Hans stroked his lip and stared at Ben. He nodded his head.

"You seem a straight-up guy. You can use my kit."

"Seriously?"

"Seriously," Hans replied. "Just get it back by four so I can go out for an hour or two."

"I can't," Ben said.

"What? Get it back?"

"No. I can't use your kit. It wouldn't be right."

"You're paying me, it'll be more than right. Anyway, the board's sweet. She's wasted sitting round all day doing nothing."

What should he do? On one hand it would be awful taking the board knowing he wouldn't return it, on the other, if he was ready to give up his life in this quest, he shouldn't have any qualms about sacrificing some kid's board.

"Thanks," he said.

Hans walked round the back of the shed and returned with a yellow Stormrider. The only time he'd seen one of those had been in a magazine, only a hundred had ever been made. Their handling was legendary. Another objection rose in his throat but he swallowed it.

Hans rigged up a five and a half metre sail and helped Ben down to the water's edge.

"Are you any good with waves?" Hans asked.

"I handled Maui well enough," he replied.

"Cool. There's a gap in the reef between two red buoys." Hans pointed to the thin strip of white foam two kilometres from the beach. "It's on the other side the fun begins. Just pull up before the waves die or you'll hit the reef." Hans patted his board. "If you see any thunderheads building in the south, get straight back to shore. They sneak up real fast and can be vicious."

"I'll keep an eye out."

He watched Hans walk back up the beach. Poor guy.

He turned his cap so the peak was facing backwards and looked towards the hotel. Vernon was talking to the young Kenyan he'd seen hanging around earlier.

It was time to get going.

He launched the board onto the water, stepped on and sheeted in. Within seconds he was on the plane and jumping the first breaker. He steered the board across the lumpy water out to the reef, gybed and returned to shore. It was easy sailing compared to the English Channel.

He repeated this several times before eleven-thirty. This left him the minimum two and a half hours he reckoned he'd need to make his flight.

He finished his last run back to shore and dropped off the board into the water to check the state of play. The Kenyan with the carvings was where he'd been all morning. He looked bored and seemed more interested in staring at a group of white girls sunbathing nearby than keeping watch on his target. Vernon was lying on a sunlounger not far from where he'd been sitting. He was sleeping off the previous night's drink.

150

He turned his back on the beach and got his kit in position to sail out again. A group of four windsurfers was nearing the shore. They gybed one after the other. He stepped onto the board and tagged onto the rear of the convoy as it skimmed across the sea towards the reef.

He hooked into his harness and looked out to sea. An ominous dark cloud was forming on the southern horizon. He leaned back and accelerated downwind.

The sailors he'd been following slowed down as the reef drew nearer, they all tacked. He pointed the nose of the board towards the reef gate then released some of the tension in the sail to give him more time to negotiate the five-metre gap.

He reached the two buoys. On either side the water churned above the razor sharp coral. One slip and he'd be pulling spines out of his legs for the next week.

Half a minute of cautious sailing brought him to the eastern edge of the reef. A new danger lay on this side. From the shore, the surf was an innocuous white line; here it was a roaring range of mountainous waves, each one capable of picking up both him and his kit and smashing everything into a mangled wreck.

He pointed the board downwind so he could cross the surf at a shallow angle.

The full force of the wind filled his sails, practically tearing his arms out of their sockets. A burst of acceleration turned the surrounding turmoil into a streaky blur of blue and white. The first breaker sped towards him. He raced the edge of its curling lip until a section of smooth surface appeared, then he cut up the liquid ramp.

The board lifted off the other side and he crashed down into a short gap before a larger wave loomed. He sped along the rolling canyon, before shooting up the curling four-metre face, jumping even higher once he reached the summit.

The next breaker was the biggest. He picked up speed, cut sharply up the slope and straightened out as he neared the top to avoid a jump that was on the edge of his abilities. He skimmed along the top of the wave, the sail felt weightless as his speed exceeded that of the wind. He finally slipped into the gentle valley beyond the surf.

He was now in the relative safety of the rolling ocean swell that had built its momentum across thousands of miles of open water to the east. He leaned back in his harness and pointed the board north, towards a group of hotels beyond the gap in the shoreline that led to Mombassa harbour.

For ten minutes he sailed parallel to the reef and the distant shore, eventually drawing level with the gap. He tacked and sped west into the shipping lane; the only other break in the reef he could see. A rusty freighter was chugging out of the harbour. Once he was on the shore side of the reef, he gybed back out of the shipping lane well before the freighter became a threat, and resumed his northerly course in line with the beach. In another five minutes he'd be nearing Nyali beach: his final destination.

He looked at his watch. Ten-to-twelve. At this rate he'd be in the airport by one; he may even have time to buy a celebration cigar in duty free.

His speed dropped and the sail slackened. Something was wrong. The shimmering water turned dull as the shadow of a huge cloud covered the sun. There was a rumble of thunder; he should've taken Hans' warning more seriously.

His board sank onto the water's surface, he stepped out of the foot straps and brought his feet close to the mast where it was easier to balance.

He cursed, the beach was still over a kilometre away. He tacked and pointed the board towards the shore. If he headed straight in he'd be well short of his target, but walking would be quicker than struggling with an empty sail. If the wind changed much more he'd end up stranded and having to swim.

The wind did change, but it didn't drop. As the darkness of the storm's centre approached, the hot mass of unstable air swirling around its base began to accelerate. For thirty seconds he was able to pick up speed again but then the wind became untameable. One second it was a gentle easterly, the next it was a roaring southerly.

A ferocious gust blasted into the sail, pulling him over the top of the board. His ribs crashed onto the boom with a crunching thud. He unhooked and slid off the sail hugging his chest. He put an arm over the board and looped his hand into the foot straps as he tried to catch his breath.

Lightning forked across the sky. Even this side of the reef the waves were threatening to engulf him. Maybe he should do a water start. Another flash split the darkness above, an explosive boom followed immediately. The centre of the storm was nearly overhead. If he tried to surf to shore he'd be the highest object around. He had to stay in the water and go with the swell. He just hoped it wouldn't drag him onto the nearby reef.

The wind increased further and brought with it sheets of rain that pounded the water and reduced visibility to no more than a few metres. Lightning continuously flashed overhead, and thunder bellowed from the towering mass of raging cloud.

He clung to the board, holding his breath every time a wave crashed over him, but the sea wanted more than that. It sent a huge wall of water towards him. He was picked up and thrown into a tumbling spin that entangled him with his kit. He let go as the mast smashed against his arm. He was rolled over and over by the tireless energy of the wave.

Everything was dark. Where was the surface? He kicked frantically, aimlessly, not knowing which way was up. His lungs screamed for air. He broke free and gasped, but the next wave was waiting for him and flung him over like a clump of seaweed.

He surfaced thirty seconds later. He couldn't see the board anywhere. Another wave towered above him.

He'd always suspected drowning would be his end: a sudden squall, a thick fog, or a wipe-out that knocked him unconscious. In the past he'd convinced himself it was a better way of going than spending his final years rotting in some old folks' home. Right now he disagreed. Millions of lives depended on his survival.

He was swamped again. This time he didn't fight; he just held his breath and waited for his buoyancy to lift him to the surface. He thought of Ruth. He had to stay alive for her; there was no way this storm was going to take him.

A blinding flash was followed by a deafening blast. He saw his mast, held up by the wind, burst into flames less than ten metres away. He turned and began swimming. He had to do something, but it was pointless really, he'd lost all sense of direction.

He stopped. He needed to conserve energy; ride out the storm.

After five long minutes of fighting the sea the sky began to brighten. The rain eased, the thunder moved away and the wind died down. A few minutes later the sun broke through and the shore became visible again.

He looked around to see if Hans' board had survived. He thrashed his legs to lift himself out of the water, but couldn't see it anywhere. It wasn't the end of the world. It would make his disappearance more plausible, and by the time Marivant found out what had really happened, he would be a few hundred miles inland.

He began swimming, and with each stroke he pulled the distant shore a little closer.

After ten minutes he stopped for a break. He trod water and looked ahead. It was about another three hundred metres to the beach, but the storm had blown him half a mile beyond the group of hotels he'd targeted. If he was going to make his flight he'd need to get a move on. He swam faster, but was stopped by the sound of a speedboat bouncing off the waves.

He turned to see it cast an arc of salty spray as it banked a few hundred metres away. It completed a circle then resumed its original course: straight at him. Suddenly it veered away towards the reef. A man standing in the rear of the boat was pointing out to sea and shouting. It was Vernon.

Chapter 19

Ben turned and began swimming again. He switched from front-crawl to breaststroke to reduce the splash. The whining of the speedboat engine was lost in the sound of his breathing as he pushed through the water.

He swam for fifty metres then looked back. It was hard to see, the water was still choppy after the storm, but he caught a glimpse of Vernon holding the mangled mast of his windsurfer.

Hans was standing on the end of the boat looking around. He needed to get underwater. He took a deep breath, dived and resumed his swim for the shore.

The watery silence was disturbed by the noise of the engine revving. The whine of the outboard above water became the thudding of the submerged propeller below and it was growing louder.

He pushed forward, but the sound was getting closer. He couldn't hold his breath any longer, he had to surface for air.

He looked around. The boat was further away than he'd expected. It was at least fifty metres to the south, steering away from him towards the shore. It looked like they were systematically sweeping the area.

While their backs were turned, he swam with his head above water, keeping one eye constantly on the boat. It neared the beach and began turning towards him again. He dived.

The water was only five metres deep. He grabbed a large strand of kelp to stop him floating back to the surface. He stayed motionless, using as little oxygen as possible. The thudding grew louder and louder. This time the ribbed hull was heading directly towards him. He held tightly to the weed, begging it not to break away from the seabed.

The boat passed within two metres of him as it continued on its course towards the reef. He waited for it to travel a safe distance beyond him then kicked hard for the surface.

He watched the boat for a few seconds. Vernon and Hans were facing away from him. He looked to the shore. Fifty metres: two lengths of a swimming pool.

The motor changed pitch again; it was turning back.

He ducked back underwater and began swimming to the beach. It was becoming shallow enough to stand up but he needed to keep below the surface. He knew he could hold his breath for one length of the local pool in Hove, could he do two?

The thudding of the motor approached rapidly.

He couldn't hold on any longer, he had to get air. He surfaced twenty metres short.

"There he is!" The accent was Vernon's. "Ben!"

He stood up in the water. After everything he'd failed.

He turned and waved at the boat; it would be pointless to continue with his escape now. He was positive he could outrun Vernon, but the other Marivant people would be mobilised within minutes. They'd be waiting for him at the station and the airport.

He'd have to come up with another idea before he got in Vernon's car that evening.

The boat pulled up alongside him. Hans killed the motor and came to the side.

"Hey dude, what are you doing all the way down here?"

"I got caught in the storm," Ben said. "Help me out would you."

Hans leaned over, reached out with his hand and pulled Ben up to the rail.

There was a loud blast. The German slumped forward; blood trickled out of his mouth. Vernon appeared behind him, pointing a pistol at Ben.

Ben put all his weight on the rail. The combination of his effort and Hans' body draped over the side was nearly enough to capsize the boat. Vernon lurched forward and tripped over the edge into the water.

Ben scrambled into the boat. He grabbed the metal boat hook lying on the floor and got to his feet. The boat rocked as Vernon tried to climb back in. Ben raised the hook and swung it down onto Vernon's head. There was a sickening crack. Vernon went limp and slipped back into the water, blood gushing from a hole in his skull.

Ben stood up and looked along the beach. It was still deserted after the storm. The nearest buildings were the hotels half a kilometre to the south. No one could have seen what happened.

He knelt down and rolled Hans over. The young windsurfer's eyes stared lifelessly back at him. He felt for a pulse, nothing. There was a bullet hole at the base of his neck. He'd been killed instantly.

He'd never have taken the kid's board if he'd known this would happen.

He stood up and looked at Vernon's body bobbing up and down in the surf. This far from the resort it might be a few hours before anyone found it. The boat was more of a problem. If he left it this close to the shore it wouldn't be long before it attracted attention. He wanted to be well clear of Mombassa before the police started sniffing around.

He took the controls and opened the throttle a notch. He turned the nose out towards the reef, jammed the boat hook in the wheel, and pulled the throttle right back. The boat surged forward. He put his left foot on the side, took one last look at Hans then jumped into the shallow water.

He waded quickly to shore and turned back. The boat was halfway to the reef already.

He glanced at his watch. It was twelve forty-five. He had to move it.

He ran up the beach then jogged next to the line of palm trees and shrubs that bordered the sand. Two minutes later he was nearing the hotels. The vegetation grew thinner and he could see a road. He pushed through the branches and high grass until he reached the tarmac.

There was a parade of tourist shops a short distance away. He hurried towards them. He needed to buy a change of clothes. One of the shops had an assortment of beachwear hanging on rails outside. He grabbed a pair of beige surf shorts, a T-shirt and a pair of sandals.

He started walking towards the cash desk and opened his bum-bag to pull out his wallet.

He looked at the contents and groaned: his phone was in pieces. It must have smashed against the boom when he catapulted over the board.

He paid for the clothes with cash and went outside. He ignored the startled looks of an elderly couple and ripped off his wet T-shirt. He put on the new one along with the pair of sandals before jogging over to the Nyali Beach Hotel. He'd change his shorts once he reached the airport.

Two taxis were waiting outside. He jumped in the one nearest the hotel entrance.

"Airport please," he said. "I'll double the fare if you make it by one-thirty."

The driver looked at his watch and nodded.

"Hold tight," he said.

* * * *

Ben touched down in Nairobi at three. Harry was waiting for him in arrivals.

"Everything go to plan?" he asked.

"Not quite, but I don't think I'm being followed any more." He handed back Harry's credit card and passport. "You were right about the airline staff not checking."

"They see a white face with a business-class ticket and that's enough," Harry said. "I've sorted the car and put your holdall in the boot."

They walked out of the busy terminal and found the rental in the Avis area of the parking lot.

Harry handed him the keys and he unlocked the door of the Land Cruiser.

"Are you going to tell me what's going on?" Harry asked.

Ben turned to face him. "Two men died today because of what I know. If I tell you, not only your life, but the lives of your wife and kids will be in danger. Still interested?"

Harry shook his head slowly.

"I wish I didn't know," Ben continued. "But I do, and I have to do something about it."

Harry nodded.

Ben climbed into the jeep, closed the door and lowered the window.

"Good luck Ben," Harry said. "Maybe you'll be able to tell me about it over a beer one day."

"I hope so." Ben started the engine. "Thanks for everything, I'd have been stuck without you."

"Anytime."

Ben reversed, waved to Harry, and then pulled away. He left the Avis compound and began his journey out of Nairobi, keeping a close eye on the rear-view mirror.

It didn't take long to break free from the squalor and pollution of the city. Shantytowns overrun by kids in rags were left behind for the open savannah of the plains surrounding the capital. Every mile or so there were small wooden huts selling drinks and tobacco. Overloaded trucks were parked alongside; their drivers sat on benches, smoking cigarettes and drinking out of mugs.

The road was as rough as he remembered. Huge potholes spanned the width of a lane. Traffic waited impatiently either side, colonial concepts of politeness forgotten in the fight to get past.

Other than car-jackers and Ethiopian bandits, Matatus were the most frightening aspect of driving in Kenya. It was like the drivers were playing a video game, and driving other cars off the road earned them extra points. But their lunacy was costly. Kenya had road kill statistics that made some of its war-torn neighbours look like safe havens. He adopted the policy of expecting every approaching lorry to have a Matatu lurking behind it, its crazy driver waiting till he was within a hundred metres before he jumped out to overtake.

Forty minutes after leaving Kenyatta airport the grassland dropped away and the road veered sharply to the right. His eyes flicked towards the two thousand-foot drop a yard away from his tyres. He gripped the wheel tighter.

There was a lay-by up ahead. He pulled over, got out of the car and stood a few feet back from the railings. There was no way his fear of heights would stop him from enjoying such an awesome view.

The floor of the Rift Valley was strewn with the grass-covered cones of extinct volcanoes. Small lakes full of wild birds and hippos broke up the grassland where zebras and giraffes roamed. On the other side of the valley, steep cliffs rose towards the Masai highlands of Western Kenya and the shores of Lake Victoria. He was insignificant in the face of such natural grandeur.

There was another purpose for stopping: he had to be certain he'd lost Marivant. Up till then there'd been no obvious signs of someone following him. Now he could make sure. No one had joined him in the lay-by during the five minutes he'd been there, any car that might be tailing him would need to pull over on the road ahead and wait for him to catch up. He'd spot them easy enough.

He returned to the jeep and waited for a long queue of traffic to pass before leaving the lay-by. It took all his concentration to keep the jeep on the road as it began winding its way down the side of the escarpment.

After ten minutes the road reached the valley floor and straightened out. He travelled for five miles before seeing another vehicle join the highway: an ancient pickup that faded in his mirror within minutes.

Marivant were nowhere to be seen; his plan had worked.

* * * *

At five-thirty he pulled up in front of the large one-storey lodge in the centre of Jake's thousand-acre ranch. He got out of the jeep, stretched, and started walking to the entrance.

The wooden front door opened and Jake appeared at the top of the steps. He hadn't changed much, maybe added a few more inches to his ever-expanding girth, and increased the tally of short grey hairs on his head. Otherwise, the ex-Kanu party official was looking well.

Ben walked up the steps.

"Jake, good to see you." He shook his old friend's hand. Two gold teeth flashed at him from the upper right-hand side of Jake's broad grin.

"You must be tired," Jake said. "Come in. Give Jonathan the keys, he'll get your bags and park the jeep."

Ben handed the car keys to the middle-aged man standing behind Jake. Officially Jonathan and his wife Elizabeth were servants, but in reality they were the closest thing to family Jake had since he'd lost his wife, and his sons had left the country.

Ben followed his friend into the house.

They walked down a dimly lit corridor. Wildlife paintings and hunting trophies hung on the cream-coloured walls. Jake led the way into the lounge, a large rectangular room with wooden French windows at the far end. Two couches covered in tribal blankets formed a square with the fireplace and a TV. In the middle lay a large zebra-skin rug. The walls were sparsely decorated with African antiquities similar to those lining the walls of the corridor. It had the feel of a hunter's lodge.

"I'll get tea organised," Jake said, and left the room.

Ben walked over to the French windows and looked out. The property was about three hundred feet up the side of a hill and overlooked Lake Nakuru. It had been built during colonial times before the area became a game reserve. Its views made the ranch one of the best pieces of real estate in Kenya.

The late afternoon sun turned the flamingo-filled waters of the lake into a haze of gold and pink. A vast black boulder yawned to reveal the gaping jaws of a wallowing hippo.

This view was the result of Jake's rank in the Kanu party. It was impossible not to hate the corruption and favouritism of the old regime, but you couldn't hate Jake. He'd just been born lucky, coming from the same Kalenjin tribe as President Moi. Jake was a pragmatist who'd adapted to the system so he could get the best for himself and his family, but he never abused his power like some of the other party members.

They'd become friends after he'd saved Jake's youngest son from malaria. Jake had promised to repay him in any way he could. It was time to call in that favour.

Jake returned. "How long did it take you to get here?" he asked.

"I left Mombassa at lunchtime."

"You were there this morning then?"

"Yes," Ben said. "Why?"

Jake walked up to him and put his hand on his shoulder.

"We're old friends, and I trust you. You don't have to tell me, but were the two deaths anything to do with you?" Jake looked him straight in the eyes.

"Deaths?" Ben said.

"Like I said, you don't have to tell me. I just heard on the news that two white men were dead and a third was missing. The police suspect foul play." Jake breathed in heavily. "I know you're into something bad after reading Esau's file. What is it?"

The boat must have been spotted hitting the reef or something. A bit more time would have helped.

"It's best you don't know," Ben said. "I haven't done anything wrong if that's what you're worried about." The image of the boat hook piercing Vernon's skull sprang up to disagree. "So you've got the info on Esau Kimani?"

Jake nodded and smiled. "When have you known me to let anyone down?"

Ben raised an eyebrow.

"But you got it a day early, that's not very Kenyan."

"My powers aren't as eroded as I thought."

An elderly maid shuffled into the room. She was carrying a silver tray with a large teapot, two cups and a few pieces of sponge cake. It rattled violently as she made her way to the table. Ben moved to help her, but Jake held his arm. She put the tray on a small table by one of the sofas.

"Thank you Elizabeth," Jake said.

"That's Elizabeth?" Ben asked quietly.

Jake nodded.

"But she's only…" He stopped and waited till she'd left the room.

"Forty-two," Jake said. "AIDS."

Ben shook his head. She'd aged twenty years since his last visit.

"Shall we?" Jake said, gesturing towards the tea tray. They both sat on the central couch. There was an A4 manila envelope by Jake's side. Jake picked it up and pulled out a few sheets of typed paper. He handed them over. "Everything we know about Esau Kimani."

"Brilliant," Ben said, taking the report.

"After you phoned I contacted Robert, an old friend from the police. He got things moving, even did a bit of searching himself."

"I knew I could count on you."

"Don't get too excited, there isn't much. You're not the only one who's been asking after Esau, and he doesn't want to be found."

"So Robert couldn't find him?"

"Not in two days, but his report might give you some clues," Jake said. "Tea?"

Ben nodded. "White, one sugar please." Tea with sugar was normally disgusting, but in Africa it was the only way to mask the taste of goat's milk.

Jake handed him a teacup.

"I'm very grateful for everything you've done," Ben said

"Well it'll give you a start. You'll need to go off road. Robert reckons this guy went bush." Jake passed Ben a piece of cake. "Were these people in Mombassa the same lot looking for Esau?"

"Almost certainly." Ben instantly kicked himself for falling into the trap.

Jake leaned back into the sofa and shook his head. "You're playing with fire Ben."

"I know." There was no point in avoiding talking about it. "I nearly got shot today."

Jake's expression darkened.

"They've killed before," Ben continued. "As many as a hundred."

"Go home," he said. "Don't fly from Nairobi. Slip over the border into Uganda. Just go home."

Temptation at every turn. His sister, Jake, the whining voice inside, even death were all trying to talk him out of it. But seeing Elizabeth, and the way she'd been ravaged by this disease were a powerful reminder of why the risks were worth it. "I can't. Not till I've spoken to Esau."

Jake slurped his tea then bit a large chunk out of his cake.

"So what does the report say?" Ben asked.

Jake put the cake down. "It makes unhappy reading," he said. "This chap Esau has lived a troubled life. His first misfortune was his birth. He's Kikuyu"

Tribalism was the plague of African politics. The Kikuyu were the majority tribe in Kenya, but because of political horse-trading in the Parliament, they'd ended up being the most oppressed.

"And as you know, he's HIV positive," Jake continued. "But so are a lot of people these days. The local police chief gave it to Esau's wife when he raped her. Esau found out and tried to kill the guy. His failure to do so was the second biggest misfortune in his life. He had nowhere left to go. The party blacklisted him and put a price on his head. He fled the country."

"Didn't have any choice by the sounds of it."

Jake nodded. "The most recent official record of Esau's movements is of his re-entry into the country three months ago."

"Wasn't he arrested?"

"No. His crime was viewed as political, and after Moi lost the election an amnesty was granted towards all political dissidents."

"What about the policeman? Surely he'd want to see Esau dead."

"He's dead himself," Jake said. "Killed by a mob after the elections. Esau should have been free to roam where he wanted, but his final great misfortune is that someone else seems to be after him. From what you're saying they're just as nasty as his old enemies."

"Nastier," Ben said. "So how far did Robert get?"

"He learned that Esau stayed with his family in Nakuru for a short while before moving to a cousin's farm on some marginal land near Nyeri. Robert visited the cousin and found out Esau only stayed a week. After that the trail goes cold. No one knows any more about him. Bribing the villagers produced nothing so Robert hauled the cousin in yesterday afternoon on false charges. After a bit of persuasion he said that Esau didn't just disappear. Some men came looking for him, he got scared and ran."

"Did he say who the men were?"

"No, but they smashed up his furniture and gave him a fat lip."

"He got off lightly," Ben said. "Do you think there's a chance they've already found Esau?"

Jake shrugged. "If we couldn't find him I think it's unlikely anyone else will, including you."

Ben frowned. He needed to meet this guy. Without him he couldn't be sure Spiravex was a cure. He only had four days.

He finished his tea and yawned.

"I'll show you to your room," Jake said.

"Thanks. I'm shattered."

"Have a rest. There's no rush for dinner."

Jake led him to the guest wing of the bungalow. He took him into a room that had a similar view to that of the lounge. Once he'd left, Ben closed the curtains, undressed and lay on the bed. Apart from his nap on the beach he hadn't slept for thirty-six hours.

No wonder he was knackered. He closed his eyes and went straight out.

* * * *

He drifted in and out of a series of abstract dreams that became increasingly disturbing. Disturbing became terrifying when he found himself back on the boat with Vernon trying to climb in. No matter how many times he hit the Australian over the head, Vernon wouldn't let go. Blood splashed everywhere until the whole ocean turned red. He awoke with the sheets soaked in sweat. He forced his tired body to sit up so he wouldn't slip back into the nightmare.

He looked at his watch. Nine-thirty. He got dressed and headed to the lounge.

The sound of the TV could be heard along the corridor. Jake was sitting on the sofa wearing a pair of half-moon glasses. He was concentrating on the programme.

"Hi," Ben said.

Jake nodded slowly without diverting his attention from the screen. He was normally more polite than that. Something was up.

"Everything alright?" He asked.

"You're famous."

"What?"

"There's been more about the Mombassa killings."

Ben walked between the two sofas and sat down facing the TV. They'd moved on to a story about a Matatu crash.

"What did they say?" he asked.

"A man was found dead on the beach. He'd been battered to death. The other was found near a boat that had crashed on the reef. He'd been shot. The third man, a windsurfer, is still missing. A man fitting the windsurfer's description was seen taking off a bloodstained T-shirt outside a shop in Mombassa. The police gave the name Ben Williams." Jake took his glasses off and looked gravely at Ben. "You're in serious trouble my friend."

Chapter 20

"Are you sure you won't change your mind?" Jake asked, leaning in through the passenger window of the jeep.

It was a question he'd asked himself a thousand times during the night, when more violent nightmares woke him and joined the other voices trying to undermine his determination.

"I'm sure," he said.

"At least take one of my guns with you."

"No thanks. How would a gun help? I've lost Marivant, who would I use it on? A policeman? I'm in enough trouble as it is."

"Go to Uganda then," Jake said.

"No. They'll check my passport at the border."

"I have a friend who runs an air-safari business. He could fly you there."

"But I still wouldn't have found Esau."

"You won't find him anyway. Listen to me Ben, you're wasting your time. I don't want you to suffer for nothing. Have you ever been to a Kenyan prison? You wouldn't live to see daylight again."

"You don't have much faith in your justice system," Ben said.

"The police don't care about justice, as long as they put someone behind bars. Anyway, you told me your fingerprints would be on the boat hook. They've got enough to lock you away for the rest of your life."

Ben started the engine. "I've got to get going. It's already eight."

"Be careful," Jake said, and stepped away from the window.

"I will. Thanks Jake."

He pulled away and began the long drive east into the heart of the highlands.

* * * *

As the road climbed out of the Rift Valley into the surrounding hills, the wild vitality of the landscape was smothered beneath a bland blanket of corporate greenery. Rows of regimented coffee bushes marched up the slopes like a soulless army, leaving only a few defiant outcrops of ancient forest as a reminder of the majesty that once was.

To some the neatness may have appeared pretty, like the English countryside could be pretty, but to Ben it felt sterile; Africa had been emasculated.

An hour after leaving Nakuru the road curved northeast as it began a semi-circular detour around the peaks of the Aberdare Mountains. Twenty miles later he passed a sign announcing his arrival in the Northern hemisphere. After another fifty miles, a similar sign welcomed him back to the Southern hemisphere.

He reached the former colonial trading post of Nyeri just before one. He was exhausted after five hours of dodging potholes, so he was ready for a rest and Nyeri was as good a spot as any to stop for lunch. He parked up outside the Central Hotel, a favourite from previous visits. As well as a good menu, it had the benefit of a guarded car park.

He looked at the menu. It might be a long time before he ate a decent meal again. He ordered steak and chips, a large side salad, bread and then a banana sundae for dessert. It was just gone two by the time he returned to the jeep. The sumptuous leather seats beckoned him to lean back and sleep off his lunch, but that wasn't an option.

He picked up the Kenyan road map provided by the hire company. The hamlet where Esau's cousin lived was thirty miles southeast of Nyeri. In England that would be less than an hour's drive, but this was Kenya. If the roads weren't too bad he'd make it in an hour and a half.

Fifteen minutes after leaving Nyeri he reached the turn-off he needed. The road was no more than a dirt track and recent rain had left deep puddles of brown water. It was a good job he had the Land Cruiser; anything without four-wheel drive wouldn't have stood a chance.

The jeep yawed from side to side as it careered through the muddy ruts. The unruly steering wheel jolted back and forth in his hands, and even though he was only trying to guide it rather than fight it, his shoulders began to stiffen.

Five miles after leaving the highway, the driving became easier as the road climbed briefly above the dense layer of bushes to reach the brow of a hill.

Ben stopped the jeep.

It just kept getting better. The road ahead turned into an endless roller coaster of ridges and gullies that had been carved out by rainwater running off the hills to the north. They didn't look any more than twenty-metres deep, but were steep and muddy.

He checked the four-wheel drive was properly engaged then crept down the sharp incline in first gear. At the bottom of the gully any pretence of this being a road had been washed away. He began climbing the other side. The field monitor quickly spun past ten, twenty, then thirty degrees. The diesel engine grunted in vain as the tyres began to lose traction. The jeep started to slide back. He engaged reverse and allowed it to roll to the bottom of the slope.

He tried a second time, but with no more success. The third attempt showed that a change of strategy was needed or he'd be stuck there all day. He looked around the plush cabin of the jeep, a sop to Kensington mothers who wanted the intimidating size. But this beast was designed for conquering rugged landscapes not bullying other drivers on the school run.

He reversed back up the slope leading into the gully. Just as the wheels began to slip he slammed the gearshift forward into second and hit the accelerator.

The two-ton Land Cruiser hurtled towards the rocky bottom of the ravine, bouncing off the boulder-strewn surface. He held tightly to the steering wheel and gunned the engine up the other side. The tyres struggled to grip the surface, but the momentum carried him past his previous attempt.

Yes! He reached the top and braked. The three-litre engine chuckled with satisfaction. He looked into the next ravine and threw the jeep down the slope.

After half an hour it stopped being fun; by three-thirty it was torture. His entire upper body ached from the continuous strain. Each jolt caused the cut from Saturday to knock against the seat; his bruised ribs sent pulses of agony across his chest. How much longer would this last?

He stopped on a crest for a break and reached for his bag on the floor behind him. He pulled out a piece of Elizabeth's sponge-cake and washed it down with mineral water.

After a few minutes his strength and will returned. In spite of all the pain and struggling this was what he loved about Africa. Life was messy, but it was real. If a problem came up you didn't whinge or moan, there was no customer services, you just found a way to overcome it.

He reached for the map on the passenger seat. He was just over halfway, so much for an hour and a half. He put the bag back and resumed his battle with the road.

For another quarter of an hour he fought his way up and down five more ravines, covering no more than a mile. Just as he felt his arms were ready to give up, the road levelled out. The surface changed from sticky clay to loose sandstone as it crossed an arid plateau. The tall bushes that had lined most of the route thinned to a patchy scrub, and he was able to get a better view of the surrounding area. A range of rocky hills gathered ahead. Thick clouds boiled up from their midst and hid the snow-capped peak of Mount Kenya.

He picked up speed and used fifth gear for the first time since hiring the jeep. By four-fifteen he was pulling up on the edge of a collection of mud houses.

It was a typical Kikuyu settlement. The one-storey huts formed a rough square. They all had corrugated-iron roofs with guttering leading to clay water butts that gathered the precious rainwater.

He turned the ignition off and stepped into the cool highland air.

The place looked deserted.

The stony ground surrounding the huts had been dug up in an attempt to grow crops, but the thin stalks looked barely capable of standing upright. They made a sorry comparison to the juicy towers of maize that rose out of the fertile lands owned by the corporations, white colonialists and government stooges to the west.

He closed the door of the jeep and locked it out of habit. He walked over to the group of huts. There were no doors on the outside of the ring. He passed through a narrow alleyway that formed the entrance to the hamlet.

A woman was sitting outside one of the huts, her back to him, washing clothes in a plastic tub. He walked towards her. She stopped scrubbing and looked round.

"Jambo," Ben said.

She jumped up, ran across the square into one of the huts and slammed the wooden door behind her. Nice to know you're welcome.

He looked around at the other huts. None of them appeared particularly inviting.

He walked over to the door the woman had disappeared into and knocked. There was no response. He tried a second time, and told her in Swahili that he was a doctor.

After a few seconds there was a muffled shout, something about her husband returning soon. In Kenya that could mean anything up to a week.

He decided to try the other huts, but it wasn't until he reached the fifth that he found someone home. A voice mumbled from inside. He knocked again.

The door was opened by a woman who could have been in her fifties or sixties. It was always hard to tell. A life of toil in the fields aged the skin early, and then there was AIDS. Either way life had been hard, her face had wrinkles so deep they looked like scars. Wary eyes peered from beneath a pink headscarf that covered her forehead.

"Jambo," Ben said.

"I speak English."

"Does Daniel Kimani live here?"

She held his gaze for a few seconds then slowly lifted her finger and pointed across the small square.

"Thank you," he said, and turned to walk away.

"But he is not there."

He turned back.

"He will not be back for a few days," she continued.

The news just kept getting better.

"You have come a long way for nothing," she said. "Would you like some tea?"

He nodded. Tea, the universal tonic for all woes as prescribed by the English.

The old woman walked into the hut. He followed her and closed the door behind him. The hut was a typical Kenyan farmworker's home. There was a large main room where all the eating, cooking and socialising took place. Three doors led off this central-living area to other rooms.

In the far corner of the main room an aluminium pot steamed over a crackling fire. Raw meat and chopped carrots lay on a plastic mat beside it.

He sat on a nearby wooden bench, put his keys down next to him and felt the blisters on his hands.

"What is your name?" the woman asked. She moved the pot along the grate to make room for an iron kettle.

"Ben Williams."

She nodded then shuffled over to a bucket near the door, pulled out two cups and washed them in a neighbouring bowl. The kettle began to whistle. She returned to the fire and poured a thick brown liquid into one of the cups. She handed the cup to Ben and poured another for herself.

He took a sip. The strong taste of goat's milk was tempered by the overpowering sweetness of raw cane sugar. It was good to have a hot drink after all the cold water.

"Why do you want to see Daniel?" she asked.

"I'm hoping he might help me find his cousin, Esau."

She gave him a wary frown.

"Why are white men looking for Esau?"

"Other white men have been here?" Ben asked.

"One, a month ago."

"What did he look like?"

"He was white."

That narrowed it down a bit. He took another sip of the tea. "Did he find Esau?"

She shook her head. There was a long silence.

"Your English is very good," Ben said.

"I used to work for an American family in Nairobi."

"Was the man who came an American?"

She eyed him suspiciously for a few moments, and then her expression softened.

"What do you do?" she asked.

"I'm a doctor."

She smiled.

"I knew you were a good man. I can tell from your eyes. The spirits have taught me who is good and bad from the eyes."

"Was this man good?"

She shook her head slowly. "I didn't need to see his eyes to know that. He hurt Martha and tried to bribe us. He and a Kenyan man hurt Daniel too."

"Who's Martha?"

"The girl who was outside when you arrived. They used her to show us they weren't afraid of hurting people. They had guns. There was nothing our men could do."

"Did you report them to the police?"

She raised her eyebrows. "You don't know Kenya very well."

"I did," Ben replied. "But I was hoping things might have changed."

"You would have to change every policeman to change Kenya. They don't come here unless they can get something. The police were looking for Esau the other day. The white man probably paid them. That's the only reason they would be interested in any of us."

"And the policeman didn't find Esau either?" He said. It was worth knowing if Robert was really as trustworthy as Jake said.

"If the white man didn't find him, he wasn't going to either."

"So you do know where he is."

The woman laughed. "No. But if I did, I wouldn't tell anyone."

Ben nodded and finished his tea. "Does Daniel know?"

The old woman shrugged. "You will have to ask him."

Ben frowned. "I hope so, I've come a long way."

She slurped her tea.

"Why is Esau so important?" she asked.

He examined her for a few moments. After all the hassle they'd attracted she deserved to know some of the story.

"The men looking for Esau want to murder him. If I talk to him first I might be able to get these people off your backs for ever."

"You can stop them hurting Esau?"

Ben nodded. "But I have to meet him, only for a few minutes, that's all."

"Are you an enemy of these men?"

"Yes. They're after me too. They tried to kill me yesterday."

172

She stood up and snatched Ben's mug from his hand.

"You should not have come here." She grabbed his arm and started pulling him up. "You must leave."

"Sorry?" Ben got to his feet but was unbalanced by her strong grip.

"You must leave now. Go back to Nyeri. I will tell Daniel you came. You tell me your hotel and he will catch a Matatu and find you."

"Why must I go?"

"If these men know you then you are in danger."

There was the sound of an engine in the distance.

"Leave my hut." The woman began pushing Ben towards the door. "You cannot be seen here. I don't want them hurting me."

"How do they know I'm here?" he asked, her panic was infectious.

"Our village has been watched since the white man came. We have seen them camped in the hills."

The noise of the engine grew louder.

"Now leave, please, I don't want trouble."

Ben opened the door and stepped out. He ran towards his jeep and felt in his pockets for his keys. They weren't there; he'd left them on the bench.

He turned to go back, but it was too late. The roar of the engine was nearly upon him. He looked round to see a Land Rover Defender bouncing along the track, a plume of dust billowing behind it.

Ben sprinted across the field towards a clump of bushes. He heard the jeep scrape to a stop in the gravel. Doors slammed and the shouting of two men followed him into the scrub. He started scrambling up a slope. The shouts were getting nearer. Halfway up Ben turned back to see a tall black man emerge from the bushes holding a gun.

Ben accelerated towards the top of the rocky slope then skidded to a halt as the ground disappeared down a precipice.

A deep ravine lay before him. There was no way across. He looked back again. The man with the gun was closing fast. He was trapped.

Chapter 21

As the man got closer he lifted his gun and pointed it at Ben. He reached the top and stopped a few paces away. Ben put his hands up. The edge of the drop pulled at his feet behind him.

Another man started running up the slope towards them.

"Don't shoot him Curtis!" he shouted in Swahili. He was stocky and much shorter than the man holding the pistol. He reached halfway up the slope then stopped, bent over and rested his hands on his knees.

"Bring him to me!" he shouted at Curtis.

Ben was pulled away from the edge of the cliff and shoved down the slope until he stood in front of the short guy.

"You Ben Williams?" he asked

Ben shook his head.

"You are lying. Show me your wallet."

"I don't have it."

He delivered a powerful blow into Ben's stomach. Ben fell to the ground and a pair of brown caterpillar boots appeared next to him. Hands rifled through his pockets. He was pulled back to his feet.

"Dom asked you for your wallet," Curtis said.

"In the car," Ben said. There was no point in lying; they'd find it sooner or later.

Dom pulled a mobile phone out of his pocket and held it up. After half a minute he shook his head and put it back.

"We need to take him back to the camp," he said. "There's no signal here."

Curtis grabbed Ben by his arm. "Walk."

Ben felt a gun being pushed into his back and he stumbled forward. He was marched down the slope, through the bushes and past the huts to his jeep.

"Keys?" the tall man asked.

Ben looked at him then put his hands in his pockets and shrugged. "They must have fallen out while you were chasing me."

The two men looked at each other.

"We'll come and get it later if we need to," Dom said. "I have to make that call."

Curtis nodded. They led him to their Land Rover, opened the back door and pushed him in. Dom climbed in beside him and shoved a gun in his ribs. Curtis walked round the front, got in and started the engine.

There was a strong smell of BO and bad breath; neither of them could have washed in days. The driver did a three-point turn and headed back along the road towards Nyeri. Ben turned round and watched his Land Cruiser recede into the distance.

* * * *

Helen handed over the collection slip to the Post Office clerk.

"I was in all morning and I never heard the door," she said. "I'm too busy to be doing your job for you."

The clerk looked up with an emotionless expression.

"Have you got any ID?" he asked.

She rustled through her new Prada handbag and found her Amex. She pushed it under the glass.

The clerk looked at it and disappeared into a room behind the counter. A few minutes later he reappeared holding a thick A4 Jiffy bag.

"Sign this please."

He pushed a form towards her and she scribbled her signature.

The clerk opened the window and handed her the parcel. She walked away, turning it over in her hands. There was no return address but she didn't need one, she recognised the writing instantly. It was from Anne.

She walked back to her apartment. Once inside she put the kettle on, dropped a teabag in a mug and ripped open the parcel. There must have been at least two hundred sheets. There was a note clipped to the front:

Helen,

I had to send you this. I think they might be on to me and I need some insurance. Keep it safe.

This information is dynamite. The first section is all about MVT084. We've only been told part of the story. It's scary stuff. It might make you feel differently about what you've been doing for Slade.

But that's not all, there's more. Much more.

Her mobile rang. She put the letter down and answered it.

"Luke," she said.

"I need you up here right away."

"But…"

"Now!" The phone went dead.

She turned the kettle off, slipped the letter back in the parcel and put it into one of the kitchen drawers.

She looked at the mug.

"Screw him," she said, and switched the kettle back on.

* * * *

She walked up the steps to the manor house and smiled at Luke's irritable expression.

"Where the hell have you been?" he asked.

"It's rush hour. The M25 was a nightmare," she replied. "What's so urgent that you need me here now?"

"Inside."

He led her to the communications room and pointed at a chair in front of one of the monitors.

"Sit here and watch the girl. I've got some business to sort out."

"You called me all the way here to baby-sit?" Helen said.

"Yes."

"Why can't Anne do it?"

Luke glared at her.

"How long will you be?" she asked.

"Long enough to need you here."

He left the room without another word.

She flicked through the security monitors and watched him walk out onto the front porch and get in his Mercedes.

176

She browsed through the other cameras till she arrived at the one positioned above the door of Ruth's cell. Ruth was sitting on the bed holding her knees like she had been the night she arrived. She stared straight ahead; her lips appeared to be moving.

Helen zoomed in on Ruth's face. She was definitely speaking.

Helen switched on the sound; all she could hear was a vague muttering. She turned up the volume, but it only increased the static. She switched the sound back off and continued to study Ruth's face. There was a small cut above her left eye and an angry bruise on her neck. She looked exhausted.

She swallowed the guilt rising inside her. She didn't even want to imagine the violations the woman on the screen had suffered. Luke was an animal when you volunteered your body to him, it didn't bare thinking about what he was capable of when there were no boundaries.

Ruth looked at the camera.

Helen got up and left the room. She went to the kitchen and made a coffee. She returned after a few minutes and lit a cigarette. Ruth was still staring out of the screen at her. Helen turned away.

She took a long drag of her cigarette. She should have brought the pills. They worked better than nicotine. She'd taken one Wednesday night when she got home. Luke had been right: she felt nothing, went straight to sleep and didn't give Ruth a second thought. But the effects only lasted as long as the drug was in her system, and just like heroin, once it had worn off she was left with a greater need than she had before. Since then her conscience had made up for lost time, all she could think of was Ruth's face as Luke closed the cell door.

She looked back at the screen. Ruth had turned away. Her eyes were closed and her lips were moving again.

Of course! She was praying. The sympathy instantly disappeared. She almost deserved what was happening to her for being so stupid.

Helen got up from her chair and crossed the passage. She entered the kitchen then walked down the steps to the basement. She peered through the window into Ruth's cell; she was still sitting on the bed. Helen entered the code into the keypad on the cell door and went in.

"Stay where you are," Helen said.

Ruth looked back with a weary expression.

"Do you think I'm capable of escaping?" Ruth asked.

"Just stay put."

Helen closed the door, folded her arms and stared at Ruth. A mixture of curiosity and a desire to ridicule her had led her down there. But now she was face to face with the battered captive, she didn't have the heart to follow through. It would be like kicking a lame dog.

"What's happened to my brother?" Ruth asked.

"He's still in Africa."

"Does he know about me?"

"Too many questions," Helen said.

There was a silence.

"Do you want anything to eat?" Helen asked.

"No. I'm fine."

She couldn't think of anything else to say. She turned round and grabbed the door handle.

"Wait," Ruth said. "Don't go."

Helen looked back.

"Please stay for a bit."

She looked terrified. "Don't worry, he's out," Helen said.

Ruth nodded with an expression of relief.

"I didn't know he'd hurt you," Helen said.

"Would it have stopped you bringing me here if you had known?"

Helen shook her head slowly. "I didn't have a choice."

"And when you get my brother, will you still have no choice?"

"Do you want me to stay or not?"

"Yes," Ruth said. "I'm sorry. I won't ask any more questions."

"Good."

"At least it bothers you."

"Pardon?"

"You must still have a conscience if it makes you feel uncomfortable," Ruth said. "I don't think your boss has a conscience."

"I don't believe in a conscience, it's redundant, like God."

Ruth shook her head.

"I find your faith ridiculous," Helen continued. "If there is a God, why isn't he helping you now?"

Ruth looked away.

Helen took a few steps closer. "How can you still believe? Maybe you have hope now, but Luke will be back soon, no matter how hard you pray. Where will your God be then?"

Ruth turned back. "The rain falls on the good and the bad. It's a part of life."

Did she really mean that? Some preacher might use that as a throw away comment when challenged about injustice, but how could she be so objective about her own suffering? She was just putting on a brave face and clinging to her comfort blanket.

"Not much of a life though," Helen said. "You'd have thought he'd make it a bit easier for his own followers."

"He does."

"How?"

"If you've never experienced what it is to know him, you wouldn't understand." Ruth said. "Jesus was tortured to death on a cross, even though he never lifted a finger against anyone. He warned his followers that life would be hard. It's not always meant to be easy, it's just meant to be whatever it is for you. Life is just life. God is God. Once you've really encountered him your life is better just for knowing him and by knowing that your soul has a different destiny in this life and after because of that relationship."

"Oh please!" Helen said. "Religion's a lie. You're so busy trying to get into a fantasy heaven you forget to make the most of reality. Wake up! There is no eternal life. This is all you get, start enjoying it before it's too late."

"You have no belief at all?" Ruth asked.

Helen shook her head. "I believed in something once, when I didn't know any better. As a child I even believed that God was telling me I would save thousands of lives. As I grew up I thought about doing medicine, but decided to study chemistry instead. I hated research and discovered nothing useful, except that science proves faith in God is obsolete. I lost any faith I had about the same time I found out the truth about Santa."

"You sound like my brother. He uses science as an excuse not to believe."

"It's not an excuse, it's a reason," Helen said. "You're not a scientist are you?"

"No, I'm not, but I've read books on science and religion. From what I can see science supports the existence of a creator rather than denying it."

"Weren't written by believers were they? I've spent half my life reading real science books and I haven't come across anything to make me believe. In fact it's been the opposite. For me evolution is conclusive: we're just the result of mutations."

"The theory of evolution might explain some things, but how does it answer the riddle of the chicken and the egg?"

"What?" Helen asked.

"Which came first, the chicken or the egg?"

She just didn't understand did she? It didn't work like that.

"It was a process over millions of years."

"But what about before that, before chickens existed? What about the origin of life?" Ruth said. "All these books say the same thing. The problem of the origin of life is the elephant in the lab for modern scientists. Once the process of evolution starts, once the process of DNA translation and replication gets underway, then Darwin's theory might make sense, but how did that mechanism start, how did the first cell come into existence, and more importantly the first piece of DNA that coded for enzymes?"

She obviously had read up about the subject, but she was just doing what previous generations of Christians had done for centuries whenever they saw a question that science hadn't yet answered, using the God of the gaps. Why did they cling so desperately to the ever shrinking island of creationism in the flood of scientific truth?

"Let me guess, God created it," she replied.

"DNA is a code for enzymes and proteins right?"

Helen rolled her eyes. She'd only spent her Ph.D. messing with these chemicals in her search for new drugs.

"But doesn't DNA itself need enzymes to grow and replicate?" Ruth continued. "That's why I used the riddle of the chicken and the egg. Which came first, the DNA, which needs the enzyme to transcribe and translate it, or the translator enzyme which is coded for by the DNA? Neither can come into existence without the other existing first."

"Have you ever read the God Delusion?" Helen said.

"I've heard of it."

"Richard Dawkins answers that exact question. If you put the chemicals that make DNA and enzymes in a lake for a few billion years, the DNA will form by itself through chance."

"All these books said that was chemically and statistically impossible, even if the entire universe was a lake full of the right ingredients and the universe was a hundred billion years old. One likened it to dropping a few pieces of wire on a sandy beach and expecting to come back in a few billion years and find a microchip."

She'd heard similar arguments before, they just didn't wash.

"If you had an objective understanding of science you'd realise it's not the same thing," she said. "That's the problem with religious scientists, they're subjective. Just because we haven't found an explanation for something, they shout God made it! Science will answer all these questions one day and then there will be no more room for faith. We cannot comprehend the time scales involved."

"Just like we cannot comprehend the statistics involved. Besides, science is equally subjective, and you need to have more faith in science and chance than I have in God to believe in what you do. The central tenet of science is that there is always a natural explanation. That is starting with an assumption that there is no God which immediately makes it a subjective study. The truth is science only explains how, not why."

"There is no why. Anyway, this is a waste of time." Helen turned to leave. She was going to disagree with Ruth on just about everything.

"Who was in the cell next door last night?" Ruth asked.

Helen looked back. "What?"

"There was a woman," Ruth replied. She looked down, her lip quivering. "She was screaming for help. I wanted to do something."

There could only be one woman who would be screaming in that cell. She opened the door and ran out. The door to the neighbouring cell was ajar. She pushed it open, felt for the light switch and flicked it on.

She lifted her hand to her mouth as she surveyed the scene. The walls and floor were splattered with blood. There was a congealed clump of hair lying on the bed. She slowly walked towards it.

"Anne," she said.

"Why do you think it was Anne?"

Helen spun round to see Luke standing in the doorway.

"Her hair," she said. "I recognised her hair."

Luke walked over to the bed, picked up the hair and held it in front of her.

"Really?"

A crippling terror rose up from inside and stole any reply that might have formed.

Luke dropped the hair. He pushed her against the wall and grabbed her by the throat.

"What did she tell you?"

Chapter 22

"She didn't tell me anything."

"Why do you think it was Anne?"

"I told you, her hair."

Luke's fingers tightened around her throat. "What did she tell you?"

"Let go," Helen said, choking. "I can't breathe."

Luke's grip loosened a fraction. "What did she tell you?"

Helen met his stare. "She said she wanted to leave Slade."

Luke let go of her throat. "And?"

"That's all. But she was scared, she said it was impossible to get out."

Luke took a step back. "Do you want to get out?"

Helen shook her head.

"Why didn't you tell me she was thinking of leaving?"

"I didn't want to get involved."

"What else did she tell you?" Luke asked.

"Nothing. Why? What's she done?"

"Looking into things she shouldn't have been," Luke said. He gave Helen a long penetrating look. "I think it's time to find out what you're really made of. I can't have anyone who's half-hearted working for me. Wait here."

Luke disappeared out of the cell.

Helen breathed out. She looked at the blood-spattered room; Anne hadn't just been taken out, she'd been tortured to death. Had she told Luke about the parcel?

Luke returned. He was holding a pistol in his right hand.

"Come with me," he said. Helen followed him to Ruth's cell. They stopped outside.

"We've got Williams," Luke said.

"When?"

"I found out just before I arrived back here. The team watching for Kimani caught him a couple of hours ago."

"So the job's finished," Helen said.

"Precisely. Which means we don't need his sister anymore."
He held the gun out. "Kill her."

She looked at the gun. The moment had arrived. It wasn't
going to be Ben, but his sister instead. If it wasn't Ruth now, it
would be someone else later. Murder was unavoidable. She took the
gun from him.

Luke opened the door of the cell and motioned for her to
go in.

Ruth was sitting in the same position she had been all
evening. Her eyes locked onto Luke.

Helen walked towards her. "Stand up," she said.

Ruth got to her feet. She was shaking.

Helen lifted the pistol and pointed it in Ruth's face. Ruth
raised her eyes and looked straight back at her.

"What are you waiting for?" Luke said. "Get on with it."

Helen lowered the gun and turned to Luke.

"I need the pills," she said.

"I want you to do this without any help," he said. "I don't
understand your problem, you've killed before."

"No I haven't."

"I've seen your medical records."

Helen shook her head. "That's not the same. It's not
murder."

"Miss Williams is a Christian, an expert on morality. Why
don't you ask her what she thinks of abortion?"

She winced at the word; the image of the bloody eighteen-
week-old foetus lying in a stainless steel dish appeared before her
minds eye. The nurse had made sure Helen saw the body parts as
she took them away.

"Well?" Luke said to Ruth. "Do you think abortion other
than for medical reasons is murder?"

Helen turned back to see Ruth looking down.

"You have your answer Helen," Luke said. "She thinks
you've crossed the line between good and evil, that you've killed a
human being."

She'd known that the moment she saw the wrinkled body
and the tiny hands. No matter what the law said, her conscience
screamed at her that she'd done something awful. She'd chosen her
freedom over the life of her growing baby. That decision was the

beginning of the downward slope that led to her standing in a room with orders to kill an innocent woman.

"This is the moment of truth Helen," Luke said. "To really believe that humans are no more than just animals, you must understand you killing your baby is no different to a lioness eating her cubs in times of hunger."

There was no good and evil. She needed to free herself from the shackles of her conscience forever.

She raised the gun and pointed it at Ruth's forehead.

"It's easier if you make them face away from you," Luke said over Helen's shoulder. "Less nightmares that way."

"Turn around," Helen said.

"My brother?" Ruth stammered.

"Turn around!" Helen shouted.

Ruth slowly turned and faced the bed. She began sobbing. Helen put the muzzle of the pistol against the back of Ruth's head.

She pulled the safety off with her thumb, and put both hands round the handle to steady her grip.

"Don't do this," Ruth said. "It's never too late."

"Why are you so scared?" Helen asked. "You're going to heaven aren't you?"

"Please don't," Ruth cried.

"Time to find out who's right," Helen said, her finger tightening round the trigger.

* * * *

Ben lay shivering on the hard floor of the tent. The flickering glow of the fire through the canvas did nothing to dispel the bone-numbing cold.

It felt like he'd been lying there forever, fears of pain and death filling every thought. He'd overheard Dom speaking on the phone after the ten-minute journey to the camp. A man was coming from Nairobi in the morning to interrogate him.

The sound of the zip from the neighbouring tent signalled Curtis and Dom going to bed.

The light from the fire grew faint. The silence of the night amplified the calls of the wildlife filling the surrounding hills.

In spite of the biting cold and the rope cutting into his wrists and ankles, he managed to drift into a semi-conscious slumber.

Suddenly he was wide awake again. A hand gripped his shoulder through a hole in the side of the tent. He rolled away, expecting to see one of the men who'd captured him. But the shadow silhouetted against the star-filled sky wasn't the right shape to be either of them. There was a flash of steel and the hole widened until most of the side fell away.

The shadow leaned forward.

"Doctor Williams?" it whispered.

Ben looked into the barely discernable eyes.

"Be very quiet," the shadow said.

"Untie me," Ben said.

A hand felt for his arm, and then moved down to the rope. The knife rubbed against his skin. The rope gave way and released his hands. He massaged his sore wrists.

"My feet are tied as well," Ben whispered.

The hand felt down his leg then cut the rope that bound his ankles.

"We must be silent," the shadow said. He leaned back out of the tent and stood up.

Ben crawled through the hole and got carefully to his feet.

It was a moonless sky, but the expanse of stars gave just enough light to make out the surrounding area. Loud snoring came from the other tent less than six feet away.

"Follow me," the man said.

Ben peered into the gloom around his feet and took a step forward. When he looked back up the man had disappeared into the shadows. He searched the murk for a human shape; a hand grabbed his arm.

"This way."

The shadow pulled Ben away from the camp and down a steep slope. Rocks and loose stones made the soles of his feet tense with the expectation of slipping. Halfway down the slope he became awake enough to become suspicious.

"Who are you?" he asked.

"Daniel Kimani," his guide replied. "We must keep moving Doctor Williams. They might wake up and check the tent."

Daniel pulled away and Ben continued to follow him down the slope. After another few hundred metres of picking their way through thorn bushes, the ground levelled out and they joined the dirt road that led from the camp.

They walked much faster as the track wound its way down the side of the hill. They'd covered less than half a mile when they were brought to a halt by the roar of an engine. Ben looked back up the hill to see a pair of headlights tearing towards them.

"This way," Daniel shouted.

He pulled Ben over the side of the track onto the steep embankment that ran below it.

"Lie down."

Ben dropped onto his front. He held his bruised ribs a couple of inches above the ground. The Land Rover sped past a few seconds later, sending a shower of shingle over them. Once the noise of its engine faded they both got to their feet and brushed off the dust.

"We must run now," Daniel said, then turned down the track and jogged away from Ben.

He followed, searching the distance for signs of the Land Rover. A flash of light emerged from a dip then bounced along the level for fifty metres before the brake lights lit up. For a moment it didn't move, then it turned right.

"They are going to the village first," Daniel shouted. "We don't have much time. We must reach the jeep before they return."

"Jeep?"

"Your jeep."

Daniel accelerated. Ben's legs were still stiff from lying on the hard floor for so long, but he was fit and kept pace as he built a rhythm. After another five minutes they reached a junction in the road. Daniel led them left, which was probably towards Nyeri. After a hundred yards Daniel whistled twice. A pair of headlamps lit up nearby and an engine started. Ben's Land Cruiser bounced out from behind some bushes and crossed the rough ground to join the track.

"We had your keys," Daniel explained.

The door of the jeep opened. Ben and Daniel walked round to the driver's side. A thin black man stepped out.

The stranger held out his hand and Ben took it.

"Doctor Williams, this is my cousin, Esau."

Chapter 23

"Esau and I cannot stay here long Doctor Williams," Daniel said. "Once those men realise your jeep is missing, they will come back this way."

"I need to speak to Esau about a drug he took in England," Ben said to Daniel. "That's why I'm here, that's why those men are after me."

Daniel looked at Esau nervously.

"My grandmother says you are good man," Esau said. "She told me you could help and I believe her."

"I can, but I need a few minutes," Ben said.

"We haven't got a few minutes," Daniel said.

Esau turned to Daniel. "Am I going to spend the rest of my life in a cave?" he asked. "Go and watch for those men while I speak with Doctor Williams."

Daniel walked away into the darkness.

"Do you know why those men want me?" Esau asked.

"I think so, but until I get some of your blood, I can't be sure."

"My blood?"

"I need to test it for HIV."

Esau smiled and shook his head. "You will not find any HIV in my blood," he said.

"Because you've been healed?" Ben said, remembering the notes in Esau's file.

"Yes, praise God."

"How long is it since you've taken any drugs?" Ben asked.

"I stopped taking them the day the Lord freed me from the disease."

"When was that?"

"Before Christmas, just before I left London," Esau said.

"And you haven't been ill since?"

"No."

"You were very sick before you took Spiravex, weren't you?"

"The doctor told me I had a CD4 count of twenty five," Esau said. "I remember the number because my birthday is the twenty-fifth of November."

No matter what had become of Esau's HIV, allowing his CD4 count to get so low would have caused irreversible damage to his immune system. Vital memory cells would have been lost forever and Esau would now be vulnerable to chronic diseases like cancer. However, the fact that Esau had not been ill since coming off therapy supported his theory about Spiravex, but he needed the blood samples to prove it beyond doubt.

"I know you believe you've been healed, but I've come all this way and risked my life to get a sample of your blood."

"Why?"

"Those men who captured me and forced you into hiding are being paid by the company who made Spiravex," he said. "I can use your blood to prove why these men are after you, and why they've killed so many others."

"They have killed others?"

"A hundred," Ben said. "By testing you for HIV I can prove my theory and you'll be safe again."

"What is your theory?"

"That Spiravex cures HIV."

Esau looked startled. He shook his head. "God has healed my HIV, not Spiravex."

Ben wanted to grab him and shake the religion out of him. Superstition was rife in rural Africa and bred ridiculous rumours. He'd seen the results of one such rumour: a six-month-old baby was raped to death because the men of her village believed sleeping with a virgin would cure their HIV. She was the only virgin left in that village; an entire community was decimated by ignorance.

"Don't you want to be sure you haven't got HIV any more?" Ben asked.

"Thou shalt not test the Lord your God."

This was lunacy, Esau's blind faith could deny millions of people a life-saving treatment.

There was a whistle from the darkness, followed by the distant roar of an engine.

Ben ran round to the back of the jeep and opened the trunk. He pulled open his holdall and found the syringe kit. He removed two sample tubes. He put one in his pocket and connected the other to a syringe.

He walked back to the front of the jeep. Daniel was running towards them.

"Esau! You must come now!" he shouted. "They will be here soon!"

Ben walked up to Esau holding the syringe in front of him.

"Please Esau. You could save millions of lives."

"It is only by faith that Africa will be saved from HIV."

"Esau, if I don't take this sample these men won't leave your village until they've killed you. Do you want them to go or not?" Ben could see the resolve in Esau's eyes weaken. The sound of the engine was getting louder.

Esau looked down. He put his hand on his left arm and slowly rolled up his sleeve.

"Thank you," Ben said.

"Esau!" Daniel shouted, and ran away from the road.

Ben held Esau's flimsy arm. He looked for a decent vein, but the man was so thin it wasn't easy.

The sound of the engine was now less than half a mile away.

He pulled Esau's arm in front of the headlights. Finally a vein appeared. He pierced the papery skin with the needle and pulled the plunger back. The vial began to fill with dark fluid.

Once it was half full Ben removed it from the needle, sealed the tube and slipped it into his pocket. He pulled the second one out.

"They're coming!" Daniel shouted from the bushes. "I can see them!"

He attached the tube and began drawing more blood. Each sample had to contain at least ten millilitres for the labs to be able to get an accurate measurement. There was a flash of headlights through the bushes.

The blood crept past eight, then nine. He handed Esau a swab.

"Hold it over the needle," Ben said.

Esau pressed the swab down and Ben withdrew the needle. He sealed the vial.

"Go!" he shouted at Esau.

Esau sprinted towards Daniel.

Ben ran to the open door and jumped in the driver's seat. Headlights rounded a corner in the rear-view mirror. He slammed the gearshift into drive and floored the accelerator.

The lights gained on him quickly. They were nearly on his bumper when the turbo of the Land Cruiser kicked in and he began to pull away from the Defender.

There was a sound like the crack of a whip, the rear window shattered and sent a hail of glass into the cabin.

Ben slewed the jeep across the road to avoid getting hit again, but it only allowed them to close the gap. He straightened the wheel and pushed as hard as he could. There was another volley of shots. The headrest on the passenger seat exploded. He ducked down, just keeping his head above the dashboard, but he didn't need to: the Defender was no match for the Land Cruiser, and the sound of the shots grew faint as the headlights rapidly dropped behind.

He'd need to put a few miles between them if he was going to stay in front through the series of ridges that lay ahead on the road back to Nyeri. The Defender would have the advantage once traction was the deciding issue.

A thin strip of red light on the horizon gave some comfort; he didn't fancy plunging down a forty-degree slope in the dark.

* * * *

Half an hour later he reached the small hill that marked the end of the plateau. On the crest of the first gully he stopped to look back. The headlights of the Land Rover were about two miles away.

He slammed the Toyota down the slope.

The sun was nearly up the way ahead was clearly visible. He used the same technique he'd employed a day earlier and scaled the other side with no problem. He repeated the process over and over again.

By seven-thirty, when the sun had risen above the trees, he reached about halfway. There'd been no sign of the Defender, but it must be closing in on him. It wasn't worth thinking about, he just had to focus on going as fast as he could. He pushed down the next slope. As he neared the bottom, a huge root sticking out of the road came into view. He slammed his foot on the brakes and just steered round it. He wouldn't have noticed it going the other way as that side wasn't so exposed, but going down the hill it stuck out of the surface by nearly a foot.

He aimed the jeep up the other side but it'd lost all its momentum; he climbed two-thirds of the way before the tires turned uselessly on the track. The huge weight of the Land Cruiser pulled it back down into the bottom of the gully.

He reversed as far as he could up the other side, slammed the gearshift forward and hurtled towards the bottom. The axle made a loud cracking sound as the tyres slammed into the root. He powered the jeep forward but didn't get any further than he had the first time. It slipped back.

He was stuck.

He'd been going as fast as he could, but the more agile Defender would have gained on him. He changed tactics and tried to climb the slope in first gear, keeping the revs low. He got nowhere and was forced to reverse back to the bottom.

He only had two or three minutes to come up with something.

He looked down the gully to his left, but a huge boulder blocked the path. The other direction looked more hopeful. Twenty yards away the gully curved behind overhanging trees. Countless small boulders and branches meant it wasn't going to be easy, but there was no choice.

He turned the Land Cruiser up the gully, pushing it hard over the uneven ground. The left tyre slipped on a large boulder, which crashed into the already wounded axle. The jeep listed over to the left. He revved the engine furiously and managed to pull up behind the cover of the trees. He turned the engine off, sending a violent judder through the jeep. The metal beneath him groaned before there was another loud crack. The axel snapped and the jeep plunged forward. He was completely stranded now.

He stepped out and looked at the rocky ravine. He'd have to stay put until the Defender had passed; the trees provided the only cover.

He looked through the leaves and watched the road. After half a minute the engine of the Defender could be heard over the rustling caused by the breeze. Twenty seconds later it careered into sight. It slid to a halt in front of the root, before gingerly climbing over it.

It started up the other side, reached halfway then slid backwards. They hadn't got any further than he had.

They tried again, but with no more success.

The doors opened and the two men got out. Curtis walked to the front of the bonnet, fiddled with the bumper then pulled out a hook that was connected to a thick wire.

They were going to use the winch.

Curtis walked up the slope, carrying the hook with him. Dom stretched then looked up the gully. Ben froze; he seemed to be looking straight at him.

He took a few steps towards him, stopped and undid his flies.

Ben stayed absolutely still, barely breathing. Dom finished, pulled his zip up and started walking back to the jeep. He stopped and looked down at the ground to his right. He took a step towards a patch of mud and crouched.

He'd seen the tyre marks.

Chapter 24

Dom straightened up and walked along the gully towards him.

Instinct screamed to run, but the only way out of the ravine was past the two men. Ben moved carefully to the edge of his cover, keeping as low as possible.

There was a clatter of pebbles nearby. He looked through the leaves to see Dom on the ground; he must have slipped on one of the stones.

Ben looked down the gully. Curtis was out of sight, probably finding a tree to secure the winch. This was the only chance he was going to get.

He charged out from behind the trees. Dom was back on his feet. He saw Ben and reached inside his jacket pocket. Ben sprang at Dom and collided with him, they both fell to the ground.

Ben could feel Dom's right arm move beneath him; the barrel of a gun scraped against his chest. Ben grabbed Dom's arm with his left hand, held it down and punched him in the face. Dom tried to break free, but Ben was much stronger.

He ran his free hand over the ground next to him. He felt a large stone and closed his fingers around it. He lifted it up quickly then swung it onto Dom's head.

Dom's body went limp. Ben pulled the chubby fingers away from the gun handle then got to his feet. He took hold of Dom's collar, dragged him behind the trees and kept watch through the branches.

He looked at the gun in his hands. It went against everything he believed in, but what choice did he have? Ultimately it was either him or them; if it was him it would be many others as well. It was a moral no-brainer.

He stared at the muddy slope, his adrenalin sharpening each second of anticipation. Curtis came into view as he scrambled down the track towards the Defender. He looked around then walked away from Ben towards the large boulder that blocked the lower end of the gully.

Ben stepped out from behind the trees and moved cautiously down to the Defender, keeping low enough to use the vehicle as cover. He reached the jeep and peered over the bonnet. Curtis was ten yards away and walking back in his direction. Their eyes met. Ben straightened up and pointed the gun straight at him.

"Don't move," Ben said.

Curtis raised his hands.

Ben stepped out from behind the jeep and walked a couple of paces nearer.

"Do what I say or you die," he said, and walked around Curtis, keeping the gun pointed at his head. He stopped behind him and checked his pockets; there was no weapon. "Rope?"

"In the jeep," Curtis replied.

"Get it."

Curtis lowered his hands then walked round to the back of the Defender. Ben followed him.

"Wait!" he shouted, as Curtis reached for the handle. "Step away." He motioned for Curtis to move to the side and held the gun pointing at him while he opened the mud-covered rear door of the Defender. An assault rifle with a wooden butt and curved clip lay on top of a crate of beer. There was a camping stove, a box full of tinned food, and a length of blue rope lying on a pile of dirty clothes. He leaned in to grab the rope.

The large shape in his peripheral vision lunged towards him. Two strong hands grabbed his arm.

Ben turned and pulled the trigger, but the shot flew harmlessly into the air. Curtis forced the gun towards him. Ben looked into his blood-shot eyes, and pushed back hard until the barrel jabbed into the stubble on the African's chin.

Sweat trickled down Curtis' forehead. Ben squeezed the trigger.

The gun recoiled in his hand and Curtis slid to the ground. A pool of blood spread out from behind his head.

Ben put the pistol in his pocket, and stared at the man he'd killed. The guy deserved what he'd got, but that didn't help with the sick feeling inside. He'd deal with his conscience later, for now he had to focus on getting Esau's blood back to the UK. He grabbed Curtis' legs and dragged him along the gully towards the Land

Cruiser. He checked on Dom; his hair was sticky with blood but he was still breathing.

He pulled his holdall out of the jeep and took the sample tubes from the front seat. He returned to the Defender, loaded his bag then walked round to the front. Land Rovers were standard issue to many of the Aid agencies in Africa; he'd driven dozens of them.

He engaged the dog clutch using a lever next to the winch then jumped in the cab. He selected second gear and increased the revs. The wire lifted up from the track and flicked mud into the air. He kept the revs at an even eight hundred until the wire went taught. He maintained the pressure on the throttle and the jeep jolted forward.

It took five minutes for the jeep to inch up the slope and level out. He put the gearshift into neutral and engaged the handbrake. He got out, untied the winch and reeled it back into its holder.

He looked down into the gully. The Land Cruiser and the two Africans were completely invisible. By the time someone discovered them he'd be long gone.

* * * *

He reached Nyeri by mid-morning. It was too early for lunch in the Central Hotel so he grabbed a few bags of crisps and a couple of chocolate bars in a grocery store, then returned to the jeep to eat his improvised breakfast and think about his next move.

Flying out of Nairobi or Mombassa wasn't an option; the Kenyan authorities would be looking for him. Going north into the bandit-infested countries of Ethiopia or Somalia was too dangerous. That left him with Dar es Salaam five hundred miles south in Tanzania, or Kampala three hundred miles west in Uganda. Dar was the furthest away, and being relatively close to Mombassa immigration on the Tanzanian border would probably be expecting him. The most sensible choice was Kampala, but he'd still need to drive through immigration. Although it should be less risky that far west there were no guarantees. If he got caught it was game over. The best way was to fly across the border in a light aircraft as Jake had suggested.

Going back to Jake's ranch and using his friend with the air-safari business was an option, but he might not have to. There was help much nearer to hand.

He finished the last chocolate bar and reached for the ignition. A knock on the window stopped him from turning the key. He looked out to see a neatly ironed khaki shirt stretched over a muscular chest. A bronze badge on the left breast pocket read 'Police'. He wound the window down and looked up to see the reflection of his face duplicated in a pair of Aviators.

"Can I help you?" he asked.

"Your number plate is covered in mud."

"I'm sorry." Ben pulled the handle of the door and tried to push it open, but the policeman held his knee against it.

"Automatic fine. Twenty US."

Ben frowned. There was nothing he could do though, bribery was a way of life out here. The first time he'd been stopped by a Kenyan policeman he couldn't understand why. He'd been pulled over for speeding while travelling on a road so riddled with potholes that the speed limit was an idle fantasy. He protested until the cop spelt it out for him and told him it was his wife's birthday. How could he argue with that? He paid up.

He reached onto the back seat and felt inside his bag for his wallet. He turned round to hand the man his twenty dollars but he wasn't there, he'd moved along the side of the Defender and was peering into the back.

The rifle!

The cop pulled a gun from a leather holster on his belt, pointed it at Ben and stepped sideways so he was in line with the driver's door. He leaned forward and pulled it open.

"Get out!" he shouted.

A small crowd had gathered on the sidewalk.

Ben stepped out of the jeep.

"Hands on your head!"

He obeyed and was spun round and pushed against the side of the jeep. The cop frisked him, his hands stopped at Ben's right pocket and pulled out Dom's gun. This wasn't going to be easy to explain.

"What's your name?" the policeman asked.

"Harry Walker," Ben replied. "I'm allowed to carry a gun."

"Not an AK-47." He grabbed Ben's wrists, cuffed him and led him to the patrol car. "Keys."

"They're in the ignition," Ben replied.

The cop opened the rear door of his car and pushed Ben headfirst into it. The African walked over to the Defender, opened the back, and pulled out the rifle along with his holdall. Ben tried to move his hands, but the metal handcuffs cut into the sores on his wrists. He had to do something; there was no way he was going to end up in a Kenyan jail.

He slid across the seat and leaned on the door handle with his elbow. Nothing happened. He looked through the window. The cop was locking the Defender. He walked back to the police car and put Ben's bag in the boot. He climbed in the front and started the engine.

Ben leaned forward. "How about a hundred dollars?"

* * * *

Helen squeezed the trigger slowly, trying to ignore the quivering vulnerability of Ruth's head. She squeezed harder. Ruth's head exploded in front of her, blood splattered across the bed and up the walls. Ruth slumped onto the floor, her head twisted towards Helen. All life left her face.

A mobile rang. Helen opened her eyes. There was a crack of light in the curtains signalling the arrival of morning. The phone continued to ring. She leaned across and read the display. Luke.

She put her head back on the pillow and waited for him to go away.

She stared at the ceiling. What had she become?

The pills. She needed to take a pill. She felt for the light switch and turned on the bedside lamp. The small plastic container was next to her phone. She lifted the cap off and shook a pill into the palm of her hand.

The ringing started again.

Go away.

But he didn't. She sighed, put the pill down and answered the phone.

"We have a problem," Luke said.

"What do you mean?"

"Williams has escaped."

"When?"

"Two hours ago. Murray was on his way to interrogate him when he found one of the men walking along the track. The other one's dead. Williams is proving a more formidable target than we thought."

"Either that or the men you're using in Kenya are useless," Helen said.

"They won't know what's hit them once this is all over. That aside, it presents us with a fresh problem. We believe Williams has contacted the target and is now trying to return to the UK."

"But surely he'll be picked up at the airport."

"If he knows the police want him he might try to escape via a neighbouring country. Interpol are useless in Africa, so we can't depend on anyone in Uganda or Tanzania watching for him. We have to assume the worst and that he'll be back in England within a day or two. We must implement our contingency plan."

"Anne mentioned something about that."

"She did all the ground work and identified three patients who would be suitable."

"For what?" she asked.

"If Williams has proof about what's happened with the Spiravex trial, we need to make sure he either keeps it to himself or is sufficiently discredited that no one will listen to him."

"Why don't we just kill him?"

"Shackleton says he wants Williams alive no matter what. He's even talking about flying him out to the States."

"Why hire us then?"

"Good question. But they pay the bills."

"What do you want me to do with these patients?" she asked.

"I've transferred fifteen thousand pounds into your account. Offer five to each patient to invent sexual assault charges against him."

"Are you serious?"

"I'm emailing the files as we speak. Make sure their stories are consistent." Luke hung up.

She got out of bed and walked to the study. She sat down at the computer and started it up. Five minutes later she was viewing Luke's email and downloading the attachments. She opened the first file.

This couldn't be right. She closed the file and opened the second. Men? The third was the same. She leaned back and shook her head. Ben was a man's man, but not in this way. It wouldn't stick.

She picked up the handset by the computer and dialled Luke's number.

"Did Anne really pick these?"

"What's the problem?"

"They're all men."

"Most of his patients are men," Luke said. "Just get on with it. You have a saying in this country, mud sticks. Throw enough at him and it will."

The phone went dead.

She knew he was right., lies worked. A lie had killed her father.

Her anger at the memory of her father's suicide was neutralised by the realisation that she was no better than the woman whose lie had destroyed him. She'd put a gun to an innocent woman's head and pulled the trigger, and now she was about to ruin the career of Ben Williams in the same way that that woman had destroyed her father.

She could tell herself she had no choice; Luke would have killed her if she hadn't followed orders, and he'd kill her if she didn't finish the job. But if she had any morals, she'd have given the gun back last night and would walk away from Slade now.

She looked at the computer screen. She'd get to work on the patients in a while, first she wanted to get on with a project she'd started the night before. Something Ruth said to her had caused an itch in her mind that needed scratching. The whole chicken and egg problem had been swirling around her head on the drive home, and by the time she'd reached Brighton she knew what she had to find out to put the issue to rest. She'd always bought into the RNA world theory. It made sense in many ways. RNA was similar to DNA in that it could store genetic information, but it could also perform tasks that proteins do. She knew that RNA was heavily involved in the translation of DNA into proteins in the ribosome, and ultimately this could kill off the chicken and egg argument. What she couldn't remember was whether the translation was directly carried out by RNA or whether a protein was still needed to mediate in the process. If no protein was needed then the problem of how or why two entirely different chemical systems communicated with each was surmountable. She'd ordered a couple of books about the origins of life on line, and began reviewing the literature available directly on the internet.

She started typing the word ribosome into the google search box. Her mobile rang from the other room.

She got up and walked to the bedroom. She reached for the phone, then froze as she saw the name on the display: Anne.

Chapter 25

Ben stared at the nameplate on the desk in front of him: 'Robert Yego'. He'd been sitting there for twenty minutes while he waited for Nyeri's Chief of Police to return from lunch.

The office dwarfed the mahogany furniture, which looked like relics from colonial times. Two fans whirred overhead, keeping the room at a pleasant temperature. There were bars on the window behind the desk. Were they there to keep prisoners in, or to protect the police from those on the outside?

He was handcuffed with his hands behind his back; a pair of ankle cuffs secured him to the wooden chair that the arresting officer had left him in. He sat as still as possible, any movement caused the metal of the handcuffs to dig into the rope burns on his wrists.

An outer door slammed and people entered the adjoining room. He recognised the voice of the policeman who'd arrested him, and there was another much deeper voice.

The door behind him opened. He tried to turn round, but was held back by the cuffs.

"Doctor Williams," the deep voice boomed. A black man in his forties, wearing a pair of round wire-rimmed glasses, appeared in front of him and sat at the desk. "That is who you are, isn't it?" He opened the British passport in his hands and moved his glasses down his nose. "Doctor Benjamin Alfred Williams."

Ben lowered his eyes.

"Why did you lie to my colleague?"

Ben looked up at the cop to his side who glared back down with folded arms. Ben turned away.

"Leave us alone," Yego said.

The officer left the room and closed the door behind him.

"Not only did you lie, but you attempted to bribe a policeman."

He had to be kidding.

"Bribery is not as common place as it used to be."

202

"You should tell your staff that," Ben said. "I wasn't the one…"

"It's irrelevant now," Yego said. He reached into a tray on his desk, pulled out a pile of papers, and looked through them. He selected a sheet of A4 and held it in front of Ben.

The name 'Ben Williams' was printed on the top above a photo-fit that didn't look anything like him. He was wanted for questioning in connection with two deaths in Mombassa on Thursday.

"I received this before lunch," Yego said. "I was going to tell the officers in the morning briefing tomorrow, but I won't need to now. On your way to Uganda were you?"

Ben didn't answer.

"It doesn't matter now, you won't be going anywhere for a long time."

"I've done nothing wrong," Ben said.

"Why were you carrying two guns?"

"The jeep isn't mine."

Yego raised his eyebrows. "You stole it?"

Ben looked at him. "In effect, yes, I did. I stole it from two men who were trying to kill me. The guns belong to them."

"You'd better come up with something more convincing for the detectives in Mombassa."

Yego picked up the phone and dialled a number.

"Inspector Wallace please," he said. "Robert Yego."

The name lingered in the ensuing silence. Robert. Ben suddenly leaned forward in his chair. "Do you know Jake Wambugu?"

Yego looked at him with a frown and held his hand over the receiver. "What if I do?"

"He asked you to look for Esau Kimani," Ben said. "That was a favour for me. Please listen to what I have to say before you tell the Mombassa police I'm here."

"Hello," Yego said into the receiver. "I was just calling about the fax I received this morning."

Ben held his breath while he watched Yego.

"How likely is it that he'll come up our way?" He paused, then nodded. "I'll make sure my officers keep their eyes open all the same."

He hung up and looked at Ben with an expectant expression.

"Phone Jake if you don't believe me," Ben said.

"I will, but you tell me what's going on first. As far as I'm concerned you're a wanted man, but the fact that you're a friend of Jake's buys you ten minutes."

"One of those men in Mombassa was trying to kill me," Ben said. "As were the men I stole the jeep from."

"There were two murders in Mombassa."

"The other guy was shot by the man who was after me."

"Why were these men chasing you?"

"It's all to do with Esau Kimani and a clinical trial I was involved in back home. An American pharmaceutical company want Esau and me dead. These men were hired by them."

"Why do they want to kill you?"

"To protect a secret," Ben said.

"What secret?"

Other than Ruth, he hadn't told anyone his suspicions about the Spiravex trial, but that had only been to protect those he was talking to. This guy was different. He was a middle-aged provincial policeman who stood in the way of exposing Marivant. The truth was the best reason he could think of to explain his involvement in the murders in Mombassa.

"One of their drugs cures HIV, but they want to cover it up."

"What?"

"It'd cost them too much money in lost revenue." Ben could see Yego getting confused. "Esau is the key to this secret. If he dies, or I'm put in prison, the cure will never become public knowledge."

Yego looked down.

"My eldest son has HIV," he said. "Many of my friends are either infected or have family members who are. What you are saying is very serious."

"You have to let me go," Ben said.

Yego looked up and shook his head. "I can't do that, you're wanted for murder."

"If you hand me over to the Mombassa police then you'll be murdering your son."

Yego's eyes filled with fury. "You expect me to believe you just because you're white?"

"What's being white got to do with anything?" Ben said. "The only way I can prove my case is to return to the UK with the samples of blood I've taken from Esau. If I'm delayed for more than a few days the samples will be no good, and I won't be able to prove anything."

"You'll be here for the rest of your life," Yego said.

"What have you got to lose?" Ben asked.

"If anyone found out I released a murderer, I'd be lynched."

"Do you really think I'm a murderer?" Ben asked. "If I get back to England there's a chance I'll save your son's life one day. If I don't, you'll never know. Just phone Jake. We've been friends for years."

Yego shook his head, reached for his Rolodex and pulled it across the desk towards him. He flicked through it, then picked up the receiver and dialled.

"Is Jake there?" he said. "It's Robert Yego."

Yego waited with his eyes fixed on a spot on the desk.

"Jambo Jake," he said. "I'm good. I have a Ben Williams here who says he's a friend of yours."

There was a long pause.

"But he's wanted for murder."

There was another pause.

"Are you sure?"

Ben caught the muffled sound of Jake's voice as Yego listened patiently. After a while Yego nodded. "Thank you Jake."

He put the phone down and stared at Ben for over a minute, and then sighed.

"You're lucky Jake and I know each other so well," he said. "You're also lucky that I'm the only one here who has seen this." He waved the A4 sheet in the air.

He stood up, walked over to Ben and unlocked the cuffs. Ben brought his hands in front of him and rolled the stiffness out of his shoulders. He looked at his wrists but didn't rub them; they were too raw.

"I'll take you back to your car myself," Yego said, "but the weapons stay here."

"Thank you," Ben replied.

* * * *

Two hours later he pulled up in Wasangi Mission. He'd spent five months there covering for one of the flying doctors while she convalesced after a bout of malaria.

There were three one-storey buildings surrounded by game reserves and Masai tribal land. The main building housed the communications equipment, a large dining room and a lounge area where the staff could rest when they weren't working. The other two buildings were boarding blocks sufficient to accommodate four single workers and two couples. The grounds were well maintained: clean stone paths criss-crossed neat lawns and modest flowerbeds.

A Cessna Skylane with a red cross painted on the fuselage was parked to the right of the main building.

The sight of the plane brought back memories of his brief stint at the mission. It had been a welcome change from working in the overcrowded hospitals of Nakuru and Nyeri; as a flying doctor his clinic covered several thousand square miles of spectacular scenery. If luck was on his side, the same pilots who'd ferried him around back then would still be here.

He stepped out of the jeep into the still warmth of the afternoon and walked over to the main building. The front door was open and he entered the lounge. It hadn't changed in the five years since he'd last seen it: a variety of ageing armchairs and sofas were dotted about the wide room. There were two bookcases full of well-thumbed paperbacks and three battered coffee tables. To the far left of the room were a short-wave radio and a computer. At the other end was a door leading to the kitchen and dining room.

There was only one person there, Ben instantly recognised him; Steve Morgan had a face you never forgot. It was dominated by a long nose, perched on a thick drooping moustache that wouldn't have looked out of place on a Mexican in a spaghetti western.

Steve sat up, his mouth open.

"No way," he said. "What the bloody hell are you doing here?" His Welsh accent hadn't weakened in the years since they'd last met.

Ben grinned; he had his lucky break. He and Steve had been good mates while he'd worked there. They were both misfits at the mission station. Neither had any faith, and both liked a good pint.

The other staff were mostly committed Christians, and whilst they were good people, they weren't always good company.

"It's a long story," Ben said, taking Steve's outstretched hand.

"I've got all day, the medics are out with the other pilots. I'm only on standby in case they need an extra plane to bring patients back."

He joined Steve on the tatty sofa. Unlike Nyeri's Chief of Police, Steve didn't need to know details about the trial that could put him in danger. He told him enough about the previous two days to highlight why he needed to leave Kenya anonymously, but no more.

Steve stroked his moustache while he appeared to consider the matter. "How soon do you need to be home?"

"I've got three days, max," Ben said.

The expression on Steve's face relaxed. "Why didn't you say? That's not urgent. I thought you needed to be back tonight or something. Now that would have been tricky." He slapped Ben on the knee. "We'll have you in Blighty by tomorrow, I'm sure of it."

"But how?"

"You'll see," Steve said. "You don't mind going via Paris do you?"

Ben shook his head.

"Good." Steve stood up and walked to the entrance of the dining room. A phone hung on the wall next to the door. He picked it up and dialled a number. He spoke in French, but the language lost all its charm as his Welsh accent barged through the syllables like an eighteen stone prop-forward through a line of ballet dancers. After a few minutes he hung up.

He walked back and smiled. "All fixed. You should be in Paris by four am local time. I've just got one more thing to check."

He walked in the other direction and grabbed a handset by the radio. "This is base, do you copy? Over."

"Monty here. Copy. Over," a voice replied.

"Monty. Can you tell me whether you're going to need me or not? I want to do a favour for an old friend and I'll be taking the plane for a few hours. Over."

"I'll check with the docs and get back to you in five. Over and out."

Steve put the handset back on its rest and smiled at Ben.

"So how will I be in Paris by tomorrow morning?" Ben asked.

"I'm friendly with a girl from Médecins Sans Frontières . They have a daily delivery. The plane returns to France empty bar a few personnel. As long you don't mind sitting in a cargo bay, you'll be home in time for a roast dinner."

"No paperwork?"

"None. You won't go anywhere near immigration. Besides, you know what the locals are like, see 'doctor' on a passport and a white face and they'll think you're God."

"Where do they fly from?"

"Nairobi. They leave at six. I can get you there with two hours to spare so you'll even be able to grab a bite to eat. There's a canteen in their hanger for crew and loaders."

The radio crackled. "Monty to base. Over."

Steve went back and picked up the handset. "What's the score fella? Over."

"All clear. There's no one here that's going to need lifting out. The docs are nearly ready to wrap up. Over."

"Nice one Monty. See you anon. Over and out." He put the handset down and grabbed a set of keys. "Let's go."

They left the main building.

"Just got to get my stuff out of the jeep," Ben said.

"You didn't mention baggage as well," Steve said, and smiled.

Ben walked over to the Defender and opened the back door. He checked the samples. They were safe and felt cool. He pushed them back in his holdall and zipped it up. He lifted the bag out and checked the front of the jeep to see whether he'd left anything behind. There were only the remains of his makeshift breakfast. He locked the jeep and walked over to Steve who was performing pre-flight checks on the Cessna.

"Where'd you get the Landy?" Steve asked.

"The two men I escaped from this morning."

"Better get rid of it then. I'll give it to one of the local lads."

Steve opened a door in the fuselage. There was more than enough space for Ben's bag. He laid it down carefully.

"The samples in there are they?"

Ben nodded.

"Must be pretty important if you've got people wanting to kill you because of them."

"About the most important piece of luggage you'll ever carry," Ben said.

Steve pulled a face like he didn't really understand, but saw the bigger picture. "Just got a few more checks then we're ready," he said. "Climb in."

Ben opened the front door of the plane and sat next to the pilot's seat. It was a while since he'd been in one of these. Back then he would have been sitting behind the pilot tending to a patient. Images of a child fighting malaria, a woman who'd been raped, and a Masai warrior with a hunting injury flashed in front of his mind's eye. The trips he hated most were to treat patients whose injuries were the result of a tribal tradition.

On one occasion he accompanied a sixteen-year-old boy who needed to be hospitalised because of an infection on his penis. It was Masai tradition for a young man who was coming of age to undergo an ancient ritual to show he was worthy to wear the robes of a warrior. A witch doctor and five elders took him into the bush where he was stripped naked. They laid him on the ground face-up and held his arms and legs. Their grip was loose; they weren't there to restrain him, but to detect any movement.

The witch doctor took a sharp blade and removed the boy's foreskin. If he flinched he was unworthy of the warrior's robes. Afterwards the wound was covered with cow's urine and mildewed dung. If he died of an infection then God had judged him too weak to protect the herds.

The boy that he treated was lucky to escape with his life, but his manhood was left behind at the hospital.

Steve clambered into the cockpit. "All set?" he asked.

Ben clipped his safety belt across his chest and nodded.

Steve flicked two black switches on the dashboard then pressed a button. Clouds of half-burnt fuel spluttered out of the propellers as the blades spun into a seamless blur, their thudding increased in pitch until all other noise was drowned out. Ben put his headset on.

"Here we go," Steve said, and pulled back on the throttle.

The small plane trundled along the grass, through a gap in a tall hedge, and onto a flat field about five hundred metres long.

Steve taxied to the end of the African runway and turned the plane. The windsock was hanging limp.

Steve pulled the throttle back. The plane edged away from its starting point and slowly built up speed. The bushes at the end of the runway came closer at an ever-increasing pace, but Ben knew the end of the story; he'd been there many times before. About two-thirds of the way along the field the Cessna lifted off the ground.

Within moments they were climbing above the wild savannah surrounding the airfield. To the south and west dry plains and hills stretched into the distance until they reached the Rift Valley. Green acacia trees speckled the golden slopes and herds of conspicuous zebra grazed in the chest-high grass.

They reached cruising height several thousand feet above the ground.

"Should be just over an hour." Steve's voice crackled in Ben's headphones.

"Great," Ben replied. Flying from Nairobi was better than he could have hoped for. No running the gauntlet of immigration in Kampala. He could sneak out of the country right under the noses of the police without them ever suspecting a thing.

Steve steered the plane just below the high cloud base, but was forced to take a more westerly course when a dark storm loomed ahead.

"Only add an extra ten minutes. You've got ages before the plane leaves," he said.

Ben nodded.

They skirted the edge of the angry-looking cloud. On the other side Nairobi became visible in the distance. The huge urban sprawl was an ugly stain on the perfectly woven tapestry of Africa. The sheer scale of the city made it easy to understand why Nairobi was known as the Capital of East Africa.

They passed over the northern outskirts and Steve contacted the tower at Kenyatta airport to arrange a landing slot. They were forced into a holding circle for ten minutes over the East of the city while a 747 took off. Kenyatta was not so adept at juggling planes as the busy airports of south-east England.

At last they were given clearance for the final approach. Steve banked the plane then straightened up with the nose pointing towards the runway. As they descended to less than a thousand feet the land started to take on more familiar proportions. A minute later the tyres were nearly skimming the corrugated-iron roofs of a dishevelled shantytown bordering the airport.

When they reached the runway it felt like the tiny plane was being swallowed up by the vast expanse of tarmac. Steve eased off the throttle, the tyres hit the surface and they bounced high into the air before landing a second time and sticking.

"Sorry about that," Steve said. "Used to grass strips, they're more forgiving."

Ben raised a hand.

Steve took the first taxiway and ran the plane to the end of the airfield towards several cavernous hangers. He stopped the Cessna in the shadow of a 767. Conveyer belts led from a gaping hole in the side of the jet; boxes were being unloaded onto them.

"Here you go mate." He stopped the plane and made some notes in his logbook then opened the door and climbed out. Ben joined him on the tarmac.

A blond-haired woman in jeans and a white blouse was walking towards them.

"Steve!" she shouted across the apron. "Bonjour mon ami!" Steve opened his arms and embraced her, then kissed her on both cheeks twice. From the way Steve kept his arm round her Ben guessed there was more than just friendship between them.

"Teresa, this is Doctor Ben Williams."

"The man who needs a lift home urgently," she said. Ben was able to get a better look at her. She was in her early thirties and petite. Square glasses framed her brown eyes. Like most of the volunteers in Africa she looked a bit on the thin side.

"I have to get back to the UK as soon as possible," he said, shaking her hand. "I need to test a blood sample I've taken from a patient out here."

Teresa frowned. "You know we're not going back to the UK? We're landing in Charles de Gaulle."

"No problem, I'll catch the Eurostar."

She nodded. "I'll show you to the canteen, but it's a bit noisy and all we can offer is a stale baguette and a coke."

"I'll head over in a minute, I just need to get my bag."

They walked round to the back of the plane. Ben unzipped his holdall and took a quick look at the vials. They'd survived the flight intact.

He turned to Steve.

"Thanks mate," he said. "I'd have been in a right fix without you."

"Think nothing of it."

Ben put his hand out. Steve pulled him forward; they hugged and patted each other on the back to ensure the gesture was sufficiently masculine.

Steve walked over to Teresa and whispered something into her ear. She grinned and Steve climbed back into the cockpit.

Ben and Teresa walked away and stood near the entrance of the hangar. They watched Steve turn the Cessna through a hundred and eighty degrees then stop while he spoke into his radio. Two minutes later he was trundling onto the runway. The plane looked lost amongst the jumbo jets and DC10s. They watched him take off.

Teresa led Ben inside the hangar and showed him to the canteen.

"Do you have a phone I can use?" he asked. "I need to call the UK."

"It's in the office at the back of the hangar. You can't always get a connection, but you're welcome to try."

He grabbed some food then headed through the noisy hangar to the office. There was no one inside. He sat down at the desk, picked up the phone and dialled Ruth's home number. Her answer phone kicked in after four rings. He was about to leave a message telling her he was on his way home when he realised it might not be just her he was telling. He hung up.

Chapter 26

Ben arrived in Charles de Gaulle at six-fifteen on Sunday morning. He transferred to the busy main terminal where he joined a long queue for immigration. After a few minutes he became aware that people were staring at him. He glanced down at his dirty clothes and felt the growth on his chin. He must have looked like a street bum.

He stepped out of the queue. He needed to smarten up before going through passport control.

The only shops were expensive designer stores, but if he was to avoid drawing attention to himself there was no choice. He bought a pair of trousers and a shirt for two hundred Euros and took them into the toilets. He stripped down to his waist, ignoring the bemused looks of other travellers, and shaved off his two-day-old stubble. He washed his face and upper body then went inside a cubicle to change into the new clothes. He packed his dirty jeans and T-shirt in his holdall.

He rejoined the queue. He passed through with no problems and took the metro to Gare du Nord, where he booked himself onto the nine-ten Eurostar to London. This gave him over an hour before he needed to go through UK passport control, the most hazardous part of his journey home.

The check-in area for the Eurostar was on the first floor, above the platforms. There was a wide concourse bordered by a number of boutiques and news-stands. A single queue snaked out of the entrance to the international lounge at the far end of the concourse.

He bought a copy of The Times and found a patisserie near the head of the queue. He ordered a double espresso and a ham croissant.

It was his first European food in nearly a week and each flaky mouthful was a reminder of why French food always tasted better when eaten in France. It was all in the preparation. Even though the beans that made his coffee probably came from Kenya, the final product served in Paris was far superior to any brew he'd been offered in the previous five days.

He finished eating, wiped the buttery residue from his lips and sat back to focus his attention on the immigration process.

After half an hour he'd seen enough people check in to know what he was up against. The biggest difference between the Eurostar border control and those found at international airports was that there were two sets of immigration officials. The first check was done by the French, then immediately afterwards the process was repeated by the British. It saved passengers having to queue twice, once in Paris and once in London. When the passengers arrived at St Pancras they were free to walk straight into the city.

It was a given that the British database would have his name flagged. If his details were entered into a terminal it would only be a matter of seconds before he found himself on the wrong end of a gun.

There was less chance of his name being in the French system. His passport had only been glanced at in Charles de Gaulle, and judging the interest of the French immigration checking the Eurostar passengers the same would happen here.

The British were much more cautious. During the quieter moments they stopped one in three passengers and scanned the barcode on their passport. Once the queue grew to more than fifty people they seemed to adopt the French policy, and only applied extra screening for passengers who didn't 'look European'. It was crude, but probably effective.

The queue grew to its longest thirty minutes before each London departure. Ben needed to time it right. He had to join the line as it was still growing to be sure there were enough people following after him to keep the guards' checks at a minimum.

He left the coffee shop and joined the queue at eight thirty-five. There were about thirty people in front of him and a steady stream of travellers ensured that it continued to lengthen behind him.

He pulled out his copy of 'The Times' and read it while he waited. It was a bad idea. When there were just three people ahead of him, he turned the page and saw a picture of himself. The headline read, 'UK Doctor goes missing after double murder in

214

Kenya'. He snapped the paper shut. There was no doubt about it, if the English checked his passport on their computers, he'd never get to the UK. But it wasn't just the authorities who knew; it would be anyone who read a newspaper or watched the news.

He edged forward, his mind churning over the implications. Ruth would be going out of her head with worry. What had she told the police? Had she talked about his theory? Would they be waiting for him when he returned?

The French guard called to the young Asian woman in front of Ben. She flashed her purple EU passport and walked straight through. The guard waved Ben forward. He put the newspaper under his arm and stepped over the yellow line. The guard took his passport and looked it at. Ben smiled, and the guard handed it back.

Ben joined the end of a much shorter queue for UK immigration a few metres beyond. He tried to focus his mind away from the article and let his thoughts drift onto the peculiarities of national boundaries. Once he passed beyond the British checkpoint, had he left France even though he was still in Paris? Would the soil he was standing on be British even though it lay in the shadow of the Sacre Coeur?

The Asian girl was called forward. The female guard took her passport and scanned it, then looked at the screen. Ben knew he was alright; there was no chance they'd suspect him of being an asylum seeker or a member of Al Qaeda.

"This way sir." Ben looked to his left. A guard was waving him over. A new booth had been opened, but he wanted to follow the girl.

"Sir!"

Ben walked over. The official held his hand out. Ben put his newspaper down and gave him the passport. He opened it and looked at Ben, then at the computer screen. Ben could see the Windows' logo flashing; it was still booting up. The man handed him back his passport and nodded him through.

He began walking away. He'd made it.

"Sir!" a voice called.

He froze then turned round. The official in the booth was holding the newspaper in the air. Ben walked back and took it from him.

"Cheers."

He walked across the narrow waiting area. The plastic seats were full of tourists reading books or newspapers. He spotted several copies of 'The Times' spread open among the crowd. It'd be safer to hang around the duty-free stores where people would be more interested in buying things than reading a newspaper.

His tactic worked and he boarded the empty first-class carriage unchallenged at five-past-nine.

Travelling on high-speed trains was awesome. In spite of the frantic activities on the platform, the only noise in the soundproofed interior was the electric hum of the air conditioning, making it feel like a cocoon of modernity. It was a completely different experience from sitting on a food-stained seat in a rattling London commuter train.

The moment Ben leaned back he closed his eyes and fell asleep.

He woke up to see the river Medway below the train window as it hurtled through Kent. He arrived in St Pancras at eleven-forty and took the tube to Victoria. From there he caught the Brighton Express back to the south coast. The carriage was full of families heading to the seaside for a day out. Two young boys sat opposite him playing on their Gameboys. On the other side of the aisle, their mother and her teenage daughter split their time between bickering and flicking through magazines. He couldn't see anyone reading a newspaper.

The bleeping of the Gameboys and the caustic exchanges of the women made sleep impossible, but his eyes were grateful to view the grass-covered hills of the Weald that lay between the outskirts of the capital and Brighton. The gentle scenery was all the more precious to him since there'd been many times in the past few days when he'd wondered whether he'd see it again.

After fifty minutes the train eased into the vaulted ironwork of the Victorian station that lay at the end of the line. He pulled the samples out of his holdall and checked his bag into left luggage. He walked fifty yards down the road that led to the sea and found a mobile phone shop. He bought a cheap pay-as-you-go phone and a twenty-pound top-up card.

The first number he dialled was Ruth's mobile. It rang twice then went through to voicemail.

"Hi, it's Ben. I'm worried about you, steer clear of Helen, she's working for Marivant. I'll try again later."

He left a similar message on her home number.

He then called the hospital.

He asked the operator to put him through to the path lab. He knew most of the techs, but it wasn't a tech who answered.

"Amanda Holborn," a woman's voice said.

He'd struck gold. Amanda was almost a friend, and more to the point a consultant virologist. She'd provided excellent council on numerous occasions when he'd been confronted with patients who had messy resistance profiles. She'd also pushed the Trust to install the latest HIV-testing hardware, which not only performed more sensitive assays, but was also much quicker.

"Amanda, hi, it's Ben Williams," he said.

"Ben?" There was a long pause. "What the hell's going on? The paper said Interpol are looking for you. Something about a murder?"

"How long have you known me Amanda?" he asked.

"Years, which is why I couldn't believe it."

"I haven't murdered anyone, but I am in trouble, and I need your help."

"What do you want me to do?"

He thought about going to the hospital, but he couldn't risk being spotted. "Can you meet me in half an hour?"

"Sure. Why?"

"I'll explain later. Do you know the Black Rock station on the Volks Railway?"

"Yes."

"I'll meet you there."

He hung up. Was Amanda as trustworthy as he thought? There was no choice but to find out. He walked towards the taxi rank, stopping in a souvenir shop on the way to pick up a baseball cap.

* * * *

Helen reread the paragraph from Paul Davies' book, The Origin of Life:

'When I set out to write this book I was convinced that science was close to wrapping up the mystery of life's origins. Having spent a year or two researching the field, I am now convinced that there remains a huge gulf in our understanding. This gulf is not merely ignorance about certain technical details, it is a major conceptual lacuna.'

It confirmed what she'd discovered for herself earlier after reading a number of papers and abstracts. It was statistically, chemically and conceptually impossible for the translation system that lies at the heart of cellular replication and production, and therefore of life itself, to come into being through natural means, either by evolving from some sort of RNA world, or by appearing spontaneously, given current knowledge. Considering that we know an enormous amount about the system, it was hard to see how a new thesis could ever be developed.

What was most disturbing was the fact that if she didn't know better, a system that contained codes and languages stank of Intelligent Design, dirty words amongst scientists, and if used out loud could marginalise someone's career. But even Dawkins, the high priest of atheism, seemed to be less confident in his assertions about the origins of life than before. She'd watched a webcast of an interview he had with Paul Davies from the Origins conference in April 2009 and couldn't help but think of Ruth's expression, 'the elephant in the lab', as her two fellow atheists struggled to find anything to support their beliefs from this area. They used words like 'catch 22' and 'chicken and egg' and recognised the impossibility of such a complex system forming naturally, without actually using the word impossible. Scientists have had fifty years to come up with a sensible proposal as to how this could occur and their sum effort was a collective shrug saying 'I dunno'.

Her mobile beeped. A text message appeared on the screen. It was from Luke. He wanted to meet her.

She looked back at the quote on the page. What if Ruth was right? What if she'd been wrong all these years? What if life wasn't the result of nature and there was a supernatural intelligence? What if it hated what she was doing as much as she did?

She shook her head. She didn't have a choice, she was in too deep now to turn back. She picked up her bag and headed out.

* * * *

"Williams is back."

"How do you know?" Helen asked.

Luke picked up a mobile and held it in front of her.

"He left a message on her phone."

He put the phone back down on the dashboard of his Mercedes

"He could have been calling from anywhere."

"It was a UK mobile number."

"It still could have come from overseas."

"It wasn't his number. How did he get a phone with a UK number from another country? He's back."

Helen looked through the windscreen. They were parked next to a dilapidated council leisure centre, facing the beach. She could see a ten-metre kite bobbing in the air as it moved across the water. That was where she wanted to be.

"How far have you got with the contingency plan?" Luke asked.

"I visited two of them yesterday. Both were up for it. They're going to the police tomorrow."

"That's good. It'll tie in nicely with the story in the newspapers. Forget about the third, you have more important work to do now."

"Do you want me to wait in his flat?"

"The police will be watching it."

"How are we going to get hold of him then?"

Luke handed her Ruth's mobile. "His number is in the call list, but wait till I get back to HQ. I have something I need to do first."

* * * *

Ben sat on a bench on the upper promenade and watched the small building at Black Rock station fifty feet below. The Volks Railway, which ran for a mile between Brighton Pier and the Marina, was the oldest electric railway in the world.

He heard voices and turned to see a couple walking towards him. He pulled down the peak of his baseball cap.

A green Renault Megane parked on the road running next to the railway. He recognised the diminutive figure that stepped out. He stood up, leaned over the railings and looked along the promenade in both directions. She was alone. He ran down a set of steps, crossed the road and caught up with Amanda as she wandered around the small building.

"Amanda," he said. He bent down and kissed the forty-year-old consultant on the cheek.

She was wearing a pink T-shirt that hung loosely on her thin frame. A short skirt made her look younger than she was.

He pulled one of the vials out of his pocket and handed it to her. He was hanging on to the other one in case she let him down.

"I need you to run tests on this," he said.

"What's going on?"

"I can't tell you."

"I won't do anything until I know more," she said.

"What have you heard about the killings?" Ben asked.

"I heard that two men had been murdered in Kenya and you were somehow involved."

"I did kill one of them," Ben said, trying to suppress the memory of Vernon's skull splitting open. "I didn't have a choice. It was either him or me. He'd already killed the other guy, who just happened to be in his way. They'll stop at nothing to get what they want. They've murdered dozens of people all over the world. If you know why I need these tests, they might come after you as well."

"What have you got yourself into?" Amanda asked, her face full of concern.

He shook his head. "A nightmare, that's what."

"Why don't you go to the police and tell them the truth?"

"Not yet." He thought about what to say. "Once I have the results I will."

Amanda looked at the tube. "What tests do you want?"

"HIV, CD4 count and presence of anti-retrovirals. How long do you think it'll take?"

"It's Sunday Ben. There's only one tech on duty. I'm just there to catch up on my paperwork."

"This is the most important sample you'll ever receive. I wouldn't ask you to do this if I didn't have to."

Amanda sighed and then put the vial in her pocket. "I'll get the tech onto it straight away. I can have the results in an hour and a half."

He pulled a credit card slip out of his wallet, scribbled down his new mobile number and handed it to her.

"Call me when he's finished," he said.

They walked to her car in silence.

"Do you need a lift anywhere?" Amanda asked.

"I'm fine. Get back to the lab, I need those results."

Amanda got in the Megane and drove away.

Ben climbed the steps back up to the main road and waited at a bus stop. After five minutes he boarded a bus to Hove. He arrived at the stop nearest his home just after one-thirty. He turned up the street to his flat. He stayed on the opposite side to his block and looked at the cars parked along the road. He continued past the building. After twenty yards he noticed two men sitting in a Vectra. He pulled his collar up and looked away as he continued walking along the pavement. He passed the car. No one got out.

He reached the end of the street and slipped into a newsagent. He picked up a magazine and pretended to flick through it as he looked out of the store's window. There was no sign of the Vectra or either of the men who'd been inside.

He couldn't be sure whether they were from Marivant or just there by coincidence. There was no way he could risk going into his flat. He put the magazine down and headed back towards the centre of Hove.

He bought a sandwich and a large Americano from Coffee Republic, then carried them down to the beach.

In spite of the sun a stiff sea breeze made it feel cold. He zipped up his jacket then sat on the shingle and leaned back against a wall looking out to sea. A kite-surfer caught the lip of a wave and launched high into the air, performing a somersault before he returned to the surface.

A seagull landed a few yards away and stared at his sandwich hopefully. He tossed it a piece of crust. Two more seagulls landed near the first and edged towards him. He finished the sandwich and put the wrapper in his jacket pocket. The birds lost interest and turned to face the sea, their white plumage ruffled by the breeze.

He looked at his watch. Two twenty-five. If Amanda had been right he should hear from her within the next half-hour. He closed his eyes. He just wanted to know for sure, then it would all be over. If the sample confirmed that Esau didn't have HIV, he had his proof that Spiravex was a cure. What he did with that proof was the next problem.

The police or a government agency were no good, they were hunting for him in connection with two murders, they wouldn't listen. The other alternative was the press. He had a contact who was an old University friend of Julia's, a reporter for 'The Telegraph'. He should jump at a story like this. It would be the biggest story since Nine-Eleven, with far wider consequences. The government and police would be forced to look into it. Once the scientists confirmed the truth, he would be pardoned.

His phone beeped.

Amanda.

He pulled it out of his pocket and opened the text. It wasn't from Amanda, it was from Ruth. 'Check your email.'

He dialled Ruth's number, but it went straight to voicemail. He frowned at the phone. Maybe she was in a gallery and couldn't talk. He finished his coffee and got to his feet. He headed back to the coffee shop, bought twenty minutes of Internet time and then headed upstairs.

There were two computer terminals by the toilets. He sat down next to a young Latin guy who was writing an email. He brought up the hospital server, typed his password and opened his inbox. There were fifty-seven new messages. He went through the list of names, but couldn't see anything from Ruth. He scanned through a second time, looking at the subject title rather than sender details. It was then that he realised it wasn't Ruth who'd sent the text.

His phone rang. He tore his eyes away from the screen and pulled out his mobile. It was a Brighton number. He answered it.

"Hello?"

"Ben?"

"Yes."

"It's Amanda, I've got the results."

Chapter 27

Ben looked at the screen again and clicked on the message.

"Ben?" Amanda said. "Do you want to know the results?"

"Yes," he replied. "I'm sorry, of course I do."

"Should I call you back?"

"No. What have you got for me?"

"What were you expecting?"

He decided not to prime her, he wanted her unbiased interpretation of the results. "I have no idea."

"It's good news," Amanda said. "There's no trace of any HIV."

"And his CD4?"

"Well, that's the weird thing. Is this guy immuno-compromised for some reason other than HIV?" Amanda asked.

"I don't think so. Why?"

"His CD4 count is only two-seventy. Has he been positive in the past but come off treatment recently?"

"Were there any drugs in his sample?" Ben asked.

"No," Amanda replied.

"Well he hasn't been on treatment then." The mouse cursor hovered over the file entitled 'ruth.jpg'. "I've got to go. Thanks Amanda."

He clicked on the file. The screen filled with a picture of Ruth. She was sitting on a bed with a gun pushed into her left temple.

"Be careful man," the guy next to him said. "That stuff's illegal."

He was in no state to come up with a reply. He closed the file, but the image would stay with him for the rest of his life.

His phone beeped. He read the message.

'Meet me in twenty minutes. King Alfred car park.'

He put the phone in his pocket and shut down his email. His little sister, the only family he had. What had he done? He should've listened to her.

He slowly got to his feet then made his way downstairs and outside.

He walked towards the seafront and tried to focus on what lay ahead. He knew for certain that Spiravex was the cure. Esau's sample was free of the virus after months without treatment, and his CD4 count had risen over two hundred since his last check-up: the virus was defeated.

He had the evidence he needed, but he couldn't touch Marivant now. The picture of Ruth overwhelmed all other thoughts. He had to save her.

He reached the seafront and turned right towards the crumbling King Alfred Leisure Centre. As well as years of neglect the art-deco building had suffered the further indignity of having a series of multi-coloured water flumes inserted into its backside.

The car park came into view. He hesitated and leaned against the wall of the swimming pool. He should walk away. The right thing to do was to sacrifice his sister for the greater cause. That just wasn't going to happen though. He pushed away from the wall and entered the car park.

A horn sounded. The sight of the stunning brunette, staring at him from a Mercedes convertible, confused him into a half-smile. The effect was short-lived. He walked over and stood by the passenger door.

"Where is she?"

"Get in."

"I'm not going anywhere until I know she's alright."

"You're not in a position to bargain," Helen said. "Get in."

"I know the truth."

"That doesn't really matter now does it?" Helen leaned over and pulled the passenger door handle. "Get in Ben."

He opened the door and sat down next to her.

She started the engine and drove out of the car park onto the road that ran along the seafront.

Under different circumstances he would have revelled in the moment. Every time Helen stopped at a set of lights day-trippers stared at them from the busy pavements; more specifically, men stared at her and the car.

"So what is the truth?" Helen asked.

"Why do I need to tell you?"

"Don't you want to know whether you're right or not?"

"Aren't you ashamed of what you've done?" he asked. "Condemning millions to death."

"You don't catch HIV from standing next to someone on a bus. These millions have condemned themselves to death."

"The children too?"

"They're better off dead. Once their parents are gone they'll be sold into slavery or something."

"I didn't take you for such a heartless bitch," he said. "I bet you'd feel differently if you or someone you loved had HIV."

"If you feel that strongly about these millions of people, why are you prepared to trade them for your sister?"

He folded his arms and looked out of the window.

"You're no better than me," she said. "You're so blinded by your genes that you'd sacrifice millions for the sake of one member of your family."

He took in a deep breath.

"Don't beat yourself up over it," she continued. "You wouldn't have got anywhere with your claims. We've already taken care of that."

He turned and looked at her.

"What do you mean?"

"You'll see."

He stared out of the passenger window in angry silence until they'd travelled about ten miles north along the A23.

"Where are we going?" he asked.

"You'll find out."

"I want to see Ruth."

"All in good time."

"You're not taking me to her now?"

She looked across at him and shook her head.

"Stop the car," Ben said.

"Why?"

"Unless I see my sister there's no point in going any further."

"Haven't you got it?" Helen said. "You don't call the shots, we do."

"How do I know she's even alive?"

"You saw the picture."

"But I don't know how old that is."

"You'll have to trust me."

"Forgive me if I find that a bit difficult," he said. But there was nothing he could do. He looked across at the woman he'd started to fall for a week earlier. "How much are they paying you for this?"

"Enough," she replied.

He shook his head. "I must be a really useless judge of character."

"You were attracted to my looks. There's a big difference."

"Do you think you're the first good-looking woman I've met? I thought I'd met someone who was smart, lively and thought the same way I do. How was I to know you were lying?"

There were a few moments silence.

"If you felt that way why were you so quick to leave last Monday?"

"I had a change of a heart," he said.

They took a turning off the A23 onto a minor A road. They wound through the Sussex countryside for a quarter of an hour, and arrived outside the Princess Royal Hospital in Haywards Heath. She turned the engine off, pulled her mobile out and dialled a number.

"Yes," she said. "The Hilton, one hour. Fine." She hung up. "We can't stay here long, but I need to show you something."

She hit a button on the dashboard. There was a dampened clunk followed by a whirring. A few seconds later the roof passed over Ben's head and fitted into place. They both got out and walked into the modern NHS hospital. Ben had passed along the bright corridors twice before to give lectures on HIV to the local GPs. The close proximity of one of the world's busiest international airports meant the area was full of promiscuous airline staff and their accompanying sexual diseases.

They walked past the bustling A & E reception to the intensive-care ward. There were five beds surrounded by an array of electronic monitors. The lights were dimmed creating a subdued atmosphere. Helen approached the Ward Sister.

"We're here to see Anne Faraday."

"I'm sorry, visiting hours are over," the Sister said. "You'll have to come back this evening."

"We don't want to wake her. We just want to check how she is."

The Sister glanced across at one of the beds. "Be very quiet. She needs all the rest she can get."

226

"Is she going to be OK?" Helen asked.

"We think so, but she's suffered a lot. Have the police any idea who did it yet?"

"No," Helen said.

They left the nurses' station and walked over to where the Sister had been looking.

The face of the woman lying on the bed was swollen with cuts and bruises. Her left arm was in a cast, and her ribs were bandaged.

"Take a good look," Helen whispered. "The man who did this is looking after your sister right now."

Ben started shaking with rage. He wanted to strangle her. He'd never felt such hatred in his life.

"Let's go," she said.

He followed her in silence to the car park. Seeing a picture of Ruth with a gun to her head was bad enough, but to think she could end up in the same condition as that woman was pushing him to the limit.

Helen started the car. "Don't ever deceive yourself that the organisation you're dealing with is anything but ruthless."

He didn't respond.

She reversed the car out of its space and put the shift into drive.

* * * *

Forty minutes later Ben was sitting in a suite at the Gatwick Hilton, staring at the coffee table in front him. He'd moved his chair so he didn't have to look at Helen, who was leaning against the window frame behind him. There was a knock at the door.

Helen walked past him, crossed the room and opened the door.

Ben recognised the visitor.

"Doctor Williams," Luke said. "You must enjoy my company, why else would you have ignored my warning?"

"I want proof my sister's OK," he said. "I'm not doing anything till I see her."

Luke glared at Helen like this was a matter she should have resolved, then looked back at Ben.

"If you don't do as we say, the last thing you will ever see will be your sister being tortured to death," Luke said. "It's only because of our client that you're alive now. But I'm not a patient man, I'd advise you to be careful."

"Why did you try to kill me in Africa?"

"Are you going to obey us?" Luke asked.

"Keep quiet about Spiravex?"

Luke smiled. "If that was all we wanted then killing you would be the most simple option," he said. "We want Kimani. You get him for us, you get your sister back."

"Get him yourself," Ben said.

Luke flicked his jacket back and pulled a pistol out. He strode over to Ben and put the gun against his head. He gripped Ben's collar and pulled him closer.

"You know damn well he's hiding," Luke said. "Just think of your sister."

Ben focused on the print of Constable's 'Haywain' hanging on the wall opposite. He wished he was the driver of the cart as he crossed the tranquil scene of lost England.

"Go on. Give me an excuse," Luke said. "I'm bored of this assignment. Let me finish it now."

He felt Luke's grip tighten on his collar.

"Will you deliver Kimani to us?" Helen asked.

Ben looked down.

Luke let go and walked a few paces away.

"My client wants to see you," he said, his back to Ben.

"Your client?"

Luke turned and looked at him as though he was stupid.

"Marivant?" he said.

"Of course Marivant." Luke put his hand inside his jacket pocket and pulled out a digital camera. "Helen, close the curtains."

She leaned behind Ben. He felt the skin of her arm brush against his neck as she pulled the curtain across.

"Sit still," Luke said.

"Like to take pictures so you can boast to your other psychopathic friends?" Ben said.

"You can't use your own passport. You're too hot after what happened in Mombassa. We need to create a fake ID."

Ben looked at the camera. The flash momentarily blinded him. He blinked the red square of light away and saw Luke looking at the display on the back of the camera.

"That'll do," Luke said, and put the camera in his pocket. "Both of you are booked on the nine am British Airways flight to Chicago."

"You want me to go too?" Helen asked.

* * * *

By three pm on Tuesday Ben and Helen were sitting in the back of a Lincoln town car. They'd barely spoken for the previous twenty-four hours, and now they sat as far apart as possible looking out of opposite windows.

The car pulled up in front of a pair of tall security gates. A slab of granite sat on a grassy mound to the left, the words 'Marivant Park' engraved on it.

An armed guard appeared out of a brick hut and spoke to the driver. Ben pulled his elbow away from the window as it lowered into the door. The guard leaned forward and looked in the back. He straightened up, patted the roof of the car and walked back to the hut. The gates began to open.

He'd heard about this place from a Marivant rep a couple of years earlier. It was supposed to be the size of a small town, covering hundreds of acres of Michigan countryside. All Marivant's US operations were sited there.

They passed through a short stretch of woodland into the main industrial campus. On either side of the road lay buildings encased within steaming pipe work; metal chimneys reached into the sky, filling the air with a sulphurous stench.

The driver navigated through a warren of roads leading towards grey buildings that housed research and production units. They followed a sign to the Global Corporate Headquarters, and passed though another section of woodland into a broad expanse of landscaped gardens. A four-storey office block, clad in blue glass, stood at the far end of a car park filled with non-descript corporate sedans.

The Lincoln stopped in front of the main entrance and the driver got out. He walked round to Helen's door and opened it.

Ben followed Helen up the steps, through a revolving door into a stone lobby. Two plasma screens hung on the walls to either side: both showing CNN. The Marivant stock price flashed on an LCD monitor above the reception desk; beneath it an animated chart displayed the company's year-to-date performance against its major competitors. It wouldn't have been there if it didn't look impressive.

That was what it was all about: shareholder value. The customers, the patients, even the staff, came second to keeping Wall Street happy.

"Helen Richardson and Ben Williams," Helen said to the young Asian receptionist. "We're here to see Doctor Shackleton."

The woman picked up her phone and dialled a number. She spoke briefly then hung up. "Take a seat. His secretary will be down in a minute."

Ben and Helen sat on one of the designer couches. He looked at the screen on the opposite wall. Tanned talking heads were speaking in cringing tones about Politics. Behind them a picture of Capitol Hill was superimposed onto the Stars and Stripes, which rippled majestically. It did nothing for him; national pride was a repugnant sentiment. Having a mother from a wealthy American oil family, a father from a mining family in the Welsh valleys, and then growing up in Africa and England, he struggled to feel loyalty for any particular nation or culture.

As a boy he'd felt like an outcast when his friends cheered for their motherland's football teams. As an adult he'd come to realise that his lack of national identity was a blessing. The whole concept of patriotism was as abstract and perverse as religion; it was slavery to an intangible and fickle master. How could anyone really think they belonged to a land or vice versa? If you believed that, then only Aborigines had the right to call themselves true Australians. History showed that entire nations of people could be displaced or obliterated, and the land possessed by a more aggressive tribe whose descendants will judge it theirs by right. So what if he was half American? It didn't mean a thing.

"Doctor Williams, Doctor Richardson?" a stern-looking woman asked as she passed through a waist-high security barrier. "Please come with me."

They got up and followed the woman back through the barrier to a bank of elevators. They rode up to the fourth floor. The door opened onto a wide semi-circular lobby presided over by another receptionist. She smiled politely at them.

They followed the secretary down a corridor, passing a number of private offices on either side. He glanced at the nameplates; all had 'Director' of this or 'Vice-president' of that after them. They reached the end of the passage and entered through the most imposing door. There was a brass plaque engraved with the words 'Dr P. Shackleton, Global Medical Director'. They were shown into a suite of rooms. The first was a small reception area. He could see through an open door into a conference room to the left. Straight ahead was a set of tall chrome double doors. The secretary walked up to them and knocked.

"Come in," a voice called from inside.

The secretary pushed one of the doors open, motioned for them to walk past her, then closed it behind them. They were left facing Shackleton, who was standing by his desk.

He had thick silver hair that was combed back neatly. His face was lean, with lines etched around the corners of his eyes and mouth from years of corporate smiling. He wore a dark grey suit tailored to his slim form.

His office had views over the surrounding parkland. The conservative decor reflected the occupant's status. Two chairs were positioned in front of a mahogany desk.

Shackleton walked towards them and extended a hand to Ben.

"Pleased to meet you at long last," he said.

Ben ignored his hand. "This is hardly a cosy business meeting."

Shackleton's smile faded and he gave Ben a begrudging nod. He turned to Helen and shook her hand. "Nice to put a face to a name."

He walked back to his desk. "Please," he said, his palms outstretched, "take a seat."

They both sat down.

"Doctor Richardson, I wanted you to be here so you could find out a little more about your assignment. I know it isn't standard practice to be so transparent in your organisation, but I felt it would be appropriate if you understood exactly what is going on, especially since you are going to be following this through to the end. But I need to make one thing clear before I say another word. Nothing I tell you can go beyond this room."

"I'm aware of the history of Spiravex," Helen said.

"I'd be very surprised if you were," Shackleton said. "Only a handful of people know the entire truth."

"It's our job to find out information," Helen said.

"We'll see." Shackleton turned to Ben. "So you've been to Kenya, Doctor Williams?"

"You know I have."

"And what did you discover?"

"You tell me."

Shackleton nodded. "I take it you found patient eighty-seven, otherwise known as Esau Kimani?"

Ben remained expressionless.

"The only patient in study MVT084 not to be accounted for," Shackleton continued.

"I think you mean murdered," Ben said.

"Doctor Williams, we've brought you here so we can co-operate. Please hear me out before you use words like murder."

"Do you really think I'm feeling co-operative? You murdered my wife and you've kidnapped my sister."

Shackleton's expression filled with concern. "I am very sorry for what's happened to your family. It is most unfortunate."

Ben let out a bitter laugh.

"I know that an apology isn't enough, but it's all I can offer at the moment," Shackleton said.

"You could order Ruth's release for a start."

"That will happen in due course, but we must be able to rely on you. We need insurance, Doctor Williams, there's a lot at stake."

"Billions if my calculations are correct," Ben said.

"Much more than that."

Ben sighed impatiently.

"So I take it you met Mister Kimani, and found out that he's HIV negative?" Shackleton said. "Am I right?"

"Why do you assume that?"

"Because you say that billions are at stake. You think we're trying to bury Spiravex because it's the cure for HIV. You believe we have suppressed the results of the trial to protect our HIV portfolio and future profitability."

He didn't answer. Shackleton's direct approach had wrong-footed him.

"How long have you been a doctor?"

"Long enough."

Shackleton pulled a file across the desk and opened it. "You qualified in ninety-two." He looked up. "You've practiced medicine for nearly two decades. You strike me as being an intelligent and balanced man, not prone to conspiracy theories. Let me ask you this. Before recent events, what was your impression of the pharmaceutical industry?"

He shrugged. "Mixed."

"In what way?"

"We depend on your drugs to treat our patients, but because pharmaceutical corporations are driven by profit, the interests of the patients sometimes appear to be forgotten."

"It is always in our interest to put the patient first," Shackleton said, "they are our end-user after all. But if, in the final analysis, patient interests come a close second to making a profit, that is the price we pay for living in a free-market democracy. We have to make money to put bread on the table."

"And pay for your company car and share options."

Shackleton turned a couple of pages in the folder.

"And your generous NHS salary buys you an Audi sports car and a private top-up pension scheme, some of which no doubt consists of pharmaceutical stock. I think it would be fair to say that anyone who works in the healthcare industry who earns more than a subsistence wage is profiting from it. That aside, Doctor Williams, in your experience would you say companies like ours operate in a reasonably ethical manner?"

He paused and thought about it. The truth was that other than the occasional over-zealous rep, the big pharma companies were ethical. He'd spent a month working on a research project in the Makerere Infectious Diseases Institute in Uganda, an organisation funded by Pfizer, so he knew the pharmaceutical industry put money back into the community. They made mistakes, and sometimes they were too slow to correct them, but in general his experience had been positive. "Most of the time, yes I would."

"That's because we are ethical, and people like me exist to ensure it stays that way. I sit on the Board of this organisation along with the Commercial, Operational and Research Directors. There is always conflict between the desire to provide life-enhancing medicines and the desire to make a profit. Like everyone else here, I have stock options, and I would be a liar if I didn't admit that I wanted them to provide for me in my old age. But at the same time, I am a man of medicine. I took the Hippocratic oath, just as you did, and I want to see people's lives improved through our products. I am very privileged to have worked on teams producing excellent drugs. I couldn't sleep at night if I wasn't sure this organisation did its best to make that its priority. Yes, we have to stay profitable, but not at any cost. There are many more men and women like myself sitting on the boards of other pharmaceutical corporations, Doctor Williams. We act as a moral brake to any reckless greed that might surface and we push for investment in philanthropic projects." He paused, his expression simmering with resentment. "Your suggestion that we would try to suppress a cure is highly offensive."

Ben held Shackleton's stare. "Righteous indignation is a bit rich coming from someone who has overseen the deaths of a hundred innocent people."

Shackleton looked down for a moment and took a breath. When he looked back up the anger had gone.

"The situation we found ourselves in with Spiravex was uniquely perilous, and presented us with a dilemma that required swift and decisive action." Shackleton leaned forward, a grave expression on his face. "Your test on Esau only revealed half the truth, Doctor Williams."

Chapter 28

"Why should I believe you?" Ben asked. "Everything points to Spiravex being a cure."

"I can understand why you think it does. A year ago we held the same belief. I remember the day we first caught a glimpse of what we thought was Spiravex's full potential. We'd been conducting tests on apes for five months. All ten had undetectable viral loads. As you're probably aware, that's not uncommon with modern anti-retrovirals. Then one of the chimpanzees developed an unrelated infection and needed treatment with antibiotics. Our protocol demands that we exclude results if other drugs are added to the regimen. We took the chimp off Spiravex, but continued to monitor the progress of the virus. Two months later the Head of Animal Research informed me that the virus hadn't returned. The results were checked and double-checked, there was no doubt about it, the chimp appeared to be cured." Shackleton smiled. "They were the best days of my career, we thought we were on the edge of one of the greatest discoveries of our time."

"Why didn't we hear about it?" Ben asked.

"You did," Shackleton replied.

"I don't remember anything."

"When I say you, I mean the scientific community. We published a paper in an obscure journal and presented the results in an ambiguous way. You'd be right to assume this was to avoid publicity. There have been many false dawns in HIV research. Remember AZT?"

"That was completely different," Ben said. "The press announced a cure on the basis of just a few weeks' data, at a time when testing techniques were much more primitive. They didn't know about HIV's ability to mutate and evolve. There was no way of predicting all the patients would develop resistance within months. Things have changed. We know a lot more about the virus now. Your discovery should have been better publicised."

"We didn't see it that way," Shackleton said. "History has a knack of repeating itself. Therefore we decided to proceed cautiously. Subsequent events have proved that decision to be wise."

"Wisdom had nothing to do with it Shackleton, it was pure selfishness. Science only progresses when people share ideas."

"I'm not saying we acted entirely without self-interest. Of course we wanted to keep our competitors ignorant for as long as possible. It wasn't just those on the outside we had to worry about either. Knowing how porous organisations like ours can be, we ensured that only the minimal number of employees within the US and UK divisions were aware that Spiravex might be a cure. The vast majority of Marivant staff were misled into believing that it was merely another promising class of anti-retroviral."

"You even lie to each other!" Ben said.

"We felt it was the right thing to do," Shackleton replied. "Anyway, the next step was to confirm it wasn't an isolated anomaly. We took all the apes off Spiravex. Two months later there wasn't a single chimp with detectable SIV."

"What's SIV?" Helen asked.

"Simian Immuno-deficiency Virus, the ape equivalent of HIV," Ben said quickly, without looking at her.

"Thank you," Shackleton said. "After this we ran a couple of brief phase-one trials. The results from these established that Spiravex was safe and gave us an idea of what happened to the drug when it was metabolized by the body. It had all the hallmarks of a blockbuster therefore we pressed ahead with phase-two trials and began recruiting for MVT084. This was the trial that would conclusively confirm whether Spiravex was a cure, since it would be tested on HIV-positive patients.

"We were nervous, but excited. We allowed ourselves to start thinking the impossible. Even the commercial directors in the loop barely mentioned the downside of losing revenue from long-term treatment. We are a vast organisation, Doctor Williams. Our HIV portfolio represents less than two percent of our annual revenue, and that proportion will become even less significant when one of our HIV drugs comes off patent in the next few years. Believe me when I say there was never any talk of burying this product."

A tremor of uncertainty rumbled in the foundations of Ben's theory. He'd only looked at MVT084 through his HIV-tunnel vision, and had never taken into account Marivant's global presence in virtually every other area of medicine.

"Nothing you tell me will excuse the murder of my wife or a hundred innocent people."

"We didn't kill those people." Shackleton looked at Helen.

"Slade did," she said.

"The CIA insisted on that path," Shackleton added.

Ben's mouth fell open. "The US Government knows about this?" he asked.

"We needed all the help we could get. They weren't directly involved for political reasons. The fact is that we were, and still might be facing a catastrophe that makes HIV look as innocuous as an outbreak of the common cold."

"Sounds like the politics of fear," Ben said. "I can't think of a disease more threatening than HIV."

Shackleton took a deep breath, sighed and looked down at the desk in front of him.

"Our hopes were crushed when we were halfway through MVT084," he shook his head. "At first there was just disappointment, huge disappointment. Can you imagine what it felt like? One minute you're part of a team of scientists who will be celebrated across the world, the next minute..." He paused and looked at Ben. The corporate façade lifted for a second to reveal eyes that had seen dreams shattered. "It was like watching the lottery, and the same numbers you've been using for years come up one by one on the screen. Just as you run to tell your wife, you remember you forgot to buy a ticket."

"What happened?" Helen asked.

"So you don't know the truth?"

"Obviously not."

"Shame on you," Shackleton said.

"I had nothing to do with the patients' deaths."

"At least your conscience is free from that." Shackleton looked down again. "I keep telling myself there was no choice." He shook his head.

"There's always a choice." This guy was responsible for killing his wife, he couldn't believe he hadn't decked him, or worse. "What possible justification is there for what you've done?"

"We first saw it in the chimps." Shackleton recovered his statesmanlike demeanour. "Every Monday morning we received a report on their status. Week after week for nearly a year we saw nothing, no trace of the virus; we barely read the reports anymore. Then one morning we received an email informing us one of the chimps had died. Within a month they were all dead. The pathologist reported the same cause in all cases, accelerated systemic apoptosis."

"Sorry?" Helen said. "What did they die of?"

"Cell apoptosis is medical jargon for cell death," Ben said. "It happens everyday inside of you, but if it becomes widespread and accelerated your internal organs literally dissolve." He turned back to Shackleton. "That sounds like Ebola. There's no way Spiravex could cause that."

"It wasn't Spiravex, but a metabolite of the drug that proved to be the cause. Spiravex is broken down in the liver into two components, both of which are active against HIV, but in different ways. They both acted as entry inhibitors stopping the viral particles entering and infecting host cells but via different co-receptors, the CXCR4 and CCR5, they also mimicked chemokines and purged the latent CD4 infected cells..."

"Wait," Helen said, holding up a hand. "You've completely lost me now. CRC5? Chemokines?"

"OK," Shackleton said. "Imagine that our CD4 immune cells have gates on their surface that allow certain chemicals to enter. Now they wouldn't just want any old rubbish wandering in and out, so these gates have locks which can only be opened by certain keys. The HIV virus has developed the ability to unlock two of these locks and enter the CD4 cell and eventually destroy it. If you jam a key into both of these locks, then the virus cannot enter. That's what these two metabolites did. Spiravex was effectively two drugs in one."

Helen nodded.

It still didn't explain why the virus was present and undetectable at the same time though.

"If the apes were undetectable for nearly a year without taking any anti-retrovirals, they couldn't have had any SIV left," Ben said. "Surely it must have been a haemorrhagic disease peculiar to chimpanzees that killed them. Ebola does come from monkeys."

Shackleton shook his head. "Just because the samples were undetectable doesn't mean the subjects didn't have any virus."

"But it does if they weren't taking any drugs. If there are no drugs then the virus can start replicating again."

"Not if the virus is somewhere hidden from normal tests. We discovered another property that distinguished the two metabolites other than the locks that they fitted. The first metabolite is less effective at crossing the blood-brain barrier, the membrane that separates the central nervous system, or CNS, from the rest of the body, but the metabolite that acted as a CXCR4 inhibitor was able to cross it at will. Although this metabolite had been working in the CNS to destroy the virus, it failed because it was now working alone. The result was the emergence of a mutant strain of virus which itself wasn't able to cross the blood brain barrier and so stayed hidden in the CNS. This meant that samples taken from normal blood would always remain undetectable."

The rumble travelled through the walls and shook dust from the rafters. Since coming up with his theory Ben had seen Marivant's request for CNS samples as evidence of the cover up. He had suspected they used the samples to determine who had been cured, then killed them once they knew. The fact that the resistant strain hid in the CNS suggested a different reason.

"How did the metabolite create this mutant virus?" Helen asked.

"Do you understand how resistance develops?" Shackleton said.

"I'm not a virologist."

"Neither am I, but I've had to think like one for the past year." Shackleton looked at Ben. "Would you mind if I explain?"

Ben shook his head. He gave the impression it was a reluctant concession, but in reality he was eager to hear what Shackleton had to say. The whole area of mutations was one that he struggled with.

"Viral resistance is really nano-scale evolution. How familiar are you with the science of evolution Doctor Richardson?"

"I've read some of Dawkins' books."

"Then you will be aware that species adapt or evolve because of selective pressure. One route by which a species can advance is when an individual is born with a genetic mutation that confers a competitive advantage over its peers. This enables it to get the best resources more effectively."

"Like the first animal that developed an eye," Helen said.

"Developing an eye in one step is impossible, but yes, the first animal that had a genetic mutation which produced a light-sensitive patch had an advantage over its peers.

"Another way that evolution works is when an individual has a mutation that enables it to cope better with sudden changes in the environment. A good illustration of this is the extinction of the dinosaurs, probably due to an event that triggered global cooling. Warm-blooded mammals, which had previously been a sideshow, were better adapted to cope with the drop in temperature. In the absence of the predatory dinosaurs, mammals were able to proliferate and rule the food chain on land.

"This last example is analogous to what happens when HIV develops resistance to drugs. HIV is a very sloppy virus and produces millions of mutations in its genetic code every day. In the absence of external environmental pressures, these mutant strains are normally less effective at competing for resources, just like mammals were when dinosaurs ruled the earth. As a result, they die off or are pushed to the sidelines.

"However, when you change the environment by adding a drug, you apply selective pressure. The drug destroys the normal virus, leaving behind a few viral particles with mutations in its code that cause the drug not to work thus making it resistant. Just as the cold didn't kill the mammals, these few mutant viral particles are unaffected by the drug and are able to flourish in the absence of the fitter virus. That is when resistance is born and why we use combinations of drugs. If you have a second or third drug present it is much less likely that a viral particle exists that has resistance to all three."

"Ok, but why would this mutation that makes it resistant to one of the lock blocking drugs stop it crossing the blood-brain barrier?" Ben asked.

"The chemical key that unlocks the host immune cell allowing the virus to enter, sits on the surface of the virus. The mutation that makes the virus resistant to the drug therefore changes the chemical structure of the virus surface. The blood-brain barrier is designed to repel certain types of chemical and this change on the surface of the virus not only made it resistant, but also made

240

it look like one of these chemicals it should repel, leaving it trapped in the CNS."

"That's why you asked for monthly CNS samples from the surviving patients," Ben said. If Shackleton was telling the truth then the results from Esau's blood test were meaningless, he needed a CNS sample too.

"It's also why the CD4 count continued to rise," Shackleton said, "the immune system outside of the CNS was able to recover."

"If the immune system wasn't being compromised how could this new virus kill the chimps?" Helen asked.

"New viral strains arise in a variety of ways and for a variety of reasons. This first mutant strain prevailed due to environmental changes brought about by the addition of Spiravex, like the mammalian example I gave earlier. But the virus was still sloppy and generated millions of mutations during its replication cycle. It was only a matter of time before it created a second mutant strain that was fitter than itself, and was therefore able to predominate."

"Like the evolutionary example with the light-sensitive patch," Helen said. "Only a new mutation occurs that gives one of these creatures, a second patch."

"Exactly like that. The virus generated a second mutation that changed its surface. This new mutation had a number of beneficial effects on its ability to interact with its surroundings. Firstly, the mutation changed the chemical appearance of the virus again and allowed it to cross back over the blood-brain barrier and infect the whole body. Secondly, it had become resistant to all other HIV drugs, and thirdly, it was able to attach to virtually every type of cell, not just immune cells, as was the case with normal HIV."

"Is that why it behaves like Ebola?" Helen asked.

"Yes, but its progress is not as quick as Ebola. For the first week or two there are no notable symptoms. During the second or third week the victim develops what appears to be a cold, which progressively worsens. It's after this that the virus reveals its true nature. The lining of your eyes start to bleed, your gums begin to dissolve, your skin peels off exposing raw flesh, and your heart collapses." Shackleton looked back and forth between Helen and Ben. "With the existing HIV it was the immune system that was destroyed, with this new strain everything it came into contact with was eventually liquefied. That is what killed the chimps and would have killed your wife."

"Why were the patients killed if they were just going to die anyway?" Helen asked.

"Let me guess," Ben said. "To avoid lawsuits."

"It would make more sense than your belief that we killed the patients to cover up a cure," Shackleton said. "As Doctor Richardson pointed out, the patients were going to die anyway, so why not stop them from suffering a hideous death and save ourselves a couple of billion dollars at the same time?"

He was tempted to nod and say 'exactly', but he knew damn well that Shackleton already had an answer to that question.

"The research on these apes had been conducted in a category A testing facility, where the scientists wore protective suits with an external air supply, so there was never any risk of the virus transferring to humans. However, in addition to the ten apes on the Spiravex trial, there had been thirty other apes undergoing tests with different drugs, all housed in separate cages."

"Had been?" Ben asked.

Shackleton nodded. "All of the apes died within a month."

"This one ape infected the other thirty-nine apes, including those not taking Spiravex?" Ben asked.

"Yes," Shackleton said, "which proved that this metabolite of Spiravex had selected a strain of HIV that was not only more deadly, but also airborne."

"How can you be sure that one of the other apes didn't have Ebola?"

"We traced the source of the new virus back to one of the original chimps in the Spiravex study," Shackleton continued. "It was the only one that had developed the HIV with two mutations. All the other chimps, including the ones taking Spiravex, died from a secondary infection caught from the first chimp. It only took one additional mutation in a single chimp to turn forty complex organisms into pools of festering slime. The fact that the advanced strain was able to bind to virtually any cell in the body meant saliva now became a suitable vector. One sneeze would contain enough virus to infect the entire population of Chicago."

"Did the other 9 chimps have SIV?" Ben asked.

"Two were healthy controls who were not taking any drugs at all, and yet they succumbed just as quickly as all the others."

"So Spiravex selected for a highly infectious killer virus?"

"I think you are beginning to understand the serious nature of this problem," Shackleton said. "To make matters worse, the pathology of this virus is very different from Ebola, making it far more insidious. For the first three to four days after the second mutation forms, as was the case with the original chimp, or a subject becomes infected, there are no symptoms and the virus is not contagious. At some point between day three and four, the virus enters the lungs and becomes airborne."

"How infectious is it?" Ben asked.

"If you were standing within a yard of someone with the second mutation and they were breathing, you'd get it."

"Even if the carrier doesn't appear to be ill?" Helen said.

"That's why it's more dangerous than Ebola, which overwhelms the patient so quickly that they become immobile and the disease cannot spread over a wide geographical area. With this mutant strain of HIV, the patient still doesn't show any symptoms during the first five to ten days after the virus becomes infectious. All that time they would be transferring it to everyone they come into contact with."

Once again no one spoke. The whole world seemed to be focused on that room. "But it was SIV. Surely the same thing wouldn't happen in humans?" Ben said.

"As soon as we found out the cause of the deaths in the apes we took CNS samples from all the patients in MVT084. Eight had already developed the strain of HIV with the first mutation."

"And it would just be a matter of time before one of them got the second mutation," Helen said. "So you called Slade in to deal with these patients and you stopped the study, citing heart attacks as the cause of death."

Shackleton nodded. He looked at Ben. "I am truly sorry, but maybe you can see now that we had no choice."

No answer came. He was back to square one. He'd given Julia a drug that caused her death. He responded to the thought as he always had. He shut it out.

"We immediately recalled the drug and tried to bury Spiravex for ever," Shackleton continued. "As well as the eight patients in the study, we had another problem to contend with, one which you brought to our attention, Doctor Richardson."

"Adam," Helen said.

"Doctor Sandford worked in our research facility in Oxford. In spite of our efforts to keep a lid on our hopes for Spiravex, he'd managed to learn about the early animal data. Like you, Doctor Williams, he made the assumption that we manufactured the heart attacks to destroy Spiravex and protect our profitability. His solution was to sell the data to a rogue generic company in India who would make the compound and supply it illegally. He believed he was doing it to help others, but if he'd succeeded, it would have been a disaster." He looked at Helen. "You may have unwittingly saved the world."

Helen looked stunned.

"Can you prove all this?" Ben asked. "I mean, how do I know you're not just making everything up to throw me off the scent?"

Shackleton nodded. "I have plenty of literature for you to examine."

The roof of Ben's theory finally caved in leaving him exposed to the harsh glare of the truth: he'd risked his life, and the life of his sister, for a half-baked theory that he hadn't properly thought through. But one hundred people had still been murdered.

"You killed the eight patients in October, what about the other ninety-two? Other than Julia, our patients only died in April."

"Initially our hope was that once Spiravex was withdrawn the chances of developing the first and second mutation would disappear with it."

"But the chimps had been taken off Spiravex and they still developed the mutations," Helen said.

"Because all our analysis was conducted through post mortems, we didn't know whether they developed the first mutation before or after Spiravex was stopped. The second mutation develops without any influence from the metabolite."

"So you gave the other patients every chance?" Helen said.

"The CIA wanted to eliminate all of them, but we pushed for a reprieve, although we couldn't take it for granted that the virus wouldn't progress, hence the requirement for CNS samples. This proved a wise decision. In late December two of the patients who hadn't taken Spiravex since October developed the first mutation."

"How?" Helen asked.

"We discovered that the metabolite which causes this mutation lingers in the CNS for months, even after the drug is stopped. By the end of February thirty patients had the first mutation. These were patients who had enrolled earlier on the trial than the remaining sixty, so it was sensible to conclude that all the patients would develop the first mutation. Once they reached this point, it was inevitable they would develop the second mutation at some later date."

"Why didn't you just quarantine them?" Ben asked.

"That was my preferred option. However, after consultation with the government, they decided it was too risky. Putting them into quarantine would have meant dealing with international bureaucracy and the delays this would have caused were unacceptable. Every day that these patients remained at large made human extinction a very real possibility. Elimination of the trial participants proved the most efficient response." Shackleton paused and looked straight at Ben. "Except one is still alive."

"Esau."

"Doctor Williams, you appear to be the only person who can reach Mister Kimani."

Ben looked at Shackleton and then at Helen. "You want me to hand him over to you so you can kill him?"

"This is about more than just one man's life." Shackleton took a deep breath. "The reality is, Doctor Williams, you hold the future of modern civilisation in your hands."

Chapter 29

Ben sat forward with his elbows on the arms of his chair and stared at the front of Shackleton's desk. If only he could turn back time two weeks. Instead of heading off the water that Tuesday afternoon, he'd race Ruth for a couple of hours and just leave Julia's memory to rest.

How was Ruth holding up? How were they treating her? At least before he heard Shackleton's story he believed it was all for a higher cause. That illusion was quickly fading.

"You said you can prove all of this," he said.

"The relevant data is sitting in the conference room waiting for you."

He nodded and leaned back. Something in his left pocket dug into him. He put his hand in to move it. His fingers closed around a plastic vial: Esau's second blood sample.

He pulled it out and looked at it. "You said it was sensible to conclude that all the patients would develop the first mutation and therefore go on to get the second mutation."

"That's correct," Shackleton replied.

"But do you know for sure whether they all did or not?"

"No, but there was a strong scientific assumption that they would."

"What about the eight apes taking Spiravex, did they all get the first mutation?"

"The thirty patients who acquired the mutation were among the first people to start the drug. There was a clear correlation between time and development of mutations."

"That wasn't my question," Ben said. "Did all ten apes get the first mutation or not?"

Shackleton raised his chin and stared at Ben. "No."

"How many didn't get it?"

"One."

"It had no HIV at all?"

"SIV," Shackleton said.

246

"Whatever, but it was cured?"

"We don't know. It may have just taken longer for it to develop."

"But all the other apes developed the first mutation within a year didn't they?"

Shackleton nodded.

"So the other one might have been cured," Ben shook his head. "That's more than ten percent."

"I don't see where this is going."

"Aside from the fact that you may have killed ten people who weren't a threat, it could be highly relevant to Esau's future." Ben held the tube up for Shackleton to see. "I have a sample of his blood."

Shackleton stared at the tube.

"I've already had it tested for HIV," Ben continued. "He's negative, which from what you're saying may not prove anything, but what if he hasn't got the mutated virus either? Surely there'd be no reason to kill him."

"That sample wouldn't tell us anything, we'd need one from the CNS to show whether he has the first mutation or not."

"But you could check whether he has the second mutation," Ben said.

"How would that help?"

"If he has then I'll take you to him."

"If he has then you might be infected, you could be a carrier."

"But he wasn't ill when I saw him."

"He still could have been infectious."

"Do the test and find out," Ben said.

"It's not that simple." Shackleton looked at the tube again. "You've only got ten mils there. It's not the standard HIV test so it would take at least forty-eight hours to generate enough DNA to determine whether it contains the second mutation. If you had a bigger sample we could do it overnight."

Ben put the tube on the desk. "That's all I have. I'll wait."

"We can't waste any more time. Kimani first took Spiravex over a year ago. Each day that passes increases the likelihood that he'll develop the second mutation. We can't afford for you to be waiting here for lab results. Our corporate jet is ready to leave O'Hare right now, and you need to be on it as soon as possible."

"Two days isn't going to hurt," Ben said.

"That could be the difference between seeing my grandchildren grow up and watching them being eaten alive by this virus."

"Just do the test. I don't want to know that I led an innocent man to his death without a very good reason."

Shackleton sighed and leaned forward to pick up the vial. "I know you don't. I had to make that decision for a hundred men and women, and in spite of your opinion of me, it goes against everything I believe in." He played with the sample in his hands. "I'll cut you a deal. Fly to Kenya and find Kimani. If the sample shows no trace of the second mutation then we'll allow you to bring him back here for further tests. But, if he's positive, you hand him over to Doctor Richardson."

Ben turned to Helen. She looked startled, like a school kid who'd been caught daydreaming by a teacher's question. She nodded.

"And if you bring him back here and he doesn't have the first mutation?" Ben asked.

"We'd let him live, but we'd want to keep him under permanent observation."

Maybe this hadn't been a waste of time. If he saved one man's life then everything would have been worth it.

"What about my sister?"

"She'll be released the moment we have Kimani."

Ben nodded.

"I want to see that evidence you've been talking about before I fly anywhere," Ben said.

"Follow me." Shackleton stood up and walked towards the door. Ben and Helen followed him into the conference room. It was larger than his private office, but the lack of windows and the long beech table lined with chairs made it feel less spacious. A plasma screen hung on the wall opposite the door. A black coffee machine sat on a sideboard next to two bottles of mineral water and a tray piled with packets of biscuits.

Three document wallets lay on the table beside a laptop. Two wires led from ports in the back and disappeared down a hole in the table. Marivant's corporate logo scrolled across the screen.

"Take a seat," Shackleton said.

Ben sat on the chair nearest the wallets and pulled them towards him. Helen sat opposite, folded her arms and looked down.

"Coffee?" Shackleton asked.

"Black, no sugar," Ben said.

"Doctor Richardson?"

Helen shook her head without looking up.

Shackleton made Ben a coffee and put it on the table.

"I'll leave you to it," he said. "The laptop is connected to the Internet. You can access any journal you like. Of course, the majority of the material is internal data."

The door closed, leaving the room silent except for the subdued wining of the laptop fan and the distant murmur of the building's air conditioning.

Ben opened the document wallet on top of the pile. The contents were mostly experiment forms and results tables. They were organised in chronological order.

The first set of data related to the chemistry used to develop the drug, and in-vitro cell culture results. He flicked through them quickly; there was one item he was looking for. He found it towards the end of the first file. It was the copy of the original paper that detailed the results from the trial in apes. It had been published in 'Anti-microbial Chemistry and Chemotherapy', a journal that he wasn't familiar with.

He pulled the laptop towards him and looked over the screen. Helen still had her arms folded; she was blinking erratically and her eyes were red.

He looked back at the laptop. If she was feeling remorse, it was way too late.

She got up and walked out of the room.

He entered the Internet and searched for the journal. It was genuine, a publication from the American Society for Microbiology. He accessed their website, pulled up the relevant issue and read the paper from the screen. He didn't trust the copy Shackleton had given him; it could have been doctored.

By the time he'd finished he knew Shackleton had told the truth about the ape study. If they'd published the data in 'Nature' or 'The Lancet', placing a clear emphasis on the potential implications, the article would have caused a frenzy of excitement. So that part of the story was true, but they still could have been trying to hide Spiravex's promise to protect their profits.

He looked at the other two files. He suspected everything in them would support Shackleton's story, otherwise they wouldn't be there. He was tired, and reading data required concentration, but he had to persevere. He wasn't going to take Shackleton at his word, no matter how plausible he might seem.

He opened the second file.

After about twenty minutes Helen returned. She made herself a coffee and sat at the far end of the table in silence. He glanced across. The tears were gone, but her eyes were puffy.

He continued reading. He reached a series of reports detailing the progression of the disease. If this strain of HIV really did exist then it was the perfect virus. The drug's effects couldn't have been more destructive if someone had sat down and designed it. The virus' slow progression during the first two weeks after the appearance of the second mutation was the key factor. It ensured the infectious carrier remained symptomless until they'd had plenty of time to spread the virus.

He pushed aside the potential relevance this information had to his meeting with Esau in the early hours of Sunday morning. He needed to focus on the task in hand: confirming beyond doubt that Shackleton was telling the truth.

An hour later he finished interpreting the final results table. He closed the wallet, breathed out and sat back.

"Well?" Helen said.

"Well what?"

"Are you satisfied with what you've seen?"

"Just get Shackleton."

She sighed, stood up and left the room. He stayed where he was until she came back with the Director.

"I trust you believe me now," Shackleton said.

"All but two of the papers were internal documents," Ben said.

"That's how organisations like ours work. We publish the minimum required to get a product licensed," Shackleton said. "That's all the hard evidence that exists."

"But I still haven't seen anything to convince me you're telling the truth." Ben picked up the document wallets and slung them across the table towards Shackleton. "These have got your company logo all over them. I don't trust you, and I don't trust Marivant."

"Didn't you read the original paper?" Shackleton asked.

"Of course I did, but it only shows me you were trying to hide the fact that Spiravex might be a cure. Rather than supporting your case, it undermines it."

Shackleton shook his head. "What will convince you, Doctor Williams?"

"Someone senior within the government. I'd need to meet them on government property so I know they're genuine."

Shackleton nodded. He didn't look surprised or annoyed, just resigned.

"I was hoping the data would be enough, but if I was in your shoes, I'd ask the same thing. A car will take you straight from here to O'Hare. Our jet will fly you to the CIA headquarters in Langley, Virginia. There you will meet with the man who has been involved with this operation from the outset." Shackleton walked to the door and pulled it open. "I only hope the delay this causes won't prove fatal."

"I'll take that chance. Just do the tests on Esau's sample and contact me the moment you get the results."

"I'll make sure you get a satellite phone before you leave O'Hare," Shackleton said. "I want to be sure we can be in touch."

* * * *

Ben took a sip of the ten-year-old malt, leaned back into the welcoming leather of his seat, and admired the view of the Appalachians thirty thousand feet below. But this 'once in a lifetime' event of flying on a private jet wasn't what it could have been. Any pleasure he might have derived from the experience was removed by the circumstances that placed him there.

He did, however, appreciate the generous interior which allowed him to sit as far away from Helen as possible. But since meeting Shackleton something about her had changed; one minute she looked confused and vulnerable, the next she appeared to be lost in thought.

The flight to Virginia took an hour and a half. They stepped out of the jet to find a car waiting on the tarmac.

Fifteen minutes later they reached the security gates of the CIA headquarters.

An armed guard took their passports and checked their names against a list on his clipboard. A second guard knelt on the ground and fed a mirror attached to the end of a telescopic pole under the chassis.

The guards stood back and waved them through. A dense layer of woodland surrounded the compound giving it a similar secluded feel to the Marivant site. But the similarities ended on the other side of the trees: no steaming pipe work or laboratories, instead the complex was fronted by a six-storey office block.

They passed through an additional security barrier at the entrance of the building and were escorted across the echoing marble lobby. They marched over a copy of the circular CIA emblem imprinted on the floor. He looked around at the countless men and women walking to and fro. Were they spies like in the films, or were they assassins like Helen, only operating under the veneer of respectability provided by the government.

They were shown into a windowless waiting room on the first floor.

After twenty minutes a tall man in his fifties walked in. He was completely bald and had a close-cropped grey goatee. He had an air of physical confidence that triggered an instinctive wariness.

"Tom Marshall," he said, extending a hand. "I'm the head of Infectious Disease Containment."

Marshall grabbed Ben's hand around the knuckles and squeezed hard. It was a power handshake designed to intimidate, not greet. This wasn't going to be fun.

"I didn't know the CIA were interested in healthcare," Ben said with a smile, refusing to let Marshall glimpse his discomfort.

"You're a doctor. Tell me which is worse, another Nine-Eleven or an outbreak of Marburg in Manhattan?"

"I'll tell you what's worse than either of those," Ben said, holding unflinching eye contact. "The millions of people who'll die this year because of your patent laws."

Marshall squeezed Ben's hand harder. "We wage war on anything that threatens our country Williams." He finally released his grip. "My personal battle is against microbes."

Marshall turned to Helen, shook her hand briefly and then led them out of the waiting room into an open-plan office. They walked along a central aisle hedged by cubicles full of workers staring at computer screens, talking on the phone or gossiping over the partition fences. They reached the end and Marshall opened the door to an office separated from the rest of the floor by a glass wall. A tidy desk stood on the left next to two chairs. A United States flag and a picture of Marshall shaking President Obama's hand dominated the rear wall. A bookcase full of neatly stacked magazines stood against the wall opposite. The top shelf boasted a series of medals and cups.

Marshall sat down behind his desk and motioned for Helen and Ben to sit in the chairs.

"I had to cancel a meeting at the United Nations to be with you Williams," Marshall said. "That is how seriously I view this situation. Before we go any further you need to sign these." He pushed two sheets of paper forward, one for Helen and one for Ben. "They're confidentiality agreements. If you break them you won't be able to enter our country again without needing to plan for a very long stay. Am I understood?"

They both nodded.

He handed them biros.

Ben read the sheet then signed at the bottom. He pushed it back to Marshall, who glanced at it and put it to one side.

Helen did the same and Marshall placed her sheet on top of Ben's.

"I'm going to get straight to the point Williams." His eyes were emotionless. "Your investigations have placed both ourselves and Marivant in an awkward position. Of course you'd never be able to prove anything, but nonetheless you have complicated matters by becoming involved."

"So you are in collusion with Marivant?" Ben asked.

Marshall glared at him. "Do you think you'd be sitting in this office if we weren't?"

"Well that's all I really came here to find out," Ben said.

"I don't think you fully understand the situation you're in," Marshall said. "This isn't about satisfying your academic curiosity. Has Shackleton clarified just how dangerous the mutated virus is?"

Ben nodded.

"Then you'll understand why it is vital that we get Esau Kimani. At the moment he is considered to be of more risk to our national security than Al Qaeda."

"Why aren't you looking for him yourselves then? Why do you need me to do your dirty work?"

Marshall narrowed his eyes. "Firstly, we are not officially involved. Secondly, it's not that simple. Since Moi fell from power our relations with the Kenyans have deteriorated. We can't just send teams of men to scour the country looking for Kimani. Until you turned up no one knew his exact location. Slade suspected he might be hiding near his cousin's village, but their men never actually saw him. You've got closer than anyone else."

"And now you want me to kill him," Ben said.

"You will lead Doctor Richardson to his hideout."

"Isn't that the same thing?"

"Answer me this Williams," Marshall said, leaning forward and putting his hands together on the table in front of him. "Imagine for a second that you were able to travel back in time, but could only go back once. What date would you choose?"

Ben shrugged. "Two weeks ago, then I could make sure I wouldn't be sitting here."

"How altruistic of you. I know exactly when I would choose. I would travel back to nineteen twenty-two. I would get on a boat and travel to Hamburg, then catch a train to Vienna. There I'd search for a young artist named Adolf Hitler and I'd shoot the arsehole right between the eyes." Marshall raised his eyebrows. "Wouldn't you do the same? Or are you too precious about human life that you'd spare him at the cost of the millions you know he'd kill?"

"If I was going to kill anyone, it'd be the idiot who discovered this drug," Ben said. "Esau Kimani is innocent, he doesn't deserve to be murdered."

"But if Kimani's allowed to live, the results will make the Nazis' Final Solution look like an episode of the Waltons." Marshall leaned back in his chair. "I'm trying to make it easy for you Williams. But it makes no difference whether it satisfies your morals or not. It has to happen."

Ben didn't reply.

Marshall stood up.

"Good day doctor Williams." He walked over to the door and called to a young woman in the office. He stepped a few paces outside, folded his arms and looked straight ahead. The woman came to the entrance and peered into the room.

"Follow me please," she said.

Helen was already on her feet.

Ben had nothing more to ask. He was in the CIA headquarters and Shackleton's story had been confirmed. Marshall clearly wasn't going to invite them to stay for tea and biscuits.

Chapter 30

Ben and Helen boarded the Marivant corporate jet at seven-thirty pm.

He'd crossed the Atlantic in business class a couple of times, but on most occasions the trip back east was a sleepless contortion act spent in coach. Not this time. Both he and Helen had private berths, a luxury he took advantage of as soon as he'd finished dinner. He put his head on the pillow just after ten, and didn't wake up until the steward knocked on his door twenty minutes before landing.

They touched down in Faro, Portugal, at nine-fifteen am European time and refuelled. After half an hour they were back in the air, climbing above the Straits of Gibraltar, then crossing the barren slopes of the Atlas Mountains. Thousands of miles of empty desert lay beyond.

The plane reached cruising altitude and he was served an American breakfast, cooked fresh in the on-board kitchen. He ate as much as he could, then settled back and watched movies on his seat's personal entertainment system.

They reached Nairobi at six forty-five pm and hired a four-wheel drive. Helen wanted to begin the journey immediately, but he knew better. The roads in Kenya were notorious for car-jackers after dark. He insisted they check into a nearby hotel and wait till the morning before they headed for Nyeri.

They left at dawn, and by early afternoon they were approaching the small group of huts where Daniel Kimani and his grandmother lived. They pulled up and got out of the jeep.

"I think it's better if you stay here," he said. He reached into the back of the jeep and grabbed the rucksack containing the equipment Shackleton had given them.

"Why?"

"The grandmother thinks she's some kind of psychic. I don't want her picking up any bad vibes from you."

Helen walked up to him and looked him in the eyes.

"She won't pick up any bad vibes," she said. "I'm coming with you."

"We can't afford to blow this. It's our one chance of finding him."

"I know. So let's get on with it."

He shook his head. He put the rucksack over his left shoulder, closed the door and began walking towards the group of huts. Helen stayed at his side.

He knocked on the door of the grandmother's hut. After a minute the old woman answered. She had a grim expression on her face.

"You have come for Esau?" she said.

He nodded.

"I knew you would be back. This is going to end now." She looked at Helen. "Who is your friend?"

"A colleague," he said. "Esau may have a very dangerous disease. We need to do more tests on his blood."

She smiled and then chuckled. "Your tests won't find anything," she said. "The King of the spirits has taken the disease away."

He looked at Helen.

"Would it hurt to be sure?" Helen asked.

"It is not good to question the spirits. If they say something is done then it is done. I do not need to hear you tell me his AIDS is no longer there. I know already."

"If we do this last test, the men who've been threatening your family will go away," Ben said.

The old woman studied Helen, and then nodded. "Go to the fields on the other side of that hill." She pointed at an area of high ground to the north of the hamlet. "You will find Daniel there. He will take you to Esau."

"Thank you," Ben said.

The hill was at least eight hundred feet high. Thick bushes slowed them down by forcing them to weave a crooked line between their thorny branches. After thirty minutes they reached the summit. They stopped and surveyed the land on the other side.

The ground fell away in a succession of shabbily constructed terraces, filled with a mixture of weeds and skinny maize stalks. A stream ran along the valley floor three hundred feet below. Further crumbling terraces climbed up the far side before giving way to a series of rocky bluffs that led to more mountainous terrain.

The terraces were fed by a network of irrigation ditches and pipes, which drew water via hand pumps from a crudely constructed mud dam five hundred yards upstream.

"Is that him?" Helen asked, pointing up the valley.

He followed the line of her finger and saw a man digging on the far slope.

"It's hard to say from here." He put his hand across his brow to shade his eyes. "I can't see anyone else."

They followed the crest of the ridge until they drew level with the man, then cut down the side of the valley and headed towards him.

At the bottom they reached the stream. It was fast flowing but shallow, and there were enough boulders scattered along its bed to find a way across without getting wet.

They climbed up the other side.

"It's him," Ben said as they drew closer.

Daniel looked up from his digging. He threw the spade down and climbed out of the ditch.

"Jambo Doctor Williams," he said with a carefree smile. "You are back quickly."

"Jambo," Ben replied, and extended his hand as he reached Daniel. They gripped the ends of each other's fingers then linked hands like arm wrestlers to complete a traditional Kenyan handshake.

"Are you here to see Esau again?" Daniel asked.

"We need to do more tests," he replied.

Daniel's smile disappeared. He nodded and looked at Helen. "Who is this lady?"

"She's a scientist I work with," Ben said. "She's here to help me."

Daniel looked down. "Esau is not well Doctor Williams."

Ben looked across at Helen. The panic in her eyes suggested she was thinking the same thing: the second mutation.

"How long has he been ill?" Ben asked.

"The day you left he started feeling bad. He is very hot and not eating the food I bring him."

"When did you see him last?" Helen said.

"This morning, and he was worse than before."

258

"You'd better take us to him," Ben said. "Maybe I can help."

Daniel turned and began climbing the hill. Ben turned to Helen. She had put her rucksack on the floor and had her hand in the bag. She pulled out a water bottle and a bottle of pills. She shook one into her hand and threw it into her mouth. She took a gulp of water, then looked up.

"You alright?" Ben asked.

"Headache," she said, then put the bottle of water and the pills back in her bag. Ben started up the hill after Daniel. Helen fell in behind him.

"It's a good job we have those masks," she whispered as she joined him.

He nodded, but his mind was already playing out the possible scenarios. If Esau's illness was due to the second mutation then he would have been highly contagious when they met four days earlier. He remembered smelling the African's strong breath. If he'd got that close then the virus may already be multiplying inside of him, invading his vital organs, preparing to liquefy them. He tried to push the thought out of his head.

They left the cultivated land and joined a track leading up through a forest of thorn bushes that reached ten feet above their heads.

He kept his eyes on Daniel's feet a few paces ahead.

If he was infected, how many others were infected? Shackleton had said the virus became contagious three to four days after catching it. Ben had seen Esau on Saturday morning; today was day four. So far the only person he had come into contact with other than Daniel and the old woman, was Helen. He looked across at her. If he had caught the virus then she had it too and there was no point in using Shackleton's protective gear. But Helen obviously hadn't done the calculations. He decided to go through with the charade when they reached Esau; he didn't want her losing her head. To contain the virus it wouldn't just be Esau who needed to die.

But what if he'd become contagious after three days? Everyone he'd been near at Marivant, Langley, and worst of all Kenyatta Airport would now be infected. If that was the case then it was already too late, all this was in vain, the virus would have a foothold in half the nations on the planet.

It was ironic that in his quest to become a hero, he could become the greatest villain in history by providing a route for the virus to escape the wilderness it was currently lost in.

The bushes came to an abrupt end at the top of the slope. Ahead of them lay a wide shelf of red rock, leading to the foot of a cliff that stretched out of sight above them. A number of ledges ran horizontally across the face, which was bisected by a narrow gorge to their right. Millions of years of rainwater flowing out of the gorge had carved a trench into the plateau.

Daniel stopped and turned. He looked at Helen, then up at the rock face.

"Don't worry about me," she said. "That's nothing. I've climbed much worse."

Ben looked up. Why did it have to be a cliff? Spiders or snakes he could handle, but not heights. He knew vertigo was all in the mind, but that didn't stop him suffering from it.

"Esau throws the rope down just before sunrise and just after sunset. He won't be expecting me now." Daniel stepped towards the rocky face and hauled himself onto it. "Keep close to me. I know an easy way up."

Easy? Ben tilted his head and examined the steep surface.

Helen scrambled up behind Daniel.

Ben pulled both straps of the rucksack over his shoulders, put his hands on the cliff and began to follow her.

Daniel was right: the actual process of climbing was simple. Ledges, fissures and knobs of rock covered the uneven face, providing plenty of hand and footholds. Except for the absence of garish colours, it could have been an artificial climbing wall in a leisure centre. He actually found himself enjoying the exertion.

As long as he didn't look down he'd be safe. He kept his eyes looking up, focusing on Helen's backside. It was a pleasant view; for a smoker she took care of her body.

After ten minutes of steady climbing, she stopped.

"Daniel!" she shouted, breathing heavily. "I need to rest for a minute!"

Ben stopped a few metres below her.

He relaxed and glanced to his side. His brain instantly latched onto the unfamiliar perspective of the horizon. He forced his eyes upwards again, but it was too late. Like a kid watching a horror movie from behind a pillow, he knew the monster was there and he had to peek.

His eyes slowly worked their way down the rock above him. They crept into the danger zone, below the horizontal, and accelerated downwards to a point well beyond his feet.

He breathed in sharply, pulling himself close to the surface. He closed his eyes and dug his fingernails into the rock. The ground was too far away.

"I'm OK now Daniel," Helen called.

Loose stones and dust fell into Ben's hair. He looked up to see Daniel resume his climb.

Ben focused on the rock above him, but once again his eyes were drawn towards the forbidden view. He looked at the rock in front of his face to stop his head from spinning.

Use your brain Ben.

He breathed deeply for a minute then looked up. Helen was already at least twenty feet above him. She pulled herself over a ridge and disappeared.

He was on his own.

There were countless handholds to help him continue climbing, but that wasn't the problem. He was frozen to the spot. His mind had put his body into lockdown. Every second felt like an hour as he clung to the surface. He could have been there just a few minutes, but it could have been twenty, nothing else existed except the void below his feet.

"Dr Williams!" Daniel shouted from above.

Ben pulled his sweating forehead away from the rock and looked up. Daniel looked frantic.

"You must come up Dr Williams, your friend," he looked behind him. "I think your friend is dead!"

Chapter 31

Dead? What the hell was he talking about, she'd been fine a few minutes before. He took a deep breath then pushed himself a few inches away from the surface. He stared at his left hand and willed it to move. His fingers, white from the pressure they were exerting, slowly loosened their grip. His hand finally released its hold on the cliff. It reached up and grabbed a sturdy-looking rock half a metre higher. He then focused on his right hand.

If the left one could do it, so could the other.

Once again he summoned his will to overcome the stubbornness of his body. After ten seconds of intense concentration both hands were reaching above him. He looked at the rock that supported his feet and began lifting his left leg. The moment his boot parted contact with the surface his right foot slipped. He felt the drop pulling him down.

He clung to the rock above and scraped his feet against the cliff. His left foot found its hold again.

He looked for a secure spot to place his right foot.

"Dr Williams!" The shout was more impatient than before. "Please come!"

"You're such a wuss Ben Williams," he muttered. They were the words his sister had used on him twenty years earlier, when he'd found himself frozen halfway up a ladder at his grandfather's house. It was the first time the spectre of his phobia had been awoken.

His sister's goading had worked on him then, and the echo of her voice from his youth worked now. There was no way an absurd fear was going to get the better of him. He reached up again.

Two minutes later he pulled himself onto a wide ledge cut into the cliff face, and stood up.

Helen was lying completely still on the ground with her eyes closed. Daniel was kneeling next to her. He looked up with a helpless expression. Ben knelt down beside her and felt for a pulse. Nothing. She really was dead. It was no loss to the world, but there was always the Hippocratic oath.

He put one hand on top of the other on her chest and started pushing hard and fast, even though the chance of her coming round without a defibrillator were tiny. He didn't use mouth to mouth as he once might have, recent research had shown that just chest compressions had a better success rate in adults. He carried on for three minutes. What had happened to her? One minute she was fine, the next she was dead. It didn't make sense. It couldn't be anything to do with the virus, if she'd caught it off him it wouldn't have been in her long enough to do any serious harm yet. He stopped for a second to check her pulse. Suddenly her chest heaved up and she breathed in deeply, then coughed. Her eyes were wide open. She looked at him with a bewildered expression.

"You need to rest," he said, turning her onto her side. She tried to say something, but he stopped her. "Just lie still." He pulled her backpack round and placed it under her head, then stood up and joined Daniel.

"Where's Esau?" he said. The Kenyan pointed to the mouth of a cave.

They walked towards it, with the cliff face on their left. They passed a long rope coiled around a stump of rock. The ledge narrowed to less than a yard then stopped four feet short of the cave. The ground disappeared in front of them. A sheer walled gorge fell to the base of the mountain two hundred and fifty feet below.

Daniel motioned for Ben to give him some space. He stepped back a couple of paces then ran and leapt forward. He landed in front of the cave, and put his arms out to steady himself against the rock.

He turned and looked at Ben.

He stared at the gap. If it had been a puddle, no problem, but the sight of the gaping chasm turned the four feet into a mile. He glanced up at Daniel, who was looking at him expectantly.

"Stand back," he said. He took two paces away from the edge of the drop, held eye contact with Daniel, and surged forward. He leapt across, landing heavily in front of him. He steadied himself inches away from Daniel's face.

Ben put the rucksack on the ground and opened it. He pulled out two facemasks with air filters, he was about to hand one to Daniel but realised it was pointless. He put the other on then took a pair of latex gloves out of a box.

"What are you doing?" Daniel asked, looking at him.

"Just a precaution," Ben said.

"But you cannot catch HIV by breathing it in."

"Is Esau in here?" Ben moved towards the entrance of the cave.

Daniel turned, knelt down in the mouth of the cave and picked up a torch. He shone it into the gloom.

Ben took a few paces inside then stopped. Esau looked as though he was already dead.

"He is worse." Daniel turned to Ben. "Can you help him Doctor Williams?"

Ben edged a few steps nearer.

Esau's chest heaved and he coughed violently. An aerosol of particles crossed the torch beam.

They were too late; Esau had the virus, which meant Ben probably caught it on Saturday morning. It was only a matter of days before they were all suffering in the same way.

"Let me have a closer look at him," he said, kneeling down. "Esau? Can you hear me?"

There was no response.

"Esau," Daniel said. "It is Doctor Williams. He has come to help you."

His cousin's words seemed to penetrate. Esau opened his eyes; they were swollen and bloodshot.

Ben leaned forward and placed his arm under Esau's right shoulder. "Take the other side," he said to Daniel. "We need to get him outside, I can't examine him in this light."

There was the sound of feet landing on the rock outside. Ben turned to see Helen enter the cave. She was supporting herself against the rock with one hand, the other was holding the pistol in front of her.

Chapter 32

"Out of the cave," Helen said to Daniel. "Get on the other side of the drop."

Daniel looked at Ben in confusion.

Ben nodded reluctantly.

Daniel's expression turned to anger. He walked out of the cave and leapt across the gap. He continued to the far end of the ledge then got down on his knees. He raised his hands high into the air and began wailing in Kikuyu.

Helen turned the gun on Ben and Esau.

He was expendable now that she had Esau. In some ways he'd prefer to go like this. He was going to die anyway, and a bullet between the eyes was far better than ending up like Esau. He could finally be at peace, his memories and the pain gone forever.

He looked at the end of the barrel. It was shaking. Was it the after effects of the heart attack? People normally needed to rest for days, but she'd got straight back to her feet. Or was it something else? Was it nerves?

Helen didn't know she might be carrying the virus and even if she did, she wouldn't have the courage or conscience to do the honourable thing. If he let her kill him then she could be in Nairobi infecting thousands by tomorrow afternoon. He had to stop her pulling the trigger.

"You don't have to do this," he said.

"Don't I?"

She had every reason to dispose of him; he'd fulfilled Slade's purpose and now he was just another liability. But her nervous eyes and shaking hands didn't match her steady voice. He needed to stall her, undermine her resolve.

"There has to be another way," he said.

"Don't make this any harder for me than it already is."

"Think about what you're doing."

"Just move out of the way Ben." Helen waved the pistol to one side.

He looked at her with surprise, then turned to Esau. He slowly stood up and stepped out of the line of fire. He moved around the edge of the cave and drew level with her.

"We've got to kill him haven't we?" Helen asked. "You heard what Shackleton said. If I don't kill him everyone will die."

Esau barely seemed aware of what was going on. He looked like a thousand pictures used by Aid agencies to raise money for African appeals. His skinny, disease-ridden body only had a few hours left anyway.

Ben turned back to Helen. If he told her that once Esau had been killed, she had to shoot Daniel, himself, everyone in the village, then herself, would she go through with it or would she just shoot everyone else and run? Could he trust her not be selfish? The hell he could.

He needed to grab the gun. She would be most off her guard immediately after shooting Esau.

"It's him or four billion others," Ben said. "It's that simple."

She nodded. Her hands steadied for a moment.

"I can't," she said. Her arms fell and the pistol dangled in her left hand. "I can't do it Ben."

She looked at him. "I've never shot anyone before. I nearly did, I pulled the trigger but Luke was just testing me, the gun wasn't loaded. I was given a second chance. If I kill Esau I go back to what I was becoming. I don't want to be that woman any more."

"What are you talking about?"

"I thought I was living a life without meaning, but now I know that I wasn't and it's not too late to change."

She'd lost it. He grabbed the pistol out of her hand and pointed it at Esau. He would be the easiest to shoot first.

He began squeezing the trigger.

"No!" Helen shouted. "Don't do it."

"What?" he said, keeping the gun pointed at Esau. "He has to die. You might be too weak, but I'm not. This is bigger than us, our consciences."

"No," Helen said. "You're a good man, if you kill Esau you'll lose that."

"What do you know about being good?" Ben said.

"You said there has to be another way."

He looked away.

"If you haven't got the stomach for this, go and join Daniel." He'd been right not to tell her what he knew. This was nothing to do with her conscience, it was a selfish act.

She stared at him for a few moments, then turned and left him alone.

He looked down the barrel. He just had to will himself to the pull the trigger.

Esau opened his eyes. For the first time he seemed to understand what was happening. He held up a hand. Ben pictured the bullet tearing through the frail skin on its way to Esau's skull.

"Please Doctor Williams."

The Kenyan's voice was barely audible, but it was loud enough to hear the words. 'Doctor Williams'. He was a doctor, not some testosterone-fuelled ex-SAS soldier with a blood lust. It violated his nature to even be pointing a gun at someone who was sick and helpless, let alone kill them. He lowered the gun. He would not kill an innocent man.

The fear induced by Shackleton subsided. He went over the situation again. He already knew that killing Esau would just be the beginning. If the illness was due to the second mutation then himself, Helen, Daniel, and everyone in the hamlet below would already have the disease. If it had spread outside of the immediate area it was out of his hands. But he had no way of knowing that yet. In the short term his first priority was containment of any potential outbreak, without shooting anyone.

The decision was made, they'd go back to the village and isolate the area. He'd contact Marivant, and get them to fly a team to Africa to find out for certain if they were infected with the lethal strain. Until then he was going to help Esau. That was who Ben Williams was.

He slipped the gun into his belt, leaned forward and gently pulled Esau up. He walked to the edge of the cave.

"Daniel!" he shouted. The African lowered his hands and turned his face to Ben. His face was covered in tears. "Give me a hand."

Helen was sitting on a rock. She smiled with relief.

Daniel sprang across the gap and they moved Esau to the edge of the ravine.

"We'll have to lower him down with the rope," Ben said. But first they needed to get him across the rift. He passed all Esau's

267

weight over to Daniel, then looked down. The dizzying drop drove all reason from him.

Don't think about it, just do it.

He reached his left foot out into the air and tipped forward. He passed the point of no return; all his balance lay over the gap. He stretched his leg as far as he could. His foot landed firmly on the rim of the ledge on the far side.

Helen had stood up and moved to just a few feet away. She was looking at him with an expression of awe.

"Do you think you'll be able to grab him?" he asked.

"He can't weigh more than me," she replied. "Pass him slowly though."

"We'd better tie him to the rope just in case," he said.

Helen ran back along the ledge and grabbed the rope. She returned and passed it to him. He swayed under its weight for a moment then passed it to Daniel.

"Be quick. I don't know how long I can stay like this."

Daniel tied the rope around his cousin's waist, putting the excess line on the ground behind him. He picked up Esau's frail body like it was a child's, and leaned forward.

Ben stretched towards him, holding his arms out. Daniel passed Esau over. The extra weight pulled Ben forward. He fought back with the muscles in his feet and calves, focusing on Esau's pitiful face in his arms. He righted himself then slowly passed Esau to Helen. She was just able to grasp enough of Esau's body to swing him onto the ledge. She pulled him towards the safety of the wider section.

Neither Helen nor Daniel had sufficient weight to act as an anchor to Ben's hundred kilos. He'd have to lever himself upright using the rope.

"Untie him," he said to Helen. "And don't hang about."

Helen did as he asked, and moved Esau clear.

"Daniel," Ben said. "Grab the loose rope and pull it taught in front of me so I can reach it." There was no way he could lean down to take hold of it; that would be suicide.

Daniel picked up the coil of rope and pulled on it. It snapped up and hit Ben's chest.

He tipped backwards an inch. He felt his left foot slip. He waved his arms to try to rebalance. It was no good. He pitched backwards, every nerve on his back felt the drop behind him. He stretched his hands out towards the rope in front of him. His fingers grasped the line.

His vision became a whirl of rocks and air as he fell into emptiness. The rope pulled taught in his hands and his body slammed into the gorge wall. The excess rope uncoiled in a spiral beneath him.

"Ben!" Helen shouted.

His left shoulder screamed in agony. He wanted to release his grip on the rope to ease the pain, but if he did, he was dead.

He looked up. Helen's face was peering over the ledge above him.

He tried to pull himself up, but couldn't move his right hand; his left arm was too badly hurt to support his full weight. He pushed the mask down with his right shoulder so he could breathe freely.

Helen's face retreated beyond the rock. A shadow passed overhead and he glimpsed Daniel's heels disappear beyond the ledge.

Half a minute later he felt himself lift a few inches. But he didn't go any higher. He dropped back, sending a shockwave of agony into his shoulder.

Helen's worried face reappeared above him.

"I'm sorry," she said. "We tried to lift you up, but we couldn't hold your weight. You're going to have to make your own way down."

Perhaps he should have thought all this through before he decided to straddle the gorge. Bit late now. He repositioned himself, wrapped his legs around the thick rope and transferred the weight to his lower body. He swayed in the still air.

He looked down and saw the end of the rope dangling ten feet above the ground.

That was odd. He was looking down and feeling nothing, the irrational fear had disappeared, it must have been shocked out of him. All that remained was the will to survive and a shed-load of adrenalin.

He loosened his grip and began sliding down the rope. The course texture burnt his skin; the rock in front of his eyes accelerated into a blur. He gripped tightly again, setting his hands on fire with pain as they halted the slide. He looked up. Helen was over twenty feet away.

He took a breath and slowly loosened the muscles in his fingers. He slipped again, unable to control the pace of the fall. His hands were raw, but he had to use them as brakes otherwise he'd never stop. He gritted his teeth as the rope bit into his flesh.

He looked down. The ground didn't feel any closer.

The hot blood in his hands made them swell against the rope.

* * * *

Ben slid deeper into the chasm. Helen winced. He didn't have a clue how to abseil.

He looked up at her again. His face was a long way down, but the drop beneath him was further still.

She held her breath as he slipped down another length of rope. Each time he stopped to look up his face filled with agony.

He repeated this over and over until he had about forty feet left to go, then suddenly his legs came away from the rope.

He was in trouble. All his weight was on his hands now.

She put her hand to her mouth. She didn't want him to die. Something had changed inside her, and that change had exposed her feelings for the man dangling on a thread a hundred and fifty feet below.

He tried to get his thighs back round the swaying line, but his hands gave way and he tumbled backwards, his arms flailing in the empty air.

She leaned forward, wanting to reach out to him.

He hit the floor of the gorge, his arms and legs spread out on the ground. He lay motionless.

"Ben!" she screamed.

There was no response.

She turned round. Daniel was right behind her.

"We've got to help him," she said.

"We must lower Esau first," he replied.

She looked back down at Ben. She wanted to go straight to him, but Daniel was right.

They pulled the rope up out of the gorge. She looked at Daniel's scrawny figure. "How are we going to do this without Ben?" There was no way she was going to strain herself after what had happened to her heart. It must have been the same thing that happened to the men in Afghanistan, combination of overdoing it and altitude.

They both looked at Esau. He was barely conscious.

"I will tie him to my back and carry him," Daniel said.

She wasn't convinced, but he'd already pulled a penknife out of his pocket and was cutting a long length of rope from the end of the line. He looped it around Esau's thighs, leaving about four foot of spare line on either side of him. Helen helped lift Esau onto Daniel piggyback style, and crossed the rope over Esau's back. She then secured them together by tying the ends of the rope around their shoulders.

"Are you going to manage?" she asked, looking at the cord cutting into Daniel's upper body.

"I will be quick," he replied.

He manoeuvred himself to the edge of the cliff. She threw the line over and passed it to Daniel. He grabbed hold of it, leaned backwards, and stepped onto the cliff face. He lowered himself one jolting step at a time.

He disappeared out of sight. She walked to the end of the ledge and looked into the gorge. Ben hadn't moved. He couldn't be dead, not now.

She returned to the rope. It stayed taught for about ten minutes, then suddenly went slack.

She pulled on it. It lifted up easily. Daniel had reached the base.

She moved to the rim of the ledge, grabbed hold of the rope, and eased herself onto the cliff face. Unlike the gorge walls the slope wasn't sheer. She decided to use the same technique of abseiling as Daniel; it'd be much quicker than trying to climb down the way she'd come up.

She leaned back with both feet on the cliff, and began walking down backwards. She transferred her weight from one arm to the other as she passed the rope through her hands.

It didn't take long to draw level with the horizon. She looked below; the rope was dangling six feet above the ground.

"Daniel!" she shouted.

There was no reply. All she could see was rock and dust.

She reached the end of the rope then jumped, bending her knees and rolling over face down in the dirt.

She put her hands on the ground to lift herself up. A ring of cold metal pushed into the back of her neck.

"Don't move."

Chapter 33

Two pairs of hands grabbed her. She was hauled upright and spun round to face three Kenyan men. One was short with a large cut on his forehead, he was pointing a pistol at her. To her left stood a guy wearing a red beret and army fatigues, on her right she was dwarfed by a man in a Masai robe who must have been at least six-foot-five. They both had assault rifles slung over their shoulders.

"Where is Ben Williams?" the short man asked.

"Are you from Slade?" she said.

"Where is the white man who went up the cliff with you?"

"If you are, you take orders from me."

The short man looked at the guy wearing the beret. He smashed his rifle into her face, sending her to the floor. She put her shaking hand to her cheek, when she pulled it away there was blood on her fingers.

"Where is the white man?" he shouted, pushing the gun into her forehead.

"He's dead. He fell into a ravine."

The short guy looked at the Masai warrior. "Kill the other two. We'll have some fun with this one." He looked back at her. "Stand up."

She slowly got to her feet. The man pushed the muzzle of his pistol in between her breasts, moved it up to a button on her blouse and smiled.

"You are making the biggest mistake of your life," she said. "Do you know Luke Martin?"

The man shook his head. "I have never heard this name. Now undress."

They had to be contractors.

"I work for the company who hired you," she pleaded.

"I told you, undress," he replied. "I do not care who you are. My orders were to watch for Esau Kimani, and when I find him, kill him and anyone he is with. You and the white man led me to Kimani. My job is done, you are my reward."

He grabbed her blouse and ripped it open.

A shot blasted from behind her. She turned to see Daniel slump to the ground, a large section of his skull missing. The Masai warrior stepped sideways to face Esau.

* * * *

Ben opened his eyes. Was that gunfire?

Another shot echoed down the ravine.

His head was splitting. He looked at the wall of rock above him and remembered what had happened.

He sat up. Nothing felt broken. He was lucky; he must have fallen flat onto the sandy ground and distributed the impact across his whole body.

He leaned forward to get on his knees and push himself up. Something solid jabbed into his stomach. The gun.

If he still had Helen's gun, who fired the shot?

He lifted himself up, fighting the pain in his muscles and shoulder. He walked cautiously to the end of the gorge. He peered out from behind the rock and looked towards the base of the cliff. He saw Dom with two other men: a guy in a red beret and a tribesman. Dom was unbuttoning his shirt while the other two pointed their rifles at someone lying out of view on the ground.

He ducked back inside the ravine.

Whatever they were doing, he wasn't going to hang around to find out. Once Helen joined her chums from Slade, they'd come looking for him.

He looked out across the plateau of flat rock that lay between the cliff and the thorn forest. There was only one way he could escape across it. He would have to crawl along the trench leading from the gorge; he was lucky it wasn't raining.

He got on his stomach, held the gun in his right hand, and began crawling along the rocky ditch. He kept as low as he could, it was no more than three feet deep.

The uneven surface scraped against him, but he moved quickly and reached a deeper section about halfway. He got to his knees, carefully peered over the rim and looked at the group assembled at the base the cliff.

Dom had his trousers round his ankles and was pointing his pistol to something out of sight. The other men had put their rifles to one side and were undoing their belts.

He hated African militia; they were animals. Everywhere they went they raped. They didn't usually bother with men though. He looked up at the cliff. No sign of Helen. Perhaps when she turned up she'd take control.

He got back on his stomach and crawled the remaining twenty feet. He arrived at the point where the rocky plateau joined the edge of the forest. From here he could move anywhere without being seen. He dashed to the cover of the thorn bushes, turned right, and ran fifteen yards to draw level with the men. He stood behind a bush and looked out through its branches.

Helen was lying on the floor naked. It didn't make sense, surely these guys were on the same side as her? Dom was standing in front of her with a smile on his face. The other two were on all fours, holding her arms.

Dom knelt down and tried to grab her legs, but she landed a kick in his face. She shouted something impossible to discern from that distance.

Dom fell away, felt his lip and looked at her with rage.

This was nothing to do with him; it was Slade's business.

He turned and started walking away. By the time they finished with their entertainment he'd be long gone.

There was a loud scream.

He stopped.

Keep moving. Just think of Ruth. How can you save her if you're dead?

Helen screamed again.

He couldn't go any further. Maybe he'd spent too much time in Sunday school and been indoctrinated with the love your enemy stuff, or maybe he was just born with a suicidal conscience, but just like he couldn't walk away from the investigation when things got tough, he couldn't leave Helen, no matter how much he hated her.

He turned round and ran back up the hill towards the clearing. He pulled the pistol out and returned to the edge of the forest.

Dom was holding Helen's legs apart and was almost on top of her. Her struggling was less violent. Blood was smeared across her face.

The rifles lay a few yards away from the group.

Ben stepped out from behind the bush and started running. The first man to go for the rifles would be his first target. He needed to get as close as possible before he fired. He was a reasonable shot with a rifle, but he was less confident at that range with a pistol.

He covered three feet then felt a vibration in his pocket. A second later the unfamiliar tone of the satellite phone filled the clearing. All three men looked straight in his direction. The guy with the beret jumped to his feet, pulled his trousers up and ran for the rifles. Ben aimed the pistol and fired two shots. Both missed.

Dom and the tribesman grabbed Helen and dragged her towards the gorge.

Ben turned and ran. He looked back to see the man in the beret reach the rifles. He accelerated into the forest, bullets spraying the surrounding bushes.

He sped down the hill, pulled his phone out and turned it off.

Another burst of gunfire shredded the branches behind him. He stopped, turned ninety degrees to his left, and ran behind a large bush. He looked through the thorny branches. The man careered down the slope. Ben watched him pass and then looked back up towards the plateau. The other two hadn't followed.

He slipped out from behind the bush and turned down the slope. The man was less than ten feet away. He'd stopped and was looking around.

Ben lifted his pistol and aimed it at the man's back. He knew that he should pull the trigger now, he knew it was the one moment where all the advantage was in his favour and that given half a chance this man would shoot him in the back, but he couldn't do it. He took a step closer.

"Drop the weapon!" he shouted.

The man spun round and lifted the rifle. Ben fired. The shot hit his shoulder. He fired repeatedly until the man was on the floor.

He walked over and grabbed the rifle. "You had your chance," he said. The man was still breathing, but he didn't have long. By nightfall the wildlife would finish him off.

Ben carefully made his way back up the hill. He neared the edge of the clearing and returned to the bush he'd used for cover a few minutes earlier.

Apart from Helen's clothes the plateau was empty. Then he noticed two lifeless forms slumped against the rock face. He'd been so focused on what was happening to Helen, he hadn't seen Daniel and Esau. They'd been shot like stray dogs.

A movement caught his eye. The tribesman was looking out from the gorge. Dom stood on the other side of the narrow opening. Both were pointing their guns across the open ground. There was no way he could get near them without taking a bullet.

Maybe if he waited long enough one of them would venture out in search of their friend with the beret. Unlikely. Then he saw another way. It wouldn't have been his first choice, but he didn't see how else he could reach them.

About fifty feet up the cliff face a change in the layer of rocks left a ledge that ran all the way to the gorge. If he could climb up to it unnoticed he might be able to attack from above.

He felt his shoulder. It was sore, but he hadn't broken anything. His hands were more of a problem. Huge blisters had swollen up across the palms and fingers. He flexed them, he'd suffered worse from windsurfing, but that hadn't kept him off the water. As long as there was flesh on his fingers he could use them. They'd heal in time.

He turned to his left and followed the edge of the thorn forest away from the gorge. He kept out of sight until he reached a point where there was only ten feet of open ground to the base of the cliff. He looked back at the gully. It was now over sixty yards away.

He ran out of the forest and reached the cliff in a few seconds.

He looked up, slung the rifle across his back and started to climb. His hands cried out for him to stop, but he didn't listen. Instead he moved up the face as quickly as he could. He arrived at a point just below the ledge and realised he'd underestimated the difficulty. Unlike the stretch he'd climbed with Helen and Daniel, the ledge overhung the cliff by about two feet.

He reached out with his right hand and grabbed the lip of the rock, compressing the fiery fluid in his blisters. It felt like someone was pushing soldering irons into his flesh. He grabbed the ledge with his other hand and was left dangling in the air.

He glanced across at the entrance to the gorge. He could see the tribesman standing at the edge, but there was no sign of Dom.

He pushed his feet against the rock and swung up. His chest landed on the ledge. He lifted his left leg onto the surface and pulled himself to safety then peered over the side. The tribesman hadn't moved. He was still staring at the forest.

He got to his feet and crept along the ledge, his back against the cliff face. After a minute he passed behind the rope that the others had used to climb down. He was near the gully now, he got down on all fours and moved slowly to the point where the rock dropped away. He'd hoped the ledge might have continued along the inside wall of the gorge, but it didn't.

He lay flat on his stomach and pushed his head over the edge.

The tribesman was still standing at the opening. Dom, who'd put his trousers on, sat on a rock a few yards behind. Helen was on the ground with her back against the wall of the gorge. She hugged her knees, covering her bare chest. Dom was staring at her.

The longer he left it, the more likely the Kenyan would feel safe enough to finish what he'd started. To shoot either of the men, he'd need to lean out, point the rifle at ninety degrees and aim for the top of their heads. A tough shot at the best of times, but it felt like a lifetime since he'd used a rifle. He didn't have a hope.

He looked at the opposite wall of the gorge. The overhang continued along the outer face, but unlike the side he was on, it hadn't been eroded on the inside. There was about fifteen feet of unbroken ledge leading into the gully.

He'd have to jump. If he made a sound, he'd blow it.

He removed his shoes and got to his feet. He looked at the drop and took two steps back then ran forward.

He landed on the other side and clung to the rock face; the ledge was much narrower than the one higher up. His whole body tried to pull him backwards. He pushed his fingers into the rock and willed his body to suck against it. His balance teetered towards the drop, then finally tipped against the cliff.

He crept to the corner of the ledge as it turned up the gully. He got on his stomach, his feet pointing into the gorge, and looked down. The scene below hadn't changed; no one had heard anything.

He reversed along the ledge. He stopped every few feet and looked behind him. He stretched to see whether any stones lay in his path. If one tumbled into the gap below he'd become target practice.

He reached the point where the ledge disappeared into the rock face. It was just far enough to get a good angle on the two men.

He pulled the rifle off his back, rested on his elbows, and aimed it up the gorge. He moved the sights from Dom to the tribesman, and then back to Dom. Dom would be first, he was nearest to Helen. He'd grab her the moment he heard a shot.

He closed his left eye and used the other to line up the sights on Dom's chest. His cadet training from school kicked in and he breathed slowly. He allowed the sight at the end of the barrel to rise up to Dom's head and then down to his waist as he breathed in and out. He held his breath as the sight returned to Dom's chest a third time. He squeezed the trigger halfway.

Helen's speech in the cave came back to him. He suspected she'd have a different view now.

He pulled the trigger home.

The butt recoiled into his right shoulder and a blast echoed through the narrow gorge.

Dom was sent flying to the ground.

The tribesman spun round and fired a volley of shots up the ravine. Bullets ricocheted against the rock around Ben.

He leaned forward and fired several shots back. The African threw himself behind a large rock near the entrance to the gully.

Stalemate.

Helen was looking up at him, then across at the body lying a few feet away. She reached over and grabbed Dom's rifle. She began crawling across the sand towards the tribesman's hiding place. She looked like an Amazon in a low-budget porn movie.

The tribesman aimed the rifle over the rock and fired a few shots in Ben's direction. He pulled back from the edge. A bullet sent a shower of stone fragments over him. The firing stopped. He peered over the rim again.

Helen lay flat on the ground at the base of the rock. The tribesman was only a few feet away on the other side.

Ben aimed his rifle just above the rock, where the guy's head had been.

Helen looked up at him. He nodded. She stood up quickly and fired twice. The gangly frame of the man fell out from behind the rock onto the floor of the gully. Helen fired again. The man's head exploded.

The echo of the last shot faded, and the ancient stillness of the sheltered gorge returned.

"Are you alright?" he shouted.

"I am now."

* * * *

Ben recovered his shoes and reached the base of the cliff ten minutes later. He walked towards the gorge and found Helen, fully dressed, smoking a cigarette. She was standing in front of Esau and Daniel.

She turned and looked at him as he approached.

"He was going to die anyway," she said.

He stopped in front of Esau. He knelt down and closed the African's eyes.

"Such a waste," he said. They'd been shot like worthless dogs, two men with mothers, wives, siblings and children. Two seconds of violence causing a lifetime of pain and loss for so many.

"At least he was spared the hideous death Shackleton described."

"It'd be good to know for sure." He pulled the syringe pack from his pocket rolled Esau over gently and pulled the African's shirt up. He plunged the needle in between two vertebrae near the base of the spine and filled the syringe with fluid. He stood back up, pocketed the vial and faced Helen. There was a large bruise under her left eye and a cut on her forehead.

"Thank you for not leaving me," she said.

He nodded. "Just make sure I get my sister back."

"I will." She looked up at the sun in the Western sky. "We'd better head back to the jeep before it gets dark." She turned and started walking away.

"Wait," He said. She stopped and looked back at him. "We can't go back to Nairobi yet."

"Don't you want to see your sister as soon as possible?"

"Not if I give her the virus."

"Sorry?"

280

"Esau may have infected me."

Helen looked confused. "But you were wearing a mask."

"It doesn't matter," he said. "He would have been contagious when I talked to him on Saturday, which means I've been contagious from this morning, if not before."

Her mouth opened to object.

"Do the maths."

She shook her head for a moment and took a deep breath. "Call Shackleton, he might have the results by now, then we'll know for sure."

The phone call, it must have been him. He pulled the mobile out of his pocket and dialled voicemail. He had one message:

"It's Paul Shackleton. I'm afraid I have some bad news. The sample you gave us had partially decayed. We'll need to perform further amplification procedures so the results won't be ready till later today. I'll call you as soon as we know. In the meantime, if you do make contact with Kimani make sure that you use the protective equipment we provided."

He put the phone in his pocket.

"What did it say?" Helen asked.

"They won't have the results till later."

"What do we do now?"

"We wait, and we make sure that no one leaves the village until we find out. I'll take another sample now in case the mutation developed since Saturday."

"What about us? What if he was infectious when you saw him?" Helen asked.

He looked down at Esau. "We'll be begging for someone to do the same to us."

Chapter 34

They reached the hamlet just after six.

The door to the grandmother's hut was open. Ben knocked on the frame and stepped inside. Helen followed. The old woman was sitting on a chair. She looked at Ben with a bleak expression.

"They have been killed," she said.

He didn't respond.

She stared at Helen. "I knew today would bring evil to my home."

Helen looked like she was about to say something but the old woman shook her head.

"I am not blaming you. It was meant to be. Unlike Western people, we do not fear death."

"I'm very sorry for what's happened," Ben said.

"It is only their bodies that have died," she continued. "Their spirits are now free. They were good boys. They will live forever."

He nodded. He didn't have the heart to say anything about the virus, not until he was absolutely certain.

"Goodbye." The old woman turned her back to them.

Helen looked at him with a questioning expression. He nodded his head towards the door. They walked out of the hut.

"What about the virus?" she asked once they were outside. "Shouldn't we tell her she's in danger?"

"Not now," he said. "We'll wait till we've had confirmation from Shackleton before we drop that one on her."

"But we've got to make sure no one leaves here."

"It's getting late. No one will be going anywhere now, and I know somewhere we can keep an eye on this place."

* * * *

"Give me your lighter. I'll get some wood and start a fire," he said, and began clearing the half-burnt branches from the patch of ground that Curtis and Dom had used while they camped there. "You get the food we bought this morning."

He wandered off into the bushes and gathered a large pile of dry branches. He built a fire and lit the kindling at its base. Within a few minutes a roaring blaze sent sparks flying into the air.

Helen sat down a few feet away. She put two plastic bags containing cakes, crisps and water between them. She laid her shoulder bag on the other side.

They ate their meal as the last remnants of twilight disappeared from the sky. They finished eating and sat in silence watching the flames paint an ever-changing masterpiece of flickering images. They could have been on safari, it was as though the death and mayhem of the past days had never happened.

He looked across at Helen. Her face glowed from the reflection of the fire. She looked a completely different woman from the one he'd met ten days earlier. The smokescreen of make-up and fashion had been washed away to reveal genuine beauty. But there was something else about her that was different.

She looked up at him.

"How are you feeling?" he asked. "Did they...hurt you?"

"Not really." she said. She pulled a packet of cigarettes out of her bag and lit one. "What about you? The way you were lying on the gully floor I thought you were dead."

"I'm fine, a bit bruised, but nothing that won't mend." He sighed. "I just wish it hadn't all been a waste of time."

There was a loud rustle from a nearby bush. He snapped his head round to look towards the source but it was pitch black. He turned back, Helen had pulled her gun out of her bag. A twig cracked and a low-pitched growl came from the darkness.

He picked up a large stone and threw it in the direction of the noise. It crashed into the branches. The undergrowth shook and a scampering of paws fled away from them.

"Don't worry," he said, turning back to the flames. "They'll leave us alone as long we keep the fire going."

Helen shuffled over to within a foot of him and put the gun down next to her.

"I don't think it's been a waste of time," she said.

"Sorry?"

"You said this had all been a waste of time."

"Oh." He turned away. "All I've achieved is to lead those men to Esau so they could kill him. On top of that there's a chance I've spread a killer virus across the world. I'd never have got involved if I'd known it would end up like this."

"You did what you thought was right." She looked down. "That's more than I've done for the past few years."

It was hard to feel hatred in the face of genuine remorse.

"You made the right choice today," he said.

"I know, I'm changing." She looked up, her expression serious. "Remember when we were in the cave and I told you I thought I'd shot someone, but I was given a second chance?" He nodded. "At first I reacted badly to it, I felt I'd sunk to a new low. I'd pulled the trigger without knowing the gun wasn't loaded. I felt as though I had actually murdered someone. The next day I was sick with guilt, but I was given the chance to put that behind me.

"The woman you saw in the hospital had been half buried near our headquarters in Surrey. Luke thought he'd killed her. He left her for dead, but she wasn't. She was able to pull her mobile out of her pocket and hit my number. She couldn't speak but it didn't matter, our phones are fitted with GPS. I knew her exact position within a minute.

"I had a choice. I could phone Luke so he could go and finish the job, or I could help her and risk being killed myself. A voice inside told me to help her at all cost. I ignored my conscience for years and I was miserable because of it, so I decided to listen for once."

"If your conscience has suddenly come back to life why haven't you got my sister away from that bastard?" he said.

"It's not that simple. I couldn't just walk out with her."

"So why can you now?"

"Esau's dead," Helen replied. "He has no reason to keep her any more."

"You'd better be right."

"Believe me, once I started to change I wanted to help you and your sister. But I couldn't do anything until we'd resolved this Spiravex business. I had to play my part, which at the time meant doing what Slade told me."

"You should have gone to the police," he said.

"That wouldn't have done any good. Slade has connections everywhere. Besides, I'm not sure it was the right thing to do. Over the past week I've started to feel that we might be placed where we are for a purpose, no matter how much we don't understand it."

"What on earth are you talking about?"

"I'm saying that I think I was meant to be in Slade. Maybe to help you, but definitely for another reason, an even greater one." She picked up a small stone and turned it over in her fingers. "Two days ago Shackleton said something that blew me away, made me look at my life completely differently. For the first time everything made sense." She looked back and held his gaze. "I betrayed someone Ben, a good man, like you. I led him to his death for money and revenge."

"The guy who was going to sell Spiravex?"

She nodded. "I hated myself for what I did, but on Monday I found out my betrayal of Adam saved millions of lives, maybe even saved the human race. What I did was wrong, I know that, and I wish I could have achieved the same result without being such a bitch, but it didn't happen that way. I'm not even sure it could have happened differently. If I'd listened to my conscience I wouldn't have been working for Slade in the first place and Adam would never have come to me. It feels like more than just a set of coincidences. It was as though my whole life had been pointing towards that one event. I can't excuse what I did, but Adam needed to be stopped somehow. Knowing that has set me free to make my future better."

How convenient. She gets to spend half her life screwing up other people's lives, then realises she has a conscience and walks away from her past. "I don't think you're taking enough notice of your conscience yet," Ben said. "If you were you wouldn't be able to dismiss all the bad things you've done by saying it was meant to be."

"I'm not dismissing them," she paused and looked down. "Something else has happened too."

She went silent and looked at the ground. Was she playing a game? Was she being dramatic? He really couldn't be bothered with it, but there was no one else to talk to. "What?"

"I feel embarrassed telling you," she said, still looking down.

"I'm a GU doctor, believe me, there is nothing you could tell me that is embarrassing."

She looked up again and smiled. It wasn't an arch smile, or an alluring smile, just a grateful, open smile, something he'd not seen her do yet. It made her look completely different, someone he might want to be with.

"Something happened to me up on the mountain."

"A lot happened up there."

"No, when I passed out."

"You didn't pass out, you were dead."

Her mouth opened to say something, but she looked away troubled.

"Did something happen to you while you weren't breathing?" he asked.

She turned back and nodded.

It was his turn to avoid eye contact and feel uncomfortable.

"I could see you giving me CPR," she said.

He knew what was coming next.

"I could see everything, and I mean everything around us, completely clearly. I saw you stuck on the cliff with your face buried in the rock, I saw Daniel look down and call to you and how you struggled to climb higher."

This wasn't the first time someone had said something like this to him. He turned back.

"Don't tell me, you went into a tunnel," he said.

She looked shocked.

"And there was someone at the end and they made you feel good." Judging by her expression he'd nailed it completely. When he'd done a rotation in Casualty as a junior doctor he'd come across a man who died of a heart attack. After they resuscitated him he claimed to have seen them working on him. He also had the tunnel experience and seen the bloke who made him feel good. When he spoke to the senior doctor about it, he was told it was quite common, and that it was probably residual brain activity. That didn't change the fact that the whole episode was quite unnerving.

"You had an NDE," he said. Her expression was blank. "A near death experience, it's just the brain firing after your heart has stopped."

"How come I could see you then?"

"I don't know, maybe it was the scene that you last saw or something." The evidence of out of body experiences provided by people who had experienced an NDE often seemed compelling. It was tempting to be suckered in by it, but until the properly controlled trial set up by emergency doctor Sam Parnia was completed, it made sense to treat the whole subject with skepticism. If that trial proved the phenomenon to be real, that would be a very big deal though, and would shake the foundations of science.

"This man, or being," she smiled. "It felt so good. So much love, I've never experienced anything like it. It felt as though he knew everything about me, and yet he didn't condemn me."

"And that's why you feel you can walk away from all the suffering you've caused with a free conscience?"

This was doing his head in.

"No, I didn't say that. I know I still have to deal with the past. I may not have felt condemned, but I wasn't forgiven either. I'm just saying that I feel like I can have a different future. It ties in with this whole feeling I'd been having of the way I was acting being necessary to make sure that things happened the way they did. Now that those things are done, I don't have to carry on being like that."

"Don't you find it a bit perverse that you saved the world by getting your ex-boyfriend murdered, whereas I got two innocent men killed and will probably die myself because I tried to do the right thing?"

"It might seem like that now, but I believe there was a reason why you became a part of this."

"No, there is no reason. There is no plan or purpose. It's all just random actions, and I screwed up."

"I believed life was random until all this happened, like I was certain the conscience was just a result of evolution, but now I'm not so sure. Even if it is just a genetic trick, I'd rather obey it and be happy than go against my nature because my intellect tells me it's OK." Helen drew her knees up to her chest and rested her chin on them. "It feels better to believe that there's a purpose to all this. It gives me peace."

"Even if it's a lie?" Ben said. "You're a scientist. You can't really believe in nonsense like that."

"I don't know what science tells me any more. I thought I did, but I'm starting to realise that what I once thought were facts were in reality only beliefs. I was convinced there was no God and that the conscience was an irrelevant by-product of evolution making the words good and bad meaningless. I'm starting to see that the evidence I was using was based on guesswork by people who were as fervent in their atheism as I was."

"Maybe you're not such a good scientist," he said. "If you don't believe there's real evidence then you can't have heard of Charles Darwin."

"Something your sister said about his theory has been bugging me. It's made me look at the problem from a different angle."

"Ruth is indoctrinated. As much as I love her, you can't take her seriously."

"You're probably right. That's why I dislike most organised religion, it seems to be all about mind control and who's the boss. Even so, she made me see something that has been staring me in the face for years, but because I was so committed to atheism I'd never noticed it."

"What? You suddenly realised that all science was a lie, the devil buried fossils to stop us believing in God, and the world is only four thousand years old?" Ben laughed. That was why he never spoke to Ruth about it. You can't reason with someone who refuses to look at the evidence rationally.

"She didn't mention any of that," she said. "She used the chicken and egg riddle to show the impossibility of spontaneous life. Which came first, DNA, which needs an enzyme to form it, or the enzyme, which is coded for by the DNA? I fobbed her off with the standard line that DNA came into existence first by chance."

"Which is possible," he said.

"Yes, but the odds against it are huge. Ruth compared it to dropping a piece of wire on a beach and coming back a billion years later to find a microchip."

"A typical creationist's response."

"That was my reaction, but I knew I'd given a superficial answer to what was really a fundamental question. I realised Ruth had only scratched the surface of the riddle about the origin of life. Life doesn't begin with DNA."

"But it's the first step."

"Not really. DNA is just information in the form of a chemical code, it's only when this code is read by translating enzymes that the processes of life begin. So the second riddle is, 'If DNA is a code for making enzymes but only enzymes can translate this code, how did the enzymes get made?' Since there are over twenty of these translating enzymes working together in a system, the problem is even more complex than the one for making a piece of DNA."

"This system could have evolved from something simpler, like the RNA world," he said.

"The RNA world theory is a red herring, a blind alley. It doesn't overcome the problem of how one chemical system, nucleic acids, came to contain a code for a completely different chemical system, amino acids, and how that code contains the instructions for a translation system."

Helen leaned backwards and put her hands on the ground behind her. Ben caught a glimpse of soft white flesh through a tear in her blouse. If only he could forgive her as quickly as she was able to forgive herself, they could quit talking about irrelevant rubbish and have some fun under the stars. There was no way he'd sink that low though, not while his sister was still in danger.

"It's like a Japanese person speaking on the phone to someone from England on how to make a machine that translates Japanese to English, when neither can speak the other's language," she continued. "For all the English person knows, he could be giving him a recipe for Sushi. The British man needs the machine before he can understand how to make the machine. For the same reason, without the translation enzymes already up and running life cannot start."

"The enzymes came into existence by chance then."

Helen laughed. "All twenty? As well as the DNA, in the same place at the same time? That would be like Ruth's example of the wire on the beach, but instead of coming back to find a silicon chip you'd find a laptop loaded with the latest version of Windows. To believe that requires more faith than it does to accept your sister's solution to the riddle."

"That God created everything?" Ben shook his head.

"I don't know." Helen looked away. "Before recently I despised the idea as much as you, but codes and language appearing at the dawn of life and containing incredibly complex instructions can only be a sign of..." she paused and widened her eyes as if looking for words, "...well, of intelligent initiation." She shook her head and smiled. "It's ironic that Darwin's famous sop to his Christian wife, Emma Wedgwood, about some creator breathing life into an original form, may have been his last stroke of genius. After today I'm not so sure there isn't some awesome being out there. Also, I'm no longer convinced that science is objective. I mean look at how we answer the questions surrounding the Big Bang theory. Physicists like Stephen Hawking have shown that the odds of the universe coming into existence in such a way that it's able to support life are smaller than trillions of trillions to one. To overcome this they have proposed the theory of a multiverse. They believe that there are trillions of other universes, all completely incapable of supporting life, to balance the statistical chances of our universe existing with life. But they have absolutely no evidence for it, and never will. It has no more basis in fact than the story of the world being created in six days, and requires an equal amount of faith to believe in it. They just create a theory to satisfy the fact that modern science always demands a natural explanation. Isn't that a subjective position?"

Ben looked up at the sky. It wasn't like the one in southern England. There was no light pollution or smog to block out the endless array of stars.

"Look up," he said. "If you'd told people a thousand years ago that there are millions of galaxies, each containing millions of suns and planets, they would have said that was ridiculous."

They both gazed at the awesome spectacle above them.

"But we can see them," Helen eventually said. "We didn't know what they were, but we could still see them, just like we didn't know why the sun was hot, but we could always feel its heat. But we'll never be able to see other universes. It's purely imagination. To believe there isn't a creating force requires at least the same amount of blind faith as it does to believe that some superior being made this crazy world and everything in it."

"So you're a convert?"

Helen shook her head.

"No, I'm not saying that. I'm only saying that what I used to believe, atheism, was as much a religion as Buddhism or Islam, but I didn't realise it. It was easy to believe the things I did because they're so rarely challenged by the modern world. Like everyone else, I accepted theories as proven facts. But they're not. The truth is, I don't know who's right, but I want to learn more. I don't let the idiots on the TV form my opinions. The media changes its view on morality and faith like MTV presenters change their hairstyles. I need to find out this stuff for myself. If Christ, or Mohammad, or

Buddha is right, and there is an eternal soul, what could be more important than learning about how to look after it?"

"Good for you. But in my opinion you're wasting your time. I think you'll find it's all a load of self-contradicting nonsense." He looked into the darkness surrounding the fire. "It's tempting to believe there's something out there, that if I die of this wretched virus I'll go to a better place, but how can I believe in a God? My parents claimed to be servants of God, yet they were murdered in cold blood. What kind of a God allows that to happen to people who only wanted to help others? And then there's Julia..." He shook his head, looked at Helen and pointed at the fire. "My parents believed in hell. They were good people, but their religion twisted their minds into thinking that anyone who didn't believe the same thing as they did was going to burn for eternity. Even if there was a God I wouldn't want anything to do with an egotistical maniac who punishes people like that. My wife didn't believe in God. Are you telling me that she's gone to hell in spite of all the good she did and because you've had some new age epiphany you get to go to a better place?"

"No, I'm not..."

The satellite phone started ringing. He pulled it out of his pocket and answered it.

"Doctor Williams?" Shackleton asked.

"Yes."

"I have the results."

"And?"

"Have you found Mister Kimani?"

"A few hours ago."

"How is he?"

"Ill," Ben replied.

"What's your diagnosis?"

"You tell me."

"Any symptoms he's suffering cannot have arisen from the mutant strain."

"Why not?"

"There is no trace of the second mutation. Our tests show he has Lyme disease."

"You don't get that in Africa," Ben replied.

"He probably caught it in England. It can lie dormant for months."

Ben fell silent.

"Doctor Williams? Are you still there?"

"Yes," he replied. "So he couldn't have been contagious on Saturday?"

"No. But we still need to get him in for observation. It is likely the mutation will develop at a later stage."

"He won't be coming in for any tests."

"But Doctor Williams," Shackleton said, "we had an agreement."

"He won't be coming in because he's dead."

He hung up and turned to Helen.

"Phone your boss and tell him to release my sister," he said. "We're going home."

* * * *

Helen pulled her mobile out of her bag and dialled Luke's number.

"What's going on?" he said. "I haven't heard anything since you left the States. Have you found Kimani?"

"Yes," Helen replied.

"And?"

"He's dead."

"Good. And Williams?"

"He's here with me now."

"Kill him. He knows too much."

"But Shackleton..."

"I don't give a damn about Shackleton. Just kill Williams. Phone me once it's done. As soon as I know he's dead we'll not need his sister any more. I'm bored of being a babysitter."

Chapter 35

Helen pulled the SLK up in front of Slade's Elizabethan mansion at ten-thirty pm. Luke was waiting for her on the steps.

She picked up her shoulder bag, got out and walked across the gravel to stand in front of him.

He grabbed her chin and turned her face to one side. "Did you learn nothing in Namibia?"

"Williams was too strong," she replied.

"How did he guess you were going to kill him?"

"Would you trust me?"

Luke examined her for a few moments then turned round and marched inside.

She followed him through the house into the communications room. They walked towards the far end of the room. She passed him and sat in the armchair that faced the LCD screens on the opposite wall. Luke sat on the sofa facing the windows.

"What do we do now?" she asked.

"We wait," Luke said. "We have his sister. He'll not expose us while he believes there's a chance he can save her."

"I don't think he'd go to the police now," she said. "He was convinced by what Shackleton told him."

"I'm not interested in what he thinks about Spiravex or Marivant. It's us, Slade, that I'm protecting. We don't let our enemies roam around at will."

She glanced down at her shoulder bag. The mobile was still visible on the top.

"Do you think Williams will just walk in here and give himself up?" she asked.

* * * *

Ben pushed the lid of the boot open. He stretched his arms over the edge and pulled himself out of the tiny space he'd been crammed into for the past ten minutes. He got to his feet, put his mobile in his pocket and picked up the Berretta. He closed the boot and looked around.

The scene was pretty much as Helen had described. An iron lantern hung over the ancient stone doorway and lit the steps below. The only other light came from four windows to the far left of the entrance. Beyond that the cloudy night sky revealed nothing but darkness.

He ran up to the door and pushed it open. He hurried across the small entrance hall, passing beneath the solitary camera, and entered a short corridor that led through the centre of the building.

He paused in the shadows.

She'd made him memorise six signals, each giving different locations for her and Luke. They were in the communications room. He pictured her diagram of the house. The comms room was located at the left-hand end of the main passage. The entrance to the cellar lay opposite the comms room in the kitchen. He knew from her signal that Luke couldn't see the security monitors or the kitchen. But that could change at any time.

He pulled the mobile out of his pocket. They were still chatting.

He put his back against the oak panelling and inched towards the end of the corridor. He stopped where it joined the main passage at right angles and peered out to the left. Luke's voice echoed from an open door at the far end.

He listened to his mobile again. Nothing had changed. He slipped it back into his pocket.

He turned left and crept towards the comms room. He stayed close to the wall, taking care not to brush against the sombre portraits that hung at six-foot intervals. His pulse raced every time his eyes caught the reflection of a face in the dark windows on the other side.

With each step he took, the voices from the end of the passage grew louder. Wisps of Helen's softer tones were all but lost beneath Luke's booming bass.

He stopped two metres short of the comms room. Was now the moment for a surprise attack? He fancied his chances; he had a gun and he was stronger than most men. But Helen had consistently ruled out a direct confrontation; she was too scared.

Luke could wait; getting his sister was all that mattered.

He looked over at the entrance to the kitchen. The door stood open.

He crossed the passage and edged along next to the windows, keeping his eyes on the comms room.

The profile of the back of an armchair came into view, then Helen's hair and face. Another pace revealed Luke's hand resting on the studded leather arm of a Chesterfield sofa. Ben took a short step and Luke's mass of black hair appeared.

Ben slipped into the kitchen, waited by the entrance, and listened.

They were still talking.

He looked to his left, grabbed the handle of the cellar door and turned it. There was a creak. He paused.

The voices had stopped.

He raised the gun in his right hand and focused on the doorway.

The conversation resumed. He breathed out and turned the handle as fast as he could.

He pulled the door open and stepped onto a stone staircase that spiralled down into the dark. He felt for the light switch and eased it on. He closed the cellar door and descended into the cold damp air.

At the bottom there was a short passage with two iron doors on either side. Each door had a small window in it, but only the cell on the far right had light coming from inside. He headed straight for it.

The room contained an iron-framed bed with two plastic buckets next to it. Ben instantly recognised the red hair of the woman curled up on the bed.

"Ruth." Relief flooded though him and washed away five days of worry.

He smiled and tapped the window.

Ruth turned her head and squinted at him.

His smile disappeared. She had a black eye and a spilt lip; grazes and bruises covered her arms.

She looked away and put her head back on the pillow.

"Ruth, it's me, Ben."

She lay still.

Maybe she thought it was someone else, someone coming to hurt her again. A fierce rage exploded inside him as he thought of Luke sitting in the room above.

"Focus," he said.

He looked at the keypad, but his mind was consumed with hate.

He shook his head.

"Think man."

It came back.

Three-five-two-six.

He entered the numbers. A red light lit up on the pad. He tried the door anyway, it didn't budge.

He was certain it was the right combination.

He punched the code in a second time, making sure the pad beeped as he pressed each number. It flashed red. He rattled the door but it stayed closed.

He looked up at the security camera in the corner

* * * *

Helen tried to ignore the screen. "Do you know the real reason why those patients had to die?"

Luke smiled. "I don't care for reasons. I'm given orders, I carry them out, and I get paid. It's that simple."

"So it wouldn't make you feel any better if you knew that millions of lives had been saved?"

He shrugged. "As long as I get my money."

The screen switched from the kitchen to the cellar.

What the hell was he doing?

Ben was still looking at the pad. His hand reached for it again. The security workstation beeped. She could see a red text box flashing.

Luke turned round and looked at it.

"I'll sort it out," Helen said. She stood up. "Probably just a pigeon tripping the alarm."

She walked over to the keyboard. There was a message: 'Incorrect code entered three times - door 27. Code entered: 3526, 3526, 3526.'

It'd worked a week ago. She minimised the window and switched the sound off. She didn't want to reset the system in case he tried again.

She turned round.

Luke was staring at the security monitor on the wall.

"All clear," Helen said. She started to walk back to him; he didn't take his eyes away from the screen. She looked up; the view changed from the kitchen to the cellar. The passage was empty, but the red flashing of the keypad betrayed the otherwise innocent scene.

Helen stopped.

Luke stood up and smiled. He reached inside his jacket pocket and pulled his gun out. "Why so nervous Helen?"

"I tend to get nervous when someone points a gun at me," she said.

Luke went over to her armchair. He picked up her shoulder bag and shook the contents onto the floor. "Where's your gun?"

"I left it in the car."

He walked towards her. "You always have your gun on you."

"Luke, I'm too tired for this."

"Enough," Luke said. "I'll deal with you later."

He lifted his arm back and smashed the butt of the gun against her temple.

* * * *

Ben held himself flat against the wall of the cell. Five minutes had passed since the keypad started flashing continuously.

How much longer should he hide? What if it hadn't triggered an alarm?

There was the sound of a light switch being turned on.

He inched closer to the window. Luke's back filled the doorway of the cell next to Ruth's. Luke lifted his hand and turned the light off.

Ben spun round and scanned the darkness for a place to hide. There was nothing, except for the bed. He crossed the room and felt for the iron frame. He dropped onto the floor and slid underneath.

A switch was flicked in the cell next to him.

He passed his hands along the invisible underside of the bed. He pushed his toes into the gap between the mattress and the rim of the iron frame.

There was another click on the neighbouring wall.

He put his hands on the inside lip of the frame above his head and lifted himself up. He pressed as close to the mattress as his strength would allow.

The door opened, sending a wedge of light across the floor. An instant later the whole room lit up.

Every muscle in Ben's body strained to full capacity. He pressed his lips closed to stifle the sound of his breathing. Itchy droplets of sweat clung to his forehead.

He looked to the side. A pair of black leather shoes took a step closer.

His arms started shaking. He stared at the mattress and willed it to stay still. Even if that didn't give him away the explosions in his heart surely would. He couldn't hold on much longer.

The shoes turned and walked back towards the door. They stopped.

His muscles screamed at him to let go.

The light went out, the shoes disappeared out of view and the door was pulled to.

He relaxed his muscles, eased himself back onto the floor, and breathed deeply. He wiped his forehead with his sleeve.

There was a loud beep and a clunk from outside.

He rolled out from under the bed, got to his feet and pulled the gun from the front of his jeans.

He crept towards the window to see Luke enter Ruth's cell.

Ben eased the door of his cell open and held the gun out in front of him. He took two paces into the passage where he had a clear view of Luke.

"Don't move," he said.

Luke took a step towards Ruth.

Ben pointed the gun above Luke's head and fired.

"I will kill you," Ben said. "I've already killed four of your men."

Luke stopped.

"Drop the gun," Ben said.

298

There was a pause before Luke released the pistol. It clattered on to the stone floor.

"Kick it away."

Luke nudged the gun towards Ruth, who was trying to sit upright on the bed.

Ben stepped into the cell. "On the floor."

Luke got on his knees, put his hands on the ground and lowered himself down.

Ben glanced at Ruth. He swallowed hard at the sight of the weeping cuts on her face and arms.

"He did this didn't he?"

Her eyes moved towards Luke and tears formed.

Ben looked at the man lying on the floor. He took a step back and launched a kick into Luke's stomach, then another. The next blow was aimed at Luke's crotch.

Each time his size-eleven boot crashed into flesh and bone, his need to inflict pain only increased. He stopped and took a step sideways. He lifted his foot and sent the toecap hurtling towards Luke's face. It struck just below the Gallic nose and sent a tooth flying across the floor.

"Ben!" Ruth's feeble voice just managed to penetrate his mushrooming rage. "Stop."

He looked at his handiwork. He was so used to putting people back together that he could hardly believe the scene was of his own making. Luke was lying still. His nose oozed blood and his upper lip was already beginning to swell.

He looked at Ruth; his breathing slowed. "Let's get out of here."

He leaned under the bed and grabbed Luke's pistol.

"Hold this." He handed it to Ruth then leaned forward and picked her up in his arms.

He carried her out of the cellar, up the stairs and into the kitchen. He stopped in front of the comms room. Helen was lying on the floor with her hands tied behind her back. Her head moved and she groaned.

He stepped inside, lowered Ruth to the floor and rested her back against the wall. He crossed the room and knelt by Helen. He undid the telephone cord tied around her wrists. Her eyes opened.

"Do you know where you are?" he asked.

She nodded.

He lifted her upright, pulled her towards the armchair and leaned her against the soft leather. He put the Beretta in her right hand and closed her fingers round it.

"I'll be back in a minute," he said.

He returned to Ruth, picked her up and walked down the passageway. He could feel the eyes of the dignitaries following him. How would they feel if they knew their home had been used for torture? Maybe they'd committed their own atrocities in the cellar, back in the days of serfdom when the landlords owned the peasants.

He stepped onto the porch and walked to the SLK.

Helen had left it unlocked with the keys in the ignition, ready for a quick escape. He opened the passenger door and put Ruth on the seat. He went round to the driver's side, started the engine and turned the heating on. It might be a summer's evening, but Ruth was shivering.

He leaned over and lifted the gun out of Ruth's lap.

"Use this if you need to," he said, and held it in front of her. She looked at Luke's gun, but didn't say anything. "Take it Ruth."

She put her left hand out and held the handle. He let go and it fell into her lap again.

"Be careful," she said.

He reached over and brushed a tear from her cheek. He turned away from her and looked up at the imposing brick façade of Slade's headquarters. He got out of the car, walked up the steps and entered the hall.

The sound of a gunshot stopped him.

Helen.

He ran to the end of the corridor and turned into the main passage.

It felt like two hundred pounds of steel slamming into him.

A second later he was lying on the floor, Luke's hand gripped his collar.

Ben tried to push himself up, but he was held tight.

Luke raised a fist and punched him hard in the face. His head jolted back onto the carpet.

"You think you're strong enough to take me out?" Luke said, and spat blood into Ben's face. He leaned forward so his black eyes filled Ben's view. "I had worse whenever I played rugby." He

300

raised his fist again, but Ben wasn't going to wait for it this time. He jerked forward and head butted Luke.

The grip on his collar loosened. He forced himself up, unbalanced Luke and sent him toppling to one side.

He scrambled away, but a hand grabbed his hair and pushed him forward. His face smashed into the floor. His nose was pressed into the musty carpet.

"Leave him alone!" Helen shouted.

His arm was twisted into an agonising angle behind his back. He was lifted to his knees and turned round. He struggled against Luke's hold. His arm was bent further; every tendon in his shoulder stretched to the point of tearing.

He was raised to his feet. He became a shield between Luke and Helen's gun. She was at the far end of the corridor, supporting herself with one arm against the wall, the other pointed the Beretta at them.

"Let him go!" Helen said. She took an unsteady step closer.

He was moved into the corridor that led to the entrance hall. They stopped. Luke's grip tightened in Ben's hair and his head was yanked back. The wood panelling accelerated towards his face, smacking into his forehead.

But Luke wasn't the only one to survive a stray boot on the sports field.

"You'll have to try harder than that," he said. He struggled against Luke's grip, but with no effect.

"As you wish."

His head was whipped back again and smashed at full force into the unyielding oak. His legs wobbled beneath him and his eyes rolled into his head. Everything went black.

Chapter 36

"Ben."

He opened his eyes and saw Helen leaning over him. "How long have I been out?"

"Two or three minutes."

He sat up and felt the lump on his forehead. "Is Ruth OK?"

Helen took a deep breath.

Something was wrong. He tried to get to his feet but nausea and dizziness pinned him down. "I left her in the car."

"Luke took it."

He closed his eyes. He'd had her in his arms. "Why didn't you stop him?"

"I couldn't. When I reached the steps he was already halfway down the drive."

He tried to stand up again. This time he succeeded. He put his hand against the wall to steady himself. It took a few seconds for his head to settle. He took two cautious steps forward, then walked to the entrance.

It was drizzling. A rectangle of drier gravel was left where Helen's SLK had been. He looked across the lawns towards a floodlit patch of drive in front of the gates. The car stood abandoned; both doors were open.

Helen joined him.

"Why did he stop there?" he asked.

"When you triggered the alarm, the system initiated a security lockdown," she said. "The perimeter's sealed until it's reset."

"They're in the house?"

"The grounds. There's over twenty acres."

He stepped onto the gravel drive and looked into the darkness on either side of the building.

"It might be easier to find them on a security camera first," Helen said, "and we need more than one gun."

He looked at the SLK and remembered the pistol he'd left in Ruth's lap. Helen was right. They'd stand a better chance if they were both armed.

They headed back into the house.

"Luke will find somewhere he can gain a strategic advantage," she said.

"Isn't having my sister enough?"

They turned left into the main passage and hurried towards the end.

"His only thought is survival. To survive he needs to kill us. He taught me to never give up my weapon, no matter what. You need to think like that too."

"I have to save Ruth," he said. "I'm ready to take her place if that's what Luke wants."

"You'd be dying for nothing. The moment we lose our weapons we're all dead. He knows that's how I'll be thinking. That's why he isn't standing in front of the house right now with a gun to her head demanding we give ourselves up."

"So what's he doing?"

They reached the comms room.

"Like I said, he's looking for a strategic advantage, and I think I know where he'll find it."

Helen walked over to a computer terminal and typed in a command. One of the security monitors switched to show the Mercedes in front of the gates. She hit a key. The image on the screen changed to a view looking down on the front door. She tapped the key again; the screen went black. Ben squinted as he examined the different shades of darkness.

Helen's sleek fingers rattled across the keyboard and the image changed. The picture remained dark except for a small red object moving away from the camera at the top of the screen.

"Infrared?" he asked.

Helen nodded and pressed another key. The image grew larger. The red shape turned into the multicoloured outline of a man running away from them. The right-hand side of the figure was much larger, like he had a humpback: he was carrying Ruth over his shoulder.

The coloured shape blurred and started to fade.

"What's happening?"

"He's taking her into the woods. He can use the cover of the trees to pick us off one at a time."

They watched the last traces of colour dissolve into the darkness.

She turned round and walked past him to a door on the opposite side of the room. She opened it and entered.

He followed her. On the wall to the left stood three metal racks loaded with electronic boxes, which were interconnected by a thicket of coloured cables. LEDs flickered frantically, and dozens of hidden fans whirred in a continuous hum as they cooled the sleepless silicon.

Two metal cabinets stood against the right-hand wall, each had a security keypad on the front. Helen typed a number into the nearest one and the door clicked opened.

"You've got to be kidding," he said.

The top half of the cabinet had at least ten pistols, eight rifles and a stash of grenades.

"There's more in the other one," Helen said.

"Isn't that enough? You could stage a coup with that lot."

Helen reached into the cupboard, grabbed a pistol and handed it to him. He automatically released the magazine and pulled the barrel back. He held the gun up to the light and checked the chamber. It was empty. He released the barrel and squeezed the trigger.

"You know your way around a gun," Helen said.

He looked down. She was crouched on the floor, a box full of ammo between her feet.

"Old habits die hard," he said. "I went to private school. Every Wednesday we played soldiers in the Cadet Force."

"They let you use real guns?"

He nodded and pushed the magazine home. He slid the barrel back and loaded a round. He checked the safety then secured the gun in the back of his trousers.

Helen handed him a spare magazine and took one for herself. He slipped it into his pocket.

She rummaged around inside the box and pulled out a clip. She stood up, grabbed a laser-sighted rifle and loaded it.

"Aren't you overdoing it?" he asked. "There are two of us."

"You don't know Luke." She slid the rifle strap over her shoulder and pushed past him.

They started to cross the room.

She stopped after a couple of yards.

"Hang on," she said, then turned back to the weapons room.

"I think we've got enough."

She ignored him.

She entered a code into the keypad on the second cupboard.

"We haven't got time for this." He said.

"Luke isn't going anywhere." She opened the cabinet and pulled out two boxes, each big enough to hold a football. She handed one to Ben.

He turned it in his hands.

"Open it," Helen said.

He crouched down, put the box on the floor and lifted the lid off. He pulled back the white crêpe paper to reveal what looked like a pair of binoculars attached to a three-way rubber strap.

"Night-vision goggles," Helen said. "Now we have the advantage."

He started to put the goggles on.

"Wait," Helen said. "You'll blind yourself in this light."

He adjusted the straps so the goggles rested on his forehead.

They left the store and went into the main passage. Helen crossed to the other side and flicked a switch next to the kitchen door. The passage lights went out.

"If Luke's watching the house he won't be able to see our movements," she said. "You can put the goggles on now."

He pulled them down over his eyes. "I can't see anything."

"There's a button on the left."

He ran his fingers along the edge of the goggles and found it. His world turned from black to green.

Everything looked alien. The blinkered view made him feel clumsy and vulnerable. He pulled the gun from his trousers. His heartbeat upped a notch and adrenalin rushed through him, burning away the fog of concussion.

He turned round. Helen was striding down the passage. He jogged after her, catching up as she passed the corridor leading to the entrance hall. She picked up her pace and they soon reached the far end of the passage.

Helen pushed open a door and he followed her into the room.

He turned his head to try to see around him. Three of the walls were lined with books. The other wall housed a set of French windows.

She walked past a low, carved table placed between two armchairs and reached the back of the room. She ran her fingers along a shelf above her head till she found what she was looking for. She crossed the room and unlocked the French windows. He followed her onto a wide patio flanked by classical sculptures.

The drizzle had turned to a steady rain. He felt water leak into his trainers as they splashed through large puddles on the stone slabs. They arrived at a set of steps and ran down onto a lawn that stretched more than a hundred yards towards an area of woodland.

He struggled to keep his footing as they sped across the slippery grass. Droplets gathered on his lenses, turning his surroundings into a green blur. He wiped them with his fingers, leaving a distorted smear.

They reached the end of the lawn and slowed to a walk. Helen started down a narrow path leading into the woods, but he put a hand on her shoulder.

She turned and looked at him. "What's the matter?" she whispered.

"This must be the same path Luke took," he said. "We should go a different way."

She turned round, looked down the muddy track and nodded. He led her along the edge of the woods until he spotted a gap in the undergrowth ten yards to the right of the path. They moved into the shelter of the trees. The drips grew less frequent and the noise of the rain subsided. The air was thick with a damp loamy smell.

They crept through the wood, stepping carefully on the layer of fallen debris. At first they took a line parallel to the path, but if they continued on it for too long they would miss Luke completely. After a few minutes they veered left, bringing them nearer the centre of the woods.

He held his gun out in front of him and scanned the ground to either side. His eyes had finally adjusted to seeing only shades of green, but the lack of definition made it hard to distinguish between shapes in the tangle of branches and tree trunks.

After about five minutes the rain grew heavier and began penetrating the thick layer of greenery high above them. A large drop splashed onto Ben's right lens. He stopped to wipe it away.

He lifted his head and glimpsed a movement to his left.

Helen drew level with him.

"Did you see that?" he whispered.

She nodded.

There was a muffled shout for help. It was Ruth.

He rushed forward.

Helen grabbed his jacket but his strength carried him out of her grip.

He crashed through the undergrowth towards the source of the cry.

Up ahead the trees thinned. He slowed down and stopped behind a bush on the edge of a clearing. He peered round it. Ruth was slumped against a fallen tree trunk; heavy rain splattered in the mud around her. He desperately wanted to run to her, but it was a trap.

Chapter 37

He wiped his goggles and surveyed the surrounding area. Trees and bushes encircled the twenty-yard wide patch of open ground. Luke was there somewhere, watching the space, waiting for one of them to run into his line of fire.

He looked at his sister again. He had to do something.

Luke was probably no further away from the clearing than he was himself, otherwise he wouldn't get a clear shot, especially without night vision. That meant he could be just a few yards away, or right round the other side. The best approach was to circle the clearing another ten yards out.

He turned and started to crawl along the damp ground.

Something hard hit his head.

He looked around but couldn't see anything. He moved forward again.

A lump of clay hit his left arm. He saw Helen looking out from behind a bush. He crawled over to her.

"What did you see?" she asked, her whisper nearly lost in the heavy drops beating on the leaves around them.

"Ruth's in the middle of the clearing straight ahead."

"A trap," Helen said.

He nodded.

"Luke has to be close. I was going to circle round to try to spot him. It'd be easier with two though." He turned and pointed to the left. "You go anticlockwise, I'll go clockwise."

He looked at Helen. She didn't seem convinced.

"Can you think of a better way?" he asked.

She shook her head reluctantly. "If you fire at him, don't miss. You'll only get one chance."

He kept low and moved to his right. He looked back. Helen was creeping the other way. She passed out of sight behind a clump of saplings.

He stayed close to the ground. His trousers were soaked with mud and covered in dead leaves. He reached about a sixth of the way round the circle and found a large tree he could use for cover. He stood up and looked out from behind it. He had a good view of the ground between himself and the clearing. He let his eyes roam over the area systematically. Luke wasn't there.

He got back down and continued his circular path. After a few minutes he realised it was much quieter. The rain had stopped.

He covered a few more yards and found another tree to hide behind. He stood up and looked out. The view seemed different, as though the wood was fluorescing. He pulled his goggles up. Moonlight filtered through the branches lighting up patches of ground.

They'd lost their advantage.

He slipped the goggles back over his face and started scanning the area in front of the tree. He moved his eyes across the scene in lines, like mowing a lawn. He didn't want to miss an inch in case only a small part of Luke was visible.

Bang!

He pulled his head back behind the tree and held his pistol up. His heart beat double time.

Another shot, followed by two more.

The firing wasn't at him; it was coming from the other side of the clearing.

Three shots, one after the other.

Helen cried out. She'd been hit.

He ran from behind the tree and sped towards the shooting. There were four more shots. He reached the edge of the clearing and stopped behind a bush. He needed to be careful; he couldn't count on Helen's cover, she could be dead. He felt an unexpected emptiness; it didn't have the chance to develop.

"Williams!" Luke shouted. "Give up or I will kill your sister."

His voice wasn't far away. He pictured the clearing as a clock face: if he was at two, Luke was at eleven.

"Do you think I'm playing games Williams?"

A shot blasted from the other side of the clearing.

Ruth screamed.

Ben looked out from behind the bush. His sister was curled up in a ball holding her ankle.

He gritted his teeth and sucked in air to try to calm himself. 'You'd be dying for nothing...' If he gave himself up then Ruth would definitely die.

The green glow dimmed. He lifted his goggles. The moon was covered in cloud again. It wasn't cave dark, but as good as. He pulled the goggles back down.

He got to his feet and left the cover of the bush. He kept low, looking ahead and holding his gun out, ready to shoot first. He reached twelve o'clock. A twig snapped nearby. Luke had moved as well.

He knelt behind a shrub and looked out. Luke was walking about fifteen feet to his right. Ben raised his pistol, aimed and fired.

He missed.

Luke dropped to the ground and fired twice. The bullets rattled through the leaves a few yards away.

Ben stood up, fired four shots, and then ran in the opposite direction to the clearing. He heard heavy footsteps following him. He kept running. It was working: he was drawing Luke away from Ruth.

He found a large tree trunk, slid behind it and crouched down at its base holding his gun ready.

Luke had stopped. All he could hear was the creaking of timber and the occasional drip from a wet branch.

The scene grew brighter again.

"Williams, you have no hope!" Luke shouted. "You have one minute to give yourself up or your sister will die."

The footsteps receded towards the clearing.

This was his last chance. Ruth was lying on the ground. As long as he fired at chest height or above there was no way she'd get hit.

He jumped out from behind the tree and ran in the direction of Luke's voice. He fired repeatedly into the green blur that lay in his path.

White flashes flared in his lenses. He felt a sharp pain in his left arm. He threw himself down and rolled onto his back. He reached up and held the wound just below his shoulder. It felt damp and warm, and stung like hell, but there wasn't any bullet. It must have just grazed him. He stretched the arm; it felt OK.

He rolled over onto his stomach and looked ahead. He saw a branch move less than ten yards away. A large shadow passed between two bushes.

He raised his pistol. He tried to aim just ahead of the target as it moved in an arc towards him. He squeezed the trigger. Nothing. He released the magazine. It made a loud scraping noise as it fell from the handle.

There was a crunch a few yards away. Luke was nearly on him.

He jumped up and ran as fast as he could, weaving from side to side through the trees.

Two shots exploded behind him.

He pulled the spare magazine out of his pocket.

The green became dimmer again. He tripped on a root and crashed to the ground; the magazine flew out of his hand. He rolled left into a bush, got up on his knees and waited.

Luke appeared a few seconds later and stopped. Ben held his breath as he watched the tall figure through the leaves. Luke stared straight towards him, then looked away.

"Williams!" he shouted. "This is your last chance. I'm going back to your sister now."

Ben charged out, leading with his right shoulder. He caught Luke full in the side, lifting him a foot into the air. His momentum pulled him down onto the Irishman. He put his elbow across Luke's throat and grabbed his right arm. He lifted it up and smashed it against a root. There was a blast as the gun went off.

He lifted Luke's hand a second time and brought it crunching down onto the wood. The gun fell to one side and slid into a gap beneath the root. He leaned over and touched the handle with his fingertips. The gun slid further out of reach into the hollow.

Luke grabbed Ben's goggles with his free arm and ripped them off.

Ben was suddenly engulfed in darkness. He tried to punch Luke but his fist hit the dirt.

Luke pushed up beneath him, throwing him backwards. He scrambled to his feet and looked around. His eyes fixed on a glint of steel in the black.

He sucked his stomach in as the blade slashed the air an inch from his skin. He reached out and grabbed Luke's arm on the follow through. He elbowed Luke in the face and drove forward.

The Irishman toppled over.

He jumped over him and ran towards the clearing.

The light increased again as the moon shone overhead.

He raced through the damp bushes, stray branches lashing every part of his body. He put over thirty yards between himself and Luke, but he still couldn't see the clearing. He stopped to get his bearings.

"Williams, I have my knife to your sister's chest!" Luke shouted. "If I do not see your face in front of me in one minute, I will kill her."

There was a rustle nearby.

"Ben!" Helen's whisper came from ground level. "Over here."

He stared into the blackness of the undergrowth. He felt something hard jab his leg. He reached down and found the end of the rifle. He knelt and saw the outline of Helen lying under a bush.

"He shot me in the leg," she said. "I had to hide, I would have been useless."

"Forty-five seconds!" Luke shouted.

She pushed something into his hands. Her goggles. He pulled them over his head; he could see clearly again. She was looking up at him. There was a dark stain spreading across her trousers. She held the rifle out.

"I've turned the laser sight on," she said.

He took the rifle, stood up and ran towards Luke's voice.

"Thirty seconds Williams!" Luke shouted.

He reached the edge of the clearing.

He saw Luke standing by the fallen tree. He had his left arm around Ruth and his knife on her stomach, ready to push up to the heart. In his other hand he held the goggles to his eyes and was looking from side to side.

"Twenty seconds Williams! Come now or I kill her and hunt you like a dog!"

Ben stayed where he was, raised the rifle and aimed it at Luke. A tiny red dot danced on Luke's forehead but the laser traced a telltale thread of light through the moisture-laden air.

Luke turned towards Ben and pulled Ruth in front of him. He'd lost his line of sight.

"Put the rifle down."

"Release my sister and I'll let you live," he shouted.

He felt along the top of the laser and found a button. He pressed it and the beam disappeared. He slowly moved a pace to his right. He aimed using the old-fashioned method he was used to, and lined up a spot on Luke's face.

"You do not call the shots Williams, I do. I have your little sister here."

"Do you think I'm stupid?" he replied. "Do you really believe I'd give up my gun in the hope that you'll let us both go?"

"That is a chance you'll have to take."

"On past form I think I'll give it a miss." He had to try one more time. "Drop the knife and you walk out of here."

"Do you think I'm stupid too?"

Stalemate.

He steadied his breathing and focused on his pulse. He had an area the size of a coin to aim at; the same size as the target on the twenty-five-metre range at school. If he took the shot there was a high chance Ruth would die, if he didn't there was a hundred percent chance.

"It's now or never Williams!" Luke said.

He breathed halfway out.

"Too late!" Luke's arm began to move.

He squeezed the trigger. The rifle jolted into his shoulder.

Luke fell back, dragging Ruth with him.

Ben sprinted towards them.

There was a hole where Luke's right eye had been.

Blood was spreading across Ruth's jumper. He slid to his knees and pulled the knife away.

"Ruth!" He pulled her jumper up. A large wound gushed blood just below her rib cage. He ripped his T-Shirt off and pressed it against the wound.

She coughed and her eyes opened.

Her lips moved but he couldn't hear her. He pulled his goggles off and leaned forward, still pressing as hard as he could against the oozing wound. He put his ear next to her mouth.

"Ben," she said. "Dad would be proud of you."

"Stay with me Ruth," he pleaded. "You're going to make it."

Her eyes closed.

This couldn't be happening, he couldn't lose everyone.

He choked involuntarily on the grief that surged up from within. The faces he loved flashed before his eyes, Julia, Mum, Dad. He couldn't be brave anymore, there was no one left to be brave for.

The lifeless face of his little sister blurred as his eyes filled with tears. He pulled her close to him, looked up and cried, "Please..."

Chapter 38

Helen followed Ben into his flat.

He looked like he hadn't shaved for days and the living room was a mess. There was an old cardboard box on the floor next to the sofa. Pictures lay scattered around the place. There were some family shots, some with a young boy and girl, others with adults, most looked like they were set in Africa.

There were other pictures too, all showing a woman of incredible natural beauty. She felt a prod of jealousy, but suppressed it quickly; bit silly being jealous of the dead.

Ben sat down on the sofa. He didn't offer her a seat. He looked up at her with weary eyes.

"Why are you here?" he asked.

This wasn't going to plan.

"I'm going back to Spain today."

"How nice for you."

"Slade pays for the flat in Hove, they want me out."

"Will they leave us alone?" he asked.

"If they've got any sense. I've left a copy of the files Anne sent me with a lawyer. If anything happens to us he'll go public."

"What's in the files?" Ben asked.

"Details of all their agents, bank accounts and training camps. There's information on jobs that would bring down half the governments in the developed world. But that's not the worst of it, Anne dug very deep."

"I don't want to know."

"Aren't you interested in finding out the truth about Spiravex?"

"What do you mean?"

"What Shackleton told us was only part of the story."

"He lied?"

"No, he didn't. Everything he said about the virus was true. It does mutate and develop a deadly strain that's undetectable," she said. "Did he phone and tell you Esau's spinal fluid had the first mutation?"

Ben nodded.

"Then you'll know that if you hadn't found Esau we could be facing the kind of global disaster he talked about."

"What are you talking about then?"

She pulled out an envelope from her shoulder bag and handed it to him. "I copied Anne's report. The first part is about Spiravex."

He turned the envelope over in his hands. "Can't you just tell me?"

She looked at her watch. "My flight leaves in two hours, I'm late already."

"Why didn't you post it then?" he asked.

This wasn't the time to tell him why she'd really come, maybe there never would be a right time. She took a deep breath. "I wanted to see you before I left, I wanted to thank you for saving my life."

He nodded.

"I also wanted to see how you were bearing up," she said.

"My sister's in intensive care and I've lost my job," he said. "I've been better."

She opened her mouth to say something, then closed it again, "I have to go."

He got to his feet and followed her to the front door.

"What are you going to do in Spain?" he asked.

"I've got some ideas," she said. "I meant what I said about learning more about faith. I'm full of questions after finding out about the origins of life and my near death experience and I need answers. One thing's for sure, I won't be doing the same stuff I have been. It's time to put something back. What about you?"

"I won't be able to work as a doctor again." He shrugged. "That's all I've ever wanted to do."

"At least Shackleton made sure the CIA cleared things up with the Kenyan police."

He opened the door. "Yes, it's such a relief to be downgraded from wanted murderer to suspected pervert."

316

Helen bowed her head and turned round. She started walking towards the lift but stopped halfway and turned back.

"I am sorry Ben. If I could go back and change everything I would."

He held her gaze. "So would I."

She turned round and continued to the lift. She pressed the button and looked back, but Ben had already closed the door. Would she ever see him again? Would she be able to convince him that she'd changed? Was she even convinced herself? All she knew was that after years of living selfishly and being miserable, she'd glimpsed a better way. Just putting a bottle of water to Anne's lips had given her greater pleasure than a hundred wild parties. She'd finally understood the truth behind the 'giving is better than receiving' proverb. There was no way she was going back to her old way of life.

The lift door opened. She looked back at Ben's apartment. If only she'd learned that lesson sooner, maybe that door would still be open for her. There was one last hope though, as long as he opened the envelope.

* * * *

Ben went back to the lounge. He sat on the sofa, the same place he'd been sitting for over a week.

He was confused. He'd tried to hate Helen, but there was such a change in her eyes it totally threw him. She'd always been beautiful, but now there seemed to be a light coming from within that made her irresistible.

He looked at the pictures of Julia scattered around him. For the first time since he'd returned to the flat and opened the box he was able to look at them and not feel complete desolation. He got on his knees and began collecting them together carefully, along with the photos of his parents. He put them back in the box and closed the lid. He'd get them out again from time to time. Now that he'd finally begun to grieve his loss, he'd never be able to push the pain back inside, but in a way, he felt better for all the tears he'd cried.

He looked at his watch. It was still a few hours before he could visit Ruth. He couldn't wait to see her, she'd been talking properly for the first time the day before and the doctors reckoned she'd be out of the ICU within a day or two.

He stood up and began walking to the bathroom then noticed the envelope Helen had left for him. He picked it up and tore it open. There was a hand written note on top:

Helen,

I had to send you this. I think they might be on to me and I need some insurance. Keep it safe.

This information is dynamite. The first section is all about MVT084. We've only been told part of the story. It's scary stuff. It might make you feel differently about what you've been doing for Slade.

But that's not all, there's more, much more.

Slade are effectively the security arm of a much bigger organisation. Their goal is to draw control of global power into the hands of a privileged few. They have infiltrated all walks of life, including the highest offices in government.

Once you've read the report you'll realise that Spiravex may have been a part of their plan to dominate everyone and everything. I'm still looking into this, but there's a whole heap of other stuff this group are into that threatens our freedoms. Call me once you've finished it.

Anne.

Two hours later Ben reached the final page:

Dear Ben,

If you've got this far then you'll know that this organisation has got to be stopped.

I gave you this report because you're the one man in the world I feel I can trust.

If there is such a thing as a selfless purpose in life, I've found it.

You have my number.

Helen.

If your interest about subjects like the Origins of Life or near death experiences has been piqued, then visit my website, www.orsonwrites.com, for more information.

Lightning Source UK Ltd.
Milton Keynes UK
01 December 2009

146960UK00002B/22/P